The
OWL'S ROOST

The
OWL'S ROOST

by
HELGA SANDBURG

...see the children sport upon the shore,
And hear the mighty waters rolling evermore.
—Wordsworth

1962
THE DIAL PRESS   NEW YORK

43,813

Oct. 1962

To
Mother and Buppong

ACKNOWLEDGMENTS

My warm gratitude to Richard Eberhart for permission to reprint his poem, "If I could Only live at the Pitch that is near Madness," which introduces the three parts of this book.

Thanks also to the Folklore Section of the Library of Congress for the use of their archives and reference collection; and to Vincent Eaton of the Information and Publications Office, Library of Congress, for ready help with the general collections. And to Alvin W. Dreier and Bill Warchol of the Chicago *Tribune* for seiche clips from their files; to Iona and Peter Opie for inspiration from their excellent *The Lore and Language of Schoolchildren* (Oxford, Clarendon Press); to W. J. Holland and Leland O. Howard, whose tomes on moths and butterflies I have used a life long; to my sisters Janet and Margaret; and my patient offspring, Karlen Paula and John Carl Steichen, for firsthand lore.

CONTENTS

Though the place and time are as real as memory and love can contrive, the people in this tale are fictitious; any resemblance to anyone living or dead is unintentional.

The

FIRST SUMMER

If I could only live at the pitch that is near madness
When everything is as it was in my childhood
Violent, vivid, and of infinite possibility:
That the sun and the moon broke over my head.

[1]

ALTHOUGH in the half-dark before day the shore was barren of people, there was a record in the sand of the movements of previous hours. There were the charred half-buried remains of the fire that the young people of Pine Beach had sat around, one of them strumming the guitar for the songs they sang:

> *Way down yonder in the meadow*
> *Lies a poor little lamby;*
> *Bees and butterflies pecking at his eyes*
> *Poor little thing cries Mammy!*

Later the smallest children had put out the fire with sand they threw sleepy, "What's black and white and red all over?" Yawning, "I don't know. What goes up when the rain comes down?"

There was a daisy crushed, fallen from the hair of Dr. Bill's wife who missed it later and wondered briefly where it was. Further, past the tracks of varied beach insects like hieroglyphics, the scuttling marks of spiders, beetles, the prints of gulls and crows, sandpipers, around which were strewn an occasional feather and a splotching of white dung, up north near the pier posts was a slash in the sand where Alan Malraux, large, loose-jointed at sixteen,

[3]

had dragged his long orange Canadian canoe up hastily when he saw the Malraux housekeeper, Mrs. Chapman, waving a telegram halfway down their beach stairs at a little past seven last night. At the water line the marks had been erased by the persistent lip-lip of the wavelets. Still readable were foot impressions from Monk Ardway's boys who'd gone for a hike, the older two bullying the slight-framed fifteen-year-old Skin, driving him up on the soft sand in half-earnest horseplay.

"Say uncle!" had roared Russ.

"Say pretty please with sugar on it," Dick seconded.

The escaping Skin cried, "Phooey, help!"

South, at the opposite border of Pine Beach, was a property fenced off and remarkable for its neatness. No litter scattered about as on Pine Beach; but no youngsters lived in the Glass House on the dune above either. The two-storey transparent walls overlooked the lake and every week or so a few gulls would hurl themselves unknowing at it, breaking their necks to the owners' distress. Beyond the Behmelmens' was the Potawatomi Bible Club beach. And on one of the sand swells were prints left by the heavy-shod county sheriff and his deputy who'd talked for a while with the camp chairman about new safety provisions and then driven away with siren sounding, to buy a case of ale at Lagerquists in Sawmill. If a storm had come sweeping there would have been none of the sand notes, and like judgment all would have been wiped clean.

The lake wasn't simple to read; not a bit. Sometimes boxes and cans floated in, or driftwood smooth and polished was vomited upon the shore during high winds to lie there in shapes of dead dolphins or fabled creatures, the sun scorching the water-soaked pulp and drying it into fine soft gray splinters. The undertow dragged objects away and the fluctuating churning surface water currents wafted them in again. Out there even now something the size of a huge fish or human being bumped softly against the jutted pier posts where the loon was approaching.

The big bird had been paddling northward all night; as the dark lifted, its brilliant geometrical pattern of spots and bars, its wide necklace of black, became distinct. It dove suddenly into the black glass, gliding several fathoms below, a sea monster broad and flat-bodied, thirty-eight inches from beak to tail. It surfaced spattering drops, swallowing a glittering trout. Then it opened its greenish-yellow pointed bill and shrieked, harsh and minor-keyed, body shaking. The melancholy sound quavered in the pine tops as if the world were young again and in close-by marshlands gross dinosaurs fed.

Long after the Paleozoic Age, glaciers, four of them, covered Michigan completely; as they moved they shoved monumental piles of sterile chewed-up stuff, drift, which the preceding glacier had ground from stone. When the last ice sheets dissolved, the lake's character and outline was determined. Along the west shore bedrock lay in tiers at the bottom and sometimes jutting from the surface, spoiling the area now for city swimmers. In the Pine Beach region the drift was deep, its top level was mainly clay and sand and gravel. Fairly recently, after the pioneers came to America, a phenomenon developed for which the southeastern shore of Lake Michigan became famous. These were the sand dunes, bleak billows of silical particles that kept in a state of flux. Even vegetation, tumbleweeds, sailed past the eye occasionally, when the wind and sea went into a rage. In the Pokagon post office and general store where Pine Beach dwellers got their mail, and on whose gray gable roof the husband of the postmistress had painted a sign: IF YOU CAN'T STOP SMILE AS YOU GO BY, was a revolving stand holding dime and quarter sepia-tinted post cards of the dunes. The captions read *Mother Nature's Playground, Outdoor Charm, Picturesque Pines.* Many were photographs of tracks of humans and insects and the wind which etched the surface in frozen ripples and waves. During turbulent winds the sand movement was like the lake water itself. And the trees coating the dunes that faced the lake resembled ragged harps, beaten by a gale which came vicious full-force across the water; the picture cards described them as *Singing Pines.*

Two or three miles southeast of Pokagon was the village of Sawmill, population three hundred and ten in the 1960 census. They had a sign too, paint-flecked and ancient, on the outskirts: IF YOU LIVED HERE YOU'D BE HOME NOW. And farther inland, about seven miles from Pokagon, was the town where the Dr. Bill Olsons lived during their winters, Ideal. It also had a slogan, on the brand-new poster put up just the past season by its Rotary Club: A LIVE WIRE TOWN WITH PROGRESS ON ITS MIND. Ideal's population of near six hundred had remained static for thirty years, to the spasmodic alarm of its merchant organization.

The mating wail of the loon in this mid-July predawn heightened the primaeval atmosphere along Lake Michigan's shore. It hunted northward, skirting the rotted posts that stuck up in the light fog like a long trap.

Now there was a set of fresh tracks, just made by the Olson daughter, Clara, who had trotted down from the boardwalk to try to glimpse the bird. Its scream had waked her when the hands of the old Donald Duck clock on the bureau stood at four-thirty. She'd lain a moment listening, and then pushed her doll and the covers aside and felt about on the floor for her sandy half-dry suit. She shut the creaky door and trod down the front stairs, over the shabby sisal rug in the big room of the summer house, the Owl's Roost, where overhead hung swollen pleated paper lanterns her father had sent long ago from Kawasaki. The screen door had slapped behind her. Nobody locked their doors at Pine Beach even when they were away for days at a time; keys were dropped in a catchall drawer and by the end of the season families often had to hunt the house over so they could return them to the proprietor, Monk Ardway.

Clara shivered, looking up the dusky shoreline; the loon had disappeared. She didn't try to read the sand. Fifteen last April, with brooding brown eyes and an even-featured classic face, Clara stared out at the water, her hair sleep-mussed, and wished she had stayed in bed. She ran her tongue over her braces. Her still-growing breasts were hurting a little but otherwise she felt disembodied, unreal. Her family lived during winter in Sawmill, but every summer since she was a baby they'd rented the Owl's Roost. And so she was used to the mystery of the foggy beach dawns. She felt severed from the world, from her parents, her brother, from the housemaid Dora, from Alan Malraux. She tried out their names whispering, and they were all strangers. The bird had fled; she thought perhaps she'd dreamed its scream, and squinted northward again. She disliked wearing glasses to the beach, but missed them now, narrowing her eyes. There was no movement. The water was deceptive; it had the look of metal or cut stone, with prisms catching the light that was struggling toward day behind her in the east in back of the dunes. She frowned, treasuring her unrest.

She spoke self-loving, to the air, free of fear that anyone might overhear and laugh:

Was it for this the wild geese spread
The gray wing upon every tide;
For this that all that blood was shed,
For this Edward Fitzgerald died,
And Robert Emmet and Wolfe Tone,
All that delirium of the brave?
Romantic Ireland's dead and gone!

She wished in a flame that she were a man and were fighting in some old horrid battle, dying in blood and gore and great pain.

Under that still surface life moved; near shore shoals of immature shad, pale crappie, sunfish, whitefish, bass, yellow perch; far out were the hunters, the lean long ones; pickerel, blue pike, the savage muskellunge, called once by the Algonquins the *maskinonge,* weighing over eighty pounds. Voracious, razor-toothed, with pointed snouts, they slunk through the deep waters and could swallow a fish half as large as themselves. On the bottom somewhere rested a few of the remaining giant sturgeons, ten-footers, that men would never catch. When the first steamship sped over Lake Michigan, the *Walk-in-the-Water,* back in 1818, white men told the Potawatomi a tale of the boat being drawn by a team of trained sturgeons. They were the prize fish and as they cruised slowly fed with their four mouth barbels dragging, to locate the organisms they lived on, shooting down their tubular mouths to suck them in.

Gus, her brother, aged thirteen, said fish didn't die of old age; they were eaten by other fish or got so large they couldn't catch enough to live on and slowed down and starved. There must be some whoppers out there, Clara thought, ones that started rumors of sea serpents. Last year the papers had reported a monster seen at the port of St. Joseph, twenty miles up the lake. A photograph, which Clara had cut out and saved, was carried in the Chicago *Trib.* It might be real, she had considered, while Mum and Daddy jeered. Often grownups were wrong; things were never what they would have you think; one went along with their fairy tales for the sake of peace.

Clara watched Jack Behmelmen come down to the lake in the distance. She called him Uncle Jack though he was no relative. He seldom missed his early dip; the two of them had the beach to themselves unless a commuter dashed down for a hasty swim from which he emerged to scurry up the dunes like a bug in the distance, part of the horde who shuttled between Chicago and a summer home using the South Shore line. There was a bus that stopped if hailed at Pokagon at 5:57 a.m., making connections in Michigan City with the *Hot Shot,* an ancient electric coach bound for Randolph Street, rattling away in the cool soot-swept summer mornings every weekday and putting its passengers into the loop at 8:10.

Uncle Jack's hand raised in her direction, desultory. He was no Mr. America, she thought. He had paused with thumbs thrust in the top of his trunks, looking down at the water, chest concave, stomach protruding. He dove under and she waited until the bald head came up, the flailing arms. Then she rushed in herself, making a great foaming before she went under. Coming up gasping she swam a few strokes. In the breathless air the sounds were musical, not as they were during the day when the beach was busy with people and noises were overcome or absorbed. She ducked seven times, no more, no less. The color of seven was purple. Three was green.

She whispered, "What did the big faucet say to the little faucet? What did the mouse say when its tooth broke? Hi squirt. Hard cheese." Her hair dripped, stringing, as she hurried out stumbling. Daddy said not to take swims alone because of cramps, but she dismissed it. A sandpiper approached along the hard-packed shore, legs moving so quickly they seemed a wheel; white-breasted, hooded in light brown, with inquiring eyes, he bobbed continually, an eye on her. She sat facing the lake and shuddered, chilled. A fly squatted on her leg, yellow speckled body and widespread wings, and stung. She swatted and it started up backward to hover soundless and hidden nearby. She shrugged, irritated. It lit on her back and she slapped again.

The pink head of the swimmer was just visible. Last summer at vacation's end when all the beach had been massed with holiday visitors, a man had been swimming far out as a water skier was being towed in to shore by a motor launch. The driver had roared in, dropped his passenger, and wheeled to run his course straight into the swimmer, gutting him and killing him instantly, abdomen snared in the propeller. Unaware, the driver had continued to his destination up the bland sunny shore. The horrified shouting onlookers had been helpless. Clara and Gus had been in Chicago to see their orthodontist and were desolate to have missed it. Entrails were found in the water. She shivered again and the sandpiper flew up, low, white wing bars a streak, "Preee–leeee!"

A flock of gulls were collecting down at the Malraux beach. Clara arose and began walking toward them, picking up small flat stones that she selected as she went along. The birds flapped up as she neared and wheeled over the water in a wide band to return and land farther north, making little running steps as they folded their wings. When they flew their wings went in deliberate flailing strokes as if the bodies were ponderous to maneuver; a few had stayed out on the lake, white bobbing pieces. In the distance the ridge of dunes and trees bordering the shore receded in shadowy tiers; nearby they were a pale green, farther off a richer emerald, and then mossy and finally quite black as they reached the fog and turned blue, gray, nothing, a blank mist. She strained her eyes to observe.

Before she came to the pier posts she stopped to skip the handful of stones. One hit the water fifteen times, she counted. She saw the thing then, mounded by the farthest post and dropped her burden from her fingers unaware. It resembled a large dead fish somewhat, one of the big fellows, the flesh white and puffy, torn in a place or two as if worried by something. Her eyes widened and she felt a thrill that pierced her parts.

"Creeps." She told herself she wasn't afraid. She wouldn't want to go out though and bring it in or touch it. In the dawn-warmed water the surface steamed slightly about it and she wondered if it might drift away. She thought it might yet be half alive and stir or roll over. And she went swiftly away into the soft beach toward the Malraux stairs, scuffling the sand which clung to her damp running lean legs. She avoided the spots of oily tar deposit that penciled the highest wave-marks, vomited there by the last storms ever since the tanker had exploded in Gary's harbor in the spring. Thirty or more men had died; some bodies were never found. She breathed harder, speeding, and when she came to the stairs she took them two at a time, not looking back. The sun was breaking shouting over the sand hills as she reached the top. The light spread over the water and banished the brooding fog and made a mirror of it to hold the white sky.

Clara stood on the brick terrace and banged the knocker; it

was a brass gargoyle, a reproduction of one of the Notre Dame fiends, the one called *Le Rongeur,* ripping something with uneven teeth; Mr. Malraux had sent it from Boulogne years ago.

The housekeeper was in the kitchen of the Sand Castle, cooking a pot of beef chunks and tomatoes and rice for Alan's dogs. Della Chapman scorned prepared food that came in cans, six to a carton with a picture of red beef on its label and a pale meal inside. She sang in a cheerful shallow voice:

> *I'm going to climb up Jacob's ladder,*
> *One of these days!*

Up since five-thirty, vigorous, heavy, with unkempt gray hair framing her round face, she stirred the kettle for the last time. She rinsed her fingers and went to answer the rap, a towel in her hands.

"Hi, Chappy. Is Alan up? Boy, there's a dead man down there."

"You don't say. Well, come in, child." She shouted into the house, "Ernie! Hey!"

"It's in the water. It might float away."

Mr. Chapman emerged from the living room where he'd been repairing a screen, hammer in his hand. "Dead man? Whoo-ee! Ain't it?" Thin and small-boned, purposed, Ernie had taught his employer's charge everything he could about canoes and guns and a few of his discoveries on morals and health; he had attempted to teach him hammer-and-nails, but the boy's interest hadn't held. Mr. Malraux had bought Alan a dandy cedar canoe, best on the market, five summers ago; now he figured to give him an aluminum one for his birthday, one with styrofoam ends to increase the flotation. Both Philip Malraux and Ernie worried about the lad's safety; he was wild, no question of it.

Mrs. Chapman queried him, "You hear, Ernie?"

"I'll call the sheriff. You better tell Alan. He'll want to see it."

"He's still in bed," Mrs. Chapman said.

Ernie lifted down the receiver of the black wall phone and spoke to the operator, who promised to try and get hold of the official, and meantime would send the ambulance right out. Clara was trailing the housekeeper to the kitchen. She plumped down on the bench of the kitchen nook. "Wonder who he is, Chappy."

"Umm."

Ernie yelled from the front door. "I'm going down to the pier. You direct them where I'm at when they get here."

"I will now!" Mrs. Chapman looked at Clara. "Can you guess what? Alan's father's coming in this evening. The land only knows where he's been, China or even some place you never heard of."

"I don't remember him."

"Well, we got the wire last evening telling about it. Reckon it's two years since he's been at Pine Beach. Every time he gets in to New York for a day he sends for Alan to have a visit maybe. Not like you and your Daddy, Clara."

"Umm." Clara didn't listen.

The woman removed the pot from the burner and set it on a rack in the window to cool. "That smells good enough to eat myself. Alan's dogs are spoiled. Was it a man or woman? Any way you could tell? Any clothes?"

"No." Clara suddenly pulled at the wet cold straps of her suit, adjusting them about her breasts. She wondered whether she would be sick in the white sink over there. "It was down by those posts all the time when I was swimming. What if I'd gone there and knocked into it!"

"What a way to die. By water. Now I wonder if it was on purpose. That'd be a sin, all right."

"Dying isn't so awful, Mrs. Chapman. I just wouldn't want a dead body to touch me. Once your breath's gone what's the diff? The fishes can have me, I say. I wouldn't care."

"You talk big setting up in the kitchen here, child."

"I mean it." Clara insisted, firm. "And I don't believe in God. And I think Reverend Thwaite is a fake." She slapped her knee, intense.

Mrs. Chapman shook her head. "Talk talk talk."

Alan appeared in the doorway. "Morning, Chappy. How come *she's* here?" He was amiable, mouth gaping. "I saw Ernie out the window and he yelled something about a dead man."

"Clara found it, Alan."

Behind Alan were two German shepherds in studded leather harnesses, who followed him as he crossed the kitchen to get an apple from a bowl on the steel counter. "Lie down," he told the dogs, who threw themselves grunting on the linoleum floor, buckles and county tags clacking. He smiled at Clara. "Cat got your tongue."

"She found it, Alan," Della Chapman repeated.

"Did you, Clara?"

"I don't know."

"I'm going down in a minute. You coming?"

She shook her head. "I have to go." She fixed her eyes on her hands, listening to Chappy going on about the happenings and about Alan's father coming in the afternoon.

"He's probably on his way now, Alan," the housekeeper said.

"No, he takes a jet, Chappy!"

The woman gave him muffins she'd baked earlier and eggs bubbling in a square iron skillet. Alan had taken a scissors to his outgrown tan pants at the thighs, and they hung ragged, tight about his loins. He was shirtless and had knotted a blue handkerchief at the neck. He was heavy-boned and due to recent rapid growth appeared thin and almost disproportioned. His dark curly hair needed a cutting; his light brown eyes were large, mouth and chin well-shaped. Handsome, he resembled his mother when she had been young; she now lived in Antibes on the Riviera. The court after the divorce, over eleven years ago, had ruled she was not to visit him or have anything to do with him against his father's will; she went out of his life. Alan wasn't aware that he missed her, for Chappy was affectionate and Ernie guided him and answered questions to some extent. Mainly Alan longed now and again to see his father, who was seldom home and traveled a lot. He was elated about his coming today. "Why do you always go to the lake so early, Clara? Man, it's really dopey." His bare foot stroked one of the dogs along the shaggy back fur. He smiled at her, engaging.

"I don't know." Her tongue clove to the roof of her mouth. This morning there'd been the loon, but she was unable to say it to him, miserable. The boy was in a grade above her and would be a senior next year. He was going to Harvard after that. Clara felt unequal and strove with him not in combat, but only to be worthy. As far as the dead body and that moment of discovery, she pushed it under whenever it neared the surface of her thinking.

"You want breakfast, Clara?" Della Chapman asked. "Go on

and call your home. Ask if you can stay; maybe your mother's worried about you."

"I'm not hungry, thanks. And anyhow," she stood frowning, "they don't worry."

Alan's mouth was full of buttered muffin. "Man, I'm going to the beach right away. This is the first decent thing to happen this season." He turned from the girl. "Chappy, let me have coffee."

"Well, Alan, maybe so." The old-fashioned housekeeper knew she indulged her charge, as she poured him a cup.

A horn blared in the drive at the bottom of the inner dune steps where the three-car garage was. Four state troopers had arrived. As Clara was leaving, they passed by her, going to the beach where Ernie guarded the flotsam. In a short time they were joined by the two ambulance drivers who carried a stretcher. Mrs. Chapman pointed the way down the creosoted beach stairs. Tiny knotty-skinned toads and shiny crickets, a pair of ground thrush, scattered soundless as the weighted feet pounded the boards. When they passed the quiet would close in like a wave and the pulse of the day resume its level beat.

The younger members of Pine Beach had by now bruited word of the discovery. People were gathering below the Sand Castle to watch the uniformed men at their task. The body had decomposed and had to be wrapped and handled carefully. Alan, with a dog on each side, sat at a distance on a low dune where he could observe what went on. He'd been reprimanded last week by Reverend Thwaite when Bosco had nipped one of the Paoli children; Alan wasn't risking another encounter. Angela Paoli had waved her husband off in their station wagon at five-thirty, and came strolling up in bright shorts and weskit, the latest baby on her shoulder, varied younger Paolis about; one, four-year-old Chris, was hopping ahead shrill-voiced, prepared for war of any sort. The Thwaite daughters, seventeen and eighteen, wearing above-the-knee white pleated tennis skirts, their rackets under their arms, were whispering together, eyes fluttering over the Ardway boys, Russ and Dick.

And up at the Sand Castle Mrs. Chapman bustled about, turning a mattress expertly and flipping out a fresh sheet:

God's going to set this world on fire
One of these days!
We are climbing Jacob's ladder
Every round going higher and higher!

Clara was returning to the Owl's Roost. On the way she stopped off the path once in the sassafras bushes and retched a small amount of bile. She felt the slight sick sweat on her face and upper arms, wiping her mouth and breathing cautiously. She broke off a sassafras leaf to chew to take away the sour taste as she went the rest of the way.

[2]

DR. BILL OLSON and Elizabeth had narrowly missed a quarrel, which accounted for their careful speech the last few minutes over their breakfast trays out on the Owl's Roost porch. It was hot already and a breeze was blowing as the cool air over the lake moved in to displace the land air. By afternoon the temperature over the water would be up and then the wind would perish. Elizabeth passed by her husband as she went into the house to heat up the coffee pot. Pausing, she fondled his clipped gray hair with her small hand, bending to kiss him. She was blonde with tanned fair skin, purplish-blue eyes, wide-set. A little slow of speech, she would seem on first meeting to be thoughtful, but it was a mannerism.

Dr. Bill caught at her fingers and leaned his head into her breasts, feeling their small longish shapes. He wore heavy horn-rim glasses; his brows were beetling, the black hairs white-flecked. "Pretty Lisa. I don't say it very often."

"Isn't that your stern Nordic blood asserting itself?" She laughed at him. "Didn't we nearly have a fight?"

"Only because you're so childish, *älskling*." He called her darling but it seemed an effort; he sensed she felt it and sat back

[15]

to fiddle with his empty coffee mug. His eyes behind the lenses flickered; in the milky white the crisscrossed veins were red, a sign of his chronic tiredness.

"Am I? Will you listen who's talking?"

He watched the little rounded hips swing, clad in fitted white shorts. She was barefoot, her waist belted tight, her blouse trim. He heard her talking to Dora in the kitchen. "Where's the jar of wheat germ?"

"It's there in the icebox, Mrs. Olson. Somewhere."

"No. This is the brewer's yeast."

"I can't keep them separated," the housemaid said. "All these new things to remember. And come to think, I forgot the doctor's vitamins."

His wife was thirty-seven, Dr. Bill thought; nine years difference between them. Feeling a momentary sweet prickling down his thighs, he vaguely wondered if he satisfied her as a husband. How long had it been? He'd lost track this time. Harried during his days and at night fatigued, he ran the circle. He remembered that once he'd been as busy, but there'd been time. There'd used to be a violent appetite too. He remained unmoving in his chair all the while Elizabeth was in the kitchen, but at her coming back, as if his thoughts were mussed, he got up abruptly. "I want to go to the Holy Mother Hospital tonight. You need the Volks for anything?"

"Here." She set the jar of vitamin capsules before him and filled his pink mug with coffee. "See how we need that second car? I'm going to ask Angela to take me shopping. And don't I know which kind I want, too."

"Lisa." He pulled off his glasses and began to polish them with a handkerchief. "It's Dora or another car. Simple as that. Now if you think you can handle the house without her, we'll do it."

"Would Dora mind taking a cut? What you think?"

"Make sense." He looked at her quizzically as he put on the horn-rims. She'd been a virgin when they met, nineteen, studying at Bryn Mawr—humanities, not housewifery. A good part of his tenderness, he considered, was due to Lisa not having grown up; his was the paternal role. He sighed; he had the malady common nowadays of investing everything with a psychological slant. "Try to be practical, Lisa."

"Well, but wouldn't you love a white Porsche!" She lingered over the words.

"Yeah."

"I think there's a new A and P opening up in that shopping center outside Michigan City. They'll be handing out free samples. I wish I didn't have to ask Angela."

He dropped a saccharin in the coffee and stirred as if impatient. "Where's Gus?"

"Angela's funny. Mike's salary is fifty-two hundred, and they have those five kids to feed. But as soon as we go in the supermarket, doesn't Angela head right for the frozen foods and pick out blueberry pies and chow mein and TV dinners? It's her vice, she says."

"Lucky for their kids they get them out of Chicago for the summers. I don't know how they manage."

"Monk said he'd never raise their cabin rent because of Al's leg and him having polio."

"Monk's one hell of a businessman and it's his prime virtue. Is Gus upstairs? Where's Clara?"

"I think so. And Clara's out someplace."

"I didn't even see him yesterday. Where was he?"

"You know Gus was down in Herb Worth's orchard, Bill."

"Christamighty, Lisa, catching butterflies." It was a hell of a note. His only son fussing with pins and cardboards and cages of bugs and rats. It seemed almost effeminate. Dr. Bill looked down at his hands that were broad and skilled. They were pale, antiseptic looking, the nails trimmed close. He was thinking how the night before last Gus had dashed in late to the supper table, his face sunburned, his blond hair nearly white; he'd produced from his shirt pocket a tiny moist toad that he held out in his grimy hand as if it were a prize or something. His fingernails were unclipped and dirt had rimmed them, and it had triggered Dr. Bill; there'd been quite a scene. Dr. Bill raised his eyebrows. "We don't organize our family very well, *älskling*. The four of us ought to be able to get together for breakfast. Lunch is impossible and half the time I seem to miss supper here with all of you."

"You're right, Bill. Why don't I speak to the children about it? You took your vitamins?" She looked absently over at the stocky man, forehead knit between lowered brows, and considered how he was energetic once, somewhat handsome. His pin-stripe summer suit was wrinkled and sweated on the back. His dark blue bow tie was knotted carefully and too tightly. She pushed away her dissatisfaction.

"Let them alone. I didn't mean that." He shook the pills out into his palm and turned into the house to get his kit and the clip of papers he carried.

She called after, mocking, "A family that prays together stays together. Dr. Thwaite said that has always been his motto on WGN yesterday. Did you know his wife actually had to read Dickens instead of bedtime stories to the girls?"

"Maybe she likes Dickens," he shouted.

"She'd read all through him by the time Pearl was eleven."

He came back on the porch. "Did you have a picnic last night?"

"Um hum. Clara and Dora and I did, that is. Gus had a sandwich here. We all wondered if you'd get home in time."

"I had a bad case. Finally called someone in for a Caesarean. The Holy Mother Hospital is run as if this were the Dark Ages. My Murdock's got more sense than the whole flock of nuns up there." Dr. Bill was fond of his office nurse and depended on her. She'd lived for years next door to them in Ideal, with her elder sister Amy. They kept an eye on the Olson house during summers when the family moved to Pine Beach. Murdock ran Dr. Bill's office, five days a week and Saturday mornings, in one wing of the winter house.

"Will you be here for supper tonight?"

"I thought I'd get in early and maybe you'd fix a picnic for me, Lisa."

She glanced up at him, blushing, recalling in the glow that brought her confidence and a feeling of well-being, the business of the daisy and Monk last night on the beach. Again she had almost, she thought, in a rush of guilt. "I'll tell Dora, Bill. Shall we have something cold? Won't it be too warm for a fire?"

He spoke as if the thing were crowding his mind, "You know Gus is blowing his summer? How old is he anyway?"

"Don't you know as well as I?" She put her elbows up, chin on palms, frowning, girded for the argument.

"I know what I was doing at his age. When I was in high school like he is."

"First year; he's only a freshman!"

"And a sophomore this coming fall. Fourteen."

"You tell me often enough, Bill; I'm tired of hearing it. I know you worked all summer, every summer, for your father. And never got any pay. And how you've worked all your life. I have the whole story start to finish." She smiled, ingratiating. "And don't I sympathize and think you're wonderful? But you aren't Gus. Why don't you understand that!"

He had turned from her and his anger lay on the air. He put his hand on the guard rails that once were white, the paint now peeling. A catbird squalled in the bushes nearby. Through the trees one could see the lake down below, past the dune. The sun poured upon it, the water soft and shiny, silken. Yellow, it picked up the sky's light. Where the sandbar ascended the color darkened to brown, wavering. Dr. Bill wanted to be stirred by the beauty, to feel a thrust of energy, of belief. He was getting old too fast, he thought; he wondered if the *pojke* loved life the way he had at almost fourteen. Hunting ducks with *Far* along the beach, getting his first girl under the lifeboat after school, the fat bright one, valedictorian that year. When he was young and lonely, he'd gone directly after what he wanted. Now with a wife, separate people to consider, a daughter, a son, simplicity was gone; there were hurdles to skirt or leap or refuse entirely. The phone was ringing in the house.

Gus came into the doorway, tallish, with fine blond hair and features, small-boned somewhat like Elizabeth. He was holding a glass of milk; they turned to him. "Mum's wanted on the phone."

"Angela about shopping." Elizabeth left them.

"You haven't said *god morgon,* Gus." Dr. Bill slurred his parents' soft tongue, clinging yet to the few remembered diminutives and salutations from the Swedish they had used.

"*God morgon.*"

"Mum and I were talking. Were you listening in?"

"I've been with Dora in the kitchen. I'm having breakfast." He gulped the milk and ran his tongue to the rubber bands on his braces, snapping them in a habit he had.

"I was telling her that you're blowing your summer."

The boy nodded, eyes on Dr. Bill's necktie. "I really ought to have a goal, Daddy. I know it. I should. You're right." He leaned back on the door arch as if he'd walked a long way, and began to swish the remaining milk in the glass.

"Don't do that. You'll spill it. Remember that talk we had the other night? What did you promise me?"

"I will, Daddy. I'll get a job. You'll see. I'll try all the stores in Sawmill first and then Ideal. I'll ride in with Mr. Ardway. I'm going to." Earnest, he rested one tennis shoe on the other. His blue jeans were cut off at the knees; his tee-shirt had a tear at the shoulder.

"Damn, I'm late." Dr. Bill went toward the steps abruptly. Clara was coming up, barefoot, in her swim suit, a sassafras leaf in her hand.

"Hi, Daddy."

"Everything all right, *Flicka?*" He paused.

"Um hum."

"You look so sad. Nothing wrong?"

"I just took a dip."

"You know I asked you not to swim alone."

"Uncle Jack was down there."

"Why do you have to go early, Clara? Can't you wait until there are people at the beach?"

"I'm careful." She had her face turned up to him, her mouth open a little so the brass and wire on her teeth glinted. Dr. Bill thought her features had got so like *Mor,* who must have been the spit of Clara once. The face that had used to be full and babyish had, in the last months, changed. Nowadays, watching her, he was continually turned back to his childhood. His daughter would be sixteen soon. He supposed a man could age and finally die and still be missing his mother. "Did you hear the loon, Daddy?"

"Just now?"

"No, when it was still dark. I wanted to see it but it was gone when I got there."

"They're shy birds. Used to nest here when the creek ran differently and made a marsh. That was forty years ago, before the Ardways dammed it."

"Gus says when the old flintlocks went out, hunters thought

they'd be able to shoot them easier. But he says a loon can dive faster than a shot."

"Maybe so."

Elizabeth came running onto the porch, breathless. "Bill, that was Jack Behmelmen. He says they found someone drowned on the beach. Washed up. Did you ever?" Gus came behind her, glass still in hand.

"Identified?"

"No. And it had been in the water for a long time. Can you imagine if one of the children had found it? And Ernie Chapman called the sheriff and they sent an ambulance to the Sand Castle. Should you go over?"

"Not as long as the sheriff's in charge. Did you see it, *Flicka?*" He turned to Clara suddenly.

She shook her head, features composed, and looked up at her brother draining his glass. "Hi, Gus!"

"Well," Dr. Bill chucked his daughter's chin as he went by. "Go on down and see the excitement. I don't have time. Murdock'll have them lined six deep. *Adjö.*" He waved back just before he got in the blue Volkswagen parked under a shaggy elm.

"Hi, Mum." Clara went past the two of them to pick up the coffee pot. "Can I help?" She spoke to Dora who was gathering the dishes onto the breakfast tray.

"What's the matter, eh?" the maid asked as they reached the kitchen. "You going back to the beach?"

"Everybody says what's the matter!" Clara went to the refrigerator and took an orange from the low drawer. She peeled it, dropping the skins into a paper bag set in the wastebasket. "What's the matter. Ugh."

"Oho, we're cross. That's what comes of gallivanting about without eating till eight in the morning."

"That all you can think about, Dora? Food?" Clara ate quickly, sitting on the counter edge, spitting the seeds into her palm.

"And what's better to think about, Miss Know-it-all? Even an engine's got to have fuel. Eh? You think that's all you're going to have now? You sit and I'll give you some cereal."

"My suit's wet. I'm getting dressed." The girl went into the hall and up the stairs. Gus came dashing after her, three steps at a time. He punched her in the ribs as he went by so hard she grunted. He wheeled into his room. When she passed his door, he had seated himself on the bed and was staring ahead at the wall, stolid. She looked at him. "What."

"I hate Daddy. Double-double-double-damn."

"Oh that." She withdrew and went to her own room. After she put on the tortoise-shell glasses that she'd left on the dresser, she wound the old toy clock and then picked up the large worn doll from the floor. She held Baby under the arms as if it were alive and set it on the bamboo seat of a chair, placing the plaster hands together in the lap. She skinned off her suit and draped it over the iron bedstead. Her adolescent body was slender, the breasts not fully formed. She had overheard Mum tell Mrs. Paoli once that she was a late-bloomer and it had angered her; it was a secret. The swim suit's outline was pale and luminous against her brownness. She pulled on faded blue shorts and a sailor-style shirt, wrinkled; she ran a comb through her hair and sauntered to her brother's room. He knelt now on a chair, leaning over his rickety table, gazing into a large green volume open to colored plates of butterflies. She demanded, "Know what?"

"Un un."

"I found that man. Me."

"Hum?" He didn't look from the page.

"That dead body. I was the one discovered it."

"See here, Clara." He pointed to the plates, tapping the reproduction with enthusiasm. "Sometimes the Tiger Swallowtail comes brownish-black like this and not yellow. You'd think it was an Eastern except it's bigger. It'd be easy to mix them. Yikes." He read, "Diamorphic female form: *glaucus*. Expanse 3.5 to 5.0 inches."

Clara came up and put her hand in mock anger on his neck. "I said! What'd I say, dope?"

"What?"

"Didn't you listen? I found that drowned man."

"Oh." He shrugged, speaking overloud, eager. "I know I saw one in Worth's orchard. I didn't take it because I was sure it was an Eastern. And I already have a set of them!"

"Me," Clara cried.

Outside the upstairs windows the heat was increasing. The white pines shivered and were still; birds fell asleep in high branches, their early feeding over. The ripples on the lake were a sheer banner that fluttered and streamed vertically to the horizon. Monk Ardway was whistling as he went along the road that wound around the summer cottages. He mimicked the birds precisely. By now the troopers had gone, preceding the whining ambulance. Monk was heading for the tennis court where the net had broken again, the rope rotten. He had set Russ and Dick to tarring the leaks in the lifeboat—which needed a paint job too. His wife Belle had set their youngest boy Skin to washing windows, rebellious. Monk swung the roll of wire easily in his hand; a pair of pliers was tucked in the belt of his well-tailored shorts. Monk dressed so the facts of his excellent physique would not be missed.

He was taking the long way around in order to look in on Mrs. Olson. She was a stunning little gal and Monk Ardway had an old wish about her. He'd known Dr. Bill and his family a long time; they'd been among his first renters when Monk's mother turned Pine Beach over to her son years ago. Mama Ardway, a sod widow in the twenties, had inherited Pine Beach from her husband; it had been his family's summer vacation spot. Cousins and relatives, moneyed and poor alike, had come there for years. Those were days of easy living when even middle classes staffed servants. The Ardways had constructed stucco cottages and tall-ceilinged large frame houses, one the Owl's Roost. They put down and leveled a grass tennis court which Monk cemented; they graveled and limed the winding roads. A sign of twisted vines was nailed up: PINE BEACH. It was in the days before income taxes and the Depression. Mama Ardway had been something of a *grande dame* locally, but after the market crash her affairs went steadily downhill until finally to Monk's private relief she said he must forego college and settle for converting Pine Beach into a public resort. They installed steam heat in the center cottage, the Lodge, and moved in.

When he was nineteen, Monk already had a wife, a country girl. The young couple waged dramatic battles; a three-cornered scar on Monk's temple was witness to where the hot iron caught him once when the young woman hurled it with her battle cry, *"Bullshitter!"* Mama Ardway moved out, taking a cottage on the

road into Sawmill and she lived there now, alone. As Monk's three
boys acquired the gift of speech, Belle set them now and then
to spying on him, and was as often rewarded as not. Monk kept
the summer houses in fair repair, although he preferred to save
himself for projects like grading a slope for winter skiing or
planning the bridge that Jimmy Fox wanted to construct over
the ravine to the Wigwam in place of the treacherous one now
there. Luck-touched, Monk did well enough with the rents,
managed to keep out of debt. He bought a yellow convertible back
in 1950 that still served. Mama Ardway enjoyed her solitary
existence. She hid her disdain for Belle as well as she could. Occasionally on hot afternoons her son drove her out to sit under an
umbrella on the beach, her old body withered, clad in a youthful-
styled suit, a novel or half-finished letter in her bag. "If they don't
want to look, they needn't," she affirmed. Only one piece of the
original land ever was sold: the broad strip at the north that ran
down to the water. Philip Malraux purchased it in the forties for
a five-figure sum too high to resist and Mama Ardway told Monk
to take it. The famous columnist had the Sand Castle built on
top of the dune, commissioning a world-known architect to
design it.

As Monk went through the hollow and approached the
Owl's Roost he glanced up at the porch, his whistle mocking a
shrill robin. He swung over to greet Elizabeth perched on the
railing. "Hi, *hausfrau!* Heard the news? Big doings on the beach.
I came over to report." He liked the way she raised her brows and
tilted her head at him.

"I know. Jack called us. What's the sheriff say?"

"They can't even locate him, so the state police sent the
ambulance. That buddy-boy's off somewhere sleeping it off."

She lit a cigarette. "Want one?"

"Throw it down." He caught it. "When he was a deputy over
in Ideal he found a dead horse on Hickory Street, but couldn't
spell hickory; so he hauled the carcass down to Elm before he
wrote it up." Monk struck a match. "I don't get in any swivet
over a body turning up, gal. Someone's always drowning up and
down this lake. Every year."

"What a thing to say!"

"Look at last year. There was that tanker blew up at Gary."

"That doesn't count."

"Well, it happened on the lake. And anyhow, counting sui-
cides there were a few." He laughed and blew the smoke up at her.

"You going to fix that old tennis net again? Why not buy a
new one?" Her voice was always slow; the red was up in her face
and her wide-apart eyes like a child's.

"Oh, it'll do a while yet. Papa Thwaite's having kittens about
it. He's set on making champions of those two gals of his."

"What's wrong with that?"

"Not a thing. I don't give a dang. Why'd you run off last
night?"

Elizabeth glanced inside where Dora was getting out the
sweeper. "Hush. And I lost your daisy too."

"You're afraid of me. No need to be."

"Hoo! Of you?"

Under the banter, as the heat of the day gathered she could
feel Monk's persistence, was eased and flattered by it. It was as if
it pushed aside, hard and steady, with fire, all the accumulated
mores. Elizabeth wanted to live! In three years wouldn't she be
forty, a hag? How would it feel to be wrinkled and ugly like old
Mrs. Ardway, saying, "They needn't look if they don't want." It
wouldn't happen to Elizabeth! Her eyes flashed at Monk. He had a
dreary wife, who had let herself go, and seemed a good deal
older than he because of it. Belle never cared for her skin or her
hair. Elizabeth couldn't understand that sort of woman.

Gus emerged from the door behind her, and she turned to
him at once. His net was in one hand, green army-surplus bag holding a cyanide jar and insect boxes swinging from a strap on his
shoulder. He was so big, taller than Clara now. She cried, as she
brushed his hair back with her hand as if teasing, her voice thick
and heavy. "Monk, look at my handsome boy!"

"Say, been down to the lake, Gus? You see the excitement?"

The boy flushed and drew away from his mother, shaking his
head. "No, sir."

"Come on over to the Lodge and take a look at Skin's gun
collection. He's got Civil War and everything."

"I know." Gus moved down the porch. "I've seen them already, Mr. Ardway. Mum, I'm going to the orchard."

She stopped him. "But what about what Daddy said? About
that job? Gus—"

"I'm going, though. I'll do it after a while."

"All right." She watched him hurry down the stairs and lope off, bag bumping, net swinging. Why didn't Bill leave him alone? All her thoughts and communication involving Gus, she was aware, were contained in a suppressing sort of love. She'd talked with Angela Paoli, who had five and would say how wonderful, extraordinary each was; even Carmen, who at twelve had an IQ of sixty, and the older game-leg boy Albert. Elizabeth's problems receded whenever she sat with Angela on a long hot afternoon. She sighed to Monk, "Bill wants him to find a summer job."

"Good notion. If you can get him to work. Belle's always putting our kids on an allowance and fining them like a western marshal. Don't do much good far as I can see; when they need money they ask and she gives it."

"And doesn't Bill ride him all the time about it, Monk?" She was relieved, saying it to someone.

"I bet Jimmy Fox would pay Gus to help us on that bridge."

"Is Jimmy going ahead with it?"

"Yeah. The old one's too dangerous to use any more."

"He wouldn't want a child, would he?" She warmed to it. "Hasn't he always got someone staying at the Wigwam? I saw two or three last weekend."

"That was his daughter and her kids, I think."

"I never did know about Jimmy's wife. What about Mrs. Fox? You ever know her?"

"Curiosity killed the cat, gal."

"I never figured Jimmy out. He's smug. You'd never think he went through a messy divorce and got fired from the University. He doesn't even seem to mind just being a high school teacher."

"Well, Jimmy says the pay's better than college. He gets more than Mike Paoli, who's a full professor. Jimmy told me the day his youngest was out of high school was when he moved out."

"Those crazy scants he wears. He'd never get away with them on a Chicago beach. Don't you bet Preacher Thwaite will start in on Jimmy next? He's a character."

"Lots of characters round here, and not all men." He stamped out his cigarette and snapped the pliers in his belt, grinning.

She leaned her head against the porch post. "Hoo."

"You heard Jimmy's latest? About this southern baby doll.

The judge had her come in to answer some questions about this hired man who was up for trial. 'Don't you be afraid to speak up,' the judge says. 'Did he rape you?' 'Judge,' she says, 'it was rape rape rape, all summer long!' Well, I got to get." His whistle floated back as he went down the path.

Elizabeth put the cigarette out on the under side of the guard rail and dropped it in the path below. She ran into the house, her bare feet light, and poked her head into the fragrant pink-trimmed kitchen. "Dora, think if there's anything to add to the shopping list."

Dora was baking a low-calorie yellow cake special for the missus and a pan of cheese rolls for the doctor. She considered, hands on hips, pale eyes reflective, "Get some new fruit if it's not too high, like berries. And some of those big beefsteak tomatoes. And say, that girl ain't had breakfast yet. She's getting wild, Mrs. Olson, I notice. Goes down to that lake too early. This morning when I heard the screen I looked and it was half-past four. It's a wonder she never happened on that spooky thing in the water, tell the truth."

"Well, she didn't, anyway. So don't worry, Dora."

"I know. But hadn't you ought to speak with her?"

"I will. I'm going to. And help me get them both in for breakfast with the doctor after this. We really ought to eat together."

Dora agreed, nodding, her wispy hair partly held in place with pins, her ungainly apron rustling with starch as she moved about. She brushed at the wood counters with a damp dishrag in her work-red hand. Dora was untanned, and she felt she knew her position and enjoyed it. She'd never change places with the missus here. Poor dissatisfied thing, and playing now with that Mr. Ardway out there. And just look how she dressed, like the young women did nowadays; bare legs and her blouse too tight.

You'd never catch Dora even in a swimming suit. Oho, just you try, she told her boy friend, Herb Worth. Look what they dragged up on the bathing beach this morning; it goes to prove. Herb had been courting Dora over a decade but she hadn't made up her mind yet. He was a widower with an old mother and two young ones not yet raised. Dora had been with the Olsons for a long time, nine years, since one winter Gus was sickly. The missus found it so handy to have help that she coaxed the doctor into keeping her. Twenty-seven dollars a week and lived in, taking Sunday off when she pleased. And then as a rule just to go over and clean up Herb's farmhouse. The children were lazy and the old mother'd been sick on and off.

Elizabeth was turning the crank on the wall phone. The Ideal Line was a private telephone company, one of the few in existence. You had to call long distance through Bell Company to get the Behmelmens' residence across the blow or the Potawatomi Bible Club, or the big cities up the lake. Sawmill and Ideal and Pine Beach and the whistle-stop of Pokagon were all on the same line. "Operator, give me the Paolis."

"Hello."

"Hi, Angela."

"Say, Elizabeth, I was just going to call. Isn't it frightening?"

"I said to Bill, what if one of the children had come on it."

"I don't know," Angela said. "I took all mine down to look. I believe in every kind of experience to prepare them for life, as they say. Maybe I've been reading too many women's magazines. Al looks a little pale."

"I hear they can't find our sheriff. Don't you bet he's off on a toot again?"

"That's the reason he's elected every term. The people feel he's one of them—good common clay."

"Now, don't get obscene. Still I'm glad it was Ernie saw it down by the pier posts."

"I nearly forgot. That's what I called about: Ernie, not that old dead man. Guess who I saw big as life in the driver's seat of a certain long black Chrysler?"

"Who?"

"Ernie sitting beside him talking like a breeze."

"Who I think?"

"Big as life and wearing a Homburg hat. I haven't seen one of those in an age. He's been away a long time from Pine Beach." Angela's voice faded. "Stop it, Carmen. There's a girl. You'll wake Baby sure as fate. . . . And I bet there's a happy boy in the Sand Castle, Elizabeth."

"Umm." Elizabeth was thoughtful.

"Did you know he was coming? I wonder if Hazel Behmelmen

knew. She used to make him the star of a party now and then, I hear. But he makes me uncomfortable. I mean, he's different, and I remember I felt a fool when I met him. Brilliant people make me think I'm being patronized. . . . Stop it, Carmen. Now see what you've done? . . . Well, if you'll pardon me, old Mrs. John Dewey's needed. Wait a sec, there's an A and P opening up outside Michigan City this afternoon. And there's sure to be all kinds of bonuses. Come along?"

"That's what I called you about."

"I'll pick you up."

"Thanks." Elizabeth hung up. "Well, what you know?" She felt the sweet tingle of the hunter that she recognized, pleased. "Philip. Mr. Malraux." She'd met the newsman who was their neighbor once or twice; but mostly she'd just nodded when their cars passed. She remembered that around him she'd not felt a child the way Bill liked her to feel.

[3]

THE next afternoon was Sunday, and it was already a quarter of five. Dr. Bill removed his sweat-soaked forest-green jacket and tossed it into the corner of the bedroom and the wash-and-wear pants after it. He picked up his glass of Scotch and ice, glancing at the clock over the rim. Over two hours ago he'd begun to undress in the same spot, planning on one July afternoon at the beach. He'd not got down there yet for a lazy stretch. Something or other managed to come up. He'd had his shoes unlaced when the phone rang this time.

Lisa had said, "There go your plans and it's nobody's fault but your own. If you were a specialist you'd be on regular hours. Go on, GP! I'm heading for the lake."

"Christamighty," he'd said, going down to answer it, listening to Monk who was in a panic, convinced that Mama Ardway was breathing her last. When Dr. Bill got there and gave her the initial glucose injection, the worn heart began at once to pump again. She was as withered and shrunk as her own blood cells, it seemed.

Dr. Bill was struggling with himself, trying to use the fading woman's human battle and his own continual amazement at the tenacity for life he'd witnessed over his years of practice as a stepping place to climb out of his depression. Last night there'd been a curled-up four-month fetus in the hospital pan deposited there with the placenta and caul; its heart beat as violently, as desirously as Mama Ardway's as the pan was carried away by the nun. Dr. Bill pulled off his steamed glasses and wiped them on a corner of the bedspread. The Black Swede, they'd called him in med school. The Gray Swede now. Over the years he still struggled to recover that fine feel of power he'd had in his twenties. *Far* had been a small farmer, an immigrant, who'd managed to send sporadic checks during Dr. Bill's schooling. He promised himself that when he was through his parents would take it easy. But then there was the war, and *Far* dead of a coronary while Dr. Bill was in Italy. *Far* was under the sod and a stone up before the letter reached Dr. Bill. He'd used to take him hunting ducks along the shore in winter; it had been their one common pleasure. His father had advised him rarely and had none of *Mor's* dedication to a God or her happy remembering of her old land, Sweden.

The sweat beaded on his forehead from the atticlike heat of the upstairs room. Alcohol was a bad idea before a swim; it was a depressant. At med school there'd been a toast with a girl he lived with until she flunked out. A capable cook, she bought the food and sometimes there was watery wine; they clinked their jelly glasses in the basement flat. Wine unto those of heavy heart! He'd been unquelled, declaring *my beloved's white and ruddy, the chiefest among ten thousand!* She was blonde with pretty green eyes and complained, But don't I wish I had a Florida tan instead, Billy. He was on fire those days.

He stripped off his shorts and undershirt and threw them on top of the crumpled suit. He stood before Elizabeth's long mirror to look glumly at the rather ordinary figure with the beginnings of a rubber tire about the waist, the thick-rimmed glasses emphasizing the intent near-black eyes. The loose sacs, shrunken, dangled. He thought it was a pretty ignoble-appearing creature, and lifted his glass to it before pulling on his swim trunks.

Out in the hall, he stopped at Gus' door, pushing it open. *Mor* had dinned the Bible into his brain. *Correct thy son,* she said, *and he shall give thee rest; yea, he shall give delight unto thy soul.* He could recall the earnest pursed face and hollow eyes and the fact that she had been a rather tall imposing person. That was Proverbs twenty-eight, he thought.

He was picking up books fallen in a heap by the bed. *All Quiet on the Western Front; Practical Taxidermy; Dating, Dancing and Decorum,* the latter inscribed last October, "Happy Thirteenth from Mummy." He lifted the spread and looked under: apple cores, a torn sock, a dirty towel, a specimen-mounting rack, pins, dust kittens, sand. What did one do? Argue, threaten, cajole? When he was young he got the belt from *Mor* if his room didn't stay in order. And it hadn't been a deadly thing between them; he was wrong and his parents not unjust, so he got the strap about his calves. No one belted children today; a public censuring ring stood at your shoulder. When he tried to talk to Gus the boy listened with eyes as if he'd pulled down a curtain and with mouth ready for appeasement. . . . I'll clean it up, Daddy. Don't you worry. I know I'm wrong to let it get this way. . . . And there was no change. Patience, the specialists advised. Don't scar him. Lisa read the books, afraid he'd warp the boy's spirit!

Under the window was a rat cage. There Dr. Bill had been firm—no breeding; he'd brought home two males from the lab. He put a finger on the wire and the fearless animals reared up softly, pointed noses sniffing, tiny front paws hugging their stomachs, snowy coats glistening. He bent closer. Gus had fenced off a corner of the cage with a piece of mesh. There an ordinary field mouse crouched. Where in hell did Gus get it and why in hell did he want it? About on the walls were glass display cases of dead insects, butterflies, moths, a gigantic curled-up spider, a vicious-jawed four-inch flying bug: a hellgrammite. And a stretched dried bat, bird feathers, pine needles arranged with labels. On a low shelf were two killing jars. Gus had followed instructions on making them up from a book he got from the Ideal Public Library, using Mason jars, plaster of Paris and lumps of potassium cyanide, which Lisa got him in the Downtown Drug Store in Ideal. Dangerous, Dr. Bill had protested. Any time Gus could stumble with the jars. He was at a clumsy stage, his feet always resting on each other, his body awriggle.

Downstairs the phone jangled; Dora's steps moved through the rooms. He thought he might try something with Gus, like saying they were old pals and should go hunting together. Once upon a time a family planted and mowed wheat or whatever it was and beat the grain out together. He wondered what the troubles were then—outside ones like existence, survival? With plenty, with pink refrigerators, housing available at a thousand down and easy mortgages, with idleness and boredom the birthright, the troubles had moved inside; one stood alone. Gus was somewhere behind curtains he drew. The *flicka* never did that to him; she made it easy to be a father.

"For you, doctor! It's that young Mrs. Paoli."

"Thanks, Dora." He went down the stairs, thinking how he was blessed in Clara. Funny how even the way she moved sometimes, if she got up quickly, her shoulders bent slightly, leaning forward, in a shambling, not ungraceful way, the odd lonesome pang for his mother shot through his bowels. He paused and let the smoky liquid flow cool down his throat.

He passed the kitchen where Dora was rummaging in the freezer that matched the pink theme, and had two payments made out of ten. Christamighty, he was pretty touchy this afternoon. He lifted down the receiver and leaned against the wall. "Yeah. I'm just leaving the house for the lake, Angela. What's wrong?"

"I'm sorry, Dr. Bill. It's Al; he's been acting sick since last night but he claims it's nothing. I didn't let him go swimming with the other three. Do you think maybe I shouldn't have insisted he come along to see that body yesterday?"

"Goddam, how would I know, Angela." He looked up at the paper globes above him, motionless and brilliant in the still heat.

"Well, don't get sore, but what do you think?"

"Look, I'm not a psychiatrist."

"I'm asking you as a friend, then."

"Your guess is as good as mine. Temperature?"

"No, but he can't hold anything down."

"Then give him ice and soda pop. That usually does the trick."

"My gosh, that's some professional prescription."

"How are you and Mike getting along?"

"If you mean is Mike still drinking, yes. And have I missed, no. But the suspense is killing us."

"I'll tell you again, majority of Catholics wear something nowadays. And if they have Caesareans they have the tubes tied. I know; my hospital happens to be Catholic. And these are religious people. You already have five, Angela. Lordamighty."

"Mike doesn't like that sort of thing. My crazy wop."

"Maybe we could do something about it between you and me. And not tell Mike," Dr. Bill said. "I've heard of that, too."

"That calendar we keep in the bedroom," Angela giggled.

"Let me know if you change your mind."

"Okay, Dr. Bill. I'm coming to the beach with the baby; see you there, maybe."

He took a short cut using Jimmy Fox's bridge and beach path. Jimmy had set new thin slabs of concrete in which he'd fixed, as it hardened, beach stones encrusted with fossil shapes. They were from a pre-man age, small water animals and plants, squares, cones, circles, many broken, millions of skeletons compacted into shale rock.

The beach was crowded with rainbow-hued umbrellas and folding chairs and paraphernalia and people. The lake was a pale blue that faded to white at the horizon where it blended imperceptibly into the sky. The water looked brackish and would be warm near to shore. One had to swim out to find the cold. Boats were busy, small canoes, a long cruiser with sail up, a kayak, sailboats, among the latter Behmelmens' white one that was maintained for Hazel's guests, *The Desire,* a blue star in her white triangle and a soaring thick yellow mast. A motorboat from the Potawatomi beach went puttering by, dragging an old sunburned gentleman on spread skis. The Pine Beach raft had been pushed out to just this side of the second sandbar in deep water and its cinder-block anchor thrown out. It was a broad clumsy plank structure with empty oil barrels strapped underneath; it was laden with children; they slipped and slid about it; the older ones, Monk's boys and the two Thwaite girls, had taken over its main flat area, lying spread-eagled, or hovering above each other, squeezing blackheads and saying what came into their minds:

"You know that new hit 'I'm Going to Be a Big Wheel Some Day'?"

"I prefer 'Only the Lonely Know how I Feel.' I always ask for that."

"Is Jimmy Fox a homo?"

"Do you think! You ought to hear what happened at Madame Moret's last year." The pair of girls attended a finishing school of international reputation for its strait-laced policy on morals and scholastic work. "Some day we might tell."

"I wonder how it feels to drown!"

"What about organizing a swim party for tomorrow night? There's a moon." And "Let's try to get Dr. Olson's lanterns for the last dance of this year. Do let's."

"You think there could be another dead person floating near?"

"I don't know, but I think girls ought to pay half when you go to the movies," Irene, eighteen, gurgled.

"Don't drowned people sink at first, Russ?" Dick said.

"Search me. Don't they have to fire a cannonball over the water to make them surface or something!"

"Beats me."

Their younger brother Skin was hiking himself up over the side. At once Russ and Dick nudged him so he plunged back into the water, watched by three of the Paoli children, sitting close together on the edge, chewing gum and paddling their feet, chanting:

> *I like coffee,*
> *I like tea,*
> *I like the movies*
> *And TV.*

Clara and Gus were practicing diving and coming up under the raft in the space between the barrels. The air smelled different there and was colored green; it was another country than outside. One had to keep his eyes open coming up so as not to bump his head; that was the secret danger. Clara pounded on a hollow rusty drum. "Bong bong bong!" Three times; three was green.

Alan's canoe shot by the raft and he saluted with his paddle, "Hi, everyone!"

"You out hunting for bodies, Alan?" someone shouted after him.

"Yeah, and guess whose freezer I'm going to put them in!" he yelled back. His dogs weren't with him as usual; he'd locked them in the Sand Castle cellar because of the preacher's berating.

Dr. Bill's feet were stung by the sand when his sandals sank in. He reached the Olsons' ten-year-old green-and-white-striped umbrella. Three pairs of legs protruded from under it. Within the hot shade were Elizabeth, Hazel Behmelmen, and Philip Malraux.

"Hello, Hazel," Dr. Bill said. "Looking as handsome and healthy as usual." He leaned to shake her hand.

"Is that a compliment? You know I hate them, darling." Hazel had a statuesque figure at near sixty; her white hair was dyed a brittle black.

"How's your patient," Elizabeth asked, "Mama Ardway?"

"Pulling through."

"Hazel's mending fences, Bill," Elizabeth said in her lazy way.

"I may not come to your beach very much, but when I do I try hard to be neighborly." Hazel smiled in her ironic way. "And I brought Mr. Malraux along to help. He just got here from Nigeria. But you two have met before."

"I don't think so," Dr. Bill said. "But welcome back anyway."

"Yes," Hazel told him, "at the Glass House; one of my parties."

Malraux was getting up to greet Dr. Bill. "It was Mrs. Olson I met, not the doctor. How do you do?"

"Hot."

"Sure is," Malraux said. "I'm afraid I'm a worse neighbor than Hazel, even."

The men's bodies were pale. There were all degrees of sunburn on the people, some related to the finely drawn social lines of the community. Monk, proprietor of the resort, was dark brown and so were the children *in toto,* and a large proportion of the wives. So was Jimmy Fox, high school teacher on vacation. Not the commuting husbands, who came out to bake on week ends and peel the rest of the time. Not Hazel, who stayed under umbrellas and had money and a glass-structured house designed by the same man who did the Sand Castle. Hazel chaired and served on numerous cultural and civic committees; she knew writers and painters and political bigwigs. Her mate Jack played host to her friends and cared for the grounds and interior of the Glass House. Jack was sunburned—even his bald head and beer-belly—from ambling about to water his petunia beds when they drooped in hot hours and to repot the coleuses into bigger tubs.

Malraux smiled as he shook hands; he was fair-skinned with red hair that stood high and mussed. "Better get in and cool off, Doctor."

"When did you get here?" Dr. Bill asked.

"Yesterday. I landed at O'Hare, but it almost took longer to get out to Pokagon by that South Shore line than it did to get to Chicago from Africa."

"That line is a rustic symbol which I hate to see go," Dr. Bill said.

"Mr. Malraux is going to stay all this summer," Elizabeth said, "unless something comes up. Aren't you?"

"I'm taking some time off. I felt I ought to get to know my son a little."

"What you think of Alan?" Dr. Bill asked. "Shot up, hasn't he? Last time he needed a doctor was for his dogs. One had a bad infection; they'd had a fight."

"My Lord, did you look at it?" Malraux grinned.

"I did. High time, too. But don't let it get around that I do vet work. I'm too busy as it is." Dr. Bill was turning from them, tired from the effort, wanting another drink. "Any of you joining me?"

Elizabeth said, "Didn't we just come out?"

"I only wear a suit," Hazel said, "to create the impression that I lie about in luxury."

Elizabeth turned to Malraux as Dr. Bill left. "But is Alan's dog all right now?"

The man sat down again between the women. His hand, concealed by her robe, had already been touching Elizabeth's. She felt how she healed the half-stranger's raw spirit and made him whole. She knew her beauty, lying beside the older woman and the famous man, like a ballad that cleaved the still hot air.

"Frankly I didn't know they'd been in a fight. My son never wrote about it." His face was beside Elizabeth's and he watched her soft lipsticked mouth. "How old are your children, did you say?"

"I didn't. They're big. Gus is almost taller than me."

"And Clara Olson's your daughter, isn't she? Alan talked about her. He even accused her of not doing much but read." Philip smiled.

"It's true. But right now she's out on the raft, noisier than anybody."

"She's a tomboy," Hazel said; "she never thinks of a boy, too, as anything special."

"Is she upset over finding that dead man?"

Hazel was shocked. "Darling? Did Clara really?"

"She couldn't have. I remember, Hazel. Uncle Jack called to tell us; he thought a doctor might be needed. And then Clara came home and we asked her."

"Maybe she got frightened, darling."

Malraux nodded. "I'm positive that Clara Olson was the name; Ernie mentioned it too."

Elizabeth said, "But Clara's so normal; she says whatever she wants. Does anything bother her?"

"Now, I was telling you about the African as an individual," Malraux said. "We're apt to want to deal with him as if he were an American Negro who, as we all know, thinks as a white man does. But the African is a son and grandson of a primitive warrior. His mind runs differently; for example, he thinks round where we think straight. He will build a round home and kraal and plant his crops in circles. Now this is sure to have significance in our understanding of him, don't you both agree?"

Of course they did, and they listened, impressed, content, as he talked his mind out.

Up the shore the Reverend Boris Thwaite came striding, the only man on the beach in a full swim suit, black. He'd spotted Olson coming down and had something to say to him. He'd thought it out thoroughly coming in on the electric after his sermon in the Chicago television studio at ten-thirty that morning. He ran his hand upon his smooth bald head, glad to get the toupee off. His eyes swept over the beach where here and there were strewn gum wrappers and Coke bottles and remains of afternoon picnics. He felt a righteous rage that satisfied him. He'd decided that Olson was his man. Monk Ardway was a boor and a simpleton who laughed when reprimanded; Fox was an eccentric one needed to be wary of approaching, and the other men, Mike Paoli and the lot, commuted all week. Thwaite felt he'd like to start off with someone he could use at any hour. He passed Olson's wife who was talking with Thwaite's next-door neighbor Malraux (whose existence Thwaite tried to ignore) and that atheistic woman of Babylon, Mrs. Behmelmen. The minister's mouth twisted, his loins hot with anger, and he walked into the water and went under.

He'd never had a mistress or even visited the red-light district in Chicago. He had taught himself, and it was arduous labor, to redirect his fervor. He swam open-eyed for yards along the clear bottom. His large round body gave an impression of softness but he worked out an hour or more on the tennis court every morning when he wasn't filling a speaking engagement away from home. He played single court against Irene and Pearl's double. The girls were on the Moret Academy crack tennis team and he insisted they improve their game. He did set-ups using a pair of dumbbells and duck pins and threw a medicine ball on his lawn. He looked ahead to the day two-year-old Ian could join him. He'd already started his swimming lessons. Poor little Ian! It galled him so his pulse quickened.

He pushed himself up to the surface and struck out in the Australian crawl that had won him a silver cup at Princeton. The trophy shone in the breakfront in their Blaine Park place. "Afternoon, Olson!" His voice was deep-toned, nasal, Oxford.

Dr. Bill was floating, eyes half-shut, on the outside slope of the sandbar. Oh you bastard, he thought, pretending he hadn't heard. Even out here the surface water was warm. He had been diving past the bar where it sloped deep and far under was fine and icy. He'd stretched his cramped limbs and muscles and was feeling a half-peace, letting his body hang in the balmy liquid. Faintly he could hear Gus screaming, "Throw it to me. Throw it, you dumb nut, can't you!" at the top of his lungs. They had a striped ball out on the raft.

"Olson. Afternoon."

Damn bastard. Dr. Bill let his feet down so they touched and squinted his nearsighted eyes, scarcely managing a smile. "Oh, Dr. Thwaite."

"Fine weather."

"Yeah, hot."

"Hot."

Out on the hazy water surface noises carried far. Even a whisper in the distance would come clear over the metallic-appearing blue. Thwaite cleared his throat. "You know every summer there's talk about organizing this community. Now it's come to a head, Olson, with this drowning."

"Yeah."

"And a matter equally important concerning my child."

"Umm."

"I wouldn't be a bit surprised if the next death along Lake Michigan occurred right at Pine Beach."

"Come now, Doctor." Dr. Bill let himself float back into the water, eyes half-closed.

"I'd like to catch this community while it's in shock over that body yesterday in this very water."

"What about your child."

"I have talked with his nurse and it seems one of those wolves of young Malraux attacked him today."

Dr. Bill looked at the angry minister. "They aren't exactly wolves. You think they're rabid?"

"No, I've looked into that. And as a matter of fact I wasn't even there; I was in Chicago with my program. I don't get back here until the 3:02. But she had Ian in the yard and the dogs were going by on the road and one charged over and bit the baby. The Malraux lad was right there to see it."

"Skin broken, Doctor?"

"The arm's badly bruised and turning color. Now see here, dogs should be leashed. Isn't this convincing proof? We need a committee here. To draw up a list of rules against any practice that's dangerous. I believe it was Mike Paoli's son who was hit in the eye with a baseball last year. The Potawatomi Bible Club doesn't allow games of that sort on their shore."

"I know. Ridiculous."

"Mark me, the next drowning will be one of us. Don't forget how Behmelmen's son died."

"Christamighty. He drowned close to forty years ago!"

"Just takes one mistake and you've got a fatality. And another thing, all this litter about!"

Dr. Bill was aware that the other man's mien was changing slightly, his affable smile still there but his eyes turning cold. A white mark appeared at the muscle on each side of his mouth; Eve Thwaite must know those spots. He remembered something in the morning *Daily News;* Thwaite had got a drubbing from some columnist. He'd used a phrase: wipe your troubles away and flush them down the drain. It was during one of his televised revival sessions. Dr. Bill had read it to Lisa, pleased at the time. But now he felt sorry for Thwaite, who must be furious about it. The bastard would have made an excellent Puritan or inquisitor or crusader; he was always anxious to spout off on his conviction that this century was going to be renowned for Christian revival. Obviously, as one of the leaders he expected to be remembered by posterity. Dr. Bill made his tone friendly, "I'm just not convinced. I'm pretty tired this afternoon. I'll think about it."

"Come, Olson. Let's catch the moment while it's ripe."

Dr. Bill wished he'd stop calling him by his surname. "Lord-amighty, I'm just not interested."

"It'd take a very small assessment to do it. You have two youngsters. Wouldn't you feel better if there were a lifeguard to keep an eye on them?"

"Ardway's usually on the beach, Doctor. He keeps track of what's going on. And Russ and Dick are on the raft whenever it's out; excellent swimmers."

"Have those young men ever had a lesson on how to pull in a drowning man? Do they know the prescribed holds? No. I've questioned them."

"Sorry." Dr. Bill gave it up. "I don't know." He felt the weakness of words against the man's fervor.

But Dr. Thwaite abruptly had lost interest. He was glaring at the raft where Pearl and Irene had dived under and disappeared, hidden in the air space between the barrels underneath. The Ardway boys were rocking the raft, one standing at each end. Soon the other children were aiding in the rhythmic movement so the plank structure rose and fell, smacking the water. The minister spoke fiercely, "You don't know, eh? Well, I know!" He shouted toward the raft, "Halloa! You stop that. You there. Halloa!" He was wading along the shallow bar, yelling, until the children heard suddenly and ceased the rough game. By now the preacher was purple-complexioned. "My daughters," he roared, pointing with a wild arm under the raft.

"Okay, sir! Okay." Russ shouted and dove over the side. Dick followed. The other children either slid into the water or grew still, their eyes on their hands or the horizon. One or two shoved at each other's sides and giggled, intimidated. The sun was a hot cauldron in the white smoky sky. A tern flew over dipping at the water, missing the fish, just skirting the heads of swimmers. Then the two girls popped up, colored caps like bird-egg shells, pale faces set and anxious.

"Come at once!" the order sounded. He waited while they swam in to him in studied breast-stroke form, their countenances mottled from chagrin and rebellion. "Is this what they teach you at Moret's!" His temper shook him. They trailed after with heads lowered, out of the water and onto the beach.

"No, Papa."

Dr. Thwaite turned them over to his small wife, Eve. She sat in an unbecoming full-skirted suit under a beach umbrella with Ian who dug with a shovel to fill a tiny bucket, and the stiff-uniformed nurse. "They are not to go in again today. This is your fault, my dear. You neglect their training. What they were doing was quite insane."

"Yes, Papa."

"They will explain and you will talk to them."

"Yes, Papa." Beside Eve Ian dumped his bucket and began to fill it again.

The minister wheeled on the two girls, his lips curved down and his face hot. "I haven't heard you say you know you were wrong."

"But we do! Sorry, Papa. Sorry."

"No dessert tonight. And we'll see later, my dear, whether they may come to Vespers tonight."

"Children!" Eve looked at the miscreants. "Whatever did you do?"

Dr. Thwaite returned to the water to finish his swim. That was the very sort of thing, he thought, that he was talking about to Olson. The rage subsided and the blood beat not so loudly in his ears. A guard would never have permitted dangerous horse-play.

Irene was in tears while her sister sat stoic. "I can never face those boys again! Dammit on dessert."

"Don't say that word, dear."

"Papa's hateful." Pearl cracked her knuckles slowly. "Some-time I'll do something to him. Why's he that way? I'd divorce him if I were you, Mama. How can you stand him? Was he always that way? Was he like that when you married him?"

Irene took a tissue from the basket and blew loudly. "Am I embarrassed! I could die. Dammit. Murder." She put her face in her hands, edged back in the shade near her little brother. "Poor Ian."

Eve got out another toy and gave it to the nurse, who jingled it for the baby. "Dam!" he chortled and hit his spade on the sand, striking the bauble aside. The bruise on his fat upper arm was slight. The dog, Eve knew, had been confused and meant him no harm; the nurse hadn't told the whole tale. Eve liked animals and always wished for a pet, a dog of her own, a collie.

She said, "Girls, Papa's thinking of you. Only of you." She trained her thoughts that way, consciously submissive. She turned hate aside. She was rather like a nun, she considered, although she differed in that she never thought of God as palpable; she never depended on Him. An old-fashioned nun: offer it up; never rebel. Eve's face was pretty in an ordinary way, she felt; her hair plain; there was a coarseness about her hands and feet that showed her peasant blood. Now Boris, son of a line of preachers, had refined limbs for all his round body; she felt she should be humble before that fact. She had excellent control; at times she came right to the brink before she stopped. Yes, Papa. Of course you're right. Always are, Papa. She knew she'd be glad, though, when the girls were married and gone. No reason to tame them, she felt, and allowed them privately to voice their pouts. "Now Papa has your best interests at heart. You know that."

"Yes, Mama." Irene's face was still hidden in her lap. "But I could die."

"He's mean. And he *doesn't* care." Pearl's fingers were toying with a gold anklet she had put on, a gift from Dick last year. She blinked her eyes rapidly, a tic manifest only when she was steamed up about something. "You couldn't drag me to Vespers this evening."

"Let's pray tomorrow's papers have nothing adverse to say about this morning's service." Eve lifted her brows and watched her beautiful daughter Pearl seethe.

One by one, as it neared six, the people were leaving the shore, the women to see that supper was under way, the men, most of them, to mix a tall drink with plenty of ice. Sunday evening was cherished by the commuters whether they took the last night connection, the 8:19, went in on the early morning *Hot Shot,* or drove into the city in their cars. The young offshore wind was blowing stronger; the boats were setting in, glinting, the voices of the passengers muffled. The sun misted over as its last hours neared. Three small brown boys with water-shining flesh and sun-white hair waded a few feet from shore, with a plank of driftwood on which they had mounted a stick and hung a torn plastic tablecloth. They held the corners so the wind could fill it and make it move. Their mouths puckered in concentration. The clear treble of Chris Paoli rose, "I have breakfast cereal every night when the little hand points at six and the big hand points at nine."

Malraux was taking leave of the Olsons and Hazel. "Now all the air a solemn stillness holds, save where the beetle wheels his droning flight. And drowsy——what's the rest of that?"

"Jack would know," Hazel said. "It's Tennyson, I think. I used to know it. Here are the children."

Dripping, Alan, Gus, and Clara emerged from the lake. They stood quiet and spent, waiting for the grown-ups to move toward food. Gus put one bare foot on the other and with his water-wrinkled finger and thumb flicked at the rubber bands on his braces. Clara knelt, scooping the dry silical grains through her hands, her cheek against her knee. Alan came close by his father and watched his face.

"I knew a lot of poetry once, didn't I, Bill?" Elizabeth appealed to him.

"Umm."

"How'd that go, Mr. Malraux? It fits this evening perfectly, doesn't it?" Elizabeth was vibrant, happy.

"Now all the air a solemn stillness holds." Malraux paused again, hands on hips, throwing his red hair back in an energetic way.

Clara began to recite from where she knelt, not looking up, her voice unclear.

> *Save where the beetle wheels his droning flight,*
> *And drowsy tinklings lull the distant folds;*
> *Save that from yonder ivy-mantled tower*
> *The moping owl does to the moon complain*
> *Of such, as wandering near her secret bower,*
> *Molest her ancient——*

She flushed. "It's just that old Gray's 'Elegy.' It takes a lot of time if you want to say every line. Phooey."

"I didn't know you knew that, Clara," Elizabeth cried.

Dr. Bill came over and ruffled the girl's hair. "Sure you don't want to come up and have a short one with us, Mr. Malraux?" He drew Clara up to stand beside him, his arm about her.

"Call me Philip, if you don't mind. We're neighbors." Malraux nodded. "No thanks. Alan and I are going over to the Summer Playhouse. Like to take a rain check, though."

Hazel asked, "It's *Gaslight* again, isn't it? They always do *Gaslight*. I'd take the drink, Philip."

Gus pointed out on the water. "They're bringing your boat in, Mrs. Behmelmen."

"Isn't *The Desire* sweet? One of my guests this week is a painter. He had a one-man show at some Mexican gallery last year, I think. Jack calls him an honest gigolo—a compliment, of course." She left them, waving, "I must hurry and get supper. I'm the cook, you know!" She went to meet the sailboat, her black hair gleaming bronze in the sun, the flesh of her long legs wobbling. Her body was aided in its contours by a corseted custom-made suit. She reached her property, along both sides of which ran a fence as far to the shore as the government allowed land to be owned. Twin signs were mounted, with old English lettering: IF THIS WERE YOUR BEACH, WOULD YOU WANT OTHERS TO USE IT? THANK YOU!

Philip and his son went toward the Sand Castle, cutting diagonally through the sand. Philip put an arm on Alan's shoulder, noting suddenly that the boy was nearly as tall as he. There was no physical resemblance between the two and they had lived apart so much that the boy hadn't picked up the mannerisms that often pass for inherited qualities. The man was freckle-skinned and had a slight burn; his eyes were gray and his hair bright; the boy, brown as an islander, had a stronger physique, and his dark features were handsome; he walked half a step behind Philip, eager to show deference.

"You didn't bring the dogs down. Why not, Alan?"

"That Dr. Thwaite."

"What?"

"He has it in for me. I'm not going to his old services any more, either. Man!"

"What happened? Bite someone? You know you promised to train them when I bought you the pair."

"Jojo nipped his little kid this morning."

"Who's fault?"

"Don't know, Father."

"Well?"

"See, I was meeting Dick Ardway at the tennis court, and the kid came toddling out of his yard. I thought a car might get him and I went to look for that woman who takes care of him. She was talking with Chappy down by the fence. The little kid must have grabbed Jojo's tail because he got spooked and nipped him and he began to yell. That's when the nurse came and took him into the house." Alan's frown lines creased. "I hate that crabby preacher."

"I remember he raised Cain about the boundaries long time ago; that's why I told the architect to have the place surveyed and stones sunk in cement along the line." His pale eyes turned amused on his son. "Has Jojo bitten anyone else important?"

"A week before you got here Bosco nipped Carmen Paoli. She's that dumb one."

"Dumb?"

"I don't know, she's sort of wacky. She's twelve but she acts more like her brothers, about four and five. I like her, though, and she's crazy about the dogs. She's real good-hearted. She was playing in the water and that always makes Bosco excited. He wants her to stay up on the beach. He tore the pants of her suit."

"My Lord!"

"But she didn't care. Angela didn't mind either; she thought it was cute he wanted to take care of Carmen."

"Who's this Angela?"

"Mrs. Paoli. Most everyone calls her Angela."

"I see. Does everyone call Mr. Paoli by his given name?"

"Sometimes Mike. He's a physics professor."

"Let's get back to the dogs. Was the minister around when the Paoli child was bitten?"

"No, but he heard about it and bawled me out and said the dogs mustn't come to the beach."

"Say anything about me? He can't do that. Why you take his guff?"

"You have to. He bosses everyone around, Father. I had the dogs trained to the canoe too." He flung his hand, building his humor. "You talk to him, Father, will you? He's very important. But he'd have to listen, because you're *more* famous."

"I'll pay him a call in the morning; straighten it out."

"Man!"

"By the way, do you play with the Olson children a lot? Their boy, what's-his-name."

"Gus? It's hard to get him to the tennis court and he's not very good. They have a canoe but it's an old one and they never use it. Gus doesn't come to the beach half the time. He collects bugs and stuff."

"And Clara? She's the one found that body."

"Yeah. She's okay for a girl. She wears glasses."

"That's not good?"

"I don't mean anything, but girls shouldn't be so brainy. Like I say, she sometimes has her nose in a book like a real show-off. And then she takes dips too before the sun's up; me, I sleep!"

"And do you call Clara's mother Elizabeth?"

"Jeeps, no."

Philip thought about the slow voice and soft body in the sand in the heated shade of the umbrella. "And the doctor? Should you have asked him to look at your sick dog, do you think?"

"But they'd had a bad fight." His changing voice creaked in his enthusiasm. "All the way down the dune steps! It was great. Ernie and me had to get the hose. Finally we pulled their tails and got them separated."

"I didn't know they fought each other."

"Just that one time. I beat them up right after. Ernie made me so they wouldn't again. But then Jojo's neck swelled; the vet gave me something to heal it, and Dr. Olson said that was wrong. He said to soak the scab off, and Chappy and me put him in the bathtub and squeezed about a cup of yellow stuff out. He got well fast; I sure thought he was going to die for a while."

"You didn't write me."

"Yes, I did, and I told you about Dr. Olson curing him too."

"Oh."

They passed the sand hummocks where sparse prickly Marram grass grew, and up the creosoted staircase that blended into the side of the dune. Around were ground myrtle and junipers and yews brought in from nurseries by Ernie Chapman. The lake side of the dune was covered with pine and hemlock; the north side was bare sliding sand.

Ernie Chapman worried about it, for inches at a time the grains were leaving on the wind and eating toward the house's foundation. Last winter Ernie had written detailed letters to Philip about the trouble and itemized the expenses necessary to correct it. The area stretching twenty miles south of Pine Beach and a few miles north composed one of America's little deserts. The people said the hills walked. The barren dunes were a product of white man's coming, for once there was a forest of giant white pines here and the land was nailed. But lumbermen came in after the pioneers and snaked out trees; they left openings into which crows would often drop acorns, but where sometimes the sand, out of control, began to drift about. In a violent windstorm the landscape's contour was recreated. The sand went wandering and overcoming timber and marsh and making of the countryside a wasteland. Even over towns it flowed, nearly in the way a volcano advances. In the small desert nothing very old grew; underbrush and trees were young and the stubborn Marram grass throve. Ancient growth to remind one of the duneland's history was sometimes manifest in the branches of a colossus tree upthrust from the top of a sand billow like a drowning man's arms. Ernie Chapman liked to worry about his war with the sand.

Alan and Philip turned to look back at the nearly deserted beach as they paused to get their breath. They heard the shrill whistles that maids and housewives blew at the supper hour to call in the children. Monk's wife Belle blew three longs, and Angela Paoli a long and a short. Della Chapman called Alan with four short wheets, though she was seldom in a hurry and he could eat just about when he pleased. Jimmy Fox blasted in his guests or visiting adult offspring with an ancient first-world-war army bugle he'd picked up. Eve Thwaite used a camel bell from Egypt presented to her husband by one of his admiring parishioners. Far down the cooling sand the four Olsons were starting up the boardwalk, Clara leading, Dr. Bill in the rear, hands loose as though he were tired.

It was later in the evening, while the land breeze leaped in fits and starts, disturbing the lake, that Dr. Bill and Elizabeth went for a walk. They had finished supper half an hour ago; Herb Worth had come to call on Dora, his big-chested frame balanced on a pink stool, bent over a bowl of her homemade lemon ice cream. Dr. Bill had persuaded his wife to come with him instead of accompanying the children to the Sunday evening vespers. Every summer Sabbath that the Reverend was in Pine Beach they were held punctually at seven-thirty. As the Olson couple came down the boardwalk they heard the singing which Irene accompanied with her guitar:

> *O Lord, it can't be so this morning*
> *O Lord, it can't be so this evening*
> *O Lord, it can't be so!*

Later on Thwaite would tell at least one parable.

The sun was gleaming red and the sky gathering its colors together. The small waves rolled on the hard-packed sand, backing off and then rushing forward to break, "Fisshh-unk, fishsh. Fishunk-unk, shshsh, fsshssh, onk!" The light dazzled as the end of a wave exploded in rainbow bubbles. The pure arc of lake swung around; the world was a circle, half water, half land. Sprinkled over the fluid surface were bars and dots of white wave that picked up the coming sunset hues. Near shore it was translucent green, urine green, almost as if orange shone through it. A band of small children passed the couple, hurrying nowhere in a zigzag course, diverted easily by driftwood or a pebble. Their skins glistened like mirrors struck by the crepuscular rays; where they padded lightly in the lake edge, the moisture twinkled. Their tones faded:

> *Oh my finger, oh my thumb,*
> *Oh my bellybutton, oh my bum!*

Elizabeth stopped. "Wait. I want to take off my shoes."

He was already barefoot, his sandals at the foot of the boardwalk. "Why didn't you leave them back there?"

She tossed them on a sand rise and swatted at a beach fly, impatient. "Don't let me forget them."

"Well." He rolled his pants cuffs.

Up ahead Jack Behmelmen was stripping off his sweater and wading in, going under. Lisa walked in the water's edge. "There's Uncle Jack having his dip. Yoo hoo!" Jack raised a hand as they passed.

"Hazel seems in fine fettle today."

"She's getting white rugs for all their downstairs, Bill. A new fabric that you can just hose off."

"She manages to keep busy."

"You mean something by that? Is it a crack?"

"No." He caught her hand, appeasing. "I'm just glad you're my wife and not Hazel."

She was unwilling, her eyes turned away. "Be nice to have her money, Bill."

"Money's not the whole world."

"It is too. I'd be good at being filthy rich; I'd throw all my clothes away every year and wear new ones."

He laughed, feeling a renewed pulse of affection for this Lisa who was a little girl; her clear skin, disarrayed blonde hair, vital and rounded body; even the old white shorts and the loose shirt with a pack of cigarettes jutting from its pocket, contributed to the effect. "But you'd be good at anything you set your mind to, *älskling.*" Gay, he put his arm about her waist. He was forcing it though and felt she knew. Vaguely he wished that she'd speak more clipped and not so drawling; and that she would not constantly sound as if she were phrasing questions; and that she were satisfied and mature and intent on him. He sighed as she drew away from his arm by bending to gather skipping stones.

She held them against her little narrow breasts that were made firm and pointed by a brassière. "One thing we need and we don't have to be rich for it. You know what I mean. I was telling Hazel and she says forget about a Porsche and buy a secondhand car. They're real cheap; the market's something-or-other."

"*Älskling,* we can't afford it. You know what the Volks cost and it isn't even half paid for. Hazel ought to know I'm not the plush kind of doctor; I'm just an old-fashioned extinct GP species. You better enlighten her. You know the subject so well." He was walking ahead of his wife.

She refused to hurry and spoke to his shirt back, brooding. "Hazel says it's smart to turn over your car every couple of years

because it's easier to sell before it's out of style. Doesn't that make
sense?"

"Let's give up the Owl's Roost next summer! Then we'll get
your car. We'll stay in Ideal." He turned around. "We're paying
for everything on a plan now, Lisa."

"Isn't it your fault though? If you'd just specialize like everyone else. General Practitioners are out just like the old family
grocer, but will *you* admit it? There'd be nothing to it, Bill. Set
up the office in Michigan City or Benton Harbor. Ideal's too small
for anyone but farmers. They'd take you right away on the staff of
that new Community Medical Center, too. Don't you know it!"

He paused, waiting until she caught up. "I will not have
patients who come to me on referral and have five or six specialists
diagnosing and treating them. I just happen not to be able to endure
pushing people back and forth like cattle. No telling where the
trend will end, but I'm not going to be a part of it."

"You're exasperating; you should have been born last century. Don't you have any pride? You should see yourself when
you go off in the morning. Will you get a new suit and give away
that old wash-and-wear? You aren't bad-looking but you sure
know how to hide it."

"Thanks," he laughed, running his trim strong hand over his
hair, glancing at her, angry. "I'm sticking with my Holy Mother
Hospital despite all medieval inefficiencies and all those maddening
old virgins with stubborn pruderies. At least they have convic-
tions. And the Lord knows they do need me. That's something,
Lisa."

"Is it?"

"And could I give up Mama Ardway? Damamighty."

"I didn't say you shouldn't keep her if you have to."

He said sharply, "Do you deliberately misunderstand me?"

Her eyes on the sand, she was intense. "Why not consider the
rest of us; not me. What about Gus and Clara? Do they go to
college?"

"I'll bet on the horses at the South Bend track."

"Don't you make me mad." She fumbled at the cigarettes in
her shirt and shook one up, catching it between her lips. The
skipping stones were still in her arm crook.

He grinned, feeling her capitulation, "And don't forget,

älskling, there are those who go from birth to grave and don't
see the way things look at three and four in the morning. *The
pride of the height, the beauty of heaven, with His glorious show.''*

She hadn't heard, scratching the match and lighting up. "And
that way wouldn't we have money for a car, at least?"

"Are you going to skip them?"

"Bill. Don't you ever listen to me?"

He pointed ahead to a cave of sand on the boat-strewn
Potawatomi Club beach. "What's that? First one I've seen in a
long time." He quickened his steps while she stayed by the water.

The sand house was lighted by the red of the west sky. The
magnificence of the dune sunsets was due partly to the light re-
fracting through the silt and smoke of Chicago and Milwaukee
across the lake. The blazing ball was falling slowly and whoever
was along the shore or in the water, Uncle Jack or the running
children, or Bill, or Elizabeth flipping her stones over the wave-
ripped surface, the bloody path would stream straight to that one
and stay with him.

Three square holes were carved in the damp sand to make
the adjoining rooms. Benches were cut in the walls and a table
mounded in the center of crumbling sand. The floor was soppy
from water seeping up. Dr. Bill stepped down in and sat on the
bench, whispering, "Lisa, it's you never listen. . . . *Lord, why art
Thou so far from the words of my roaring?''* He laid his hand on
the table, which gave way and split over his bare feet. He leaned
back, arms rested up on the dry sand surface. *"I cry out in the
day time and in the night season, and am not silent.''*

"What you mumbling about?" She appeared at the rim edge,
cigarette in her fingers. "They won't skip. Water's too wavy."

"Umm."

"Know what Philip told me?"

"Who." He dug with his toes in the puddle of water forming.

"Malraux." She was brittle.

"Oh. What?"

"Clara found that drowned man."

He looked up. "No. Chapman found it." He looked away to
the colored sky. "You sure?"

"Isn't it what I'm saying to you?"

"I remember she did look different when she came home."

"You realize that she lied to you. Didn't you ask her directly?"

"Poor child. I'll have a talk with her at breakfast, Lisa. I'll try to straighten it out." He scowled, half-absent.

"And that's all? If it were Gus you'd be perfectly furious. What about next time? How will you know when she's telling the truth!"

"I said I'd attend to it."

"Bill, you go about like a pendulum. One moment we're not strict enough parents and then too strict. Or is it me? I'm the one gets criticized."

"Lisa."

"We quarrel all the time."

"That's marriage for you." His anger matched hers now. And it wasn't so about Gus, he thought. He'd have felt the same about either of his children. He was a just man, his faults lay in other matters. The lovely light stood about them, the man seated in the playhouse, the barelegged woman shaking her head, standing at his shoulder shredding the tobacco with a violent unhappy movement and throwing it in the small breeze. In the two of them the feeling of human betrayal lay deep and barely acknowledged. They turned their faces to the last red edge of the ball as it was sucked under and the gaudy colors abandoned to fade by themselves. Dr. Bill stood. "Say, I'm sorry, though. Don't be cross, Lisa." He climbed up on the beach and slipped his arm about her shoulders.

She shrugged, "Well."

He pointed to the white-painted lifeguard stand above a twelve-foot ladder. A dilapidated red square hung from a pole over the chair. "Reverend Thwaite wants to organize us again this year. He's on the warpath; he wants Pine Beach to have one of those."

They looked at the sign mounted on one side of the structure, listing names—Camp Chairman, Beach Chairman, auxiliary officers; it specified that Potawatomi Bible Clubbers were to restrict themselves to the area designated by markers, and no dogs or ball playing was permitted; it noted hours during which the man was on duty:

Saturday and Sunday: 10:30–1:00
2:00–6:00

Wednesday: Not on duty
Other Weekdays: *10:30–12:30*
                        2:00–5:30

And in heavy lettering:

RED FLAG INDICATES LIFEGUARD NOT ON DUTY.
YELLOW FLAG INDICATES LIFEGUARD ON DUTY BUT
SWIMMING NOT SAFE.
GREEN FLAG INDICATES LIFEGUARD ON DUTY AND
SWIMMING SAFE.

Lisa put her arm about Dr. Bill's waist and leaned against him. "I don't think their lifeguard could save anyone. You ever see him up close, Bill?"

"No."

"Looks like a baby beef."

"Well, I hope Monk doesn't put one on our beach, Lisa. Thwaite was a little nasty." They were heading back toward Pine Beach. "What does he do at Vespers, Lisa, besides healing the halt and the blind?"

"I don't know."

"Come on."

"We sing."

"Not even one Bible verse?"

"Oh sure, and a parable for the children. They love it; he should have been an actor; they all get open-mouthed."

"He does all right, judging from this afternoon, and he'd up-stage the competition." He grinned.

She was scuffing at the sand as if restless and he felt her receding from him. When they reached her shoes she dropped her embracing arm and turned into the shallow water, splashing, her sandals swinging in her hand. Dr. Bill's mind went to Mama Ardway and how her eyes were when she'd opened them in the sweltering midafternoon. Let me go, Dr. Bill, let me pass on this time! He'd seen the glint of humor in the watery pale depths. They got along well; he clung to her life and she felt it.

They were nearing Pine Beach; only a few strips of mauve and violet remained in the sky. Sounds floated from the group ahead on the sand hillock below Thwaite's Linden House:

By thy rivers gently flowing, Illinois!
O'er thy prairies verdant growing, Illinois.
Comes an echo on the breeze
Rustling through the leafy trees
And it's mellow tones are these: Illinois!

A small figure detached itself from the group, Chris Paoli, four, running down the sand slope to meet the pair.

Marilyn Monroe fell down in the snow;
Her dress went up
And all the boys said oh!

"Hi," Dr. Bill said. "How's it going?"

"My daddy came home, Dr. Bill. Mike came home."

"That's good."

"My daddy and my mama aren't talking. I'm the interpreter."

"Heavens," Elizabeth told him. "You don't have to broadcast it. Bill, Angela would die!"

"Oh I doubt it." He laughed.

"Don't care, don't care. And when my daddy went away he took a bottle of whisky and his golf clubs. That was all he had. I like Mike and I wish my mama was deaded."

"Chris, don't say that."

Dr. Bill laughed, "Let him be, Lisa. He doesn't mean it."

"Really, Bill. What's got into you?"

"Dead dead." Chris was dashing back to the others.

I love cocoa, I love tea;
I love to sit on a white Protestant's knee!

Elizabeth's mouth was firm. "You're contrary as an old mule tonight, Bill. You spoil everything. Don't you."

"Everybody's taught the art of concealment," he said shortly, drily, "the minute they acquire their first grain of reason."

"Would you rather everyone behaved like a bunch of peasants?"

"Peasants are the most convention-bound of all."

"Let's all be savages, then." She gestured to the gathered people. "Are you coming? You want to show your face to your neighbors one time?" The song had ceased and the revivalist was relating the story of *The Golden Windows,* gold as seen sun-illumined from afar.

"No, thanks."

He watched her go. At the boardwalk he slipped on his sandals. As he passed through the twilight he felt the hovering peace of the dark trees overhead, some a century old, and more. Sagged in a hollow beside the walk were the remains of an ancient cabin. Children wearing rolled paper bags for hats and playing spacemen sometimes crawled in and out the windows and dug in the sand drifted deep:

> *Catch a falling satellite,*
> *Put it in a milkjar,*
> *Send it to the USSR!*

The wind shuddered through the high leaves and needles. Frogs and night insects trilled. And hidden, a Great Horned Owl, two feet tall, asked in a quavering bass, "Hoo-hoo—who-o-o-o? Huh–huh–hoo-o?"

Dr. Bill halted, the quiet rushing in waves upon his ears, over his mind. Heal me of my ineptitudes, he prayed to someone. Stir me from my ignorance; forgive me my guilts. He had no faith in his mother's deity; *Mor* had failed in her real intent. *The fool hath said in his heart, there is no god,* she'd read to him. She questioned him when he came home to visit and they were alone, you don't believe, do you, *Pojke?* Not really? Dr. Bill thought how as time crept over his bones he was sinking more and more into the past, remembering, pulling up old Bible phrases and dim scenes. He held to whatever would make him part to the ageless moving tide of men. He felt how death like a great wheel of doom roamed above him.

The Pere Marquette railroad lay a mile away in Pokagon and the horn of a diesel monster running on the track exploded in a series of unlovely bawls. Alan's German shepherds on the Sand Castle terrace pricked up their ears and sat on their haunches, accompanying the sound with long and sorrowful howls. Dr. Bill drank in the night's stillness as he made his way to the Owl's Roost where Dora and her farmer friend sat in the lighted kitchen, talking.

[4]

IN THE morning Clara was at the beach before seven. The air was warm and misty as if it would rain soon. She hesitated at the water edge for a while and then sat on the sand, unable to go in. This was the first time she'd come down early since she'd seen it in the water. She preferred to swim when the water was crowded. The beach was bare of life now, the lake oppressive, the surface ruffled with waves too small to break, blue-green on their shadowed sides. Along the bar the water turned pink-white. Pale streaks paralleled the horizon. The moon on its journey appeared cut of white paper in an imperfect circle, blue-mottled where its shadows merged. A gull passed solitary; the flailing strokes sliced the moist air. Clara shivered; she glanced down at her side where a bug was on its back in a sand depression, legs waving.

Her dream of an hour ago would not be shoved away; the vision of death and concealment stayed with her, the climbing through an oozy horrid tunnel that grew ever narrower, funneling, dimming, foul. Her mind went on it unwilling. No wonder, she thought, men long ago made up Hades and devils. They must have believed they'd been visited by evil when slipping into that kind of nightmare. Clara had one recurring dream in which swimming, she bumped into that fish-pecked lump, and the man turned over, opened his eyes and smiled, evil and secret. She couldn't forget, though she assured herself that she'd made it up and every bit dwelt only in her mind. It remained as scary as if there were some-one unknown who wished her real harm. She shook at the terror to rid herself of it, unable to lose the haunting feel of claustrophobia and despair.

Far off Alan's dogs barked. She saw him dashing pell-mell down the distant stairs, and trot to the water, the shepherds circling with crazy joy about him. His hand waved toward her just as he hit in a slapping splash. The dogs stood to their leg joints watching and one paddled out after him and back. Clara gazed at the beetle near her hand trapped in the sand grains, a design of two colors, its body black, thorax and six legs orange with black tips, the feel-ers and biting jaws a brilliant orange too. She pushed a finger under it to assist it and when it had regained its legs, it sped toward the lake. A wave came lapping to wash it away, so it disappeared. Per-haps it would float up against dead things out there, or sea beasts that snaked through the brown-green depths. Who knew for sure?

Alan was swimming toward her beach in his free-swinging style. "Hi!" His voice echoed in the air. The dogs galloped up to swish their tails and nudge Clara with cold leather-tipped noses, shaking themselves, sprinkling water. She grabbed at their studded harnesses.

"Hey, Jojo, Bosco! Quit."

"Aren't you going in?"

"No." Unable to move.

"Watch me do the dead man's float!" He turned face-down on the surface, his body straight.

She put her head against Jojo's wet coat. "You smell good, boy; you smell like a puppy."

Alan gasped at the surface again. "Here come Skin and Mr. Ardway!" He started turning backward somersaults and stayed under every time until his breath gave out.

A pair of sandpipers skimmed ahead of the approaching fig-ures, "Pr-lee, pr-lee! Pre-teee, tee-tee-teee." The dogs rushed at the birds, who teased, dipping along the water. When the pursuers gave up, the pipers would land and run along the wet sand, inviting the renewed chase. The game would be repeated endlessly throughout the years' days.

Monk stood above Clara. "Say, little gal, water too cold for you?"

Skin was there too. "Clara."

"No." She smiled up at Monk, who noted her last-year's suit was too tight, her young breasts constricted. Her flanks were tan and smooth, her face serious, her brows low. She was in no way like Elizabeth, ready for frivolity with an infectious laugh. The girl took after the sobersides doctor.

Alan was fanning the foaming water, seated on the sandbar, chin at water level. "Coming in, Skin?"

Skin raised high his bucket of warm tar to explain, "And I don't want to get my trunks wet."

"Going to rain," Alan yelled. "Hope it thunders and lightnings. Hope there's an awful storm. Man!"

"Looks like a drizzle to me, kid," Monk bawled back.

Clara ran sand through her fingers. "Mr. Ardway, you going to patch that old lifeboat again? Can I go fishing next time you go?"

"Yeah. You can and we are. And you tell your mother Jimmy Fox is going to tear down the Wigwam bridge. He wants your brother to help. He'll pay twenty-five cents an hour. You think he'll come for that?"

"I guess."

"You tell your mama."

"Okay. Gus is in Dutch; he'll be glad."

"Take care, gal. Come on, Skin." Monk went over to the ancient boat, pulling two scrapers out of the back pocket of his Bermudas.

Skin waited beside Clara a moment, feeling he appeared frail in contrast to the figure of his father. His chest was bony and his leg muscles knotty; his face that missed being good looking was angular, his eyes deep blue. He wore a hand-down pair of swim trunks; Monk sported brand-new shorts, bought by the dozen at the beginning of the summer at an ancient dusty department store in Ideal. Skin whispered, intense, "Penny for your thoughts."

"A quarter an hour isn't anything; I get sixty cents just baby sitting."

"You're miles away, Clara."

"Why patch that dumb boat again?"

"Yeah." He giggled. "Won't do any good."

"He ought to buy a new one."

"Why aren't you going in the lake, Clara? Go ahead."

"Why aren't you going in! Everybody wants to know. Why does everyone ask questions all the time?"

"Alan came down to go swimming with you, I know. You like him because he's a year older."

"Who cares what you say?"

> *Alan Malraux lost his drawers*
> *Clara Olson lent him hers!*

She made no reply and he tried again to stir her in some way. "Your hair; it's pretty, Clara."

She felt she hated it when Skin pestered about. He had a crush. "No, it's not."

"Grow it, Clara. Will you? Like that top-ten tune: 'Her Long Black Tresses!' "

"I don't care what I look like."

Skin was used to being low dog of three brothers and had learned persistence. He didn't mind disputing with Clara or her being nettled. "Grow it, Clara. Huh?"

"Rain'll be here soon!" Monk was beckoning, jerking his head. "Let's us get this over."

"And be my girl. Why won't you?"

"You weirdo!" Wrath stirred her, and she kept her gaze from him, fixing it on the swift swimming shape of the boy in the water heading back to his own beach. The two dogs barked down by the gray-headed pier posts. "Go away."

"You know why a gull stands on one leg when it's asleep?" He gripped the bail of the tar bucket.

"Go away, will you?"

"If it lifted the other up, it'd fall down." Skin strolled off.

She whispered, "That dumb drip," and rose and went to the water edge. Yesterday she'd watched Pearl Thwaite leave another mush note to Skin's brother, Dick, in the hollow tree in the ravine. She read it and then folded and put it back, memorized:

A pound of love, a pound of kisses;
I hope some day you'll be my missus.
Let's do what we did yesterday
Under the lifeboat, Sweetyface.

Clara wondered what they did; what was a kiss really; was that what they did? Or did Dick use his teapot like the girls at Ideal High said married people did. She felt the confusion, the undone riddle. The orange-and-black beetle had been tossed up again and was half-buried in the wave line. She urged it out with her toe and kicked it up onto the beach. But it scurried back to the water.

"Okay. Drown, dodo."

"Hey Clara!" Skin came running over. "I know something you don't know."

"Cheers."

"I'm going to count to ten and if you don't ask me I won't tell."

"Somebody give him a medal, a prize."

"You'll die when you hear." He nudged her shoulder, edging against her. Sometimes they fought getting out of the water onto the raft, leaning against each other, Clara gritting her teeth and Skin using his hard arms to keep her in the water. "It was a teen-ager from the Potawatomi Bible Club that they found in the lake day before yesterday."

She looked at him startled. "I have to go on up to breakfast."

He wanted to push her, to rumple her hair, anything to rouse her to contend with him. "Can you feature it? And it was a girl too. She was about sixteen."

"Who says?"

"That crazy sheriff. He came over to our cottage last night. Said she'd been missing a week and her mother didn't report for a while because she'd run away from home before."

"I hate it." She frowned, laid her hand soft on his arm. "It's like it was us, Skin?" She made a question of it.

"I thought you'd die." He was victorious. "And now they're trying to find if she did it on purpose!"

"But I have to go home." She hurried to the boardwalk.

"Bye," Skin shouted after her.

She didn't turn. The mist was becoming rain almost imperceptibly as she reached the Owl's Roost. Dora met her in the entryway, in her hands a wood tray laden with thick mugs and coffee pot, a crystal saccharin dish, a pitcher of cream from Worth's Jerseys, and a napkin-covered plate of breakfast-cake squares. "You wet, eh?" she demanded.

"No, I'm not wet, eh! Can't you see?" She mimicked, rude, baring her braces, hugging Dora.

"Watch out. You go change and come eat."

"Okay."

"Where's your brother, too?"

"Haven't seen him."

"Well, you come right to the porch. I'll have your cocoa. This family's like a bunch of babies. I told Gus to be here. He don't listen, more than you. The Doctor has to leave early to go see that Mrs. Ardway too."

"I felt a drop of rain." Clara leaned her head back against the door frame. "Think it's starting, Dora?"

"Hustle up." Dora went around the porch corner to the other side.

"Is that Clara?" Dr. Bill was on the cane couch, his forehead knotted over his papers. The six-year-old chintz cushions propped behind him were frayed and worn to the shapes of bodies. They were slightly damp from the night dew and the humidity. He felt harried; his practice was too full; there would be a dozen farmers and wives under Murdock's eye when he got there.

"I told her to get a move on, Dr. Bill. Want me to pour for you?" She set the tray on the unsteady wicker table.

"Umm."

"And the boy's out I guess; least he's not in his room that I can find."

"Lisa?"

"The missus goes shopping today."

"Lordamighty, I forgot again. She can drive me in."

The woman retreated; Dr. Bill leaned over to take the saccharin from the tray. He shook a pill out and it dropped on the floor. He muttered while fishing for another to put in the mug; it sizzled effervescent. From the porch he could see the gray water, hedged with a layer of nimbostratus cloud. The drizzle turned to a uniform downrush with abruptness. The lake was barred, long stripes of black and of light and dark green wavered. Along the horizon was penciled a white blaze as if under the earth globe there were clear skies. Thunder moaned; the air was sweet and soft so the man's nerves tingled. He thought how it was like the action of adrenalin. *Blessed of the Lord be his land. Mor* had always talked of Sweden, the *hemlandet.* She'd lived in the country- side called *Lilla Östergarten,* and wouldn't forget it.

Elizabeth came out, dressed in pink, a bottle of nail polish in her hand. "You remember, I'm taking the Volks today." She leaned to kiss his cheek.

"I know. Pick me up a little late for lunch. I'll take the car back with me. Smell the air, Lisa." *As for man, his days are as the grass. For the wind passes over and it is gone; and the place thereof shall know it no more.* He felt the smiting of nostalgia and blamed himself for sentimentality.

She was pouring her mug of coffee, adding cream. "If you go to the hospital you'll be late for supper?" She said it in a question.

"I won't be back at all. I can eat there."

"And Dora was planning a chicken mousse—your favorite, the cold one."

"Tomorrow, tell her."

"All right."

"I had a dream last night. I was on an enormous bridge, Lisa."

"Where's Clara?"

"I couldn't get to the end of it, to solid ground."

Clara came to join them, carrying a cup of cocoa; she'd changed to green gym shorts and a white V-neck shirt with *Ideal High* sewn in green script on the pocket. She wouldn't wear the bras Elizabeth got her, and the young form showed firm. "Don't you adore rain, Daddy!" She bent to hug him, balancing her drink. "Woops!" His coffee splashed on the gray-painted flooring as he moved it from over his seersucker pants.

Elizabeth's voice was tolerant as she looked at them. "Clara, we're fifteen, a big girl. Hum?"

"But I *love* Daddy!"

Elizabeth said, "Have some of Dora's cake."

Clara took a piece in her fingers. "Can I eat it standing?"

Dr. Bill said, "Over by the rail."

"Honestly, you two!" Elizabeth smiled from the rocker, her mug on the floor by her. With a thumbnail she pried the last of the red polish from the nails of one hand. She flicked the tiny peelings aside. "You spoil her; when's Clara going to learn any manners?" She watched him lift a piece of cake and sup his coffee, making a noise. Why did he do that? Hadn't she mentioned it carefully a hundred times? Tactful. And why not tell Clara to get off that banister and sit in a chair. And why too, hadn't Gus got home? He was off in that silly orchard, caught no doubt in the downpour. If he had any sense he'd wait in Herb Worth's barn and arrive after Bill and she had driven off. But not Gus, who'd be certain to come dashing in drenched like a puppy just as they were leaving. And then there'd be one of the famous scenes. She'd explained to Gus last night plainly that he musn't miss breakfast. She shook the bottle of pink nail polish to blend it and, balancing it on her skirt, began applying it. "Bill, you said you were going to speak to Clara this morning."

"Umm. Listen, *min flicka.*" He turned sharply on his wife. "What a godawful smell that stuff has. What is it? Acetone?"

"Sorry." Her face was expressionless. "Be finished in a minute; I didn't think."

Clara frowned, her brows heavy and black like her father's. The frames of her glasses gave her face a look of concentration that it didn't have when she forgot to wear them, as she often did. She was perched on the rail, mouth half-full. She spoke forcibly. "Why don't you say what you want to say!"

"Alan's father told Mum that you found that body."

The rain beat a muffled tattoo and thunder coughed beyond the silver liquid wall. The warm water fell on the dusty sand around the old frame house, spattering mud against the ground-level wavy-glassed cellar windows. "Well, I did then."

"But why not tell us, *Flicka?*"

"And Daddy asked you specially." Elizabeth didn't look up from her task. "If you'd seen anything. You lied. I was embarrassed when I found out the truth in front of my friends."

"Lisa, will you wait a minute, please?"

"Sure. Please give me some coffee?" She reached for her mug and held it out, careful of her wet nails.

He filled it and then his. "You see, *Flicka,*" he began.

Small shrieks of glee interrupted the trio. On the path outside some youngsters went by, wet scant clothes clinging to them,
the long brown hair of Carmen, the tallest, sopping; the small
boys with open mouths held up to catch the water:

> *I gave him back his peaches,*
> *I gave him back his pears!*

Leaping on their spindly limbs, they were swallowed by the falling water.

> *Jelly on the table,*
> *Crackers on the shelf!*

Clara turned on her mother. "Well I don't call it lying! Daddy
didn't call it that. Why did you say I lied?"

"Because isn't that what you did?" Elizabeth blew on her
nails and hoped for an early peace.

"I went straight to tell Mr. Chapman, Mum. That was the
right thing to do."

"Clara." Dr. Bill stopped her. "We aren't talking about right
and wrong; but we want your confidence."

"Mum thinks I was wrong. She does. Always." Clara heard
the tears in her voice and knew the self-pity that came with them.

"What was the condition of the body?" Dr. Bill asked her.
"Tell us about it."

"I don't remember. But fishes had got at it, I guess."

"For Heaven's sake!" Elizabeth sipped her coffee.

"It had surfaced?" Dr. Bill prodded.

"Yes. It was by the old pier. It must have washed in. I don't
want to talk about it, Daddy. I wish you'd let me alone."

"Now, *Flicka.*"

"I know what you think. That it's good to talk about it. It's
not; it's silly."

"You won't lie again to us, dear, will you?" Elizabeth asked.

"No, Mum." Clara looked across the porch at her mother, and
her smooth sunbrown face was devoted.

"Tell me, *Flicka,*" Dr. Bill said, "do you have any bad dreams
about it?"

"He sounds like a psychiatrist," Elizabeth said. "What about
your bridge you wanted to get off?"

"No, I don't," Clara said.

"You still take a dawn dip?"

"Umm."

"This morning, for instance?"

"Sure."

He felt her lie and ran his fingers through his short gray hair and rested his hand on the back of his neck. He worked at the muscles there, his face thoughtful as if he had more to say.

Lisa rocked and the chair squeaked. "Another thing, Clara. Will you not go to the lake early, please?" She got up.

"Clara? Not afraid of the water?" Dr. Bill pressed.

She was shaking her head. "I am not. But I'll tell you something else. Skin says it was some girl from the Potawatomi Club and they think she committed suicide."

"I'm damned," Dr. Bill said.

"I'll be glad when everybody forgets about this whole business." Elizabeth was restless.

"Well, that ought to put Preacher Thwaite back on his heels. All those beach rules those people have!"

"Isn't it time to go, Bill, if you want to stop for the mail?"

"I'm ready." Dr. Bill gulped the last of his coffee and stood heavily, the clip of papers under his arm.

"I'll get my purse and keys." Elizabeth was cheerful, her pink dress becoming her English blondness.

Clara swung her legs, sullen. "I said it to Ernie Chapman. I didn't lie."

"I know, dear." Elizabeth hurried off, calling, "Dora, think if there's anything else we need! What you think?"

Dr. Bill was pulling off his glasses, cleaning them on a paper napkin. "Why defend yourself to Mum like that?"

"She's always saying things to me. Why don't people just leave me alone?" Her brown eyes burned as if she were going to cry. She jumped off the rail. "Why!"

"I'm not interested in what you and Mum call lies or truths. That's not what matters. I don't want your brain cluttered up with garbage, that's all."

She slapped a mosquito and looked at him, resentful. "I wouldn't care if I found another body. Any time. Or if I was out swimming when I did. It's exciting."

"Yeah." He put on his glasses, somewhat irritated.

Through the barrier of rain where the children had leaped a while ago, a figure dashed, hunched over, the sack of equipment at his breast, the dripping net waving. He stumbled up the steps. "Hi, everybody." He paused. "Had breakfast?" A pool of water formed under him.

"Hell of a time to hunt bugs, Gus." Dr. Bill swung on him. "Or so it seems to me. You crazy?"

"I kept thinking it would clear up, Daddy."

Dr. Bill felt the rage move over him and endeavored to control it, not quite understanding why his son affected him so strongly. He watched Gus bending to shake at the old army rucksack of Dr. Bill's. Drops of rain ran down Gus' bony legs; the handkerchief around his neck was matted to the skin; sandburs were caught on the laces of his tennis shoes. "That a jar of cyanide in there, Gus?"

"Sure, Daddy. But it's wrapped up good."

"I haven't a doubt in one of Mum's best towels. Now, what was the catch out there this morning? What exotic butterfly was flitting about in the shower? Hum? And why not come over here when I'm talking to you!"

"Okay." The boy reached down at his side for the bag and net.

"And leave those goddam things by the door."

"Okay."

"Let me see your hands. Look at your nails, will you?"

"I clipped them last night, though. I'll go wash up."

"Wait. You know what you're going to do today? First place, you leave that sack of junk where it is now until I say you may touch it again. Understand? Now, you're to go on into Ideal, by bus or with Mr. Ardway. You figure out how. And bring me a coherent report on job possibilities at supper. Hellamighty, I won't be home. At breakfast tomorrow then. On each store—and I'll check up on you, too. Stock boy or whatever they offer. Hear me!"

Gus was watching him with the shades drawn over his gray-blue eyes. He put his hand to his teeth and snapped the rubber bands. "Okay. Sure."

"Stop making that noise, please."

"Okay." As if his bones hurt him, Gus supported one wet

canvas shoe on the other. And as if his blood were needled, his body shifted restively, changing position. He tore off a string hanging from his shortened jeans, rubbed his fingers through his fine curls.

"You need a haircut too. Have any money?"

"No."

Dr. Bill told Clara, "Go tell Mum I want two dollars for him." He looked out at the diminishing shower. "See if you can dress decently for once when you go. And breakfast is seven-thirty sharp. Understand me?"

Elizabeth had come in the doorway, opening her purse. "Here's your money."

"Creeps," Clara cried from behind her. "I was supposed to tell Gus. I forgot. Mr. Ardway was at the beach and says Jimmy Fox wants Gus to help on that bridge for the Wigwam. Quarter an hour."

Dr. Bill looked mildly at Clara. "Why didn't you say so before, *Flicka?*"

"All the fuss you make about putting Gus to work!" Elizabeth snapped her purse shut.

"Mum," Gus said, "will you let Daddy and me talk for once?"

"No. I have just as much right as anyone in this house to speak!"

"Mum, stop butting in, please." Gus protested, hopeless.

"Why must you always be picking on him, Bill?"

"Lisa!" Dr. Bill roared. "If I mention anything that lets your son out of diapers, you get on your high horse."

"One of these days, won't I do something!" she cried. "Oh!"

"Mum," Gus pleaded.

"What a drippy family." Clara went to hoist herself on the wood rail, apart from the three who now faced each other. She whispered, "And I think Mr. Fox is a cheapskate. I wouldn't babysit for that. Not me!" She thumped her heels seven times. The color of seven was purple and very strong; four was pink and pale. She sucked her teeth; whenever Gus snapped his bands, Clara wished she still used the rubber pieces. Her braces were due to come off this fall and in winter she would wear only a retainer at night. She watched Mum as her soft mouth turned down and her underlip trembled, her pretty eyes filled with tears and with a sob she left the porch. Poor thing, insisting that Gus was wonderful even when he acted like an all-American goof. As soon as Mum was gone the voices of the two males automatically lowered.

"How about it, *Pojke?*" Dr. Bill grinned. "You go nail Jimmy's job before some other kid does."

"I will. And I'll go to Sawmill and get a haircut first chance too, Daddy." He was buoyant. "I better change now."

"And then eat breakfast. Don't forget. You need some fat on you."

"He will, Daddy," Clara said. "But food, food is that all grownups think about?"

"You have a good day, Daddy." Gus nodded, good-natured.

Dr. Bill didn't answer, thinking he's got no idea of work; his life is one indolent undirected mess. The boy was a jellyfish. And at thirteen, almost fourteen. He picked up his notes and went in, calling up the staircase, "Lisa, I'm late. Come on. I'm sorry." He waited, leaning on the banister until she descended the stairs, chin high, lips yet offended, the full pink skirt fluttering.

"I apologize, I do," he coaxed her.

"Aren't you mean?" But she smiled. Poor Bill, and he had such a long day ahead. Why did he always start a row? "Now where's my umbrella? Dora!" She smoothed her blouse, wrinkled from where she'd lain face down on the bed.

Dr. Bill went ahead in the rain to the car; as he passed through the porch he spoke coldly. "Still standing in the same spot, Gus? And remember, you're not to touch that bag till I say you may."

"Sure. Okay." Gus went into the house.

Dora stopped him, "Come on in here, eh?"

"What you got for me, Dora?"

"Apple cake. I saved some warm back for you."

He followed and perched on a stool while the woman opened the oven door and took out a hot plate to set before him. Under the wide-limbed elm outside, the Volkswagen engine was starting up. The child felt the muscles of his abdomen relax. As the car pulled down the hollow and splashed along the sandy road, he became at ease. "Dora, I had good luck this morning. Promise not to tell and I'll say what."

She watched him affectionately, a soapy rag in one hand mopping over the cabinet fronts. "I won't."

"I caught a rare one."

"That's nice. Was it one you needed?" The maid knew some of the right questions.

"Was it!"

"Hear you're going to help build a bridge for that Mr. Jimmy Fox, too. Oho."

"Umm. I guess."

"Now it sounds like that'd be interesting."

"Dora, when you were my age, did you get to do what you wanted?"

"What you mean? Did I enjoy myself? Well, my mother had twenty of us and sixteen lived."

"Which are you?"

"And there's fourteen of us yet today. Sometimes I study to remember where we all live at."

"Which one are you!"

"Third. That way I raised most of us, eh?"

"Tell about it, Dora."

She gave the refrigerator a swift lick, pleased. "You got to get out of those wet clothes. Why you always want to hear?"

"Not this second. Tell, Dora."

"No. But I had a nice childhood, as they say. I enjoy a farm. Maybe you saw that Herb this morning when you were at the orchard."

"I never. You going to marry him? Why don't you, Dora? You'd have a farm. You'd like that."

"Oho. Want to get rid of me?" she teased him, leaning over and mussing his hair about. "Eh?"

"No." He blushed, gulping the rest of the milk to wash down the sweet bread. He got up hastily and went to the porch where Clara was sprawled on the cane couch with a book propped on her stomach; her shirt hung out of her shorts. He went to his knapsack and opened it.

She looked at him. "Daddy said not."

"Shut your big face."

"Suit yourself."

He unrolled the poison jar carefully from Mum's new monogrammed towel and unscrewed the lid. He lightly breathed the rather almond-scented vapors while reaching two slender gentle fingers in. Using them as tweezers, he picked up a huge dark-brownish butterfly by the dead curled legs, careful not to harm its wing scales. Red-orange dots and a dusting of violet-blue hemmed the underside of the hind wings, tipped by fragile swallow-tails. The upper side was almost black. Screwing on the cap, he fastened the bag clumsily and kicked it back into the corner. He walked so the breeze he made wouldn't disturb the specimen, up the creaky stairs to his room.

In a while the rain eased and ceased, and Clara followed his steps, entering her own room, picking up her doll from the bureau, and then coming to see what her brother had. He was standing above his desk, the insect's body now in position on the mounting rack. The wings had been adjusted and were held in place with cardboard strips tacked at the ends into the board. It would remain there stretched, until dry, and then be placed in one of the cotton-filled glass-front Riker cases Mum bought him in Chicago.

Holding Baby against her shoulder and swinging her body rhythmically, she thrust a thumb in the back of her shorts. "What is it?" she queried negligently.

His face was alert. "Remember me telling how the Tiger female comes in dimorphic form too?"

"Di—what?" She was going over to the rat cage under the half-open window. Water had come in a puddle on the rain-washed floor; the air was humid, steamy.

"It means different. The yellow Tiger's eggs produce blacks once in a while, especially in southern states. They're never seen up in this region, according to the book."

"Then what's it doing here?"

"Clara, why don't you ask how I caught it in the rain!"

"How?"

"I was in the barn. And there was the imago hanging on the rafters fanning its wings. I was there early and I saw it develop. So it's a perfect specimen; I gave it plenty of time. Crazy, the luck I have sometimes." He sighed, replete.

She squinted into the wire mesh of the cage. "Yeah."

He dug in his pocket. "I brought the chrysalis. See?" He

produced a leaflike sack, pointed at one end, two-horned at the other.

"You know your wild mouse has a nest?"

He came to join her. "Had them a week ago."

"How many?"

"Four. I'll probably sell them."

"Who'd buy a drippy mouse? White rats are different. I can see the sense to them." She scratched upon the cage wire so the rats lifted their tiny paws, curious.

"I'll find somebody. Maybe Al Paoli. Or even Alan."

"*Even* is right; his dogs would eat them." She tossed the doll into the air and caught it under its arms.

"No, they wouldn't, Clara. Where you going?"

She was edging out of the room. "I got a book."

"Stay and talk."

"No."

"Please."

"And you better change those wet things, Gus."

"Golly, I thought I had already."

"Did anyone ever tell you that you're a mess? I hate to be the first to break the news!"

His face lit up and as he reached for a pillow from the bed to fire at her, he yelled a football cheer:

> *Knock them down, kill them,*
> *Hold that line;*
> *Ideal High School*
> *Will slaughter them just fine!*

It hit the slamming door and bounced to the floor. Gus laid back the lid of the cage and lifted the two white rats out by their soft neck scruffs. He set them down to give them the run of the room; they waddled over the old wood, sniffing knotholes and cracks. He shut the cage door and began to remove his tee-shirt and pants which itched his skin as they dried. He let them fall by the chair and untied the handkerchief from his neck and kicked off the soft shoes. He stood naked, looking down at himself while time ceased inching and the vacuum sweeper purred out on the stairs and the two rats rustled. He was wondering at the excitement in his loins that had come in almost the identical way when his father shouted furiously at him, and when Dora reached over and rumpled his hair the way she always did. Who wanted to help build a dumb-nut bridge anyway? He frowned, scornful, and turned once more to look at the noble catch glistening in the rack upon his desk.

[5]

By NOONTIME the sun emerged in a furious white stare. At midafternoon it was ninety-eight at the tennis court. The burning cement could be felt through shoe soles. Jimmy Fox and his houseguest finished their third set. They went behind the high backstop and tramped around, hunting in the weeds of the destitute soil for two balls that had been whacked over. They picked up one with sandburs stuck in the fuzz. "If they weren't brand-new I'd let them go," Jimmy said. "It's too hot."

"I don't know what's the matter with my underhand. I was swinging wild, Jimmy."

"Let's take a swim." They went back up the road to the Wigwam. Already the washed leaves of trees had become dust-drenched as cars passed. Sweat poured from the bodies of the two men in their shorts and thin shirts. They looked forward to a swim. Jimmy, who'd rounded fifty, was in prime shape, exercised consistently, drank juices for breakfast, and tried to limit his cocktails to two. Mr. Wheeler, on two weeks' leave from a position as major-domo at Anatole's in the Loop, was in poor shape.

They came upon Gus sitting by the bridge, unsmiling, apprehensive, in fresh-ironed clothes. "Hi, Mr. Fox!"

"This is Wheeler, Gus."

"Deus vobiscum."

"Don't mind him, Gus. He's friendly. His hobby's Latin law."

Gus couldn't look at either of them; he gazed at the brittle ancient vines that made the bridge rail. "My sister said I could work for you, Mr. Fox."

"Work?"

"On the bridge you're going to put up, and tearing this one down." He stamped on the crumbling boards.

"Oh sure. Did I say I'd pay you? It's too blessed hot now, though. After supper we'll start."

"Twenty-five cents an hour."

"Is that okay with you, Gus?"

"Yeah."

"Come on. Want to see what Wheeler brought along? New member of the family."

"Okay."

The bridge trembled under their combined footfalls. Narrow, it spanned the deep ravine and had been put up over forty years before by one of the original Ardways. Above the door to the barn-red cottage was nailed a triangle of sticks, and the name WIGWAM was spelled. Just inside the meal-call bugle hung by a dirty gold cord. From under the striped canvas porch swing came a black standard poodle, clipped, beady eyes friendly. "This is Chouchou."

"Neat," Gus said, kneeling. "Cripes, he sure is."

"She. And she cost a hundred bucks too. First pooch I've had in years. Wheeler knows all about her blood lines. He owns half her sire."

"International champion." Wheeler stood with hands on city-soft hips.

Gus stood up, awkward. "Guess I'll go if you don't want me to come till tonight."

"We'll put in time when it's cool, I figure. I got some ideas about the new bridge that I want to work out. See what you think about them, Gus. I thought we'd put in a light, maybe."

"Some life you lead, Jimmy." Wheeler shrugged. "I envy you."

"I do all right. First half was hell on wheels, though." Jimmy threw himself into the swing, grinning. "I had to get burned first. Now I take the women and let them go. There's always a new one coming along. What you know about girls, Gus?"

"Nothing."

"Haven't you got a steady? I thought that was the thing with you teens."

"I'm going to be like you, Mr. Fox. I'm never going to marry."

"It's the summers off I wish I had," Wheeler said.

"Wheeler'd use them," Jimmy said. "He's a true scholar, Gus."

Chouchou trotted over to the screen and looked out, whining. *"Quid vis?"* said Wheeler. "We got company; the evangelist."

"For god sake." Jimmy stretched his legs out.

Boris Thwaite was in a hurry; his hard heavy body was dressed in a bright plaid shirt which hung outside his yellow Bermudas. He peered through the sun-glazed wire mesh at those inside. "Fox, that you? Stopped by here an hour ago."

"Tennis," Jimmy grunted. "But come in. Meet Wheeler."

"Hello. You teach high school too?" Thwaite spotted Chouchou as he stepped in. "What's this? Didn't know you had a dog, Fox."

"Just got her." Jimmy shifted, half-hostile. "And Wheeler's the *maître d'* at Anatole's in the Loop; you know that high-class place. I can't afford it."

"Gentle?"

"I don't know. Show dog, though. Won a puppy blue already. Best bitch in the pup class."

"Well, I've just been through a session with Malraux. He came over to my place to talk about those two he owns. I don't know how you see our common problem, but I'm urging this community to get together and formulate some rules, Fox. We're growing, you know, no question of it; and now there's this tragic drowning which underscores the need."

"What did Malraux say to that?" Jimmy asked.

"Pretty averse to each of my suggestions. It's plain he's been away too much to understand what goes on at Pine Beach. Hard fellow to convince. Egocentric, bull-headed. Not married, you know. Divorced for years; sensitive about it, which is natural."

"Me too," Jimmy smiled genially.

"Malraux's rather a bit left of center in his column, don't you find?" Thwaite felt his slip.

"That doesn't have any connotation any more, Doctor. I will

say I like the way his mind works; I buy the *Daily News* just to read it. The *Trib* doesn't carry it; the Republicans can't stomach him. Right?" Jimmy pulled out a handkerchief and mopped his blunt Irish face, reddened with his dislike as much as the heat. The poodle pushed her nose in his hand. Now and then over the years Jimmy had caught the minister's radio and television programs, embarrassed by their Madison Avenue techniques. He joked with the rest of the community about them and the toupee Thwaite sported to enhance his masculine allure. Self-conscious before the minister, Jimmy jabbed at him. "Saw you got another mention in the *News* today." It had been a satire on the gymnastics Thwaite used to emphasize a sermon titled *Is God a Liar?*

The preacher was cold. "I sent a rebuttal too, which they're going to print. I'm not going to let the thing drop. I'm a fighter. It's a fact about those eggheads who ridicule me that half of them go regularly to their psychiatrists while I'm the one who keeps the housewives and businessmen out of the asylums and doctors' offices. I'm the one who rescues the derelicts too; I give them hope. My detractors can't deny it. I'm using an old principle that was first employed in Galilee! My interest is in saving souls for my Maker and I'll employ any means, fair or foul. I'll not play parchesi with a bunch of pedants." He was florid with ardor.

"Now what about Malraux?" Jimmy said, a little intimidated by the other's pulpit manner.

Thwaite unfolded a paper from his shirt pocket. "I have a carbon here for you to look over. Pearl and Irene typed them for me this morning. Did anyone tell you about my son being bitten a week ago?"

"No." Jimmy took the sheet.

"By Malraux's dog; I hope this one's quiet. I trust you are civic-minded enough to see the logic in my suggestions in this paper, which includes other points, as for example the black-topping of our roads and the straightening of a few of the dangerous curves. And we ought to have a litterbug patrol."

"Pretty radical," Wheeler said.

Thwaite ignored him. "I want to have a meeting one night this week. Thursday suit you?"

Wheeler took up a magazine and sat on a camp chair. "We got that bridge, Jimmy. If you want my help. I'll only be here ten days."

"What bridge?" Thwaite asked.

"The one you just came over."

"Ridiculous, Fox. First things first. Come now. I promise it'll only take an hour of your time. Thursday, Fox." He urged it.

"I'll try. But you better nail Malraux while he's still here. You ought to have his signature. He and Monk Ardway are the only year-round residents Pine Beach has."

Thwaite stepped brusquely into the sun, and Gus followed. "I'm after Mrs. Paoli next. Good-bye, gentlemen."

"*Vale.*" Wheeler's overloud laugh and whisper in mimic of Thwaite's accent carried on the hot air. "*Mihi non persuasum est,* Jimmy!"

Jimmy's brutal voice ignored any softness. "Crap, I'd like to have got on the subject of his Republican parishioners, those Indo-European white Protestant status-mongering bastards!"

Reverend Thwaite spoke over his shoulder to Gus as they were crossing the bridge. "Dislike that type; atheistic, just like Fox. Tell your parents, youngster, that I expect them on Thursday. Seven-thirty. Don't forget."

Gus made a face, screwing up his mouth at the back and bald head before him. "Okay, sir."

They said no more, separating on the dusty road, Gus trotting one way and Thwaite moving in the other with unmutilated enthusiasm. He was anxious to convince Angela Paoli. It being Monday, her husband was in Chicago teaching a summer seminar. Thwaite looked forward to the encounter with the little woman, who was smart, and charming too, her black short hair brushed from her triangular face. Her husband was a hard worker and a consistent drinker—typical modern intellectual.

The minister felt that most of the resorters—in common with the rest of the world—belonged in the category of drunks, idiots, or children. That fact gave his crusades a firm basis; he was necessary. Mrs. Paoli no doubt had a lot to put up with; perhaps fornication besides the alcohol problem. Thwaite himself was a faithful husband and, he thought, no hypocrite when he preached fidelity. One thing he prided himself on: he was a superior husband and father. He'd married below himself; Eve was intelligent and often supplied him with a well-conceived phrase. But breeding? No; the fact had always made Thwaite arrogant, and once in a while he prayed for humility about the sin if he remembered. He mused scornfully on that stupid Fox. He sang under his breath:

Take my life and let it be
Consecrated, God, to Thee;
Take my silver and my gold;
Not a piece would I withhold!

He rapped on the screen. But no one was in; he called through the doorway and the Eyrie was empty. The dust rose from his tracks as he headed away and back to Linden House, to change into his swim suit and see whether he could find the woman perhaps at the beach and corner her.

He ran up his back steps, soft tennis shoes noiseless. He had a springing gait, lightfooted; it was characteristic of him since an early age, and was due to his interest in athletics. It no doubt contributed to his appeal when he strode buoyantly up and down the platform exhorting his audiences. He was conscious of it, of course, and often liked to slip up on people. He stood quietly outside the kitchen door. His daughters were inside with Eve. Dressed in their swim wear, they were making a meal to take to the beach in the evening, mixing mayonnaise and things into the cold potatoes, frosting a pound cake they had taken from the freezer, slicing a cold canned ham.

"The meals there aren't bad, Mama," Pearl said, "but everyone at Moret's gripes about them anyway. It's the fad. You sort of sit down at the big round tables and pick away."

"And if there are two pancakes you nibble a little out of each," Irene giggled, "and kind of leave the remainder standing mutilated and unloved. It's a game to see who doesn't care about calories the most."

"And we're right on top of the non-carers."

"Keeps you ravenous from morning till night."

"And from night till morning."

Eve worried, "Where did Papa go?"

"Do we have to wait for him to go to the beach?"

"Where's Papa," Irene sang, "Oh where, oh where, can Papa be!"

And Pearl dared:

We don't care if it rains or freezes;
We'll be safe in the arms of Jesus;
If we lose our skirts and britches——

Eve sighed, serious, indulgent. "Girls, what am I going to do with you? You're incorrigible; you know better. I ought to spank the two of you."

"Mama," Pearl said, quiet and utterly sober, "some minutes I'm so happy I could die. And before I know it I'm down in the dumps again!"

"Pearl's a subconscious death-wisher," Irene said. "Did you ever think, as the hearse goes by!"

"I never finished," Pearl interrupted, shoving her sister, pushing her knuckles in Irene's ribs so she had to giggle:

He'll still love us sons of bitches!

"Now girls," Irene spoke severely, mocking Papa's Oxford accent. "You may not go to Vespers tonight. And most awful besides: I might not let you have dessert."

"Yes, Papa," Pearl moaned, hilarious.

"I'm going to collapse," Irene cried.

"You're so funny."

The minister decided it was time to end it; he had reached a point of breathlessness. His rage was such that it was close upon ecstasy. He simply stepped into the room.

"Oh my gosh," Irene said; Pearl only blinked her eyes in their spasmodic rapid tic and waited for the sky to fall as it had done before with milder provocation.

"Go into the living room," he said; the muscles at the sides of his mouth jumped, the skin white over them. "And you stay in here, my dear."

Eve heard the slaps, and the muffled small noises. Irene returned, her eyes narrow, her face prepared for weeping. "That Pearl; she won't say anything. And it just makes Papa worse. She's holding her mouth tight. Mama, she makes me so mad sometimes."

"What's he say?"

"Oh, the usual. We're empty-headed and fools. I agree to

anything he says. Pearl doesn't know how to handle Papa. Was I dumb, singing like that. Wow."

There was a knocking at the door. "I can't answer it, Irene," Eve breathed.

They heard over the repeated soft rap, the hysterical man-voice in the other room; and a lamp fell, crashing. The muted words were undistinguishable. Eve thought, offer it up; herself, the nun. She did not understand her husband, and felt a mingling of fright and something near laughter. It was as if she were dead and looking at a comedy played on a stage. She wondered whether Ian was asleep and would remember if he heard. She didn't mind about the nurse who had witnessed other displays since they had employed her. In the upstairs master bedroom was a gash in the plaster where a radio was hurled one night. And here in the kitchen were stains on the imitation-pine panel wallpaper where food had landed. She told her daughter, "Go on and get the door."

"But what'll I say, Mama?" The two murmured under their breaths.

"Act as if nothing's wrong." Eve giggled.

"Okay." Irene shrugged, wan, half-smiling, in league with her mother.

And her false voice came. "Hullo there. Oh thank you." After a few minutes she returned, almost laughing. "Honest, he's still standing there but I think he'll go away." It was the husband of the postmistress, with a special delivery for the minister. "He wants to talk. You know how he stands and sniffs, Mama. He wants to know if it's true that Mr. Fox bought a pair of poodles; he'd like a puppy for his wife. I just walked away while he was talking."

Eve took the packet, which was expected and contained notes from the writers and helpers for a revival rally to be held for three days, starting Saturday in the mammoth Chicago Coliseum. "Papa's just upset because this is very important," she said.

"Dammit." Irene's tears welled. "Just dammit anyhow. I could die. I'll never be able to face that post office again."

Eve hesitated and looked toward the room where Pearl was, feeling the new silence. "Perhaps I'll go in now."

"Better not." Irene sniffled, red-eyed.

But Eve walked through the doorway; the suddenness, the stillness, indicated that the master had moved on to his studio. She hoped his ego was unimpaired; she wanted him unwounded. She felt if he were ever too hurt or insulted he could be dangerous. "Pearl?"

"Oh, hi!" Pearl was by the fallen floor lamp, very erect, her shoulders stiff; she pulled her knuckles to crack them, deliberately. "If you won't divorce him," she whispered, "you ought to have him see a psychoanalyst at least. I'll sure be glad when I leave this home for good and all."

"Let's get the broom." Eve kept her voice low. "And I'll give him this. I'll slip it under the door." She tiptoed into the hall. It was so quiet upstairs where Ian was that she felt positive he wasn't awake.

As she approached Papa's study, the door opened. Impassive, towering, he seemed; she felt the charge of emotion all through the house! The man, silent, still-faced, accepted the envelope and closed the door. She returned to where the girls were tidying up. Pearl held the pan and Irene swept the bits of glass shattered about on the polished wood floor. "We'll go along to the beach, dears. Irene, go tell nurse to bring Ian when he wakes from his nap. I'll put the food in the fridge."

"Not me," Pearl said, blinking. "I go to my room and stay till I'm sorry."

"Go tell him you are," Irene urged.

"Not me."

"You're exasperating. Mama, make her."

"No," Pearl said. "It's the principle of it."

Eve thought how fragile her daughter looked in her blue suit, the V-neck accenting the tiny breasts, the slim neck; she sighed; it was hot. "Dear."

"I'm like him some ways, Mama. That's why I can see through Papa. No one's going to push me around." Pearl turned away. "This is a free country."

"What are you proving?" Irene asked.

Pearl felt that nothing would ever make her cry. She thought of her boy friend, Dick Ardway, and the notes they wrote. She felt her worth, unflinching. "I'm staying up in my room till Doomsday comes." She said it and left.

[6]

As THE husband at Thwaite's kitchen stairs went away somewhat satisfied, back to the post office in Pokagon, the heat shimmered above his jeep's tire tracks. The cremating sun reached every place. Down at the lake matrons stood with breasts just above the water line. Near them the smallest children paddled and sat in the wet, clad in bright-colored tight jersey that contrasted with their mothers' staid costumes, skirted to conceal fleshy thighs and ample shaking hips, or worn loosely upon unlovely bones as if their owners finally had outreasoned bodily hope and pride, no longer bearing rancor even for the slim youthful babes in fashion-dictated pastels or plaids, skin-slick. A man walking in the deep water carried a child on his shoulders, the plump body lackadaisical, the sleepy head in blue-and-white bathing cap with a rubber pompon, tilted on one side. Everyone not under umbrellas or water was hot; their exposed skin burned. Someone called in warning, "It's over your head out to the second bar!" And people, hearing the hollow ringing voice, couldn't find energy even to turn their heads to see who shouted.

A swarm of children were launching the unwieldy lifeboat. *"Hoh! Hoh!"* they sang in rhythmic unison, tugging. Far on the

hazy water two or three canoes drifted. No breeze came and sailboats piled like unwanted skeletons along the beach. Finally the
boat was floating on the shallow brackish water; the children
scrambled over its blistering metal sides. Skin purposefully bumped
against Clara.

"Watch out," she told him crossly.

"Go soak your head." He was happy.

Monk handed the oars to his son, who fixed them in the locks.
"Stay inside the sandbar, Skin, and no monkey business. Too many
little kids in there."

"I know, Dad."

"Let's go, weirdo," Clara said.

Monk watched Skin row slowly up the shore. Chris and
Georgie and Carmen Paoli dragged their hands in the warm surface, green-scummed in places. The voices of the group going off
were hushed; flies stung and were brushed away lazily. It seemed
as if passion and vigor had been absorbed; as if danger and death
were unknown. And yet, Monk thought, on a day similar to this
last summer, a man up the beach had been gutted and killed by a
launch propeller as he was treading water alone past the bar.

Elizabeth Olson glided up to him with slow strokes. "Hi,
Admiral."

He looked down into the indigo eyes accented by the matching cap. He grinned. "Matter of fact, I was hunting you, *hausfrau*.
It's about my boys."

"Clara's going to the show with them tonight, I hear. And the
Thwaites and some of the Paolis too."

"They play their days away, gal. Well, they told me to ask
you about the tennis court dance tomorrow night. This is the big-
shot one and they want it fancy. You think the doctor'll let them
use those big Chinese lanterns you hang in the Owl's Roost?"

"Japanese. Sure. Anything else?" She stood up, her suit clinging. "Dora's going to want to do something."

"Since you asked, Belle said to accept cakes or cookies if
offered."

"Dora'll bring something over in the morning. But you come
get the lanterns yourself."

"Good. Hope the man of the house isn't home."

"Monk, you old lecher!"

"I'll be there."

Elizabeth laughed, dropping back into the water, her eyes slanting up the beach where Philip Malraux lay reading, a towel thrown over his freckled legs and wearing a huge straw hat. She swam under and surfaced, blinking the water from her eyes. In his narrow-banded nylon scants, Jimmy Fox came grinning, plunging into the water near her, staying under until far out and then swimming swiftly to the raft. He was trailed by a hesitant untanned stranger, who entered slowly, scooping the liquid over his knees, shoulders, and finally sinking in with a long grunt.

"Hoo," Elizabeth said to Monk, "look at the Boy Scout. Where does Jimmy ever find his dumb friends?"

When the lifeboat had pulled even with the Malraux beach, Alan's long orange canoe met it, flashing in from the deep water, the two dogs standing panting between the thwarts in the craft's midsection. Alan called, "Like a ride, Clara?"

"Yeah!"

"You can't," Skin told her.

"Why?" Clara laughed and began to rock the lifeboat from side to side; the glister suddenly in her brown eyes made them almost red in the hot glare.

The other children squealed in mock panic, snickering; Skin stood up, pushing at her angrily. "Sometimes I can't stand you, Clara Olson. You need you head shrunk." She grappled with him; they struggled and Clara lost her footing. Skin nearly followed her over the side but succeeded in evading the clutching hands. She dropped with a call of defeat.

"Goon!" she snorted, water up her nose.

"And you can't come in my dad's boat again!" Skin settled the oars, wishing he had his hands on her one more time, shoving at the active hard limbs. "She's nuts, Georgie." He trembled with fury.

"Um hum," the child agreed easily, palms caressing the lake as they rowed northward inside the blazing day.

Alan took Clara out a long way past the last sandbar, where the water was three and four and more times over one's head. She had to squint to see the beach where the people were ants that crawled. "It makes my ears tingle when we get this deep," she said low, turning to face Alan in the stern seat, his chest wide and brown, his shoulders standing out thin. "Ugh. I get afraid." She turned to the prow again. Daddy'd never get over Alan paddling out this far; it was dangerous she knew.

"The canoe won't sink, so you're safe. It's cedar and Ernie says it'd float for months before it logged. My father's going to get me an aluminum canoe next, a Grumman that's self-righting. He fusses when I go out this far, but I can't help it, Clara. You ever get that way; you feel like the world's right under you?" He split the blue with the paddle energetically.

"But how would they see you? Suppose we tipped over this minute and you got cramps. Suppose you hung on to the sides. Then night came. Big fish came up and bit at us."

"There aren't any fish that big out here."

But she thought about sea serpents approaching, heads visible just above the surface like the photograph in the paper that time. The water was glass-clear out here and the sand shining far below. Sometimes a shoal of brownish-backed sunfish or crappie minnows darted, changing direction swiftly. No telling what was the depth, whether they were near the surface or at the bottom; there was no sense of perspective. She felt light-headed, looking down through the water. "No one would know we had tipped and soon we'd slip under and drown."

"No, we'd have pushed the canoe in by then. It doesn't weigh even fifty pounds." He laughed and she turned to look at him, and for an instant, to think how beautiful the boy was, and unattainable. The water odors, which stamped it as a different land, rose about them.

"What about the dogs, Alan?"

"They can swim for miles. I've trained them. Want to see? I'll send them over now and they can follow us in. It's not too far for them."

"No!" It was cruel to consider. Jojo and Bosco were on the floor, their moist mouths open, puffing slightly, in the hot shade of the painted canvas sides. "Let them be, Alan." She said suddenly, "You know that drowned girl was dead a week in this very water."

"Jeeps, more things have been happening this summer! This has been the best one ever."

"They say it's a suicide."

"Maybe there's someone else in it now, Clara. Probably is,

when you think of the size of Lake Michigan. Maybe my paddle will run into someone now. Watch out!"

"Don't, Alan."

"Here goes." He knelt to get more power and dipped furiously so they sped along, rocking a little.

She held to the sides and bent her head to look between her knees at the varnished slatted bottom of the bow. She hoped dully that she wouldn't throw up here; Alan would never get over it. White-faced she endured the clammy feel of her shoulders' skin, the sickness in her belly. The idea of it being a girl that died by her own desire somehow was worse to Clara than if it had been a male and an enigma; she found it simpler to identify with; it was more tangible, farther removed from nightmare and nearer reality.

"We'll follow the beach a ways north and then turn around. Okay?" He was slowing his pace.

She didn't answer, her breath caught and released faintly. A half-hour later she was in control. They had said little. When they returned, the craft fluttering through the waveless fluid, they heard over the water three long blasts from Belle Ardway's whistle, calling her three sons and husband to supper. The sun languished a little lower in the overturned white bowl. The canoe grated upon the sand and the dogs sprang into the shallow depths; the clatter of Thwaite's camel bell sounded from the top of Linden House's beach stairs. Clara felt her legs firm on land again. "That was fun out there. Thanks for the ride." She helped him drag the craft up and turn it over on the baked sand, which was holding the heat like a stoked oven.

Philip Malraux was finshing his book, pleased the task was done. He'd been in and out of the water all afternoon and looked forward to his bourbon and iced water. He watched the approaching two and knew suddenly that he was bored and lonely. His evening would hold no more than half-hearted work spent on a long piece he'd begun and which wouldn't get off the ground. Alan, almost alarmingly, resembled his mother when she was young; Philip was aware the boy didn't know it, and anyone who saw his wife now, gross, coarse-featured, would not believe it. The present woman was in and out of the tony Riviera hospitals, varying psychiatrists at will, spending the limit of her alimony month on month. Alan had her reckless abandon too, which Philip had once

thought the loveliest thing in the world. All the same it was Alan
standing there, the paddles like spears on his shoulders, his dark
features strong, his white teeth flashing as he laughed. He would be
off to Harvard winter after next. Philip hoped his grades were
decent, but knew he'd get him in some way; he wished the boy were
steadier, realizing that he didn't know his own son. No more than
he knew that girl there; what was her name, Elizabeth Olson's
girl? "Well, children? I think you went out too far again, Alan."

"Hi, Mr. Malraux." Clara dropped down on the sand. "What
you reading?"

He handed the book to her. He took off his big straw hat
which left a deep crease on his pink forehead and gave him a
worried appearance. He gazed up at Alan, his smile crinkling.
"Meet the preacher today?"

"No, Father. I been in the canoe all day."

"I've talked to him and you're to stand up to him if he makes
any cracks. You remember."

"I will." Alan's eyes hung upon the man, adoring, wanting to
serve, anxious. The wet animals, harness rings clinking against
the metal tax discs, laid their noses in his hand, rubbed their heads
against his trunks.

Philip looked over the near-empty beach. "Everyone's gone
up. What time is it, I wonder?"

"A little after six," Clara said. "Because Mrs. Thwaite rings
her bell six on the dot. This is a good book. Mum would like it.
She's always saying she wants to travel. Me too. I'm going to see
the world some day."

"Ever been anyplace?"

"Only to Chicago to my orthodontist. Summers we come here
and winters we're in Ideal. My father's office is in our house there.
He has to work all the time; and he goes to Michigan City where
the hospital is. That's where he'll have supper tonight." She felt her
father's heroism.

"Sounds busy."

"He likes it. He says a long time ago there was a man who
thought he had a frog in his stomach. He began studying to find
a cure and he was the first doctor."

"He was ribbing you, Clara," Alan said.

"Maybe not," Philip said.

Clara shrugged. *"Honor a physician,* Alan, *with the honor*

due him for the uses which ye may have of him." Her face was close
to the pages of the book; it was a habit she'd formed before Dr.
Bill discovered her astigmatism. "That's the Bible, drippy."

"I told you she was crazy, Father."

Philip stood and removed the colored glasses he wore for
reading, tucking them into one of his beach shoes so the dogs
wouldn't step on them. "I'm going to take a dive and then we'll
go on up. You think your mother would like to read this book,
child? Maybe I'll bring it by tonight. Will she be home?"

"I guess." She didn't heed him.

"Tell her I may pay a social call. Will you?" he pressed.

"Far as I know she's home." Clara looked up from the page
as he walked away and submerged cleanly in the silky calm. "Your
father's pretty nice."

"He's okay, I guess." Alan was casual.

"But I've got to *go!*" She dropped the book abruptly, feeling
a quick flow of vitality, stretching her arms, her limbs. "I'm going
to the show tonight with the kids. It's Victor Hugo. Oh, brave
Jean Valjean!" She began to run down the beach, faster and
faster, vain of her speed should any eye see. At the boardwalk she
slowed, and then because of another gushing nearly unbearable,
plunged up the grade, welcoming any new kind of strain on her
body, trying its strength. Would she ever, she wondered, have her
fill of anything! She was going to be sixteen next April and that
left her at least sixty-five years. People were living longer than ever
nowadays. She might go past a hundred, which meant she had about
eighty-five years! They would never pass by. She felt immortal; she
pitied everybody over fifteen.

And that evening Philip did bring the book over to the Owl's
Roost, going down the road that wound about Pine Beach, from
the Sand Castle that blended harmoniously into its dune to the
Olsons' dilapidated roomy frame structure, put up sometime before
the first world war. He was offered a lift halfway by two of the new
generation, Dick and Russ, who braked beside him in their rattle-
trap Olds. They were heading over to pick up Clara, and then the
others, to drive over to Ideal's Emporium Theatre. "Where you
going to put all the bodies, boys? Thanks just the same but I'll
walk."

"Plenty room in this heap," Dick said, and reached up to

twiddle the giant cubes of dice that hung from the rear-view mirror.

"Come with us next time, sir," Russ said. "But make it this summer. You know they're closing the Emporium down in fall."

"For good," Dick said. "And Sawmill did the same thing last year. Closest movie house will be Michigan City. Twenty miles."

"What you fellows going to do?"

"We'll be away. I'm going to Michigan State this fall like Russ. We don't care. But Skin wants Dad to get a TV set." Dick gunned the motor again.

"Where's your brother tonight?" Malraux asked.

"He's reading an old book he found in the attic. Skin's bats over the past. He keeps fighting the Civil War or building an Indian tent or reading up on flintlock guns or swords or something." Russ, good-humored, made a circle in the air about his ear with his finger.

"Your TV and Dr. Thwaite's are the only ones in Pine Beach," Dick said.

"I didn't know. Come up and watch any time, boys."

"Thanks, sir!" They clattered on their way, the dice slinging from side to side.

Philip turned off the path to wait for the dust to settle and the exhaust to dissipate. He was excited about seeing this woman with the wideset eyes, who'd seemed to accept his approaches. He'd had brief, fairly pleasing affairs, now and then since his divorce long ago. He thought that doctors might make unsuitable husbands for restless women, if they were away much and their energies directed into their work. Something was wrong with a social system that required parasitical lovers for domestic satisfaction. The African women, intelligent and beauty-loving, acknowledging the carnal disposition of male and female alike, had handled their marital position somewhat better. That is, they had in the years before acculturation, before apartheid came stalking, and ancestral law was ridiculed, bastardized, confounded. Philip was keyed up and as he resumed the path felt he welcomed the future, the riddle, unsure of its pattern.

His hair that had been combed and flattened a quarter-hour past went its own rough fashion now. He ran his hand over it, and then slowed and stopped. He thought he appeared rather absurd, not only shy of his ugly hair and face, but of the position of stammering swain. Overhead came crows, sweeping in a silent dark way, like the Widow Birds of the continent he'd just come from. There were three; they flapped toward the lake and cawed. The trees lining the road that ran through the hollow held their green arms out quietly. He heard Jimmy Fox shouting by the Wigwam.

"Chouchou! Here, Chouchou! For crying out loud, I think the damn pooch is coming in heat, Wheeler! Here girl."

"Head her off. Gus, see if you can corner her!"

"Here, Chouchou," Gus squealed. "Yikes!"

Philip was sweating slightly in the evening heat, his clothes dampish. Before many days there'd be a storm; it was building to one. Monk had planted kudzu to hold the sand incline that dipped into the ravine before the Wigwam. The lush vine was blooming and smelled like purple penny candy or grape jam boiling. Ernie Chapman wouldn't put kudzu in to hold the moving dune by the Sand Castle; he had ideas for planting sucker trees and low-growing evergreens. The vine's flowers were deep purple in bud, orchid in old bloom; they hid under enormous elephantine leaves which resembled tropical growth. The boys' motor rumbled in the distance as it left the Olsons and headed toward Paolis' Eyrie. The sound urged Philip into uneasy movement.

He went up the Owl's Roost back steps. Dora came in answer to his rap at the screen. "The missus said show you in the big room. She'll be down."

Elizabeth hurried over the long stairs that ended near where Philip was stooping over the low bookcase. "Mr. Malraux."

"Philip. Remember?"

"Philip."

"Your daughter said you might care to read this. I'm doing a review of it."

"Clara mentioned it." She accepted the volume and sat on the low cot, covered with a rumpled India print spread; she tucked her feet under her white silken skirt. She read aloud, *"Africa For Whom,"* and fanned the pages.

"Like to read?"

"Umm. Some."

"I have a lot of my books out here. You're welcome to borrow any you want. Only be sure and fill out the card for my file; Chappy knows about it."

"You *don't* have a system? You aren't that kind of person?"

"Stop laughing at me." He sat down by her and pulled the Cellophane from a pack of cigarettes, his hand trembling slightly.

"Hoo," she said softly, accepting one and bending to the lighter flame in his fair freckled hand, noticing the tapered fingers. "Want some coffee? A drink?"

"No. But tell me about yourself."

"What's to tell? I don't do anything or go anywhere. I envy Hazel, who's rich, as much as my other friend Angela, who's always broke. My husband's middle-aged and loves his work like a mistress. I have a nice son, and a moody daughter who's twice as clever as me." Elizabeth was speaking as if angry, looking down at her blouse, plucking at one of the buttons on the front of the sleeveless white silk which fit snugly over her little breasts made into cups by a bra. She drew the smoke in and out; her mouth pouted as if she were going to smile. Her brilliant bronzed skin contrasted with the white she wore.

She didn't lift her eyes, and when she felt him waiting, continued. "He's a GP, and I detest it; I want him to specialize. But he doesn't think of money; he won't. Life goes so fast. You must agree? And we can't afford a second car, and we have to take the children to Chicago for orthodontia because we get it free from a college friend of his. Professional courtesy." She laughed, her breath catching. "I'm spoiled and neurotic and childish!"

"What you mean by middle-aged?"

"Forty-six. But he might as well be fifty-six."

"I'd get you a car, whatever you wanted."

She felt the swoon of love. "You would?" Weren't her grievances spoken and done?

"And how pretty you are!"

"I'm not though."

He reached his hand awkwardly to hers and left it lying on her silk-covered thigh. "And you don't mean half of what you said."

"Doesn't Bill treat me as if I were a little girl?"

"You aren't; it's the first thing that attracted me to you. I never cared for gawky young things with *all the wild summer in their gaze!*"

"But still it's dull out here in Pine Beach sometimes," she cried.

"I haven't felt that. But then I've had you to watch. I like everything you do. The way you walk and the way you swim. I saw you from my beach. I wanted desperately to come over. I kept waiting for you to come to me."

"Really?"

"And I thought if she does, I'll take her in my arms; I won't be able to help it. In front of all those people and her husband, too."

"Did you."

"I like the way you hold that book." He stated it like a litany.

"Why?" she wanted to know. She felt how magnificent he was. If Hazel could see her now. She waited for what might come.

He put his face to hers and his mouth came over her unresisting one. He moved his tongue upon her teeth in a way that she had known a time or two before; it was something Bill never did. Desire came through her in a wave; she felt how she would follow the man's cues. She parted her teeth. "Oh."

"I like your beautiful mouth."

She whispered, "Dora's in there."

"I'm sorry." He started and took his arm from her knee.

"Is this a good book?"

"Yes it's lively. I'm reviewing it."

She laughed at him. "You keep telling me that."

He ran his hand through his hair, grinning. "I'm confused. My Lord. You say something about a drink?"

"Scotch and water?"

"All right. Or bourbon."

"Let's go sit out on the porch, Philip."

"Wait a minute." He put out his hand. "I don't want a drink. Come on."

They went through the door and down the stairs into the night. Fireflies began to flick among the trees. He held her tightly about the waist and she was as if carried along, passive, denying thought. At the head of the dune among the trees they stopped. "I can't even see the lake, Philip."

"It's there."

Its scent lay on the air, the feeling of the vast empty meadow of water close by them. Some heat lightning blinked in the north-west. And Philip picked her up all in his arms and took her over to the soft sand under one of the dark pine trees. "Love and love," he said.

"And it's so new." She was surprised.

When Dr. Bill came home at ten the two were out on the porch in the wicker chairs. Dr. Bill hailed them and then went upstairs to change to his trunks. Elizabeth sighed and got up and brushed Philip's cheek as she went to the kitchen to make weak whiskies and ice for the three of them. Dr. Bill came down with an old terry-cloth robe over his shoulders.

Gus arrived from Fox's, banging the screen, reporting that the first activity that evening had been to chase the new poodle about because she was coming in season, and finally lock her in the Wigwam. They'd only had time while it was light to take down the railing of the bridge and knock a few boards loose. They'd quit and played checkers, one game after another. Gus muttered, "I'm sleepy." Going up the stairs to his room, "What a way to build a bridge."

Philip rose from his seat reluctantly and said good-bye. The moon was rising pale red in the east, tangling in the branches over the hill on the other side of the Owl's Roost. As he walked down the sand path, the young Ardways, horn hooting, were returning Clara. She dashed by, full of her excitement. She hurried to where her parents sat in the small noise of bugs at the screen, fluttering and hitting, now and then a huge death-watch beetle buzzing as it let go of the wire and fell to the ground below. She hurled her sweater on the chair. "Certain parts they had all wrong. I'm going to stay up all night reading *Les Misérables* again."

"Better get some sleep too," Elizabeth said. "Tomorrow night's the dance."

"Okay. But boy! Especially the part where Javert's supposed to dare that Monsieur Madeleine to lift that wagon up!" She groaned, "Was it murder! I can't get over it. Al and me were plenty mad with it!"

"Don't start hashing it over, *Flicka*," Dr. Bill grinned. "Spare us this time."

"The things they left out, Daddy!"

"I'm going to take some soap and go down for a dip," Dr. Bill said. "Who's coming with?"

"I have to read or I sure would," Clara said vehemently.

Elizabeth shrugged. "I'm too tired. You don't mind?"

She went up, unbuttoning and throwing the white material aside. She examined the spot of pine pitch that she would get off in the morning. She sat on the edge of the bed before getting into her transparent nylon baby dolls. The table lamp was on and she lifted off its shade so the eyeball glared at her. She picked up her hand mirror and saw the small shades of lines about her eyes. "Well, I'm glad anyway," she said.

That morning as usual she'd pulled out a few threads of gray from her blonde hair. She smiled to her image as if she were somebody else who had a lover. She noted critically the tiny crease that came when she laughed and remained and was never erased. She ran her finger over it, her pulse beating in resentment. Elizabeth felt how she fought the trap; she tried hard to feel objective about her body. She put out the light. As she lay in the washing of moonlight, all the worry retreated and she was content, soothed. She knew, as the man had said, how pretty she was!

[7]

BOSCO, the next morning, tried Mrs. Chapman's good nature. He refused to touch the pan of fresh-cooked rice and kidney. And he growled at his brother. Chappy studied him and said to Ernie, "You run him out on the leash then."

"What for!"

"I figure there's a girl-dog coming in somewhere. Bosco gets himself worked up every time. He's smart that way."

"I got no time," Ernie said. "I got the garage to wash out, ain't it?"

"No, you do it. I promised Mrs. Ardway I'd do a cake up for that party tonight."

"How can you tell for sure?"

"I know the signs. And Alan's had his share of trouble with the dogs this year," she coaxed him.

Grumbling, he went.

When Alan got up at nine, they had already warned Philip about the doors. Chappy told Alan what she figured and he said, "It's that little poodle of Mr. Fox's, I bet."

The large male dog paced in the hallway, patient. He went

down to the cellar and snuffed about the doorways to see if one
had been left free. He felt the humans' strategy, alert; he padded
back up the stairs, bristled at his brother and would not heed
Alan's words, even avoiding the patting hand.

"I'd turn him out," Ernie said. "He'd mix good with that
black bitch."

"Sure," Philip said in the doorway. "He looks miserable,
Alan."

"Heck, Father, you just talked to the preacher about how
obedient he is. Just my luck for trouble today!"

They watched the dog go, toes ticking on the hardwood and
linoleum in the different rooms. He lay down with a click of the
harness, and whining, rose; he stalked to the door and scratched.
His tongue hung out and his nose was dry and hot as if he had a
temperature. Alan gave him a pan of water; he lapped it, the drops
spilling; he smacked and sniffed and walked away, sighing. He
threw himself on the floor as if he were going to sleep and rose instantly again.

When Alan went to the lake at eleven-thirty, as Chappy was
beating up the icing for her cake, he took only the well-behaved
younger dog, Jojo. He locked Bosco in the basement. "Everyone
remember," he said. "And I'll walk him on the leash this aft." As
he left mournful howls followed.

At the same time another cake was being frosted in the Owl's
Roost fragrant kitchen. Dora had baked an elaborate three-layer,
pink, green, and white. Clara was decorating it, using a kit from the
food store. She placed the green roses and Dora criticized her.
"They're all uneven, girl."

"That's supposed to be on purpose, Dora. But what'll I wear?
I tried on last year's best dress and I can't get in it and it's too
short anyway, I think."

"What about your seersucker skirt?"

"That!"

"It's very nice."

"This is supposed to be a dance. I sure don't know what I
should go for. I dance lousy; I got D in gym for it. I wish I was
Pearl. Irene and Pearl learned how at Madame This-and-that's!"

"You can dance as good as those two any day." Dora bristled.

"Pearl is beautiful, Dora. I'm so ugly. Do you think I'll grow out of it? You should see the note Dick left in the tree for Pearl."

"Don't read other people's mail. What did it say?"

"Sweet-face. Isn't that silly? One thing, Dora. Will I ever act like they do?"

"Oho. I expect any day now you'll be trotting about the house ga-ga. I think you might have your eye already on a boy I know. He's not that nice Al Paoli, either."

Clara pushed a green rose into the sweet soft stuff on the cake. "Does it look okay?"

"I'm going to take it over to Ardway's right away. Poor Mrs. Ardway; she has her hands full. And she never does anything right, poor soul. That's because she was raised in town. She can't keep her kitchen in order. I might stay and red up. You tell your mother if I'm late back for lunch that's where I'm at."

Clara leaned on the counter in the bare room, watching Dora pack the cake and go out. In the heat she was aware, indolent and empty, of voices in the other part of the house. Mr. Ardway was clattering about with his stepladder in the big room, taking down Daddy's paper lanterns that hung from the dusty rafters. Some of them were tattered and Elizabeth was folding them along the pleats carefully, stacking them in the pasteboard box Monk had brought. The pair perspired in the unmoving air.

"Dang, it'll be the boys' luck if it fixes to storm," Monk said. "It sure is sultry. I got a notion to tell them to call it off. What you think?"

"The sky's blue, isn't it? Why would it storm?"

"All this heat's making one up, I figure."

"Making what up, Monk?"

"You're the absent-minded professor this morning, gal." He glanced at Elizabeth sharply. "You're looking pretty feisty for an old married gal this morning. Making up a storm, I figure."

"Oh." A horn beeped outside. "That'll be Bill for lunch. We're just going to have a sandwich. Stay, Monk. I'm going to fix it."

"I have to keep moving."

"Won't you?" she urged, frowning.

"No. See, Belle's on my tail, gal. She wouldn't like me staying to eat. I swore I'd have the net rolled and a table of sorts down there before four, so she can plan how she'll set her things out. She's in a swivet and that's the truth."

"Don't you just want a sandwich?"

"And the boys'll be sure to louse up that record-player connection. Dick thinks he's an engineer and he isn't." He laughed, descending the ladder. "Even when you show him he's wrong, he still won't believe it, dang it all."

Dr. Bill and Clara were coming in together. "What's this?" Dr. Bill was shirt-sleeved, his dark wash-and-wear pants wrinkled. He demanded, "Why you taking them down, Lisa!"

"Hi, Bill," she said lightly. "The dance. Don't you remember?"

"Take good care of them, Monk. I got them in the war."

"Oh, I will, Doctor. Don't you worry about a thing." Monk picked up the box and hiked it under his arm so the lanterns slanted against each other sidewise. He held the weight of the folded wood ladder easily. "See you, folks. And thanks. The boys'll bring them back safe." He was out the door in his swift pigeon-toed fashion, the ladder thudding on the casing as he went through.

"Hell, Lisa. I don't want him using those! A little wind and they'll go to pieces. Or he'll burn them. What the hell."

"Bill, aren't you silly? It's practically a community thing; we have to do something, don't we?"

"I saw Dora and Mrs. Chapman going into the Lodge with an armful of something. I suppose that means no lunch. Dora for one will feel the need to clean up Belle's kitchen." He sank into a chair. "I have to be back by one. Promised Murdock."

"I'll fix something right now. Why don't you change to a fresh shirt, hum?" She hurried to the kitchen.

"Hot, isn't it, Daddy?" Clara bounced down on the couch and propped her feet on the back, her head hanging to the floor, her short dark hair free.

"Got those in Kawasaki on V-J Day. You don't even know what V-J Day is."

"Yes, I do, Daddy."

"Where's Gus?"

"Fox's. He'll be back to eat, I think."

Dr. Bill closed his eyes. "Whenever I hang those lanterns up in the spring I think about that time and the way it was. Nineteen forty-five. The second of September. Everything ahead had meaning again." He was mumbling.

"Are you mad, Daddy?"

"Just generally cross. Murdock discovered one corker of a cancer case for me; dug him up out in the country. Do I sound mad?"

"Sort of. I sometimes get like that, so I hate everything. Especially myself." She swung her feet down and stood, as if fatigued. "I better go help Mum. Am I a weirdo this summer! Boy!"

He lifted his tired lids to watch her cross the room in her quick, rather graceless way, and go through the door. He sat without movement, feeling the heavy pulsing in his wrists and in his chest. He thought with suddenness how Lisa had no right to do that with something of his! The screen on the porch slapped and Gus came in, looked toward him from the doorway and turned away.

"Hey!" Dr. Bill said.

"Yeah?" Gus' shorts and jersey were dusty and smeared from sawdust and dirt on the new lumber he'd helped unload. One knee had a black-caked scratch where a board had slipped across it.

"What kind of manners you call that? Can't you speak?"

"Well, you didn't. I thought you were resting."

"Speak to someone when you come into a room."

"Okay."

"I notice you're in your usual state of the Great Unwashed. Go scrape some of it off as a favor to me, please." Gus started up the steps at one end of the large room. When he was halfway up, Dr. Bill asked, "How's the job?"

"Okay."

At the stairhead, Gus walked down the uncarpeted hall and into his room. There he examined the *Papilio turnus* still in the mounting rack, wondering if it were ready to remove yet. With slim fingers he unpinned the cardboard strips expertly from the wings on the left side. They shifted slightly at the body juncture, and he decided to return the fastenings for a few days longer. He picked up a pin to hook the upper edge of the swallowtail's forewing and to move it. At that moment there was a creak on the boards in the hall outside. Realizing it was his father nearing, and that he wasn't scrubbed and was guilty of other unremembered sins, he dropped the pin in haste and thrust the rack beneath the bed. His heartbeat quickened; he flushed, straightening his back as the door opened, and gripping the iron bedstead with a hand. "Hi."

"Say, Gus," Dr. Bill smiled, "don't mind me if I'm edgy today, will you? I didn't mean to sound cross down there." Dr. Bill came in, rubbing his neck muscles, his wrinkled shirt pulled open at the collar, his bow tie loosened. "I was wondering how the work went, whether you plan on sticking with it."

"Sure. I like it fine." Gus reached his foot over and put it on the rail of the desk chair; he stared at his father.

"I worry about you sometimes, *Pojke*. Maybe a thing's bothering you that you ought to talk to me about. Hum?"

"No."

"I think we ought to get together more. Maybe this winter we'll do some hunting. Would you enjoy that? I might give you a shotgun of your own this Christmas, too."

"Sure, Daddy." Gus vowed to himself that he'd never touch a gun. Never. He'd shoot with a camera instead, like the article he'd torn from *National Geographic:* "Bagging Your Prey a Better Way." He might collect birdskins if he got interested, for specimens. But only one or two, only what was needed for science. Otherwise he felt he'd photograph the way that man had done. He thought how his father was brutal, wished he'd go. When sliding the mounting rack under, he recalled, the flap of the bedspread touched it. Was there any damage to the *glaucus?* "Thanks, Daddy," he said, patient, working his tennis shoe up and down so it squeaked.

Dr. Bill walked over to the cage. "How are the rats?"

"Fine."

"I noticed that this mouse had young."

"Yeah."

"How old are they?"

"Week."

"Bill? Gus?" Elizabeth was at the foot of the stairs. "We have your trays out on the porch. Want to come now? It's twenty of one, Bill!"

Dr. Bill said, "Wash and let's eat. I'll give you a ride in the Volks over to the Wigwam." He put his arm on his son's unyielding shoulder.

"Okay."

Together they went down the hall. Gus turned into the bath-room. Running water hastily over his hands, he dried them on a towel, leaving smudges. From the bathroom door he watched until his father's back was descending far down the stairs. Then he dashed to his room. He brought the rack out from under the bed. The brownish-black insect had been folded over by the cloth which had brushed it onto the pin-fastened side, exposing the paler underwings with their bright red-orange spots and blue marginal color. The wings were broken in an uneven line. Gus worked the specimen carefully back into its original position, using long pins.

He whispered while he busied himself frantically, "It'll hardly show under glass." The lump of rage was gathering in his throat, the sweat of frustration beginning. There was no time to remount it now. When he put it back on the shelf he almost threw it, not caring really if further damage were caused. He went down the steps without haste.

A high hot breeze had begun to stir, ruffling the tops of pines near the Owl's Roost and down along the creek where it joined the lake, forming a delta. There the shore was pinpointed with a hundred gulls, some balanced on a leg half-sleeping, others strut-ting about; their white and olive mute spotted the sand. The water was disturbed, lines of green, black, brown, purple, shifting con-tinually. Boats were heading back to land all along the beach. *The Desire* sped in steadily, seeming scarcely to move, her canvas billowed, the blue star etched clear. On the high side singing a Gaucho song rode the new painter of Hazel's, who had a handsome full beard and who had spent his morning with an easel on the inner dune, throwing grains of sand now and then into the oil; at the tiller was a Democratic ward man from the South Side who knew a lot about sailing. He said it was going to be a big one and was a couple of hours off.

Hazel was sniffing the new breeze gratefully in the kitchen of the Glass House, as she cut vegetables for the lunch salad. A chunk of salmon for an aspic was boiling on one of the burners sunk into the steel counter. Jack had Chopin *études* on the player and they tinkled over and over, waiting for him to change them.

Through the opened tall window she could see *The Desire* and the specks of her guests. She felt a strong maternal surge that they inspired. On the paneled wall across her kitchen counter, in the living-room area, was the uncompleted painting of a four-year-old in a blue smock; it was many years—forty—since Robin had drowned. Jack was plucking wilted heads from his petunias and grubbing out weeds. A near empty can of Holland beer was atop the gatepost by him. She called, "They're bringing her in!"

"All right, Pet." His hands lingered on the young blooms. He remembered that old day almost every morning when he woke in his small room. And the way the gulls had swarmed out over the lake, in their crying way sounding like children. He and Hazel never spoke of the storm or any part of the affairs of that worn-out day.

"Let's go to the tennis court dance over at Pine Beach this evening!" Hazel always invited him and he never came. "It'll be cute. Monk asked us."

"That's pretty formal of him," Jack called.

"I think they'd enjoy it." She referred to her houseguests. "If you don't object to being left alone."

"Not at all." Jack came around the house and through the open glass louver doors. There were no inner walls to the structure. He carried a great bunch of snapdragons which he put on the floor while he turned the record over. "Need anything? I'm going down to Pokagon for the mail in a few minutes."

"Pick up a case of Scotch."

"Last one went fast."

"And some soda. And there's a kind of brandy my *voluntario* wants. I have the name here; he wrote it down. He knows how to mix a special apéritif. But he has to have this brand to do it just right. Artists like it."

"They only have standard fare at Lagerquists. You know that, Hazel." He came over to empty the flowers from an English china vase on the sill in front of the sink. His breath, strong-scented from the beer, his third since ten o'clock, mingled with the odor of stale flowers and their water. "Sure you wouldn't like to send me after five peacock tears and a spoon of sweat from a hydra?"

"Well, do try anyway, Jack. And a pint of double cream, too. For a Hungarian dessert we're trying out tonight." Hazel rummaged about in a drawer. "It was written on a note here if I can find it."

Jack set the vase of snapdragons up. "If you didn't give a drink to everyone who came by, Pet, you'd find you had no friends left."

"Look at the gulls." She pointed. "Like angels!"

They watched the hundred taking off, the mature white ones in loaded flight; the young, whose gray baby fluff made them appear larger than their parents, flapped after. In the glazing sun, they stayed a few feet above the water so it was difficult to tell which were twinkling combers and which flying birds, all the movement commingled. Most of the flock returned to shore in a great determined curve, screaming in an almost human sound, their hooked bills gaping. A few remained to ride the waves, white bobbing pieces. The tracks of those landing resembled duck-webs, strung by thin wires where their toes dragged.

"I forgot. I need some money." Jack turned from the window and went up the circular stairs to the master bedroom where Hazel slept in one of the pair of oversized beds covered with Swedish hand-blocked prints.

She called to him, "Here it is. I found it, Jack!"

"All right," he answered, still hearing the gulls. He took two fifties from the drawer and slipped them into his gold clip. On the dresser was a silver-framed Picasso ink drawing of a baby and next to it, on a pedestal, a Jacob Epstein sculptured head of a child. He went downstairs.

Driving out of their evergreen-bordered road, he passed his cutting garden where delphiniums and glads stood brilliant and tall; his roses insisted upon dying no matter how much black soil and peat he dumped on the sand base. He was reading up on it, expected a new brochure from the U.S. Department of Agriculture in the mail any day. When he dialed the combination and opened the metal door to Box 16, it had come, he noted. Also in the compartment were announcements of sales in clothing and food and hardware stores, two letters for Hazel, *The New York Times* book section, magazines, the Ideal *Clarion,* the Chicago *Daily News,* a card announcing that parcels were being held for him. While the husband of the postmistress hunted them out, Jack leafed through the Chicago paper, reading the advertisement on the third page of a three-day Evangelistic Convocation starting Saturday. There was a news story too, telling of the huge crowds expected, of the facilities provided, and how the crusade was to be engineered by the Reverend Boris Thwaite and his team of experienced helpers. A high number of salvations was anticipated, Dr. Thwaite was quoted as stating. The secretary gave out that in his travels so far the leader had preached face to face to no less than five million people. More souls, through his radio and television ministries, had made their decisions for Christ, than through another revivalist alive. Dr. Thwaite believed that this century would be noted for a great resurgence of belief in Jesus' Word and His entrance into a record count of saved souls. The number of the latter would exceed, the doctor predicted, the figure claimed by Wesley and Moody combined. Jack folded the paper and took his packages of books. He went on his way to get the brandy for the guest and the case of Scotch.

Meanwhile Dr. Bill dropped both Clara and Gus off at the Wigwam path on his way back to the office. "What's the matter with you?" Clara demanded when the car had left them in a swirling of dust. "You sure are crabby, Gus. Ugh. Everybody is today."

"It's Daddy," Gus said. "I hate him. Double-double-damn."

"I think it's the weather. Maybe Mr. Fox'll say it's too hot to work."

But Jimmy was rolling a strut down the steep grade with the help of Wheeler. They'd got it up to the head of the kudzu-clothed hill with the aid of two smooth logs placed under it; now they guided its descent to the spot where it would be raised. Jimmy's enthusiasm was roused and he hoped to get the supports sunk before nightfall. Chouchou was under a tree, her soft pink tongue lolling, a stout rope from her round blue collar wound and knotted to the trunk. Clara saw that sandburs were matted in her leg pompons and sat down by the bitch to work them out, tearing the hair apart carefully. Chouchou tried to help, drawing her black lips back daintily and nibbling. Clara pushed her nose away. "Watch out, girl."

Jimmy shouted up to Gus to lend a hand, and in half an hour they had dug the hole and set the post. Monk appeared and they welcomed his muscles in hauling the next support over. "Why you in such an all-fired hurry, Jimmy?" Monk said. "You'll be a month building the bridge. You don't have to finish it till you please."

"That's true," Jimmy said. "I get carried away. Have a cigarette."

"I didn't come by to do this anyway," Monk said. "I got my own hands full."

Wheeler struck a match for their smokes. Jimmy asked Gus, "Want one?"

The boy blushed, "No thanks." He sniffed their smoke, leaning back on a small haw tree nearby. The northeast breeze was pushing a nimbus cloud at the blazing sun.

"This man was on a crowded bus," Jimmy said, "and he had three bananas."

"I've heard it," Wheeler said.

"Not me," Monk told him.

"He lost two of them and to save the last he put it in his back pocket. Things got bumpy and he lost his hold but got it again. When they reached a stop a man behind him says, you can let go now; this is where I get off." Jimmy glanced over at Gus. "Ever heard that?"

Gus refused to reply, shaking his head. A joke or discussions pertaining to sex perturbed him exceedingly; he was equally drawn and repelled. He tasted the men's tobacco, wished he were one of them.

"Dang it," Monk said, "I wish Belle wasn't riding me about that shindig."

"It's tonight, isn't it?" Wheeler said.

"Supposed to be. If it storms they'll be rained out. What you think? Should I call it off, Jimmy?"

"I would," Jimmy told him. "Didn't you feel that wind change? It's coming straight over Benton Harbor. The barometer must have zoomed down."

"But it's moving too fast to rain. Suppose it blows over or goes round? They'd throw a fit."

"Let them."

"Easy for you to say. But my wife's siding with them. And you don't know her when she gets something on you."

"I was born a seventh son." Jimmy kicked the post with ardor. "I can always tell."

Wheeler began, "This couple decided to go on a second honeymoon . . ."

Monk sighed, "And it ends, the fellow says it was just exactly like the first night except this time it was me went into the bathroom and cried."

"All right. I'll stick my neck out and try another," Wheeler said. *"Gloriandi causa."*

"We got company," Jimmy said.

"Phew," said Wheeler, "the stench of sanctity. Amen."

They looked up the vine-green hill to Thwaite, who waved. "Hallo, men! Ardway, I'd like to see you for a moment!"

"What for?"

Wheeler whispered, "The Litterbug Corps for the big happy family."

"Shut up," Jimmy said softly. "Better go talk with him, Monk. Time we get through fooling around, he'll have things going his way. Persistent bastard."

Monk stuck his cigarette in his mouth and leaped up the hill in powerful easy strides. He wore no shirt and his sun-browned hairy chest was soiled from handling the log. "Yes, sir, Reverend," he shouted happily.

Thwaite began to talk. Monk shifted his feet, his mind on other things; on his wife's heavy tongue, how she'd yelled, "Bullshitter," in a morning rage, changing the word but not the volume to "b.s." when Olson's maid and Malraux's housekeeper came in with cakes; Belle was a trial. Monk thought of Mrs. Olson's pretty ways when he'd cut down the lanterns. He had sensed somehow that she was friendlier, different; at least he'd felt a carnal attraction. The wind was just lulled, and the air become still. The boats had been coming in, he'd noted as he came over to the Wigwam; their owners read their barometers and got the Weather Bureau warnings over their radios. He came to his decision; he'd bust up the plans the boys had made.

Thwaite was eying him, expectant. "Well, what you say, Ardway?"

"Afraid I wasn't paying too good attention, Reverend. You want to do what?"

"I explained rather carefully." Thwaite spoke in a hard tone.

He felt that he fought for self-control, because of one more blasted empty-headed moron. "I'm thinking of the common welfare, of the community. Can you understand!"

"And also that I don't run my own resort right?"

"There are points to go into, my good man."

"Don't my-good-man me." Monk threw caution from him. "You can rent somewheres else if it doesn't suit you here like it is."

"I've been coming here with my family for ten years! Don't lose your control with me, Ardway."

The two men turned their heads as a panting dog shot by at full speed—Bosco. Just five minutes ago Philip had gone to the Sand Castle front door and left it wide open as he welcomed an unexpected guest whom he led to the library. Mrs. Chapman came up from the cellar with jars in her arms that she'd selected from the jam room; Bosco slid expertly past her skirts and down the hallway and out; in a lope he'd headed for the Wigwam.

He plunged up, bumping against the tied poodle, eager, growling. Clara scrambled out of the way as Chouchou pulled backward, twisting her head, the collar slipping over her clipped neck and off. The beasts reared and tussled as if at war, snarling, squealing.

"There you are!" the evangelist roared, finger pointed. "Dogfight!"

"Let them be," Monk said, beginning to laugh. "You got a thistle up you? What's the matter?"

"They're rabid, you idiot!" Thwaite ran soft-footed toward them and the bitch fled, heading for the narrow wood span over the ravine, familiar to her.

"The bridge ain't any good any more, Reverend!" Monk yelled. "Come on back, dang it!"

White-faced, in the kind of temper Eve Thwaite knew in the home where she and Pearl and Irene had viewed chairs and dishes thrown about, the breakfast platter of eggs and bacon or the supper bowl of peas splattered against the wallpaper, the man, fleet, pursued the dogs, needing to lay his hands on them. His arms ached in hunger to feel the soft fur give beneath his fingers. Chouchou, halfway across, wheeled suddenly enticing. Bosco leaped upon her, stiff-legged, neck arched. Thwaite thudded, the boards shuddering beneath him so Chouchou scrambled to resume her flight, hampered by the male clinging to her.

Thwaite leaned to grasp at them, clutching. His foot cracked through a board, and awkwardly flailing the air he was plunging over the edge bereft of its grapevine railing. The dogs skidded away into the brush. The preacher fell heavily, his breath expelled in a grunt, on his bald head, the neck snapping as the spinal cord severed. "For the Jesus Christ," Monk said in awe and it was the one prayer said for the man of God as the spirit fled the shell.

The two other men, in the ravine, ran to the figure, bending. Jimmy hollered, "Wait a sec, Monk!"

Monk shouted from above, "Is he dead?"

Gus stayed poised by the sapling, looking away, listening to gulls' human cries down by the lake, a hundred of them, rising once more from the sand to rush out through sun-glittered air where surf churned with greater violence. The boy smelled the crushed kudzu flowers like purple cheap candy. Breathing unsteadily, letting the men do their work, willing to respond if needed.

Clara stood without thinking. Then there came the urgent wish to tell Alan what had happened. She worshiped the boy in steadfast secret. Mr. Ardway and Mr. Fox were yelling to each other, and Mr. Fox cried, "He's dead. Don't tell his wife yet. Let's think first. Come here now, Monk!"

Clara ran, her strong legs swift, toward the Sand Castle. Her breasts bobbing slightly, talking to herself, making a face. "Boy, I hate it. Don't worry about the dogs any more, Alan; he's dead. I wonder what Alan will say?" She dashed up the terrace steps and entered without knocking. There was no one in the kitchen.

"Chappy!" she said softly. "Mrs. Chapman?" The house seemed deserted. She ran headlong into the dining room, the empty hall, feeling the hysteria rising, as if the place around her had become ominous, as if the preacher or his ghost were perhaps hunting her, reaching out for her. Or if that swelled piece of drowned flesh, that Potawatomi Bible Club girl, that still occupied her dreams, were coming after her to do harm! She rushed to the library at the end of the hall. "Mr. Chapman. Alan! *Where is everybody?*" She banged open the door, crying out the words.

Philip Malraux and Mum were turning their faces to her. Mum lay on the low Danish sofa and the man sat beside her and over her. The pillows were cast on the floor and Mum's blouse was open, and she had no bra. Clara halted. "Where's Alan?"

Mum put her fingers to her buttons and buttonholes. "Clara," she whispered.

"What's the matter, child?" Philip demanded as he rose. "Now come in here a moment. Come along."

"It's nothing," Clara stuttered. "No." Outside the warm noisy wind charged, so doors went banging throughout the Sand Castle. She ran away, forgetting why she'd come. Out the front door where the gargoyle knocker leered, down the beach stairs. At the bottom she saw the distant Alan throwing sticks into the choppy sea for Jojo to retrieve. She veered aside so as not to meet him, taking the inner duneway where there was no path. She required only to be alone; let the others figure everything out. Pine branches waved wildly in a spurting of wind; clouds had swallowed the sun; thunder groaned. She stumbled onto a group of children.

"Hi, Clara! Hi-hi."

"You better go home," she muttered. "It's going to storm soon."

"Okay." They resumed their make-believe serious-faced, hair-tousled:

> *Ice cream soda,*
> *Lemonade punch,*
> *Tell me the name of my honey bunch.*
> *A B C D E F G*
> *H I J K L M N O P !*

Clara stayed within the line of hillocks at the foot of the tall dunes, continuing until she reached the creek. She followed the cold trickle inland until she was in the woods. She slipped into a place she knew inside a circle of spruces, broad and feathery. In the brown-needled spot the sun never reached she sat and crossed her legs, her head on her knees, her hands over her hair, fingers linked. She gazed at the ground; her glasses were filthy, she thought, but who cared?

> *Mama, mama, I am ill*
> *Send for the doctor on the hill.*
> *Q R S T U and V*
> *W X and Y and Z !*

Dry-eyed now, thinking, just let her alone, that was all she asked. The rain outside was beginning to hit in large drops. Almost unable to make a decision, inclined to remain and yet to stand up, she wandered back to the Owl's Roost, climbing to her own room.

She pulled off her wet things and left them in a heap. Slipping naked into the sheets, smelling their dampness, their difference from the winter ones in the Ideal home; there were rips repaired in these sometimes too, making coarse edges, and they tore easily. She reached and pulled the doll in with her. She shut her eyes. When Dora called again and again that supper was ready, Clara would not come. She hoped no one knew she was home; she held Baby against her, beginning to come wide awake.

She heard her mother marching up the stairs and to her room, down the hall, the small steps quick and angry. Clara felt the temper before Mum opened her door. She knew her sin in discovery. That was the worst: finding Mum out. Clara had no direct censoring opinion, and still accepted adults' folklore on a separate plane from her own. Her eyes were closed as Mum slammed in. "Well, young lady?"

Mum kept talking and Clara didn't move. "I know you're not asleep; you don't fool me."

Elizabeth exploded with her emotion, her wide-apart eyes cold and slightly frightened. "What you mean entering someone's house that way without being asked in! How did you dare? Even if a bomb were dropped, it wouldn't be cause for manners like that. No cause at all. Well?"

Clara turned over in bed, her eyes beginning to swim, absorbing Elizabeth's, the lip quivering finally and the child-sobs overtaking her. "The preacher got killed," she said in a small voice.

"What!"

"Dr. Thwaite," she whined, "at the Wigwam. The bridge went through. Mum!"

She put her arms up and in the habit of mothers Elizabeth was comforting her, seated at the bedside, the bare trembling figure clutching hers. "There there. Hoo. It's all right. It's all right."

"It's terrible, Mum. It's too terrible."

"No. I'll explain to Philip, to Mr. Malraux."

That was not what Clara meant. But she understood Mum's fear. She wanted to allay it. "I only came in like that because I had to tell Alan. It was so awful!" Clara wept.

"I'll mention you were upset. It's all right." But Elizabeth knew it was not. She frowned, bewildered. Both of them knew they would not touch upon the thing that was bright as a torch in both minds: the two on that sofa.

Later that night the rain poured about Linden House in torrents. In their own room the Thwaite daughters were talking. Pearl, seated on the bed, blinked her eyes in her nervous fashion. "I'm sick about it, Irene. But all I can think of is, I wish we could have had the dance before this happened." She stopped cracking her knuckles. "Poor Papa. Gone to Our Father."

Irene was in front of the mirror; she leaned forward and squeezed a tiny whitehead mechanically. She examined her face critically, as if she disliked its features. "Wonder if we'll stay at Pine Beach the rest of the summer."

"Poor Papa." Pearl felt an enormous guilt that she tried to reason her way out of; she had wished Papa dead. Many times. Did that make it her fault? Our Father, she prayed inwardly, she hadn't intended it really. She only said it when Papa was mean and hateful. He was strict, Our Father knew that, surely. Papa was the strictest person! All the other girls at Madame Moret's had parents who let them have their way once in a while. Could she have killed him by wishing? She said, "Dick was going to take me to the dance, Irene. I was getting pretty far with him. Now it's all spoiled. Why did it have to happen!"

"I bet we go back to Chicago pretty soon. And never come here to the beach again."

Pearl again pulled at one finger after the other, making little popping noises. "How did he fall, do you think?"

"Trying to stop those dogs from fighting, Mr. Fox told Mama."

"No, I mean, I bet he was mad. I bet—" she twisted her body, leaning on an elbow, her lips quivering.

"Pearl, you think Papa sees us now? Can he hear us?"

"I don't know!" Pearl began to cry, looking over at her sister who was patting a Kleenex upon the little sore on her chin.

"He taught me the best overhand serve of anybody!" Irene declared.

"Our brother never will know him; he won't even remember him at all."

"When Ian gets big enough I'll learn him that serve; I'll tell him it's the same as Papa teaching it."

"You're just saying that out loud, Irene, because you're afraid Papa can hear. That's sneaky."

"How do you know but he can!"

"I don't and couldn't care less." Their eyes flared hotly at each other. Pearl said warily, "Are you afraid to go to bed?"

"No. I think I can sleep now."

They undressed and lay separate in the sheets. The storm had driven off the heat and it was almost cold. Lightning flashed past the window. "Here it comes," Pearl said, and the thunder clapped nearby. Irene covered her ears but Pearl wanted to hear all the noise that was in it.

Downstairs, Eve Thwaite paid the turmoil outside no heed. She sat in the rocker, pushing back and forth, Ian asleep in her arms. She'd sent the nurse to her room. First thing in the morning Eve planned to ask her to pack her starched white clothes and take the South Shore back to the city, away for good. Eve intended to care for Ian herself after this; for a good while anyway until she got busy at something. She breathed evenly; later she would decide other matters, whether the girls must continue in the Academy, the question of a steady income, where they would live. Now Eve felt almost as if for the first time a prayer was granted. She didn't understand this feeling, but wondered at her strength and her ease with decisions. She looked down at Ian, who was a beautiful child and like Papa in some ways; his nose showed signs that it would be well-shaped and his fingers were a little longish even with their chubbiness; it was a comfort that he hadn't inherited her coarseness. Ian might attend Princeton if he liked; perhaps he'd want to study for the ministry too. She looked into the future and then let it go.

Papa's body was in the small mortuary in Ideal. It would have to go to Blaine Park for the funeral that she would announce was open to the public. That would be necessary for the sake of his following. He'd lie in state in his new British linen suit, toupee in place, hands crossed piously, body stilled for once. She nodded her head, her hair loosed of the pins, feeling not robbed. She wondered who would grieve in Pine Beach for Boris Thwaite. It was only when Papa was, so to speak, on stage, that he'd seemed truly happy, fulfilled. In the Blaine Park parish they would mourn, women and men alike, and so would the regular watchers of his television program and his radio listeners. She circled back to the scheduled Evangelistic Crusade he'd been contracted to lead. Thousands were counting on it. She would have to find a sensible answer to that problem. She examined Ian's arm where the Malraux dog had nipped him. The animals were gentle she knew; she had petted them, while they stood tolerant by their young master, their eyes looking through and beyond Eve. She thought she might get a collie. He would be a purebred with a massive brown-and-white coat of hair! She stood up, holding Ian, her step steady, carrying him back to his crib, grateful.

[8]

AT FIRST the preacher's death was on everyone's lips. "Wasn't he insistent down at the beach one day to me that the next death would happen at Pine Beach," said Dr. Bill. "He was afraid of a drowning."

"Or a dog bite!" But people were careful generally and spoke well of their former neighbor. Everyone wondered how the widow was getting on. Mr. Malraux had offered his assistance and so when Eve sent her daughters back to Pine Beach after keeping them in Chicago for a week or so, Chappy was delegated to keep an eye on them and Linden House. Irene drove the five-year-old gray Buick; Ian of course stayed with his mother.

The two girls offered to make fudge and pop some corn one evening, and Chappy told them where things were in the Sand Castle kitchen before she followed Ernie up to their large bedroom on the second floor. Alan had gone the rounds on the beach in the afternoon recruiting people to play murder and poker in his cellar that night. "Come on, and we'll do something dumb like make the four of clubs and the nine of diamonds and the king of hearts wild. Maybe more. Okay?"

"Can't we have one game of parchesi?" Carmen asked. "One. Please!"

"Please!" her small brother Georgie echoed.

Alan told him, "You're not even invited. Only Carmen and Al from your family. And we're not going to play parchesi."

"Oh," Georgie said.

Pearl and Clara and Gus were sitting on the kitchen nook benches. They watched Irene as the fudge bubbled darkly. "I can't do fudge," Pearl said. "It tastes burned or it won't set."

"Me neither," Clara said.

"It takes intuition to know just when to pour."

"Dora uses a cup of cold water. She puts a drop of fudge in it, and if it stays in a ball, it's ready. But I can't do it."

"Irene feels it," Pearl urged.

"One thing I love," Irene said, "is to make fudge. I taste it and scald my mouth." She took the pan from the fire, frowning, beat it and poured it into the buttered plate. It hardened almost at once in shiny swirls. "I hate to say it," she congratulated herself, relieved, "but I'm a genius. It's always a surprise to me."

"I'll do the corn, if you want," Clara offered. And it was a good thing because the kids had begun to arrive and Pearl, seeing Dick and Russ, fled the kitchen.

In the sand-gritty basement, dampsmelling, they gathered. Alan had dragged out two card tables and put them together. He lit the candles and they turned out the lights. He divided the red, white, and blue chips; by then the corn was done and the girls brought it with a dish of fudge squares. Alan was considered one of the best cheats at Pine Beach, but he usually negated his advantage because he couldn't keep a straight face, so everyone knew what kind of cards he had. He in fact managed to get the best hand of the evening, but whooped so that nobody stayed in. At this point an argument started and everybody decided to quit and play murder.

"First who'll make some more fudge?" Alan said.

"Don't look at me," Irene told him. But she consented under praise and Skin offered to keep her company.

While Irene climbed on a stool to get down the chocolate, Skin, who had to go to the bathroom, went down the dark hall. He was passing the library door, under which a light faintly glowed, and heard the voice of Clara's mother within. He glanced back to the kitchen, bright-lit at the other end of the corridor. He bent, with a hand on a knee, and looked through the keyhole.

"Really I must go," the one was saying without conviction, and the other was holding her and kissing her neck. Nearby one of the dogs slept flat on his side on a rug. Mrs. Olson was facing the door and stared directly at the keyhole, so Skin fled back to the kitchen, forgetting his errand.

A little later, at the game downstairs, Skin was hidden in the jam cellar. Al was there and his sister Carmen. "Shhh," the boys cautioned the girl, "you dumb bunny."

The room overhead was the library; a finger of light shone through a knothole. Skin strained to hear but all that came was a low growling sound from the dog up there. "Boy, what I saw," he whispered, but didn't tell. Skin, upon instructions from his mother, had watched Monk at two or three rendezvous when he was small, and had seen a lot more than a kiss. Now, somewhat blasé, he held what he had seen more as a curiosity than a scandal; he had no adult prurience or moral viewpoint. He planned to watch those two at every opportunity. Perhaps he'd learn something. His loins still tingled; he smelled Carmen's fragrant hair. Sly, he let the back of his arm as if accidentally go against her budding breasts. He thought wildly that he sure would like to undress Carmen. He wondered if she would mind. He pinned his eyes to the tiny light above. The dog growled again.

Upstairs the two together in the room lit by a small lamp glanced at Jojo, who had slunk, self-amused and sheepish, to an Oriental teak chest over which a mirror was mounted. It was the way of the German shepherds to rear up and gaze at their reflections now and then, front paws resting on the lace cloth. In Jojo's throat the rumble fell and rose. "Why's he do that?" Elizabeth said.

"Think he knows it's himself?"

"I better go."

"I know."

"Because it's dangerous." She asked it.

"The most beautiful mouth. I've never known anybody with a mouth like yours."

"Especially with the children here tonight. It was a bad idea.

Did you lock the door good? Mrs. Chapman might not think it was all right."

"That my neighbor visit me? Why not?" He laughed at her.

"It's indiscreet. Is it *really* beautiful?" She put her hands on his bare chest, on the soft red hairs.

"Beautiful," he sighed. The polished tables and chairs, the chest where the dog was, glinted highlighted by the faint electric bulb. The visages of furniture shone like mirrors; edges were black, all curves noted, the brightest spots being at the instant where dark met light, like crises.

The dog dropped down to the floor and went softly to the door. He scratched. Elizabeth whispered, "Jojo." The animal didn't heed.

"Here." Philip snapped his fingers.

The dog gazed back at the two on the couch. He breathed heavily and snuffed under the door, needing to be with his master, catching Alan's squeal in the cellar; he stood with head lowered, waiting. Philip came and let him out to run down the hall. They opened the front door, the man's fingers guiding Elizabeth's arm, down to the road. There she ran lightly back to the Owl's Roost, safe again.

And suddenly it was the last week end of the summer season. Angela Paoli had piled her five into the beat-up station wagon to meet Mike on the 5:07 bus. Jack Behmelmen was already parked beside Highway 12; he beamed from Hazel's new red Pontiac; he was picking up her guests for the Labor Day holiday. "How about one?" He lifted his hand which held a tiny Dixie cup. "I'll bring it over; I'm keeping it hid from the postmistress!"

"No, stay there. I'll come get it." Angela gave the baby to Albert, who put him on his shriveled knee and popped bubble gum for his amusement.

Jack handed Angela the paper cup. "There now. Jack Daniels."

"I hope it's not very much. We're going for a swim the minute Mike gets here."

He leaned against the yellow seat covers. "Make you float. I like you, Angela. You aren't a whore like most of the female dogs around here. You're a real fine wife."

"And you're drunk, Jack." She was amused.

"Hazel'll be sore at me. Said I wouldn't."

"Your wife's never sore at you. She treats you like a piece of glass."

"Ho." He sipped again, his breath pungent. "I like you, Angela. I want you to know I respect you, which is even more important. I mean that sincerely. I feel like a father to you."

"The South Shore's late again this afternoon."

"She's our sole means of transportation; what's the hurry too?" He removed the bottle from the glove compartment and re-filled his container. "You know, I wonder if you realize how much I think of you, Angela. I've got the utmost respect. You're no bitch like some I could mention."

"And you're not going to be able to drive your guests home at all pretty soon." She grinned.

"Yes, I am. Wait. There's something I want to show you. Take it to show Mike." He propped himself up and fumbled about on the seat behind him, at last getting the evening paper and turning through the pages. He folded a section and passed it through the window.

"Well, I'll be goshdarned. And it's a month, just about, since the minister was killed."

"Here it is." The blue-windowed machine came roaring down the four-lane cement. "Take it." Jack climbed out, bandy-legged in striped shorts.

When Angela was driving Mike home, he read it, perched in back, Carmen on his lap, Georgie and his guinea pig squeezed on one side, Chris on the other. The news account stated that the widow of Dr. Boris Thwaite, after successfully leading a gigantic revival staged in the Coliseum during the first week of August, had been approached about a television series designed for housewife appeal. She'd signed a contract that involved a five-figure undisclosed sum; and was quoted, "My husband would have approved of my doing this. He would have wished me to carry on his philosophies and beliefs." There was a photograph; Eve had a corsage pinned at her lapel and Ian was on her lap.

"My God," Mike said. "She's cut her hair, too."

"I want a ize-crean-comb," Carmen said.

"Me too." Georgie scratched the pig's stomach as it lay on its back against him, content.

"No, you'll get cramps," Angela said.

"I want a guinea pig like Georgie," said Chris. "Daddy-daddy-daddy."

"Lots of things you want," said Angela. "Ever think of that?"

"Spotted too," Chris declared, "and I hate you, Mama."

"If you're all good," Angela said, "you can come to the Labor Day picnic Saturday night, though. There'll be fireworks: pinwheels maybe, and things."

"Whose party?" Mike asked.

"Our news commentator, no less. Philip's immensely enjoyed his summer."

"Oh. Who?"

"Little pitchers," she said. "I hope Eve Thwaite comes to the doings. Monk said she wrote she might. I'm perishing of curiosity to see her firsthand."

When they got to the beach, Mike had a cigar in his teeth and the children were in a variety of swim suits from previous years. They slung sweaters and skimpy towels over their shoulders. A south-moving wind tide, perhaps fifteen feet high the preceding night, had left a wavering line of small bits of debris, yellow-green pieces of seaweed, broken twigs, bottles and bottle caps, a crumpled Monarch butterfly, dead fish, grass stems, shoals of multihued tiny stones, and perhaps a billion ladybugs, most drowned, but many alive and clustering in piles that clothed sticks and broken boards. They were sometimes pink or yellow, but mostly orange, with black dots. Sandpipers ran on splinters of legs; worried crows strutted about or shouted and fled down the beach, landing by the old pier. The waves were long and plunged foaming against shelves formed of sand in some places, biting at them until they crumbled and caved. The horizon was clear, the air with a taint of autumn so everyone already felt the nostalgia of a season dead. The ragged yellow banner over the lifeguard stand on the Potawatomi Bible Club beach signaled *swimming not safe*. The guard there had organized a game of one-old-cat baseball for the smaller children. In black trunks, swaying like a bear over his bright-suited charges, he directed them in a false jolly voice, hustling so the dark-tanned, smooth flesh about his middle shook.

"We can't possibly let the kids go in," Angela said. "There's a bad undertow today."

"You going to try it?" Mike puffed at his cigar end, his afternoon beard shadowed.

"If you come too."

"Yeah." He told their offspring, "Go on play in the creek today. And Al, take the baby for a while. Give your ma a rest."

"Sure." The children trailed off.

"Now the little pitchers are gone," Mike said.

"Well, can't you guess, though!"

"Elizabeth's looking for trouble."

"It's her own affair, still," Angela said.

"It's a little bit Dr. Bill's." He switched his cigar to the other side of his mouth, amused.

"Well, maybe." She put her lower lip between her teeth, glancing at Mike sidewise, thinking how attractive he was, wondering whether to bring up the letter she'd received from one of her PTA friends who'd seen Mike with a University girl last week, eating in a cafe. It was probably nothing; Angela didn't want to get shirty and throw Mike into her arms. "Maybe, Mike."

"Just don't get any notions of your own." He pinched her buttock and took her hand.

"Race you in!"

"Okay." He dashed, cigar and all, at the cold sea.

A crowd of teen-agers were bringing the raft back for the last time of the year. When there was a storm, the strong current, ignoring the drag of the cinder-block anchor, would sometimes wash the raft a mile down the shore, grounding it up on the beach. Then the Ardway boys would bring shovels and spades, and the children trudge in a group down to dig it out and bring it back. They came shouting, Alan's dogs accompanying them along the shore. They pushed the ponderous wood thing against the southeast-running waves. When the girls got tired, they lay on it while the others shoved. They sang duets unless they got the giggles and the boys dumped them in the water:

> *Not without thy wondrous story, Illinois!*
> *Can be writ the nation's glory, Illinois.*
> *On the record of thy years*
> *Abraham Lincoln's name appears,*
> *Grant and Logan and our tears, Illinois!*

When they got the raft home it was beached and its anchor staked high on shore. Some day when the beach was hard-packed after a rain, Monk would drag it up under the dune with his old yellow roadster. The Potawatomi Clubbers had a surplus government black-rubber raft, which they deflated around the puffed outer edge when it was time to store it. These children scorned the device. "Haven't they put away their old inner tube yet!"

"Alan, your dogs are eating dead fish."

"Let them."

"They'll get sick."

"No."

"Remember the dead-fish fight at the creek on Labor Day last summer!"

"Who won?"

"The boys."

"They didn't; the girls won."

"That was the fight at the shack, dopey, another year. The boys won the dead-fish fight."

"What about that crazy shack fight! That was the year before the year before last."

"Un un. It was the year before that!"

"I got this scar in it," Clara said. "On my eyebrow. Russ hit me with a plank, I think."

"Knocked you out, too," Skin said. "Honest, that was the best fight ever."

"Our shack got torn down, but we won anyway."

"The dead-fish fight was best. Where'd all those fish come from anyway?"

"Storm threw them up. And the sun made them stink."

"I went home bawling," Clara remembered. "And Dora was going to beat everyone up." The prospect had frightened Clara from her tears at the time.

"The raft's safe now. Let's go into the lake again. One more time!"

"One last time. Out to the bar."

Yelling, holding hands in a long line, they advanced into the beating sea, leaping high when a wave curved above. Before they reached the sandbar, Clara slipped and water went up her nose; she felt dizzy, desperate, choking. A roller charged over her completely while she caught her breath. Everyone down the line was laughing and she held hard to the fingers of those on each side, not daring to call out her fright. At last they reached the bar where it was shallow and the surf crashed around their legs. They got their breath and then formed, linked again, to struggle through the suck of undercurrent, and at last stagger giggling up on shore. "Oh my gosh!" They sprawled in the cold sand.

"It's cold when the air hits you. The water's warm."

"I forgot to bring a sweater down."

"Here, Sweetyface," Dick told Pearl, "take mine."

She slipped into his heavy gray one, the waistline reaching her slim upper legs. "You going to write?" she whispered, on her knees beside him.

"Yeah. And maybe I can come into Chicago on vacation. You think your mother'd let me take you out? I can stay at a hotel."

"Maybe she'd even let me invite you to our place." Pearl fastened on her thin gold anklet chain which she always took off when she went in. "Maybe Christmas."

"Yeah."

"But write, Dickey," she insisted, blinking her black eyes. "I love having a boy who's a college freshman!"

"Sure. Dad says your mother's going to be on TV."

"I know. Papa's program." Her mouth shook a little. "Everything's so quiet now in the house. Since it happened. I hate it, I think."

"You know if you'll be coming to the beach next summer?"

"Far as I know. But it's lonesome without Papa."

"Because I don't want a broken romance, Sweetyface!"

"Sing our song, Dick."

"You too."

They thought their voices went well together; all the long season they'd sung a thousand songs brought to them by the radio hit festivals, tunes their parents never heard, most dying swiftly, charitably; a few, seemingly indistinguishable from the others, survived and all the children of the land learned the words and music.

> *Don't throw away those teardrops,*
> *Don't throw away those sweet dreams,*
> *I know the feeling of a broken romance!*

Thwaites' camel bell clattered; six o'clock on the dot. The Paolis trudged up in a line, Mike chewing on a cold cigar, a child astride his neck. The sun would go down in half an hour behind the dishwater sky, out of sight. Clara stood and brushed off the grains that stuck to her legs, slapped at a stinging fly, feeling the damp irritation on her skin where her drying suit clung. Everyone, chilled, moved with reluctance toward their steps or the community boardwalk, where some of the slats were splintered and rotted; Monk planned to replace them in fall.

Somebody shouted, "So long!"

"See you at Malraux's picnic tomorrow night," somebody's answer came back.

The next day was brilliant, balmy. In the Owl's Roost they were rolling up the sisal rugs. Dora knelt in her smudged apron, and Elizabeth by her, blonde hair mussed, in a tight pair of white sailor slacks and a purple sweater with sleeves pushed up. "Roll it even," Dora said.

"It *is* even."

Dr. Bill appeared in the porch door in khaki paint-daubed pants and a frayed-collared shirt. He had the mattress from the porch couch in his arms and was going to stack it in the closet under the stairs. "If you roll sisal crooked it won't lay flat next year."

"Do you want to do it? Say if you do!" Elizabeth taunted him. "Isn't that right, Dora?"

"Heaven forbid." The phone rang and Dr. Bill took the receiver from the wall box. "Yes. Yes. Give her aspirin. Well, give her a couple more. My dear woman, your daughter's the one wanted her nose changed. A little suffering in the process will do her good." He hung up with a clack. "Keep her from feeling guilty about her good luck," he grinned to the women. "Child's having her teeth and nose straightened and her hair kinked."

"I believe it's right though, don't you?" Elizabeth said.

"People never satisfied with themselves," Dora said. "Always wanting to look like the next person."

"That's right," Elizabeth said. "Don't I want a figure like Angela Paoli? I have to lose ten pounds this time."

"I've been hearing that since I can remember," Dr. Bill said.

"Seems to me it's always the same poundage on and off. You look thin enough. What you say, Dora?"

"Oh go on. Look at these slacks bulge! I didn't used to be this fat and you know it."

The phone jangled again. "You take it," Dr. Bill said. "I've just left for parts unknown."

"Dr. Olson's residence," Dora said. "Yes, she's here. It's that Mrs. Paoli." Dora went to help the doctor tie up the rug.

"Yeah, Angela. Do we want a what? . . . Bill," she shouted, "Angela has a globe. She wants to know if we want it. Some book company just sent Mike a new one that lights up. They're going to give him a set of encyclopedia too."

"Sure. We'll put it in Gus's room."

She spoke into the phone. "Thanks, and I'll send one of the kids for it if they ever turn up. How you getting along? Bill's taking the day off to help on the heavy stuff."

In the old-fashioned pantry off the kitchen, Dr. Bill was tying one end of the rug and Dora the other. "Gus ought to be helping, Dora. I suppose he's over at Worth's."

"Oho, sure, Dr. Bill. I got up at five to get the summer china packed away and he was in the kitchen already. Says he lost so much time while they were putting up that bridge for Mr. Fox that he'll never catch up. The fruit's rotting in the grass and it's what's bringing all the bugs. Apples and sickle pears; they smell like honey. Herb and I took a walk down there other Sunday."

"The boy's not a bit like me is he, Dora?" They put the rug with others on a shelf. Dr. Bill looked out the tiny window at eye level beside him. "Gus is hostile lately. I don't understand."

"Children get that way. He'll change. You'll see."

"With us it's as if we spoke different tongues." Frowning, black eyes squinting, he rubbed his back.

The woman was busying herself while she waited for the doctor to finish talking. She wanted to get this house done today, tomorrow at the latest. She had to go open the winter house next. School started Friday; there was a world to be done. She began putting the few remaining glasses of strawberry jelly that she'd made in July into a pasteboard box, and then checked to see what else she might want from the shelves. The flowered self-stick paper needed to be removed; that would be a good job for the girl. She'd catch Clara when she came in and set her at it. The girl had slipped off as fast as the boy. Dora thought children could smell work; she chuckled softly.

"Dora, ever have that kind of trouble with your folks?" Dr. Bill asked. "Or were you close to them?"

"If I did, I wouldn't remember. There were so many of us and we had to scrabble to make a living. We never stopped to think about how we felt. People were different then, I reckon."

But he wasn't heeding her answer and walked out. "I'll go bring the canoe down."

"Need a hand?"

"No."

The canoe was a rather shabby green twelve-footer, tarpaper-patched. On the preceding evening Dr. Bill had brought it from the beach where it had lain overturned, scarcely used, all summer. He'd carried it on his back, puffing, alone. He thought resentfully that his children seemed to prefer lolling on a raft with others to some effort by themselves. When he was a boy he'd envied anyone who owned a boat and had time for it. The only sport he'd been permitted was hunting ducks, and that was a short season, *Far* and himself catching the last migrants going south to winter feed grounds in Illinois and Indiana. Now he grunted as he hoisted the boat on his shoulders. He went down by the outside stone steps; the ramshackle doors that covered them had been folded back onto the ground. He squinted his eyes in the dirt-floored place, letting the canoe down on a pair of sawhorses. He turned the knurled switch knob and a small light came from the flyspecked forty-watt bulb that dangled from a spider-webbed cord. Dora was calling outside, "Clara. Clara, your mother wants you!" Unfolding an old canvas, he spread it over the canoe and turned to go up the outside stairs again.

He heard a rustle from the small closet in one corner. Thinking it was a squirrel or perhaps a rat, he hurried over and pulled open the narrow door. His daughter was crouched on a cane-backed child's chair in the limited space. On the shelf beside her burned a guttering candle, stuck in an R-C bottle. There was ringed about it an assortment of skipping stones. Nearby was a small jar, an India-ink pen, and a school-paper binder. Clara looked as if she'd been crying.

"What the hellamighty you think you're doing!"

"Why." Almost cowering, she stared up at him.

"Of course you can't hear Dora yelling her lungs out."

"I was just going."

"Well, get! And march over to Paolis' first. They have an old globe they want to get rid of. And then you see what Mum and Dora want you to do. I'm surprised."

"Gus isn't helping."

"I'll get to Gus later," he told her grimly. "Does that make it even?"

"Don't be so sarcastic, Daddy."

"Don't advise me what to do," he roared. "And you tell Angela Paoli if Mike wants our canoe next year for his kids, he's welcome. Someone ought to get use out of it. You two don't."

"I had it out on the lake this year, Daddy. Gus and me both had it out."

"One time, maybe. Now go on. And I'm throwing this candle away. How many times you think I've said this childish stuff is dangerous? You're a big girl now, almost adult. Let's try and act like it."

Her chin quivered and she cried, "Okay, okay. I will." She ducked past and out into the sun-drenched light.

"These glasses." He pulled them off and glanced at the film of dust, though he'd cleaned them at breakfast time. He set them back on roughly, not caring. "Lordamighty." Leaning over, he blew out the flame and dashed aside the matching flat stones, not noticing that there were three concentric rings, arranged with precision as if for a primitive ritual. He regretted his anger. The *flicka* was probably unhappy because the year was over; who could fathom the ways of a child? The ways of anyone, even oneself, he reflected. He chucked the candle into the wood trash barrel outside, and went to set up the ladder and take down his lanterns; the red paper was a little more torn since Monk had hauled them hither and yon. He was packing them in crushed newspaper in a crate. "Lisa!" He wanted to caution her about lending them out. "Dora, where's the missus?"

"Getting her plants, on the hill in back."

"Why didn't she do that last week?"

Elizabeth was on her knees, shaking a geranium from its pot, fondling the leaves and roots, looking for worms. She put the ball back in the clay container. Didn't she love everything? Not wisely but well. She loved plants and the sun; green things were easy to satisfy; they didn't ask questions or talk back. If you wanted to throw one out it was as simple as that to do. They wanted to be kept dampish and to have the right soil for their feet; you couldn't appease them with sugar pills. Every spring she brought her flower pots out here and sank them in the shady hillside. They didn't even need water most of the time. Once in a while she came out in a hot forenoon and squirted the hose up there. She tapped another pot and shook out the plant, pushing from its roots a wriggling worm. She'd pinch the buds of this one and let it rest a few weeks. Then she'd put it in the window to bloom; by Thanksgiving it would be all in pink in the winter bay window.

Elizabeth carried the plants to set them in a row on the porch steps. They would have to be hosed off later. From the cellar she got a battered tin bushel, and went up on the hill again to dig mold and loam, to which she'd add beach sand and make up winter pot-ting soil. Sitting back on her hips, she looked at the sky where clouds in ponderous white shapes slowly and continually readjusted themselves. She had a sensation of well-being, of joy, half-shutting her eyes, remembering how Philip loved. Hadn't his hand that first time come fast to lie on her silk thigh? Hadn't it all been a surprise, a lovely shocking thing? And in the days just thereafter, in the vio-lence of their newness, Elizabeth had felt like a newlywed; and it had stood like an assurance to her of Philip's devotion.

It crossed her mind how her daughter had run shouting into the library of the Sand Castle, looking like a wild witch. Elizabeth still burned with shame that the girl had dared use someone else's house like that. Weren't her two children boors? She gave them up, wished them luck in growing to adulthood, guided by Bill's lax dis-cipline. Whatever Elizabeth did with them Bill seemed to fault. He seemed to know what was the correct procedure, and believed his method undeniably the right and only one. She resented her hus-band; wouldn't she rather she were Mrs. Malraux? She wrestled with her loyalty a little; and she thought only love, love, love; she wanted to keep young and beautiful. She dismissed the reality of aging in the same way she wouldn't remember that Clara saw her blouse unbuttoned that time; Elizabeth thought she had been only a little disheveled. She held the soil-covered trowel tensely, watching the kaleidoscopic cumulus clouds.

Dr. Bill came out on the back porch. He thought, seeing Lisa, how pretty she was. Today, there should be time for them to be together; but all their tasks seemed to take them apart. Today of all days, when she could have finished it long ago, she had to linger with digging a bucket of dirt! A hundred things must be done; Dora was harried, his arms ached, holding a large box to add to the stack on the porch that Herb Worth would haul over to Ideal in his pickup. And there knelt Lisa in a dream!

She turned her head and dropped her tool, waving her hand, her frown clearing. "It's a beautiful day, Bill. Are you happy today?"

"I need your help, Lisa. And I want to tell you something."

"Hope it's as fine tonight for the Labor Day celebration."

"Please. Don't let anyone borrow my lanterns again, Lisa. They're all bashed up!"

"Okay. You need me this minute? I'm almost through." She dug into the ground gaily.

Dr. Bill didn't want to go that night to the picnic; he felt he'd not come near doing all he'd set for himself. He wanted to sip a can of beer, dwelling on the turning of seasons, reading the paper again maybe. He'd set a big carton in each of the children's rooms; this year they were to pack themselves. Elizabeth stood with raised eyebrows while Gus remonstrated in a voice that ended in a squeak, "I ought to have two small boxes. My glass stuff'll get broke sliding around in that goofy thing."

"Should have thought of that sometime before today, my boy. Get a hustle on."

"It's four o'clock already," Elizabeth warned. "Getting late."

"You make such a thing of it, Mummy. It won't take me half an hour."

"Well, do it!" Clara called from the chair where she was reading. "And stop talking so much."

"Put that book down, Clara," Dr. Bill said. "You insisted you wanted to help and look!"

"I thought this book was lost!" Clara told him. "All summer I've been hunting for it. I was positive it had a green cover and it turns out to be brown. Boy, am I dumb."

Gus reluctantly mounted the stairs. When he'd packed his drawer contents in the bottom half of the box, he stacked his collections on top. The last case contained the *Papilio turnus glaucus*. He studied it. The lousy pasted-together specimen! Wishing he'd never caught it. He pulled on a fresh pair of short jeans that Dora had starched before ironing. The torn ends stuck out, looking, he thought, pretty corny. Why couldn't she just plain wash them and give them back? Why, in fact, were all his clothes taken away as soon as they felt comfortable and a part of him? They were returned to his drawer, harsh to the touch, alien. He put his feet into the dirty sneakers, wiggling his toes that were wearing a hole in the canvas sides. In the distant future Gus saw himself doing as he pleased. Free! Alone. Listen to them yelling at him right now, for instance.

"Gus! Come on. We're going ahead. Aren't you coming? We can't wait *all* night for him, Lisa. Come on!"

He pitched down the stairway. "I've *been* ready."

They took the short cut through Jimmy Fox's. Jimmy had gone early to help Mr. Malraux and Alan make the fire. Ernie Chapman was in charge of setting up the pinwheel and handling the display. The sun had gone down an hour ago at six-thirty and in the twilight the bonfire blazed and cracked. The lake was placid, its only movement at the very shoreline where the slow water touched and withdrew soundlessly. Else it was all a glass reflecting the colorless sky that had no ending and went out and out beyond. The grownups sat on pieces of driftwood dragged over by the men. Philip went about with paper cups and thermos bottles, one of martini, and the other watered bourbon. "Watch out for the sand in the olives," he said. "And there's a chest of beer over there if you prefer. Soft drinks too."

"Wonderful."

Beside the chest were two torches, tall iron sticks topped with kerosene-fed flames. The fuel was spiked with citronella to keep insects away; every now and then a sootish gasp came from them; they stank. People swatted at flies and mosquitoes that remained undeterred, hardy. Up in the wooded side of the dune above where the children played and where mists were being produced, a bird sang one strain and then was silent. Della Chapman had a huge covered black brazier of baked beans she'd started from scratch on Friday. She kept it nearby in a shallow

trench where Ernie raked some coals for her. The onion and ham
pieces sticking up from the surface were blackened and the perfume of the drying beans rose about the woman.

Chappy knew she had forgot something; she mused over her
knotted handkerchief. Now what was that for? She was always
tying it and then couldn't remember. On the weather-washed old
table was a yellow checkered clothful of fat frankfurters from
the Sawmill butcher. And the rolls she'd baked that morning,
long and crisp. Della would have none of these new notions you
could get at the A & P ready-fixed; she had her ideas on the
subject. She stood holding a long fork, its handle held together
with black electrician's tape. She gazed at the ketchups, mustards,
sauces, paper plates and napkins, the long platter of beefsteak
tomatoes from Herb Worth's place, weighing some of them a
pound each, their meat pink and juicy and rare. "Now, reckon
what it'll be this time?" She spoke to herself or one of the dogs
lounging nearby. "Knives? Salt? No. Well, never mind." She kept
one eye on Alan, playing tug-of-war with a noisy bunch. He was
sixteen, and in a year, not long, would be gone away to school
for every winter. She was preparing herself for it. She would miss
him, but he was not gone yet. She hummed, content, while she
pushed things about and waited to serve.

The smaller children had gone up on the dune by themselves.
"One–two–three–four–five–six–seven–eight–nine–ten–*red light!*"

"Chris Paoli peeked on green light."

"No, I never. Never!"

The teen-agers had linked hands about each other's waists.
Alan's voice soared down near the water, "Pull!" His dogs barked,
seconding him.

"Knock them down, kill them, hold that line," screamed
Gus Olson. "Can't you!"

" 'Ray! We won."

"No, you didn't."

"We won, we won, we won." The victorious team went
screaming down the shore, their enthusiasm catching to the losers
who raced after:

> *You're cuckoo, you're nuts, you're crazy.*
> *Why don't you join the navy?*

"Let's try it again. Double-dare!"

The adults in a crude circle sat or leaned against logs, smoking, sipping from paper cups, sometimes holding one up for more. Elizabeth felt light-headed; she smoothed the pleated apricot skirt that matched her sweater and scarf and set off her fairness. "There was this man in the supermarket; he waited on line for fifteen minutes. He asked the manager to put on another checker and he wouldn't. Finally he said, I'll leave that shopping cart right there. And stalked out furious. Everyone just looked at him; nobody cared."

Monk offered in the silence, "One of the boys is making a dugout canoe this winter."

Philip said, "Good for him. I've seen hundreds of them at a time on the Congo, one villager in each."

"Nobody minded at all," Elizabeth giggled. "The manager never even looked."

Philip turned to Monk, "On the west coast of Africa, I've watched the dugouts they use for fishing and for landing the cocoa cargoes from the ships. It takes a dozen men to handle one of them. Our American Indians used fire just like the Africans, to hollow out their canoes."

Dr. Bill chided his wife. "Lisa, everyone doesn't want to hear about your shopping adventures." He wondered why Philip Malraux didn't like Lisa, and was rude whenever she spoke, or interrupted her prattle. Lisa was just feeling the alcohol. Dr. Bill was uncomfortable as a rule in groups, felt easier alone; he wished he were on the Owl's Roost porch.

His wife's slow voice came. "Well, I'll have a bit more then, Philip. And will you light me up?"

Their host was pouring a little in her cup, almost as if impatient, and flashing his lighter. Already he inquired of the next guest, "Bourbon and branch water, Mrs. Ardway?"

Monk was saying, "That's right, Mr. Malraux. The Algonquins that used to live around here burned them out like that, just enough to get them in the shape of a boat. They finished up with stone axes or shells. I don't know about the niggers off there in Africa."

"In Canada," Mike said and lifted his cup to Malraux for more. "Fill her up. They got war canoes sixty feet long. Queen Charlotte's Islands. Remember our honeymoon trip, Angela?"

Fondly she said, "Last one we took. Take it easy, too."

"That so?" Monk said. "Well, I haven't a doubt Skin knows about that kind of canoe too. He's forever harping on the subject some way."

"Skin burned off the base of a tree last winter," Jimmy Fox said. "It's dead by now; he's starting at the beginning. That's the way I'd do it." He patted the black poodle leashed at his feet.

"What kind of tree?" Dr. Bill asked.

"Takes courage to shop nowadays," Elizabeth laughed. "Doesn't it, Angela?"

"Umm." Angela blew smoke from her cigarette up at Mike, absent.

"White pine," Monk said. "Plenty of them hereabouts." His eyes went sidewise on Elizabeth Olson, more glowing then he could remember. He wondered if it were the color of her clothes that did it in the firelight. He counted the men present; who was it? Not Fox, surely. Not Malraux. He waited, shrewd.

"You b.s., I say it's dangerous," Belle told Monk, and smiled, hostile. She appealed to the group. "They'll burn up Pine Beach yet. But the boys do what they please. Three Big *I*'s; four counting their father!"

"Now, now," Monk patted her on the back, reaching over, affable. "Don't start in on me, Mom."

"My two are strong-minded too, Belle," Elizabeth offered. "Three, counting Bill."

"Mine too," Mike said. "My five. Especially Chris, though. He's got guts. You should see him sock a golf ball. Four years old."

"Oh Mike," Angela objected, her silk blouse and slacks and her brushed hair picking up the flicking light. "You just think he's great because he's in the stage where he approves of everything you do, and hates the sight of me. Georgie's got every bit as much guts."

"Help," Mike said. "Say, isn't Elizabeth Olson looking pretty tonight, Angela?"

"Umm."

Elizabeth smiled at Mike. "But wait till Chris gets Gus' age. Then the problems start. I wish Gus was a baby again."

Jimmy Fox drained the last of his can of beer and his broad features broke in a grin. "I'll vouch for Gus Olson any day. He's a

damn good worker. When he gets his mind going one way he's
a hard kid to turn. He tell you, Bill, about us laying the electric
line for the two-way switch we put under the bridge? Whew!"

"No. Does it work?" Dr. Bill asked.

"Purely by accident, I'm convinced. The fellow at the Sawmill hardware drew up a schema for us, but it was wrong. At
least it didn't work, and Gus and me had to figure how to do it
from number zero. We blew a box of fuses."

"The bridge is finished, isn't it?" Angela inquired.

"All but the creosoting. First week end I get out from the
city I'll do it."

"Hell, let's give the brushes to my boys," Monk suggested.

"No. I'm proud of that bridge and I want all the credit."

"Wasn't it awful about Reverend Thwaite," Angela said.
"Why don't you name the bridge after him, Jimmy? Thwaite's
Bridge! What do you say?"

"His missus never came back out to Pine Beach," Belle said.
"She just sent her daughters. What you make of that?"

"I don't blame her," Elizabeth said. "Eve knows how curious
we are. I wouldn't want to be stared at if something happened to
Bill."

"Thanks a lot," Dr. Bill grinned at her.

"Oh, you know what I mean!"

Philip Malraux laughed sharply before the protest was
quite out of her mouth. "I doubt Mrs. Thwaite's staying away
for that reason, Elizabeth."

"Hoo," Elizabeth said, "what you know about women?"

"Philip means that Eve's not just the minister-from-Blaine-
Park's wife any more," Angela said. "She's a public personality."

Philip turned to Angela. "Right."

Dr. Bill watched how Malraux's cuts were unnoticed by
Lisa. He felt a surge of affection, near-pity, for his childlike wife.
It was half-dark now and Lisa's face, lit by the flames, was, as
was the moon, cut in half, the dark side obliterated, the rest
luminous.

Elizabeth said, "Monk, I hear Mama Ardway gave you a
scare today."

"Sure did, gal. Dang it. I went by to see if she wanted to

come to the beach, and she was in bed. She doesn't do that in the daytime for a bellyache. What's the matter, Doc?"

"She's feeling punk. That's the way it is at her age. She's over seventy. Now quit worrying." Dr. Bill shrugged.

"Well, she was down at the beach a week ago." Monk scowled. "I don't like it."

The children were straggling back to the fire as the dark advanced. Out in it they'd been able to see well enough, but when they came into the ring of the bonfire, all outside appeared blackness. Alan tugged at the olive-green kerchief tied around his neck. "Can we start the eats, Chappy?" The frown-bars on his forehead were shadowed. The children crowded behind him in a line.

"Well, I see what I forgot," the housekeeper said. "It's the marshmallows. Alan, you run. They're in a paper carton; middle of the kitchen floor."

He was off at a lope. "And you can start," she told the children. "Because Alan has to go to the end of the line anyway. Isn't this his party?" She began spooning out the crumbly hot beans and lifting a forkful of the dripping shredded slaw on the plates beside, and handing them about. "There's forks for roasting franks around someplace. Ernie," she called happily, "hey!"

"Mama, do I have to spit out my gum while I eat?" Georgie Paoli yelled.

"Save it," his sister Carmen told him. "Put it under the table. Put it under the table." Her wide eyes flashed darkly.

Then the grownups began to come over, reluctant, wishing to linger where they were grouped, for one more smoke, another olive, a last drop. The children would be done with their food and telling ghost stories and toasting marshmallows on the other side of the fire, before their parents were half through.

"Got a light?" Angela asked Dr. Bill, as they went over. "I'm mad at Elizabeth."

"Why?" He hunted through his pockets.

"Everyone says pretty things about her tonight."

"Everyone meaning Mike?" Dr. Bill grinned.

"I keep seeing him gadding about in Chicago while I'm stuck out here."

"Maybe he sees you that way too."

"No. Husbands are different from wives. Wives don't gad, they're slaves." She laughed, her black hair bright about her small face.

"Hellamighty, I can't seem to find a match." He fumbled about.

"Let it go; we're going to eat anyway. Does Mike ever speak with you menfolks about girls or anything?"

Bill laughed at her, "Honestly, Angela. With all the things you ought to worry about and you pick that."

"What a help you are!" Angela tucked her cigarette back in the package. She had seen Philip and Elizabeth lingering, and still felt a twinge of jealousy because of Mike's saying her friend was so pretty tonight.

Philip didn't look at Elizabeth; he was speaking softly, gathering some paper napkins that had fallen. "I have to see you later."

"Oh?"

"When you think they'll break it up?"

"Don't you imagine before midnight? Oh, think, Philip. Tomorrow I'll be back in Ideal. When will I see you!"

"Can you get away and meet me?"

"Bill never worries. He'll think I stopped off somewhere for a nightcap. Sometimes I do, you know."

"Twelve-thirty. Won't be a moon. I looked it up; it's already set."

"The efficient Philip." She laughed at him.

"Have you a flash?"

"Bill does."

"My Lord, dear one, I mean a pocket one." He said it as if cross. "For tonight."

She shook her head, pleased. "Un un."

"Take this one." He slipped her his pencil flash, pressing her fingers fierce.

She saw his forehead a little sweated, the pale unhandsome features; she felt his anxiety, putting the instrument in the pocket of her skirt, shaking her head. "Can you believe the summer is over?"

"Twelve-thirty then." He walked from her, his red hair standing up, his face appearing disdainful.

"Hoo." She stayed and smiled down at her hands. She'd had to file the nails after working on the hillside, forgetting, as always, to wear gloves. She'd put on a polish called Orange Devil. The nails were short like a child's, and the hands soft; she stroked one with the other, half-loving. Didn't she hate to think the skin would ever become loose and wrinkled? Didn't she want to be young and pretty forever! Philip was dear, and now wasn't that almost over? She went slowly to the others, already mourning a little her lover not yet separated from her.

The fireworks had begun; a pinwheel sputtered and gasped and finally whirled buzzing, sparks multicolored. Everyone shouted. "Splendid, Ernie! Grand! Look, there goes another!"

The hamburgers were being grilled within metal holders, and the franks were spitted on green switches Ernie cut or on the rusted long picnic forks Angela had brought. Over the coals they fizzled and blackened; they were tucked into toasted rolls and on them spooned mustard and tomato sauce and chopped pickles. Whatever got dropped the children offered to the dogs. "Here, Jojo. Here, stupid!"

"He doesn't want it. It's all sandy."

"Yes, he does too," Gus insisted. "He hasn't seen it. Here." He pointed again.

The dog, to be obliging, drew back his lips and gingerly plucked the piece of food from the sand. He took it over to place on the corner of a blanket, nudge it about, and finally walk away from it. Carmen chewed her first bite from a hamburger when Bosco came to stand before her; saliva slipped from the sides of his mouth. Their brown eyes gazed into each other's; she held the handful of food out and the animal accepted it gravely, to wolf it in spasmodic swallows.

"Why'd you do that, Carmen?" Mike Paoli asked his daughter, laying a hand on her long hair. "It's wasteful."

"He was hungry, wasn't he, Daddy? He was hungry. He was hungry." She was satisfied for the moment, gazing up at the man. "Bosco *was* hungry."

"My gosh, I'll get you another."

Rockets whizzed and, halting high in the air, dissolved in a shower of red or blue sparks that fell earthward. Firecrackers barked staccato and another pinwheel was touched off. Then it was over. The younger people groaned. "Is that *all* there are, Ernie!"

They slit open the boxes of marshmallows. The older girls would patiently toast the confection until a delicate tan and crusty, and the middle gooey and hot. The boys and youngsters would thrust them over the hottest coals or directly into a flame so they caught fire and had to be blown out, centers cold, outsides black and slick.

"Does anyone know a decent ghost story?"

"I got a horror one," Alan offered, "that's true too."

"Tell it."

"A long time ago, in the last hundred years I guess, the mother of one of the Zulu chieftains died and this head man wanted everyone in his kingdom to go into mourning. The way he did it, he had thousands of the people put to death. And then he decided to have the gall bladder cut out of all the calves while they were still alive, so they'd have to yell and bellow about."

"Ugh," Pearl said. "Make Alan stop." She gave Dick, whose head rested against her knee, a marshmallow she'd taken practically fifteen minutes to toast.

"No," Alan protested. "This really happened, Pearl. Six thousand of the nation were killed. Everybody had to cry. That was the idea; that was what the chief wanted, see?"

"Some son," Russ Ardway yawned. "Wow."

"How nauseous can you get?" Irene asked. "Doesn't anyone know what I call a *real* ghost story? What about a werewolf? What about someone changing himself to a wolf?" She sighed. "I don't mean a true-to-life story. I hate them."

"Think of one," they said.

Gus started to sing in his voice that was turning, and others joined in:

> *In nineteen hundred and fifty-nine*
> *Comrade Khrushchev went to dine.*
> *He lost his pants in the middle of the dance,*
> *In the year of fifty-nine!*

Irene added another line because it was a timeworn fad with the Academy girls: "And our class won the Bible!"

"This is a comparatively recent sick one," Russ offered;

"Do you mind crossing your legs, sir? We have only three nails."

"I don't think jokes about religion are funny." Irene was scathing.

"I was trying to figure what it'd take to get a rise out of her," Russ told Dick.

"I've already eaten ten marshmallows," Skin boasted to Clara. He wore on his head, to slick down his hair, a greased nylon stocking, full of runs, tied in a knot, its toe hanging down in back. "I intend to stop counting from now on."

Clara was sitting cross-legged, allowing her marshmallow to burn, like the children did, in a blue flame, the skin shriveling. She blew its fire out lazily and nibbled the charred sweet. "I might come to see that dopey canoe this winter, if you ever finish it."

"I wish it was two hundred years ago and me a purebred Algonquin."

"Well, it's not." She thought about the candle Daddy had thrown out; it wasn't his property! She'd fished it up out of the trash barrel. "But I sure know what you mean, Skin." Her eyes flashed over to Mum warily. She'd seen her talking to Mr. Malraux a while ago. For that reason Clara was plenty glad school was starting Friday and her family had to leave the resort. She felt the danger if Daddy knew Mum and Alan's father liked each other. "I wouldn't mind being a squaw," she said to Skin, "except they didn't know how to read. They didn't know anything about anything."

"Yes they did. There were all kinds of stories they recited just like books."

"But I like to read by myself. And lots of times I read the ending first if I can't stand it any longer. What about that?"

"You're funny, Clara." Daringly he put his hand on her neck. "The things you can think of to bring up!"

She leaned away abruptly to avoid his touch, dropping her marshmallow, pulling off his stocking, pushing hard in his lean rib cage. She always enjoyed a fight with Skin because she couldn't bear him really. He was ugly; he was an especial mess this summer, she considered. They stopped scuffling, and she looked at her half-buried, sand-coated sweet. "You double dope, you about broke my glasses. Go get me another."

"Get it for yourself," he told her and smiled, still feeling her soft breast in his mind. "And bring me one back too. I command you, squaw." He slicked back his smooth oily hair with his hand and hunted for his stocking, shaking it out.

"The heck I will."

"Remind me to give you my arguments on the superiority of one sex over the other," he said as obnoxiously as he was able.

Mike Paoli had brought with him a box of sparklers left over from the Fourth, and he distributed them among the younger children who ran zigzagging, their lights flickering as if independently propelled. "I'm satellite seven-six-nine-eleven!"

"I'm a planet bumping into you!"

And then people began gathering their children and saying good-bye. Pearl walked home with Dick Ardway. "Remember to write from college." Irene was driving them back into Chicago in the morning. The big Buick was already packed.

"You write first, Sweetyface."

"Well, okay."

"It's easier that way," he said, holding her hand, uninspired, feeling already away at a strange dorm in East Lansing. They stood without talking until Irene arrived, and then he dropped his hand and went away, "Good night, Pearl."

"Bye," she sighed, turning in to Linden House that was empty, with no one to care if they got in at any hour. It had been different before Papa went to Our Father. She felt the presence in the hollow rooms, where there were marks witness to his unstable patience on the walls and furniture, and perhaps on the people of the household too; here his voice once thundered. But Pearl felt the loneliness, forgetting Papa's tyranny, remembering the loss. "What about that Zulu chief who wanted everyone to feel bad because he died," she cried to her sister.

It was a quarter of one when Philip Malraux studied his radium dial, and peered once more into the pitch dark. Then her steps were on the sand, the needle of light flickering vaguely, her small voice laughing, "Philip?"

The stars were very dim. He pulled her to him with almost severity, so she dropped the tiny flash, her hands up in protest.

He sensed her sudden soft reluctance and whispered, *"A woman of so shining loveliness.* Didn't Yeats write that, Lisa?"

"You're so wild?" she asked it. His passion was too much, she felt, avoiding his body, his fervor. "Will you not say Lisa?"

"Why not?"

"It's Bill's name for me. Don't you see? Please."

"Now we must settle this, dear one. I get as much pleasure in running about corners like this as you do. I've decided I can't get on without you. I want to marry you."

"Oh." She was aghast, almost angered. "You do?"

"I've thought it out. I've watched you and Bill. He'd get on without you, Lisa. Beautifully. He's absorbed in other things; you're an appendage to him."

"Philip."

"And me, I've been cheated. I'll adore you; I'll value everything you are. I can do anything for you. My work! You'll see how I'll produce."

She pulled away, cold. "Philip, I can't stay if you're going to go on like this."

"But you're only shying from scandal. And that's ridiculous, dear one. Everyone divorces nowadays. Do you know the figures on the subject?"

She tried to sound amused. "Sure I'm flattered. But you're simply crazy; you can't mean it."

"Of course. Now, see here."

She interrupted, scornful. "You've thought about the children? Gus, Clara? Alan? About them?"

"You'll have custody; the wife's always favored in these cases. Even if the man sues. Bill can see them when he wants."

"How could I think of doing that to them?"

"Lisa, children survive; they lead their own lives. Look at Alan. He hasn't had a mother, except Chappy, for ten years. As normal a boy as you can find. Isn't he now?"

She started away, into the blackness, slightly frightened. "I'm going. I'm not going to listen."

He came swiftly after, hand on her arm, viselike, as if she would disappear. "Lisa."

"And don't call me that. Didn't I say!" she hissed, quick.

"Didn't I? Will you let me go?" Their faces were invisible almost, their forms felt shapes in the chilly night.

"Darling. Please."

She heard the crying in his voice, his desperation, tears. It touched her, and wasn't she sorry for him? "Can't you be reasonable, Philip?" She drew away from his hand gripping her. "What about Bill? Haven't I always been faithful all the time, till you?"

"That's why," he said harshly. "You love *me* now."

"Don't you know Bill needs me? Doesn't he love me?"

"After the things you've said about him, how he treats you like a child?" Philip mimicked the other man, " 'Nobody wants to hear about your shopping adventures, dear!' Everyone heard."

She folded her sweater tightly about her. "It's all in your head, not mine. I couldn't think of it."

His voice rang into the stillness. "You'll never see me again if you walk away now. I swear I'll sell the Sand Castle."

"You'd hurt Alan; you'd do that to your son—"

"I'll hurt anyone if I can't have you." He was loud.

She felt the listening ears in the night, the seeing eyes ringed about them. "Be quiet, won't you, Philip. Someone'll hear."

"He doesn't care a fig about you."

"What you know about that?"

"And probably senses a lot more than you think he does as far as we're concerned. Dammit to hell, I wouldn't be surprised if Bill knew precisely what was going on between us."

"How could he? No. Do you think!"

"If I were your husband, I'd know. I'd watch you all the time, darling. And you could have anything you wanted, anything. You said a little white foreign car, a Porsche. I'll take you everywhere with me, Lisa!"

She was embarrassed, worried. "Did I ever have any idea you felt this way?" Her voice quivered and she tried to make it strong. "Will you listen? I'm going to forget all this right away!"

"How have you felt? Nothing? Not all these weeks?"

"Well, certainly not falling in love, like a grade-B movie. I've had fun, haven't I?" She strove to hurt him. "It's been exciting."

"Shut up."

"Aren't you a dear thing. And you're famous, Philip, you know?"

"Don't say things like that!"

She tried to see his long thin face, feeling a sudden revulsion toward him, complete. She thought she'd been an imbecile, a perfect one. She moved away. "Besides, don't I know lots of men? It means nothing to Bill; he just doesn't care."

"What I ought to do to you." The voice groped from the darkness near her. She felt his sudden withdrawal, his contumacy.

"You're acting like I said I slept with them. Did I say that? They're my friends; I know them and like them. Didn't I tell you I'd been true to Bill all these years?"

"I don't believe it." The new unfamiliar insulting voice struck her. "The village bitch."

"Think whatever you want; I'm glad. It'll make you stop saying those crazy things." She was yelling too, she noticed. Suppose there were someone around to hear? What if someone heard! She felt the impending disaster but couldn't stop her raised voice in complaint. "Will I ever forgive you for what you just said. I'll remember what you called me till I die! I hate you, though. Oh."

"You love me; hate's next door to love. You feel strongly about me. You care!"

"No. Not any more."

He caught her to him, gentle, winning. "Please. There's no hurry. Think about it. Write me; I'll give you my New York address; they can reach me any time. What I'm asking is good; I can't do it any more alone. Please take your time."

She felt her weakness, disdaining herself. She was allowing him to embrace her. Always didn't she lean toward what needed her and her healing? She heard herself whimper a little, even, as if she wanted to sink down and make love. She thought, am I really what he called me; in my wish if not in my doing? Am I that name? She roused her energies and pushed him. "No." Running, knowing the path, hearing him follow.

He caught up as she turned onto the road in the hollow. He held her arm down when she raised it to strike. "Wait."

"What? Oh." The tears were there now.

"I see it's no good to beg, Lisa. I don't hate you and I

don't want to harm you. But I'll have the last word. I'd have cherished you; I haven't been playing a game. But you're a little girl playing at dolls. I suppose Bill already knows that. I'm sorry for him; it must be difficult for your children."

He let her go and abruptly was swallowed into the night, his footsteps fading. She listened to them. Wasn't she glad it was finished at last? He'd spoiled everything, though, ruined all their lovely times and made them shabby. Why? She wilted beside the path, weeping, unable to bear her confusion. The village bitch. Like he said. She didn't even know now whether she loved Bill. Or her children. How she despised herself. All because she'd wanted to make the most of her fleeting days! Why was nobody ever what you thought they were; why did everybody stay within the walls of themselves?

Autumn was almost here. A chill lay on the unlit new morning. The wind was changing and coming from the west now; each day the sun was swinging farther in its arc away from the earth, setting sooner, rising later. The dark seemed hostile as it closed in upon itself, apart from her.

The

WINTER

Then I cast time out of the trees and fields,
Then I stood immaculate in the Ego;
Then I eyed the world with all delight,
Reality was the perfection of my sight.

[9]

ANCIENT Roman augurers used to prophesy according to the migrations of birds, which varied in character but which were dependable. In September the flights began, first feeble-winged timid warblers, traveling only at night, feeding at day, their cries tseeping in the high branches where brilliant autumn leaves hid them. Later sparrows came through, scattering up in loose flocks from the dry autumn stubble, filling their crops with weed seeds, increasing their body layer of fat until their breasts began to round, then fluttering away in a close group, almost a mile above the earth, on the trackless highway. Some species, orioles and bobolinks, were traveling as far as Central America and Brazil. Bold strong-winged varieties, robins and blackbirds, moved in daylight unafraid; and long-winged ones, hawks and swallows, when they chose, careless of any hour, following the lake coastline. When the season was in its height, at mid-month, myriads of passengers formed a continuous high-flowing stream, unnoticed mainly by earth-dwellers, unless they were driven to land by fog or storm. Their voices made a murmur absorbed into the air, except huge heavy-bodied waterfowl. Then the gabbling of those trailing the old gander who made the point of the V was audible to humans, to children who rushed out of screen doors to watch the flock fading away. "There go the Canadian geese! We saw them this year. Didn't you think we'd missed them!" Migrants sometimes crashed against the windows of the Glass House, so Jack and Hazel picked them up, a thrush or dove, glassy-eyed, growing cold. They cursed the beautiful transparent walls, pained by the tender death. By late October, the few winter birds who would stay over the season at Pine Beach came drifting in from the cold-locked north. Wrens and juncos, brown creepers, and gulls in abundance.

Leaves burned on the dunesides in combinations of red and purple and yellow, and were released finally and swirled in the wind, to disintegrate in the tedious fall rains. Insects, having cast their eggs, gluing them to twigs or sprinkling them under trees, dug underground or wrapped themselves in casings that resembled vegetation. Groundhogs crawled into caves they formed far below the roots of trees; chipmunks and squirrels bustled and quarreled, hunting out witch hazels and acorns they'd missed, in a timeless pattern.

During Thanksgiving vacation, when the older boys were home from Michigan State, the whitefish ran spawning up the creek. After dusk Monk got out his Coleman gasoline lantern, and he and the boys dipped into the water with nets and threw the swarming flapping catch up on land. They cleaned the fish that night before Belle would let them into the house. They sat on the screen porch that edged the front of the Lodge, leaning forward in worn feeble-legged chairs, newspapers spread before them, gutting and scraping. The porch light wasn't very bright; there were no insects, and the wind was brisk, mingling with the sharp fish stench. The boys were given to sudden happy gestures, stamping their boots, sensing their positive immortality. And Monk, reaching into himself for his own youth, was satisfied somehow. Belle froze most of the catch and fed her family the rest, frying them in mushrooms and onions, or baking the roe in sour cream or buttermilk with sprinkles of chives that she cut with scissors from the winter pots that sat in an old baking pan in her window sill.

The creek froze over the last month of the year, in a thin sheet under which minnows and crawfish hardly moved or fed,

huddling near the brown muddy banks. Where the stream reached
the shoreline it fanned shallow, and since the fall rains had spread
so it covered an area far greater than the narrow skein of summer.
All at once on a clear night, the surface froze smooth enough for
skating. Often it congealed instead in a rough crystalline mass
mixed in spots with drifted sleet and snow so the local boys gave
up and took their skates back home. But on this December afternoon three were down there, Skin and Dick and Alan. The wind
was blowing in concentric gusts carrying a little snow in it that
clung to their parka jackets and pants. They yelled in hoarse
tones, deadened against the white blanket about. They swung
their arms and when they came skimming to a stop, they pounded
their skates to keep the blood stirring in their toes.

The cold weather had persisted earlier in the season, and
the snow had fallen heavily on the sand. Waves washed upon it,
each successive dash freezing. This process gradually built an
uneven line of frosty humps along the water line. Then storms
came and the vicious westerly wind churned the surf, which was
filled with ground ice; as it beat upon the formations it made
concave walls in many of them. The spray, leaping into the air,
fell on the other side and added frozen layer after layer, to raise
the height of the structures. Then the water fell back, calm again,
and in following days an even shelf of ice built out onto the lake.
The process was repeated so that row on row of these miniature
glacierlike mounds, interspersed with flat stretches of yard-thick
ice, crept out from the shore. Sometimes when the winter sun
shone hard, a space between the bergs would melt and become
a small pond which froze over to make fair skating.

Alan, since he was small and the Sand Castle was first
built, had found the winter beach an exciting place to play, a
miniature wasteland north country. As pups Jojo and Bosco, six
years ago, had drawn a sled down there. Ernie Chapman had
ordered a harness made for them from the Shoe Fixery in Sawmill one Christmas. The willing shepherds ran barking before
Alan, who shouted, "Mush, boys!" leaping the small fissures after
them. In the hollowed-out side of an ice hill, like a half-igloo, they
rested, sheltered. Seated on the ice ledge, the child was a hero,
who patted his huskies. "Down, Buck." Ernie, recognizing Alan's
inclination to rashness, tried to teach him the kinds of dangers

there were, and then let him go, warning the child only to stay within the farthest line of frozen knolls.

A few times Alan had gone through the ice sheet and returned, teeth chattering and clothes freezing, to the frightened Chappy. Ernie had given out long lectures. Alan nodded but forgot. In the same way in summers Alan would swim in the lake when an electric storm was raging, although Ernie flatly forbade it. Ernie even got his boss to write Alan a letter confirming his directives. "Everyone knows people draw lightning," was Ernie's repetitive protest. But still Alan, agreeing, slipped down, loving rampaging heavens, blizzards, and the brooding sea.

On week ends certain avid sportsmen would come out to the Potawatomi Bible Club beach and dig holes in the ice, fishing Indian-fashion with spear and net or with baited hook and line for walleyes and perch, chub and trout. Sometimes the prize had sea-lamprey wounds on it, ugly fleshy scars dug into the scales with a horny-tooth tongue. Often one or more of the eels would be attached, their sucker mouths releasing chemicals that would keep the fish's blood from coagulating and allow a steady stream to enter the parasite's intestinal canal. The writhing lampreys were sometimes longer than their exhausted host. The fishermen flung these infested things away, repelled, and screaming herring gulls dipped after them.

This Saturday the beach was barren but for Alan's German shepherds and the skaters who bent their heads to the whirling wind. "I hear you juniors had a History pop quiz, Skin. How'd you do?" Alan yelled.

"Don't mention the subject!"

"Guess who got A-plus? Clara Olson."

"She makes me urpy," Skin said, spinning in a figure eight, skillful. "And I'm forward on the basketball team."

> *Two bits, four bits, six bits, a dollar.*
> *All for Ideal High,*
> *Stand up and holler!*

His brother Dick bore down on him from the rear, colliding roughly. They lost their balance and went sliding, scuffling on the slick surface. When they gained their feet, Skin fled before Dick, over the ice. He reached Alan at the other end of the rink and circled, dodging, breathing fast. "I give up! Phooey." He scrabbled off the ice, blades digging into the snow, collapsing rolling in a drift. "Uncle!"

Dick triumphant, returned. "Look at me, Alan. I'm in the ballet ice-capades." He held his arms in exaggerated grace, mittens outstretched. "I'm going into Chicago Christmas week. I've got a girl in the big city!"

"Pearl?" Alan asked.

"Who might accompany me to Roseland. We might go see some belly-dancing beauties, too. I know where there are some." Dick had already concluded that if it got romantic enough he'd ask Pearl to his hotel room. Russ, anxious to initiate his sibling properly into the new scholastic surroundings, as soon as he arrived at State in September, had given him a carton of a dozen rolled rubber prophylactics, each neatly packaged in foil; a notification on the packet said *Buy 3 dozen and save 90¢.* Dick figured he might take advantage of that buy when he purchased his own. Out of the corner of his eye, he saw Skin regain the ice; out of habit he headed for him, face in the wind:

> *I'm looking under*
> *A skirt and wonder*
> *Why I never looked before!*

Overhead a trio of mallards flew, their stiffened wings whistling; they descended to light on the open water beyond the ice ridges where five or six others were already bedding. These were transients that would remain a week or two before drifting south to join the great wintering flocks. Farther along the beach two figures were approaching into the wind, Gus and Dr. Bill Olson, the latter carrying a Winchester shotgun. They quickened their steps on seeing the wildfowl aloft.

In the morning Dr. Bill had waked late after a long harried night; his last stop had been a farmhouse; as he'd stepped from the back porch into the floodlit yard, he'd seen a rose-madder ball of moon seated in the trees and at first mistaken it for a distant fire. By the time he'd driven to Ideal it was three and the planet had become gleaming ivory. Its outer curve was circled with a white band, its mountains and crevices deeply mottled. He had felt clearly his part in a pattern. *Oh Lord,* Dr. Bill had thought, *at Thy Word the light goes forth and Thou turnest the shadow of night into morning. Out of silence the mountains utter song to mountains.* This was his time of living, in a small while he'd be dust blowing in space, nothing. He reached for his usual weariness and sensed in place a rich gratitude.

The hard wind had cut and swirled as he fumbled with his key at the kitchen door and then hung his coat dripping in the entry. He removed a few vials from his bag and placed them in the refrigerator. He took a can of ale out and cheese, and got down crackers from the cabinet. He leaned over the food, mind too active for sleep. He pulled off his tie, his bones and flesh warming in the close air. He rubbed his eyes and looked at his arms. There was the place where he'd slashed a vein open with a sickle, cutting weeds in the path as a boy; there he'd hooked the soft part of his hand on a barbed wire strand; there a terrier bit him once. The bodily wounds left marks he could touch and say, I recall this and this and the terror. The spirit was hid, and its sores as well. Here his parents died, here Lisa was dishonest or he jealous, before the pair learned to make it up in the domestic bed and in fights and during breakfasts and walks along the lake shore or on the town sidewalks. And here his first patient's heart stopped, though the diagnosis had been correct, as he verified every time he still circled back about it; here his latest, with the throat malignancy primed on morphine. Bearing our wounds we make our way to our grave.

He glanced at the calendar. Tomorrow was Saturday; the weather would hold; the few mallards up north would be finding the water locking them in and would be starting down the shore, moving toward the Kankakee region where they'd join the hordes of other ducks, teal, geese, wood duck. He felt a stirring of interest. He owed himself a day off. He had the Winchester, a single-barrel, *Far's* token on a distant birthday; time whirled by. Here was his own boy who'd never even held the gun, much less had any knowledge of how to clean or shoot it. Gus was fourteen now and Dr. Bill wished he'd given him a gun for his birthday in October. He decided to tell Gus in the morning that they'd go after ducks. The season would be over in a few days. They'd make it a holiday.

And then he'd overslept, waking near ten, groggy, a little cross, his pleasure in the plan weakened. He went in his old robe to the kitchen for coffee. While Dora heated the pot, he walked into the living room. Gus was reading the funnies, hunched down on his backbone. "*God morgon,* Gus."

"*God morgon,* Daddy."

"Go get into your heavy outside duds, *Pojke.* You're going to get your first lesson in hunting today."

"Paper says snow."

"Fine; that's the best duck weather. We're going after green-heads." Dr. Bill tied the sash to his robe and clasped his hands behind him, comradely.

"Okay. But I got a lot of homework." Gus sat straight and folded the paper, his tongue in its custom beginning to move over his braces.

"You can do it tomorrow. What you say?" Dora brought a steaming cup which she set nearby on an end table. "Dora, would you make up some thick sandwiches for the boy and me? Fried eggs or meat, something that'll stay with us."

"Oho." Dora beamed, hands akimbo. "Bet you're going over to Pine Beach with him."

"Will you look how this youngster's shot up, Dora, the past year? We'll have a man on our hands before we know it." Dr. Bill went to clap his arm about Gus.

The boy stood awkward, submitting, thinking how he disliked his father's sleepy breath and body smell in the morning, his rare embarrassing attempts at camaraderie.

"I don't know why I haven't found time to teach you how to handle a shotgun. But I've told you before that when you were old enough, I'd get you one of your own. Remember? Christmas maybe I will." He looked down at the slender figure. "Nothing cheap either. And not a beginner's model."

"Gus'll like that, Dr. Bill." Dora nodded, approving. "Now I'll get you a good breakfast." She left.

Dr. Bill patted Gus' shoulder before turning to sit and take up his cup. "Any big news?" He drank the coffee with pleasure.

Gus sat on the arm of the chair as if tired. "I didn't see anything special, Daddy."

"Probably because you were concentrating as usual on the

stimulating and provocative comic section." Dr. Bill glanced over the headlines and opened the paper to the editorial page. "Christamighty!"

"What?"

"Read it for yourself." Then he smiled appeasingly. "One morning you'll get interested in these columns and looking at that junk will seem pretty dull. You'll kick yourself for wasting all these years, Gus."

"You read the funnies sometimes."

"Sure; it's all right to follow a couple. But put the rest of your time on the solid stuff. What's the point talking to you though? I run out of breath and you don't hear me anyway. Hum?"

"I do." Gus wondered why talking with Daddy always involved a war of sorts. It didn't happen with anyone else; as soon as Daddy looked his way be began finding fault.

"You understand me? It's important." Dr. Bill thought how he loved the boy and more than anything wished to bring him up whole, entire, armed with knowledge of all sides of the complex culture about him. He glanced over Philip Malraux's biweekly strip; the dateline of this one was Pakistan. His comments were well done, a little inclined to the sensational with half a chance.

Elizabeth entered with his tray. "Want to eat at the table, Bill, or over there? Comfortable?"

"Right here. Thanks." He smiled at her. "You're a pretty sight, *älskling*."

She stroked his forehead. "Are you two going hunting? Dora says you are."

Dr. Bill looked at Gus who was staring at his shoes and rubbing them together in rhythmic squeaks. "What's the matter with our sportsman?" Dr. Bill raised his eyebrows, and bent from Elizabeth's hand to sip noisily.

"Well, I want to go with Daddy, but I have this theme in English due. Cripes, Mum."

"Will you please not say *cripes* all the time," Elizabeth said automatically.

"And I don't know what I'm going to write about yet."

"Stay home then," Dr. Bill said crisply. "Can't your homework wait once? No telling when I can take you again; the season's about done."

Gus moved all at once, rising. "I want to go. I'll get dressed. When we leaving?"

"Three-quarters of an hour. All right?" He attacked his breakfast, munching the bacon, dipping the pumpernickle toast in the egg yolk, spreading the dark honey and the butter the farmer had pressed on him last night.

"Sure!" Gus dashed out, leaping up the stairs.

Elizabeth was poking about the roots of the plants in the bay window. "These are ready for bigger pots."

"Did you see Malraux's column, Lisa? He's doing a fine series."

She shook her head. "Un un."

"On trouble spots."

"Why is it geraniums don't like to be fed? Do you know if you starve them, they bloom best? Doesn't that sound cruel?"

"You never liked him, did you, Lisa? I noticed it."

"Didn't I?"

"Suppose he'll be out again in the summer? It's a shame Alan doesn't see more of him. The Chapmans are solid country people, though. I'd trust them the same as Philip if I were in his shoes, I guess." He shrugged. "I liked him."

"Bill, you know what? On the Early Bird Show this morning, Eve Thwaite was interviewed."

"On her book?"

"She's calling it *A Woman's Answer,* and there's a lot of stuff she says about Reverend Thwaite too. I can't wait, can you? Suppose she'll say anything about her neighbors in Pine Beach?"

"When's it due?"

"But do you think we might be mentioned, Bill? I've ordered a copy; it'll be out in spring."

He laughed, rising, "She certainly has succeeded in reversing the role of small brown wren."

"She had on a fur stole too, Bill, and a heavenly beaver hat. Can you believe six months ago I met her shopping in the A and P? And today she's famous."

Gus' voice came from upstairs, breathless. "You got twenty minutes, Daddy. Daddy!"

"Now remember, we'll be back late." He hurried up the stairs.

And as they went down the white-shrouded winter desert shore, the wind was whipping the snow about them. They passed the Behmelmens' fence where the white dusted over the signs, IF THIS WERE YOUR BEACH WOULD YOU WANT OTHERS TO USE IT? THANK YOU! Then the mallards flew over the figures of the skaters and dipped below the ice onto the lake. "Hurry," Dr. Bill said. They went out onto the rough ice, making their devious path toward the water, skirting the pointed mounds, sleet-packed on the north side where the wind prevailed, snowdrifted on the opposite slopes and in the caves the waves had made. Behind the last iceberg they halted, keeping out of sight of the bedding ducks.

"Want to try it?" Dr. Bill grunted. "You can."

Gus was firm. "No, I can't shoot. You."

Dr. Bill set the recoil pad against his armpit and stepped into view. The startled birds rose in throaty chorus, "Quawk-wawk-wawk-wawk." He swung for a wing-shot and the noise reverberated on the watery expanse. A greenhead staggered in midair, a few feathers drifting, regained its speed and followed the others upshore, its green-yellow bill and white neck ring extended; it was two feet long, beak to tail. It dipped once and again, as the wounded muscles failed.

"He's hurt," Gus accused. "You hurt him."

"Hellamighty." Dr. Bill reloaded and fired again knowing it was pointless at their range. "Why you think we're out hunting? To keep from harming one? What's the matter with you? What's a gun for?"

"I know."

"Did you see how fast they bounded up? And obliquely like that. I forget every time that trick of the greenheads. Trouble with me I'm an amateur. I underestimated how fast he was moving, see? I didn't swing near far enough ahead of him." He peered up the shore, shielding his glasses against the ice glare. "They're circling! I bet they settle. I'm ready now. See?"

Gus squinted. "No."

"Say, I'm sorry. You want to carry the gun?"

"Okay." Gus took it, keeping the muzzle pointed down.

"You handle it very well, *Pojke*. Later, when we get inland, we'll let you take a dozen practice shots. Burn up some shells. I'll set a target on the hill in back of the Owl's Roost."

"I guess I might as well; I ought to know how to shoot."

"Beginning to enjoy it, now? Many an afternoon I spent up and down this beach with my father. Lots of wildfowl nested here then; deer too, even a few elk and turkey. Long time ago."

"Um." Gus wasn't listening; his toes were numb; he was hungry again; he tried to remember whether he'd eaten breakfast.

"*Far* was a good shot. But I could beat him plucking and cleaning game. That's a part of the sport that's important, too. Mallards are the king's own duck for the table. Even a canvasback won't taste sweeter." He smiled, turning, and sobered. "You making a face at me, Gus!"

"My jaws are stiff. The wind's cold, Daddy."

"Don't know why I bother with you at all."

Gus flushed. "Well, you hurt that bird!"

Dr. Bill stopped in his tracks. "What, if I may inquire, is the difference between killing birds and bugs? Hum? All summer long you murder hundreds of happy insects, prevent them from perpetuating their kind or cage them while they're doing so, stretch their carcasses and appendages on your racks and then exhibit their corpses all over your private cell." His glance was withering. "How about all that crap?"

"You don't understand, Daddy." Gus's voice became high-pitched. "And I want to learn to shoot. I really do. I do."

Dr. Bill shook his head. "Then will you stop telling me that I'm hurting the game we're after. Like a damn girl; although that's not fair to the sex, is it?" He peered through his snow-flecked lenses, irritated that he'd lost his temper; he felt his unreason, his loudness, his tyranny.

They continued over the uneven surface, heading toward the beach where they'd make better speed. Gus was turning over in his mind that he definitely should acquire the skill of shooting; a naturalist would need it to make a bird collection. Specimens had to be skinned, which was difficult and sounded like fun. He'd read about it. You retained the beak and legs and stuffed them with cotton, hanging a label on the feet. First thing you had to wad something in the beak and nostrils to keep the blood from the feathers. Gus thought he'd rather stick with butterflies and moths, whose body fluid was colorless or just stained with yellow. It never made you sick, or seldom. Insects were simple to handle and you didn't need permission of the law to collect them. If Daddy did bag a duck or two, Gus was resolved not to eat them. He refused the thought, wrinkling his nose; he'd have a stomach ache. He had a bat hide on his wall in a glass case, the wings stretched; and he'd skinned house rats Dora trapped at the Owl's Roost, nailing the tiny furs underside up to boards and rubbing them with salt and alum according to the government bulletin, finally dumping them out. He stumbled after his father, wishing he were home in a warm room, with a book about it.

Alan Malraux was striding over the snow with Bosco and Jojo to meet them, his skates discarded up by the ice rink where the Ardway boys waved. "Could I come with you, Dr. Olson?"

"If the dogs behave."

"Heel." Alan gestured and they dropped behind him. "Thanks a lot." He looked at the gun that Gus carried. "Hi, Gus. Man, is that a Sears gun? Ernie has two of them."

"Sears probably handles Winchesters," Dr. Bill said. "But this is an old-timer, a single-barrel."

"The ducks landed up there. You see them?" Alan pointed with a mitten. "I thought they'd been scared off for good when I heard you shoot."

"It's the weather," Dr. Bill said. "They know it's going to snow and want to stay down."

"Birds are dumb," Gus said, to contribute.

"Yeah." Alan motioned to the dogs. "Bosco's a father."

"How come?" Dr. Bill asked.

"Chouchou, that poodle of Mr. Fox's. I got a card this morning, with a stork on it and it said

> *Little Prince Charming has appeared on the scene,*
> *We're his royal slaves, the king and the queen.*

He said there were four whopping princes, and I should tell Chappie to give Bosco a beefsteak."

"Lordamighty," Dr. Bill said. "I forgot about that."

Over on their right was the wasted north side of the dune on which the Sand Castle perched. Strips of red slats laced with wire were set in parallel rows across its bare face; they were white-drifted, some nearly covered. "The new snow fences," Alan said.

"Mr. Chapman's been busy," Dr. Bill said.

"Ernie's going to leave them up all year round. Father had a government man out to talk to Ernie. They're going to plant things next summer, too. That dune is really walking!" Alan swung his arms with energy, leaped over a frosted driftwood. "Ernie's supposed to do anything he likes to stop it."

"Did you help set up the fence?" Dr. Bill asked.

"I can't; coach made me captain of the basketball team this year. Ernie wanted me to, but I don't have the time. Being high in sports is important for college, too, Dr. Olson. You have to be well-rounded; that's what the advisers that come around told us; just being brainboxes isn't enough."

Dr. Bill asked, "You going to Harvard?"

"Father says." Alan reached down and scooped snow to make a ball which he threw as hard as he could. He laughed, feeling the young strength in him.

"I saw his column in the *News;* he's in Pakistan. Good series he's doing. Lots of thought."

Alan looked at the gun Gus carried. "He goes to Turkey next; I've got the schedule stuck on my wall. Could I heft that once, Gus?"

"Take it." Gus was ready.

"Is it loaded, Dr. Olson?"

"You always load right after you fire, Alan. But it's on safety."

"Like a camera," Gus said, "always turn to the next number. Isn't that right, Daddy."

Alan hesitated, eager. "I don't suppose you'd let me shoot, would you? Seeing as this is your last chance at ducks today."

"I don't know. What you say, Gus?" Dr. Bill grinned. "He's not much for hunting, Alan, I'm beginning to find out. But can you hit anything?"

"Ernie makes me do target practice every Saturday morning. He's strict about it. And he takes me with him to shoot crows. You ever go crow-hopping, Dr. Olson?"

"I got a few as a boy on the farm. What's the season on them?"

"Late spring and summer, when the big bands get together. There'll be sixty or more. We went out one sunrise and put on camouflage clothes. We even covered our faces because crows are smart. Ernie has a call he bought; he can sound like the bellering a baby crow does if he's in trouble; and then Ernie can make a noisy hack just identical to a riled old crow. Well, when he has them both going that's when the fun gets going." Alan's handsome face was flushed as he talked, animated. "And pretty soon there's a crowd coming over to find junior crying his little black head off. Then you start popping. We must have got a dozen right off."

"You or Ernie?" Dr. Bill grinned. "How good's your aim?"

"I banged a few down." Alan shrugged.

Dr. Bill put his fur-gloved hand on Alan's shoulder. "All right, *Pojke,* you take a crack first." He gripped the flesh through the youth's parka jacket. He turned to Gus, "We'll let him, hum?"

"Sure." Gus thought crow-hopping was dirty stinking rot. He let his resentful thoughts simmer.

They stayed in back of the last berg. On the lake the mallards were behaving in a nervous fashion, due to the impending storm. They moved about a good deal; some were dull-feathered females, the males white-necklaced, chestnut-breasted, with glossy green heads and necks. They jabbered to themselves in low tones, shaking their heads, stretching their beaks, flapping their wings when the snow powdered them thickly. Unbothered by the frigid temperature, it was only when ice crept close to them on ponds or inland lakes that they became inclined to leave. They preferred the safety of a big quiet water to the land. Alan stuffed his mittens in his pocket; he stepped out and lifted the shotgun. The birds fluttered, squawked, splashed, taking off wildly. The shot rang; he reloaded swiftly and fired again while Dr. Bill and Gus waited. A greenhead plummeted heavily on the ice up ahead. Bosco darted forward.

"Stay, Jojo," Alan cautioned but the dog plunged after his fellow, yapping.

"Will he fetch it back safe?" Dr. Bill asked. "Good shot. Nice job of reloading."

"That's because of Ernie; he said to." Alan laughed exultant. "Bosco!" The larger dog, black eyebrows giving him a quizzical frown, returned trotting, the two-pound weight making his neck

crest; his tail swayed proudly. Jojo ran at his side, nipping play-
fully at his shoulder fur.

"Well done," Dr. Bill said. "We used to have an Irish setter
didn't do near that well, and he was bred for it."

"Drop it, Bosco. Good boy." Alan patted the dog while accepting the bird. He handed it by the legs, to Dr. Bill, then
knelt to rub off the bit of red stain on his fingers with snow. He
slid his mittens back on, his brown eyes hot.

In the dusk of the evening, as they drove home in the Volkswagen, Dr. Bill wondered what progress he'd made toward being
pals. He'd praised Gus overabundantly while he popped a box
of shells at a tin can they set up in the hollow. Now the snow
fluttered, deceiving the eyes. The wipers were going; the headbeams seemed weak in the late half-light. The gun stood between
Gus' knees and their game was on the floor at his boots.

"How can two hunters go out and neither get anything and
return with a duck for dinner? That's the riddle, Gus."

Gus smiled. "Yeah." He ran his tongue in his mouth, missing
the bands that had come off a few weeks ago. Sometimes he had
used to wear out a rubber just from pulling on it with his tongue
until it snapped finally; then he would chew it for hours, like
gum. He wished his father would talk more to him now.

"Have you any idea where you'd like to go to college, Gus?
Have you thought of what you'd like to do?"

The boy sighed. "Don't know."

Dr. Bill was considering Alan Malraux, whom they'd run
across casually. So boylike in his approach to sports, happy in
his talk. His brown eyes had gleamed when he shot the bird
but he made no boast. Dr. Bill remembered that. The youth appealed strongly to him; he felt bonded, and wished—without
quite realizing it—impossibilities. Within himself, half-knowing,
he censured his son for being woolly-headed, for clamming up,
for having no drive at all. When he was that age, fourteen! he
thought. But then, poor little Gus; Dr. Bill's feelings for the
child always involved pity, even for the delicate-boned structure
that was very like Lisa's. He seemed more hers than his. And his
mind returned to the image of Alan, parka hood back, snow in
the heavy dark hair, his movements dynamic. He'd been like a

Viking prince! Dr. Bill smiled at Gus beside him and strained his eyes again upon the narrow country road.

Perhaps he and Lisa should have had more children. There might have been one who fitted better into his father's dreams. What was the old saying among the country folk he tended? "Sometimes a man has more joy of one of his apple trees that he's raised than of his son."

[10]

IN MID-JANUARY there was
a thaw and the outer row of ice humps broke loose, floating and
bumping near the edge. The gray winter lake rose and fell in swells
like molten metal; there were no windstorms all through the month.
For the first time in the memory of the present generation of local
dwellers an iceberg drifted within sight from the north, on which
crowded a small flock of whitetail deer, seven or eight. Reporters
came over from Michigan City and Benton Harbor and took photographs and the event was written up in the Chicago papers. Jack
Behmelmen strained to see them through his binoculars; there was
no way to get hay or grain to them, nothing to be done. Jack put
down the glasses and drank his breakfast Irish coffee, unhappy. He
was tending a roast on low heat in the stainless steel wall oven; it
was a huge cut of beef for the party Hazel was staging that night.
At the last minute Jack planned to sear the whole thing dramatically
in the fireplace, across the Glass House in a pit in the living-room
area. He had Mahler going on the record player; he took up the
glasses again. "One of them's slipping, Hazel. He's falling off!"

"No. What a pity. I feel so helpless." Hazel had brown paper
pasted above her eyebrows to keep frown-wrinkles from forming;
she rubbed at it.

"There he goes. He can't get back on; he's struggling too. I can only see his head. The others don't even look at him. He's gone under."

"They're just starving to death anyway." She put her hands on her hips. "Where'd they ever come from? What'll happen to them?"

"There he is again. He's heading for shore."

"Makes me sore the way humans think the world's made by the Lord God just for them. Wildlife hasn't anywhere to go any more, has it?"

"He's gone again." Jack turned to the oven. "Ridiculous to care." He basted the meat, the succulent blood-brown grease hissing. "I'm going to make some more of this highbrow coffee. Join me?" He went to the cupboard and poured a measure of brandy into his cup, and added coffee, his ruddy hands trembling slightly.

"No thanks. And you will remember I need your help tonight."

"Don't I always help, Pet?"

"Of course you do. Would you change the record to something a little more lively? I'm feeling festive, seeing this is my first real occasion since the holidays." She was on the broad ledge below the glass windows, a pencil and lists in her lap. She patted at the paper on her forehead. "Do you think it was a *faux pas* to ask Belle and Monk Ardway? I've never done it here and I thought it would be quaint. Perhaps it was a mistake."

"I don't think so." Jack put on a recording of poetry being read by the authors. "You ought to know Monk better."

"But he's likely to do anything, you know. And I'm afraid Belle will be uncomfortable with my other guests. My girl sculptor from Michigan City especially. Belle will be wearing something dowdy and she'll glare at that girl's bosom, and there'll be my trouble." She tore at the sticky paper, removing it slowly from her forehead, grimacing. "You know I'm right."

"Pet, you're the limit." Thinking how entirely attractive Hazel was, swinging her crossed legs, her figure trim. Jack knew he'd gone to pot and looked older than his sixty years; Hazel looked ten years younger than hers. Some women managed it. Others seemed the mothers of their husbands, like Belle. Jack felt that all he had left was Hazel and music and his garden and the Glass House. He had made his peace, but he felt the jabbing of self-scorn. There were photographs of the black-headed Hazel all over the place, done by her photographer friends who wanted nothing better than to catch her out on the Captain's Walk that jutted from one angle of the house toward the lake. If one suggested snapping Jack, he declared quietly he'd smash the camera. He looked through the binoculars again at the deer huddled.

"Anything?" Hazel inquired.

He shook his head. The poets droned on. The dead whitetail would sink to the bottom, Jack thought, and later rise and float, washing up somewhere, frozen-furred, glass-eyed, to be discovered and poked at, finally dragged away by a county disposal squad. How soon before another slid off the floe? Its edges were being nibbled slowly by the water, the area diminishing. And the deer were restive.

> *Dear God, you come again behind my shoulder,*

claimed the poet,

> *I had forgot.*
> *I hear you breathe, you are bolder*
> *Than once when you made no sound!*

"I'm going after the mail," Jack said. "Want anything?"

"The postmistress has a watermelon put away for me on ice."

"Watermelon in January?"

"I'm going to do a thing with it."

The poet cried,

> *But then I never felt the darkness, the wound;*
> *How you need me!*

Jack pulled on his mackinaw and stumped out. Hazel went up to make the beds in the separate rooms and to put out tiny Portuguese organdy Swiss-embroidered towels that read *Monsieur* and *Madame*. The house below was silent except for an occasional sizzle from the oven and the rising and falling voice from the sound box built into the long blond sideboard:

> *And rest your tired head upon my love*
> *Forever, God, needing my pity more than I need yours.*

Hazel told Elizabeth that night when she admired the melon, "It's just for conversation, darling. But it's chummy, don't you think?" Hazel had cut triangle plugs out of the top of the melon and poured a jigger of bourbon into each, inserting colored straws marked with the names of the guests.

"You're clever, Hazel!"

"Well, aren't you going to try it?"

"Um hum." Elizabeth sipped, obedient. Wearing white, full-skirted, tight-bodiced, with a pearl choker, she looked very young.

Hazel hurried away as the door-chime sounded, her pale hostess gown trailing on the white rugs, her hand resting on the huge Peruvian brooch at her bosom, confident. Angela and Mike Paoli had arrived, driving out from Chicago in their ancient station wagon for the party; they would stay overnight in one of Hazel's extra rooms. They came in holding hands. And oh dear, here was Belle, Hazel thought, and it *was* a mistake. And Monk, whose black suit fit him ill, though his pink satin tie and pearl stud carried assertion. Belle was incredible, out of a British late-show movie on TV, in rayon print, her hair circled with a ribbon of green velvet. Hazel directed everyone to the candelabra-lit table where the melon held the center. "Find your own straws, now. It's yummy! Jack will be right along to take your orders."

Hazel had invited two politicos out from Chicago. She intended to glean all the latest gossip available about the leaders of both parties. They had brought with them a Democrat from Texas who would run for the state House for the first time next year. He wore boots that glistened as if spit-shined and a shoestring tie. She persuaded him to part with his ten-gallon and it perched on top of the Henry Moore that she and Jack called *Auntie,* just inside the Glass House door. She called over to the Texan, "Bret, there's someone I want you to meet." She led him over to Elizabeth. "Mrs. Olson."

"Aren't you tall?" Elizabeth said in her leisurely voice. "Hoo."

"Believe I've already met your husband, ma'am. He's the doctor over there."

"What you do?"

"Oil and natural gas. I'm about to take a jump into the political pudding."

"Republican?"

"Ma'am, that's a fighting word in my country."

Elizabeth laughed, as Clara came up, interrupting. "Hi, Mum," and slipping an arm about her mother, glancing artlessly to Bret. Clara wore a tight-fitted wool beige sheath and Elizabeth suddenly realized that it was much too old for the child. Her daughter had new glasses; she'd needed stronger lenses and was to wear them all the time. Elizabeth had been happy for the opportunity to select a newer style; these were brown and trimmed with metal, inlaid with rhinestones. They flared at the sides; quite becoming, she thought. And the child had let her dark brown hair grow over the fall, brushing it up in a loose high way. Her teeth were almost even now, and she wore a wax retainer only at night; the slight crookedness that remained would be a stubborn problem to her orthodontist.

"My daughter," Elizabeth said. "Clara."

"Surely not, ma'am! I'd have said your sister. Wouldn't you, Hazel?" He appealed to his hostess.

"Elizabeth Olson was a child bride, darling," Hazel said in her dry plain way, smiling.

"She must have been!" He handled his shoestring tie, his face florid with ardor.

Elizabeth felt Clara's arm tightening about her, and wondered if she were old enough to compete, to feel jealousy. She dismissed it. Over the months since summer's end, the girl had grown particularly demonstrative. If she had thought of comparing dates, she would have noted that the change coincided with the day of the preacher's death. But it was a stage, Elizabeth felt, and hoped it soon would be done. "Why not see if you can help, Clara. Isn't there something she can do, Hazel?"

"Want me to pass something?" Clara offered.

"Go ask Uncle Jack, dear," Hazel said.

The three watched Clara move swiftly away, in her swift style, somewhat awkward as if her legs were sticks above her high heels; she joined Jack who was carrying a silver tray of glasses, his face suffused, his smile stiff.

"Don't they change abruptly?" Elizabeth cried. "You never know where you are. Clara thinks she's an adult all at once!"

"Perhaps she'd had some experiences," Hazel said.

"That I doubt," Elizabeth said. "She's what I call a late-bloomer." She gazed at her daughter. "Why, she wouldn't even walk till she was almost eighteen months old."

"Ho, ho," Bret said, jolly, leering as he watched Jack Behmelmen approach with the martinis, iced, the little lemon twists lying in them like brittle jewels. "What mothers never know would make a book, I hear."

"Don't insult motherhood, darling," Hazel told him. "That's one of the first rules a campaigning congressman has to follow."

"And didn't Gus walk at ten months?" Elizabeth took one of the bright glasses and sipped happily.

"Not practicing politics tonight, ma'am."

"Well, you ought to get into the right habits, darling."

"For Heaven's sake, doesn't everybody insult the American Mom anyway?" Elizabeth asked. "It's the vogue to deride anything heartwarmy. That's true."

Hazel saw Clara frown as she waited for Jack, poised. "I just thought of something. I could kick myself, Elizabeth. Now why didn't I tell Monk to bring along that boy of his, the one that goes to high school with Clara. Then she would enjoy herself."

"Hoo," Elizabeth said. "You're the incorrigible hostess. Isn't she, Bret!"

"Or that nice little Alan Malraux," Hazel went on. "I don't know about mixing the generations. She ought to have a boy her age. I'm so mad at myself. She's probably having a perfectly hideous evening. And where's Gus?"

"Oh, he and Jimmy are over there on the camel saddles. Probably discussing high frequency." She smiled up at the Texan. "What's high frequency?"

"Let me explain, ma'am. Excuse us, Hazel." He led her to the low cushioned benches above the fireplace pit. They chinked their drinks and laughed. When Elizabeth's eyes skimmed over the room, they passed over Dr. Bill, seated on the piano bench, as if she hadn't seen him. She saw Mike Paoli and smiled at him and at Angela at his side.

Jack was feeling fine. He accepted Clara's offer of help and she followed as he took the empty tray back behind the brass and wood counters. "You're a fine girl. I like you, Clara, did you know that? You're my girl."

"Umm." Clara settled on a tall-legged chair to watch him run the ice-cracking machine and fill the bucket. She slipped her shoes off and moved her cramped toes about, resting them on the round rungs. Jack poured and shook with an expert hand.

"A real fine girl that I respect." He took a drink from the jelly tumbler he kept on the window sill, by the little jar of bright straw-flowers he'd grown. "What are you having?"

"A Coke. In there somewhere." Stockingfooted, she slid off the stool. "I'll go find the glass."

"No, no, sit back up there. Glasses all over the place." He went to the refrigerator and took out a bottle.

"Thank you, Uncle Jack."

"A fine sweet girl, Mademoiselle Clara." He patted her knee covered by the tight wool; he leaned over and kissed her firm cheek with his thin mouth. "Sincerely. I mean it."

She stirred on her chair, a little discomfited, and pulled on her shoes again, smoothing her skirt, gesturing with the bottle. "You better finish with that stuff, Uncle Jack."

"Hazel's going to be sore. Everybody's probably dry already. You notice how loud they're all talking, Clara? Nothing to what it'll sound like in half an hour from now. Just you listen; I'll be wearing my legs out trotting about." He grinned.

"I like parties. You have a lot of them, don't you?"

"Hazel enjoys people around her; it keeps her happy."

"You're a very merry person, Uncle Jack. You know, I didn't used to think you were, but I think so now."

"I'm a clown, a buffoon. I'm Hazel's little puppy dog."

Clara was startled to see that he was about to cry. She wished firmly that grownups wouldn't drink. That is, unless they could hold it. Like Daddy, she thought; he could take a drink and you never knew it; his breath didn't even smell very badly. Uncle Jack's, when he kissed her, was extremely strong. Mum got silly too, when she had more than a cocktail. Daddy always chucked her chin and said, "Don't you forget," when they left for a party like tonight. The man had stopped what he was doing and was gazing directly at her, his eyes watery; she felt queer. She intended never to begin drinking. She and Gus discussed it often; that and smoking; they'd never drink or smoke. Uncle Jack touched her knee again, lightly.

"You know who that is?" She followed his hand indicating the painting across the chattering room, of the child in the blue smock. "That's my little boy, Robin. You didn't know I had a little boy, did you?"

"Yes I did," she whispered.

But he paid no heed. "I was having his portrait done for a birthday present for Hazel. Over forty years."

"I know. You always tell about it."

He looked in Clara's eyes. "It was one of those things. He was there and then he wasn't."

"I know, Uncle Jack. I know."

"That's the way it was." He sighed. "You're a very nice girl and you stay that way. Stay fresh and sweet, Clara."

"You better tend to that stuff for the company," she pleaded.

"I will. Hazel'll be sore." He shuffled over to the table. "It was right after the war. We'd just came here for a month. Things were different those days; you don't realize. We had a little cabin then. There were the three of us. Snug as three bugs in a rug." The tears swam slowly down Jack's cheeks. He poured the right measure into each glass with a little fillip at the end so none spilled on the counter. He pulled open a drawer and took out a striped kitchen towel to dab his eyes. He lifted the silver tray. "Now, open the icebox, that other one over there; take out the salver that I fixed and you can pass it around. Oh, I'm a handy man to have around, Mademoiselle Clara!"

She laughed, catching her breath. "You!" Uncle Jack always made her feel so alive, so beautiful! So lucky.

He bowed to her. "Follow me, men. Didn't I promise you they'd all be talking louder than they were? They always do, in direct ratio to booze consumption." He raised his voice as they approached a group so she could catch his words. "This time around we don't have to be so careful about who gets what, either." He paused before a group. "Highball anyone? Speak up."

The girl sculptor laughed and accepted a glass. She selected a tiny sandwich from Clara's plate. "Hello, darling. Hazel," she cried, "have you seen this sweet child here? How old are you, darling?"

"Sixteen, April."

"She's only fifteen. Incredible age. Jack, was I ever fifteen?"

Clara, following slowly, wished Uncle Jack hadn't confided in her. She turned her mind from it, wrinkling her nose as she offered the tray to her brother and Mr. Fox.

Jimmy was telling one of the beatnik jokes which were very popular in Chicago. The priest said to the beats as they left his church, "See you next Sunday, same spot on the dial. Only try to remember it's the Father, the Son, and the Holy Ghost, not daddio, laddio and the spook."

Gus smiled a little. "I know a beat one you can tell, Jimmy, if I can remember right."

Clara advised them, "Ugh, don't choose those black triangle ones. They've got too much salt."

Jimmy took one. "Caviar. Salt's healthy. I'm using sea-kelp this winter for the first time; iodine in the natural state. You want to know one to tone these muscles in the abdomen, Gus?" Jimmy stood to demonstrate, his athletic body constricted by his ill-fitting mass-produced clothes.

"Yeah." Gus, sitting on the Egyptian saddle, relaxed his hunched form.

"How are Chouchou's puppies, Mr. Fox?" Clara asked.

Jimmy grunted, as he swung his upper torso. "Little monsters. Wheeler's feeding them for me while I'm out here. The Behmelmens are going to take one off my hands soon as they're weaned. Poodle and German shepherd's a good cross."

"Are they pretty?"

Jimmy said, "Afraid not; matter of opinion. I might give one to the Pokagon postmistress, too. It was a blow to Wheeler." He laughed, "See, he's a fancier and thinks it's a calamitous waste of blue blood. Me, I'm more interested in the pooch's character. Right? I think the experience was good for Chouchou!" His figure stretched and then bent, his fingers sweeping the floor. "Come on. Try this one, Gus."

"Not now." It was inconceivable to Gus that one could exhibit oneself in motion or ever do more than endure, stagnant-bodied, if strangers were about.

Clara had moved on. Hazel's bearded painter who had been a summer guest had come for the party and brought a girl whom Hazel insisted on calling his *cocotte* at every opportunity. Both wore sandals and dressed casually, the man with an idol of wood slung on his chest on a chain. They had discovered a collection of dance records in the cabinet and were playing them one by one. They turned up the volume and shuffled around a while. They were joined by others. When Clara offered Monk Ardway the plate of *hors d'oeuvres,* he grinned engagingly and gulped two. "How about taking a turn with me, little gal?"

"Okay, Mr. Ardway. But I can't dance." She smiled to Mrs. Ardway apologetically. She set the tray down, feeling daring; nothing with grown-up implications was impossible.

"Neither can I, so stop having kittens."

They went across the room to the dancing; Mum and Jimmy Fox were there. Mr. Ardway's breath was like Uncle Jack's, but she didn't mind because he was very handsome, she thought. She liked his pink necktie and the enormously broad male shoulders. Her hand, on the cloth of his coat, felt the iron bands of muscle beneath. She felt she was attractive at last, a success. She liked the way her heels gave her height, maturity. She'd have given a good deal at that moment if Alan were there to see; it'd be no use telling him about it; he wouldn't listen. Mr. Ardway had ceased to be Skin's father and had been transformed into a romantic bookish image. She had stumbled. "It's my heels. I'm so sorry."

"You step too quick for me, pretty gal. Let's rest for a minute." Monk urged her around the woven reed partition into the entry area where the steps led upstairs. "Let's sit here."

"No. Wait a sec." She laughed, hesitating, feeling the child's obligation to obey the elder, yet afraid in an indefinable way. She wanted to remain; she paused to see if he would persuade her.

"Come on." He was pulling her a little roughly, not letting her fingers go.

"Okay." She was on the seat and then his arm came about her familiarly. She realized that Mr. Ardway was sometimes in Dutch with his wife because he fancied other women, and she had caught the stories bruited about ever since she'd been at Pine Beach, of fights Monk and Belle Ardway had. Once she herself had heard shrieking and wild bass-toned words from the Lodge on an evening when she came to see Skin. She'd hurried away, putting the thing from her, forcing herself to forget. Her parents quarreled, of course, but not with primitive frightening freedom. Skin said his mother nearly killed his father once, hurling a hot iron at his forehead, making a wound. And Skin had spied on his father too, only a few years ago, when Belle thought Monk was sleeping with one of his tenant's wives. Russ and Dick had rebelled at the assignment, but Skin was persuaded with a bribe. Clara didn't remember how the incident ended, but Skin seemed to bear for neither parent a grudge. He confided casually to Clara. Now she felt an intense need to find what it was all about. Men and women. Certain girls talked about it, loud and sly, at school in the rest rooms, of the coming together of male and female, of bat-and-balls and cherries. Clara hated it, insecure of discussion or retort. She was unable to accept the descriptions she'd read, or even the health-class movie. She felt something remained hidden. There was something more in it; there had to be. Mr. Ardway's heavy hand was on her shoulder. She couldn't leave, she thought, if something were going to happen. She didn't mind his hand, although she was apprehensive lest they be discovered there. She giggled.

"What's funny, gal? You like this?" He hugged her softness, thinking, very young meat. The imperative fire coursed down through his strong thighs. Elizabeth Olson would kill him if she knew he was here right now with a hard on. And the doctor! Monk resolved he'd stop in half a minute. This was crazy; he'd only come to the dang woman's shindig because Belle was in a sweat to see the house. It was pretty swaggy, and the liquor okay; he'd had a good deal too much. He shook his head, trying to clear it and looked down at the kid. He was looped, he thought, and better get back into the other room. First though, just one teaser with this little four-eyed baby. Monk argued confusedly with himself. She was obviously old enough and had likely been laid a few times. He ached to think of rolling a virgin! Immediately he put his calloused fingers to the nipple of one small soft breast. He began kissing her, noticing her quick surprised intake and how awkward she was about letting her glasses get in the way and not turning her face. He opened his mouth a moment over hers and then lurched awkwardly to his feet. He put his hands out, palms up, excusing himself. "Whew, dang it, little gal. Don't take me serious." He swayed.

She got up brightly. "That's perfectly all right, Mr. Ardway. I don't mind, Mr. Ardway."

"Look." He spoke gutturally. "I'm going back in. But you better wait, see? Your mama might think something funny if she saw us come out together. Now you mind." He straightened his satin tie and rubbed the back of his neck as if he'd forgot her as he left.

Clara felt the tears gush. She kicked off her shoes and rubbed her feet, her mind on how he'd touched her. It flashed through her mind and she erased it that Mum had let Alan's father do something like that last summer. Loneliness was awful, she considered. All the fine webs and ties she'd sensed to those people inside were broken. It seemed impossible that she could break again through the invisible wall she must encounter by going back. Someone was singing inside, that *cocotte:* "In thee Bahay-mas ev-er-eee day, you laugh and you seeng and you all-ways play!" She checked her tears and held her head up and her face in a smile in case someone happened on her sitting on the stair. She hoped Mr. Ardway had done her no harm; she crossed her fingers and knocked on the floor seven times. She liked him and hoped he wouldn't feel awkward now in her presence.

Her mind ran on to her doll that she'd packed away when school began. Mum had made her, saying at fifteen one had to. But Clara had plenty of girl friends who had dolls and big white lambs and bears and anything they wanted on their beds. She hankered for the big plaster doll, Baby, as if it had died. But it was worse, she thought, for Baby hadn't. When Uncle Jack was sad for Robin, there was nothing he could do. She could go to the attic and get it from the carton where it lay with tissue paper over its face. It had a kind of reality that she'd breathed into it. She should not have to give it up until she had a live baby of her own! Her eyes widened a little, considering if for sure she were the same as before the man kissed her. She pulled her brows in a heavy line. How silly could you get!

Mrs. Behmelmen was crying, "Come along, everybody! Jack's going to do the roast. You have to see it. Wonderful! Come along, darlings." The voices were changed, hushing, eager, the guests forgetting the words they had just been saying. Clara slipped into the tight shoes again. She got her lipstick from the beaded bag Mum had given her because she didn't like it. She repaired her mouth brilliantly. She smoothed the soft clinging wool of the beige dress as she went through the unseen barrier into the room. Almost at once she caught Belle Ardway's eyes, which seemed jealous and coarse, the mouth scornful; she wondered if she imagined it. She looked about for Mum, wanting to be next to her. Mum was dancing with the Texas politician; they weren't paying any attention to Hazel.

The bearded artist was defending himself. "But *I* think it's good and *that's* what's important, isn't it?"

"Besides," Hazel told her protégé's harassers, "Gauguin himself said nothing resembles a daub so much as a masterpiece. Isn't that so, *cocotte?*"

"I suppose so," the girl breathed, meek.

Jack plunged his spitted roast into the flames to let it blaze a moment before depositing it blackened on a great Mexican flat bowl. He began to carve, standing down in the pit, the roast before him on the floor. "Ab, the cave man," he said. "Homo sapiens has made the complete cycle." He drank from his tumbler on the bricks nearby.

Hazel smiled leniently at him. "Are you still using that old jelly jar?" She had heaped the potatoes, roasted in aluminum foil over the coals, into an Italian basket. She poured dressing over the salad she'd let chill out on the porch. She had new Belgian pottery plates, which she filled and handed about. A new sound was coming over the room, the spirited talking ceasing, the chinking of knives and forks replacing it. Hazel listened and sighed with heavy repletion. She sat on the sofa by Mike Paoli. "Where's Angela, darling?"

"Don't you know husbands and wives are supposed to forget each other as soon as they arrive at a party? That's the nice part, Hazel."

She balanced the plate on her knees. "How are the babies? Have any gossip about anything at all? The husband of the postmistress is lying fallow during this season."

Mike considered, "Well, I'll try. Angela and I had a big row coming out here. Seems she saw me having lemonade with some girl students, whose dresses she says are easily lifted." Mike's speech was slightly slurred and he made a moue at Hazel, a bit drunk.

"But you were hand-holding when you came. I saw you."

"We were?" Across the room the Texan was bending over Angela to light her cigarette. It was the wrong end of a filter-tip and it flared. Mike heard the raised sounds of excitement, his wife's chuckle. Dr. Bill brought a cup of coffee over to Elizabeth, and Mike remembered the story told around the summer community about her and Malraux. He wondered if the doctor and Elizabeth rowed about it. As for the business in Chicago, Mike liked young chicks; most men did. He liked women. But he liked the booze also; and he liked work, driving himself at top speed easily. And then he liked his little woman Angela. She was the center on which Mike spun. It was the thing the poets wrote about, how man wanders and swaggers, but in the end must return as the child is brought. That was the core: Angela was the mother of his children.

Dr. Bill was sitting by his daughter. Pretty and grave, her hair was smoothed from her face like a nun's. She spoke well and led her class. Mike thought about his one daughter, Carmen, three years younger as time was reckoned. Because she would never mature properly she was no problem to him. He never had to judge Carmen; he never resented her; continually she made something break slowly inside of Mike in a deep kind of eternal love.

Beside him Hazel was congratulating herself on a successful party; it would break up around one or two; Jack would have long since retired to his narrow bed in the small cell he liked, white-painted. Most of the guests would have their shoes off; Hazel would show the overnight ones to their rooms and wave good-bye to the others. She felt wonderful and put her hand to her chin to stifle an impulse to lean back her head and open and close her mouth, an exercise she often practised during the day to strengthen and tone the muscles and prevent dewlaps. She turned to Mike to pat his arm affectionately. Hazel had seen many marriages rock during their middle years; she expected the Paolis to settle down as others did. Love was a variation, as Ovid had observed, on war; sometimes it took a lifetime to adjust. The fire sparked and Hazel felt its warmth, and the good will of the gathered people within her glass walls.

Out on the lake the dark water licked at the gelid floating ice cake where the whitetails were clustered. They pushed each other, shifting their footing on the slippery surface. Their muscles ached from disuse over the past week; the gnaw of hunger troubled them. Their brown oval eyes stared over the watery prairie that they knew to be a danger. One of the younger deer, at the edge, snorted restive and attempted to wheel about. Disturbed, the heavy buck beside her butted his little antlers in an instinctive downward movement, striking her shoulder. She lost her balance and almost without a splash entered the deep. She surfaced in a moment, gasping, spewing water from her lungs. Then silently she submerged. The buck sighed uncomprehending, yearning for firm ground and his old role of leader.

[11]

ALTHOUGH the Great Lake was not subject to tides as was the ocean, its surface did rise and fall consistently, the lowest stage prevailing during winter. There were also occasional oscillations of varying amount and duration known as seiches. These unpredictable phenomena could cause the water to rush like tidal waves upon the shores from one side to the other of the lake basin. They rarely were violent, as a rule performing so gently that they were noted only by the measuring of recording scientists.

But every once and again a seiche would rage like an Armageddon upon Lake Michigan. As a storm died the water would have been piled by the gale up at one end of the huge body. And with a dash it would come rushing back in a fury of tremendous waves and swells. These would climb swiftly up the opposite shore, and a series of swings would continue as the natural force which had been set out of equilibrium stabilized itself. The first danger of the seiche was its sudden nature, its victims caught off guard, perhaps even convinced the storm had passed. The last major seiche had occurred six years earlier.

In February there was a spurt of warm weather; most of the ice bordering the Pine Beach shore melted, separating the outer icebergs from the land, and giving the effect of a bay running a

hundred yards out, flanked by hills. And since blowing sand had
been ingrained gradually into the ice, they resembled a line of
dunes. Five members of the Polar Bear Club came down to the
beach and were photographed by an AP man, so their pictures appeared all over the world. They gamboled in the twenty-five-degree
surf, and one wag even hiked himself up on an ice chunk that
floated free.

Skin hooted when he saw the picture in the *Trib,* for he'd
been down, diving, dashing blue-lipped to the Lodge, a week before these Polar Bears. He'd even written Albert Paoli a letter
about it in lemon juice. He and Al corresponded that way over
the years, using a candle flame to bring out the brown words,
sometimes burning the missive if it were highly secret and involved codes or plans for a private club. Every year he and Al
would invent a new club. In this letter he'd also mentioned his
newest acquisition, a pair of flintlock pistols, for which he'd traded
his lousy set of old sabers. Then Skin went into his dugout canoe,
telling how he was afraid the project was a flop. His brothers
were home for the midterm weekend and had jeered at it. Clara
Olson and Gus and Alan Malraux had been invited this afternoon
for the maple sap boiling.

Monk liked now and then to tap the trees for a lark; he'd
get out the dusty tin pails and the rigs he'd ordered once from
Monkey-Ward's. They were stored in the rickety firehouse shed.
Years ago Monk had purchased an old fire-wagon from the Sawmill City Council for the protection of the Pine Beach residents.
There had never been a fire, and the little red machine was driven
out and its bell donged only once or twice a year; the Fourth
and Memorial Day maybe. Skin stuck by his father's side all
through the sap running. They'd been gathering it for three weeks
now, sometimes two or three gallons a day from larger trees. Skin
waited for the guests. He hoped he'd get over his case on Clara
Olson soon. She was the top student in the junior class. Some
guys didn't admire that; if they even saw a girl with glasses, which
was the best way to tell an egghead, they used her for homework
and sympathy. Lots of them called Clara *Mother.* "What's wrong
today, son?" Clara would ask. And about six of them at a time
would take her over to the basketball games. They'd pour into
her ear their problems with their empty-headed giggling love-buns

and she'd try to console them. Not Skin; he watched from afar; he went for brains.

The seasonable weather had sent the sap rushing up and now the watery fluid almost ceased to drip through the metal tubes into the little buckets that hung from their spout-hooks, "Pink, pink, ping!" At night the dripping would stop altogether, to begin when the warm morning wind blew forth. Monk figured he'd do well to fill a five-gallon tin of thick syrup in the end. He didn't care how small the yield was; already he'd begun to lose interest in the whole affair. He watched his son pour the last of the sap

into the huge metal vat. Skin wore a threadbare mackinaw that had served an elder brother; he had on a bright blue wool stocking cap, the color of his eyes. Neither was aware how Monk, in contrast, sported his new leather jacket and tight hunter's breeches; they took for granted Monk's dandy ways. Crumpled in Skin's coat pocket was a paper where he'd worked out his and Clara Olson's destiny, cancelling their common letters:
The remaining letters, to the oracular formula *love-marry-hate-adore,* predicted they would detest each other. He was nettled and planned to ask her middle name, which might give them a better future.

"People used to go through these shenanigans every year for sugar," Monk said. "Four pounds from a big tree. But that size maples are gone. Don't get that big any more for some reason."

"I know. I've read on it. The county history. Sugar was ten cents a pound at the Saint Joe trading station. Honest, I wish I'd lived then. I hate life now."

"If wishes were horses, the beggers would ride, your mom says."

They were building the fire under the syrup vat, using logs and no-good pieces of lumber from the pile of half-rotted stuff that had accumulated as repairs were made on the cottages and board-walks and wood bridges about the resort. Then the Volkswagen scuttled up and Dr. Bill waved and shouted to Monk. Clara was beside him and Gus in the back seat; he dropped them off and drove away. After a while Alan came, pushing along in the melting snow on his Christmas skis, the varnished poles in either hand. "This is new to me!" he shouted. His shepherds bounded ahead barking. And then Russ and Dick meandered down from the Lodge, shoving at each other, hands in pockets, lackadaisical. The sap began to boil and the steam clouded up. Monk stirred with the scrubbed oar that had once belonged to the lifeboat.

"If two fat men were sitting under an umbrella that was very little," Gus asked, "why didn't they get wet?"

"I don't know."

"It wasn't raining," Gus said. "And I know another: supposing there were three crows in a tree and two flew away. How many were left?"

"One?" Skin inquired.

"Stupid," Dick mocked, "you heard Gus say *supposing.*"

"Oh."

"That's dumb, Gus," Clara hiked her hands in the belt of her boy's blue jeans, the fly in front, the garb all the girls affected.

"I heard you got sent to the principal's office on account of your rats, Gus," Dick said.

"Golly, Dick, he said it's okay. There's no rule about rats and lockers, he said. Just some girl got scared. I take Davy every once in a while in my jacket. He likes the locker."

"Can anyone jump over that fire?" Russ drawled, "syrup kettle and all?" Russ felt keenly how he and Dick had only come to join this set of high-schoolers out of boredom, which fact he tried to make clear. "I bet I can."

"Bet you can't." Alan took him up on it. "I bet!"

"Give me a dime and I'll jump over it." Russ took Alan's coin and hopping over, pocketed it.

Clara scuffed her boots in the slush. "Show me that crazy canoe," she whispered to Skin. She'd been hoping that Mr. Ardway

had forgot the incident at Uncle Jack's a few weeks ago, but he'd
just winked at her now and she realized nothing ever stayed the
same. She felt pride that he'd acted as if she were an adult, but
discomfort because he probably knew she'd never been treated
that way before. She sensed his eyes and strode off as if she were
a boy, unbuttoning her car-coat to the chill sweet wind. She
didn't care one hoot-nanny, she thought, about that good-looking
senior, Alan, being around, or anything; she only wanted to get
out of the sight of Skin's father.

"We're going to look at my dumb dugout," Skin told Monk.

"The birchbark, Hiawatha?" Dick sniffed the fragrant rising
steam. "By the shores of Gitchi-gumi?"

The two trudged away, hasty, down the path. "You have a
middle name?" Skin asked Clara.

"No. Why?" The wet black oaks were letting their burdens
of snow fall in pieces with a gentle continual noise; Clara shook
some ground-low boughs of spruces that were buried, and they
sprang free, green and high, relieved.

"It's a sort of a flop," Skin told her, standing before the tree
trunk which had been set across two logs down in the ravine in
the woods. The hollowing process, Skin said, was done by building
a fire on the log. "And you're supposed to keep the edges wet to
prevent burning. But I don't see how they managed to. I'm fazed.
It's ruined at that spot there."

"Why not just chop it out?"

"I wanted to do it Indian style. With fire. I won't have it
any other way." He'd set his young vulnerable mouth, his blue eyes
turning tragic upon her. "I wish you had a middle name!"

Clara glanced at Skin through the corner of her lenses, seeing suddenly, a new aspect of the boy; he was her age, near sixteen; they were both juniors. She watched him run his hands
over the rough-shaped bow. "You'll probably get it right yet, Skin.
Takes a lot of time."

"Umm." He sensed the encouragement in her voice, a little
startled. He was used to sparring with the girl, gaining his satisfaction in her company through steady, sometimes sharp, warfare.

"Let's us go see if Jimmy Fox's cottage is open," she proposed.

"Yeah."

They walked up the steep ravine and past the Owl's Roost, down into the hollow where the melting snow of the summer road was unmarred by track of man or machine. They turned off and crossed the Wigwam's spanking new bridge.

"Thwaite's Bridge!" Skin said, stamping.

"Yeah."

A creosote odor rose pungent as the ice on the planking dissolved and the damp wood lay exposed in the cold sun. The porch screen was open but the house door was locked. They hunted for the key, finally finding it in the wren's box that swung under the eaves from a rusty wire. "Someone's been here before us," Clara said. "Ugh." Another had thought to look in the tiny bird's house too and returned the key. Drawers were opened in the bedroom chests and kitchen cupboards; there were empty tin cans in the sink and soiled silverware. "Wonder if whoever it was just left, Skin? I'm scared. Should we go?"

"No. See, the food's crusted on the cans."

The sweetish unused scent of the place was like a rodent's nest. Skin went onto the porch to probe in a hole he found in the swing mattress ticking to see if any field mice were wintering there. Clara half-knelt on the moist cold floor beside him, her dark brows contracted. She tugged off her mittens and held them tightly. "Tell me."

"What."

"You ever kiss?"

"Well, sure," he lied promptly, off guard, forgetting the mattress.

"Well kiss me then. You want?"

"Okay."

"We better go in, though. Someone might come."

"Yeah."

"Should I take off my glasses?"

"It's up to you." They stood, boots touching, their jeans styled alike. He felt her slim shoulders through the wool of her short coat. His ragged mackinaw sleeve had pulled up, exposing the chapped wrist; his blue cap rode sidewise on his straight fair hair. Hesitant, he pressed her lips, feeling the rims of her glasses. She pulled them off; he looked at her eyebrows like dark furry wings, her open eyes vacant unseeing. The blood beat in his ears and Skin felt he played a part, imitating movies he'd seen of lovers whose mouths came together. Clara shut her eyes, and feeling her authority and experience he did the same, but opened them to watch her, curious, unsure.

She spoke matter-of-fact. "You ever sleep with anybody, Skin?"

"Not much," he said.

"I never did." She was frank. "Some ways I'd sure like to, but I'm afraid."

"You'd have a baby, I guess."

"That's what I mean. It's different with boys; they don't have to watch out."

"I never *really* did." He felt better, seeing that she recognized his sex's advantage. "And I might as well tell you that this is the first time I've kissed."

She pitied him. "Not me, Skin." Clara had kissed with four boys this winter now, counting Skin, and one man; she tallied them up, one and one.

"I know." He was humble. "You're popular, Clara. You're the prettiest girl in school. I like you even better with glasses on." It was the ultimate he could say.

"What about Pearl Thwaite!" she challenged, wary.

"Pearl's different. She's like an actress and she works on it, too. She uses eye stuff even that makes her lids blue. But you're what I call beautiful. Nice-looking, you know?"

She was dissatisfied with the compliment but held her peace. She already had a tiny case of mascara and an eyebrow pencil under her slips in her dresser and was beginning to use them before going to school. Mum hadn't noticed yet that she knew of. Clara was going to get some pancake makeup next. Just wait and see, she swore to herself, triumphant. She tried out something else now, a new thing she'd thought of: flattery. "You never noticed I grew my hair, Skin." She smiled beguiling, put her hand to her hair and pulled the pins from the chignon, fluffing the falling waves. She'd read of someone doing that once.

"It's nice."

"But you don't remember. Last summer. You were the one asked me to grow it!"

"I did?"

She gave up, and reached for her glasses that she'd dropped on the lumpy rust-stained hide-a-bed chair beside them.

"Tell about boys, Skin."

"I will if you will. The thing I want to know about is girls getting the curse."

"Don't you know about that?"

"My brothers gave me a book and they explained some stuff, but I can't understand."

"Okay. Boy, I'll never forget the time I was in biology, my first class, and I had to wait till everybody left the room and then Mr. Rumplemeyer gave me an excuse to go home. Creeps, was I lucky I wore my long slicker; when the halls got empty I went to my locker and got it." Abruptly she asked, "You want to kiss again?" Their cold lips met, and then she had a moment of panic. "What if someone comes!"

"Everybody's sure to be at the syrup fire still. We'd hear them; they'd never come to the Wigwam anyway." He was plaintive. "Clara."

"Okay." She felt that she was as pretty as Skin had said. It was a lot of work having long hair and doing it up. All the junior girls were wearing it that way. The seniors were starting to cut theirs short and slick. She drew away.

"I have to fix myself!" She went into the bedroom. "Is that all Mr. Fox's got for a mirror?" There was a tiny square glass on the wall and beside it on a built-in shelf a few scattered bobbypins. She wondered if Mr. Fox's daughter used them or a girl friend. She took her comb from her coat pocket, holding the hairpins in her mouth.

He stood watching, the red mounting in his face. He pushed out the words, fingering the fortune note in his pocket; he and she would hate each other, it said. "You want to do anything else, Clara?" Wishing at once that he hadn't said it.

She looked at the reflection and saw it was most beautiful; the lips were parted and even the slightly uneven teeth were charming, she thought. She dallied with the idea that she'd like to kiss with Alan, too. He had taken a girl to the Christmas hop and she was sure he must know all about things and what to do. She felt grateful to Skin. "Like what?"

"Well, I'd like to see. If you don't mind, that is."

"Didn't you ever see a girl?"

"No, just Carmen Paoli when she took her suit off that time a couple of summers ago. And it wasn't anything." Skin's mother was secretive about her body. Even in her most dynamic early nights with Monk he'd never got Belle to remove her nightdress; she felt it stood between herself and shame. The three sons, once toilet-trained, never revealed that part of themselves to her again.

In the Olson household, as the two grew, Dr. Bill and his wife purposely went about unclothed occasionally, because he believed that might help answer questions later. And it was true, of course, that Clara had none of Skin's curiosity about external characteristics. She patted the replaced smooth heavy knot of hair and stuck her hands in her pants pockets. "I will sometime," she promised. "But now we better go."

"Are you my girl?"

She shook her head and smeared her mouth without looking in the mirror. "Clara Olson isn't anybody's girl. Not me!" She was exultant.

"Roses are red, lettuce is green; my face may be funny, but yours is a scream." He gripped her arm and punched her shoulder with his fist in the old way. She ducked and tore off the cap that matched his brilliant eyes. He twisted her wrist in back of her in the style his brothers used on him. "Say uncle."

"Uncle," she pronounced calmly, feeling the new power. One didn't have to fight, she thought; that was kid stuff.

He dropped his grip, assuaged, and pulled his cap about his ears. He leaned to kiss her, but she shook her head and walked away. "Clara."

"Come on, dope." She banged the screen door as she went.

"Okay. But listen!"

"What." She was on the path.

He called, "I can tell you something." Hoping to hold her with him longer. "I got a secret, Clara."

"Hooray."

"No. It's about your mother, Clara!"

"Well, what." She faced him, fingers in her pants pocket, curled tight about the lipstick tube.

He shrugged. "Just I saw her kiss somebody."

"Who? Snoopy."

"Alan's father. One time when we were playing murder in the Sand Castle cellar. I was helping Irene pop corn. You remember? Well, your mother was there, too."

"I don't believe it."

"I haven't told anyone, Clara."

"But if it is so, don't you go around yakking about it, Skin. You hear? Or I'll kill you."

He protested. "Not ever. I wouldn't. Black and blue; lay me down and cut me in two."

"Not even if you were mad with me; because if you did and I found out you'd be plenty sorry."

"Look." He threw his hands. "I don't care if you're not even speaking to me."

She began to giggle and ran to hug him and nuzzle his cheek. Boy, she ought to watch out for Skin. She was perishing for the gory details, but sensed the folly of giving Skin satisfaction. Now if he had happened to be a girl it would be different. "Come on, let's hurry."

"Yeah."

When they reached the fire near the storage shed, nobody was there. They stirred the boiling thickening sap with the tall paddle and went up to the Lodge. Belle had baked a moist heavy devil's food cake in a great pan, topping it with a double recipe of chocolate icing. Monk and the boys, Russ, Dick, Alan, and Gus, sat with slabs of it on plates before them. Alan and Russ were playing chess and Dick was kibitzing. "I know how you could put him in double check, Alan."

"Pipe down, ass," Russ said.

"Don't say that, boy," Belle complained. She had given them coffee and hot milk. "Where you been?" she demanded of Skin, her eyes glancing over the Olson girl.

"To see the dugout, Mom. And we went to look if anyone had been in Fox's cottage. And they had. Some tramp."

Belle was overly courteous. "Come in, Clara. Lay your coat in the kitchen." Her mouth turned down in derision; she'd tackled Monk about his behavior that night at Mrs. Behmelmen's party; Belle had her opinion of a schoolgirl who led on a man old enough to be her father!

"My gosh, Mom." Skin was disconcerted. He adored his

mother but she sure could embarrass him sometimes, he thought. Russ and Dick always laughed, not caring, but Skin died inwardly every time; he wondered if things would come easy for him some day. The agony of adolescence overwhelmed him. Now he had an increased pain too in his relationship with Clara, who'd played with him since they were four, casually at school and in the long vacations. It seemed all his games with her had been a prelude to this afternoon in the Wigwam. He thought he was in love and mistook for deep happiness the huge empty hurt within him. He refused to eat the cake Mom offered, seeing only the girl's serious face as she cut her piece in two, so as to watch her weight. Clara was so cute, skirting his father, half-nodding, as she crossed the cowskin on the floor to sit by Gus on the overstuffed sofa. She didn't even glance at the chess-player, Alan. Skin knew the two of them had kissed; he was positive. The hate turned over in him sickly.

Alan pursed his mouth before he moved his queen and took the rook. "Sorry."

"The hell you are," Russ said. "This is going to be a case of total destruction."

"Watch it," Monk said. "That all they teach you up there at college? How to cuss? I can learn you that here." He'd noted Skin's discomfiture and wondered where the pair had been. And if the boy had had success of any kind. Skin had good sense, better than Dick, running after the tail of that half-cocked preacher's daughter. But not a one of his sons was small-balled. When it came to his own wife he'd done well enough. Dang it, Belle didn't need a maid, and she fed them, kept the boys clothed. Sometimes he wished she were women he'd known, tall handsome wives of his renters, or fun-loving like Elizabeth Olson. He grinned over his coffee, remembering a secret about her and a little flashlight she'd dropped, on a moonless night. "Say, Alan, is your father going to get you that aluminum canoe he promised?"

"I don't know, Mr. Ardway. . . . And that is check again, Russ."

"But not the beautiful double check I was thinking of," Dick commented, disdainful.

"I couldn't care less," Russ sighed. "Wow. What a disaster."

"Your father coming this summer?" Monk pursued, knowing

the answer before Alan spoke it; Malraux wouldn't be back for a time.

"Father wrote he'll be overseas for a while, Mr. Ardway. He's going to take a flat in Paris. He might have me over to stay for a month when he has a vacation. Maybe August."

"Paris?" Clara looked at Alan's mouth. "How wonderful, Alan." She didn't mind Skin telling that thing about Mum. Look what she, Clara, had seen; worse than kissing. There was the vivid impress on her mind: Mum's white breasts and the swim-suit line of bronze above; the man's head above her and his hands on her—Alan's father's hands, too. Clara felt how she was in love with Alan; a new thing that was not like her former puppy devotion.

"This backache'll be my death," Belle said. "I'm going to have a little more cake."

"Go to bed and rest it, gal. Who's stopping you?" Monk put on his leather jacket. "I'll go stir up the vat."

"You just want me out the way," Belle told him.

She was a grump, Monk thought, half-affectionate. "You kids can come as soon as you finish the game. It ought to be thick enough to pour. Dang it, I wager there won't even be a five-gallon tin." He slammed out, not even wearing gloves against the cold.

"He's sick and tired of that maple syrup." Belle plunged her fork into the dark sweet contents. "Tomorrow he's going to grade the hill out there, he says, for skiing; and then he wants to dig a pond for the little kids to keep their minnows and tadpoles in. I wouldn't mind except he never finishes anything. That b.s.!"

Her sons ignored her, except for Skin, who giggled unhappily. "Mom."

"I think I'll grow a beard next summer," Dick said.

"You're not concentrating," Alan told his opponent. "The battle's going on over here; why'd you take that pawn in that nearby town? You want to concede?"

"Not in this house you won't grow one," Belle told her middle one, rough but fond.

"Yes, I might too, Mom." Dick rubbed his weekend stubble and grinned at his mother, at ease.

Skin watched them and wished to be almost anybody but himself.

[12]

THERE was a spit of snow in April, the flakes falling heavy like blossoms and melting on reaching the ground. The dampness that rose had an odor of renewal which drifted on the wind. The sun shone hot and strange; birds sang. By the end of the month the migrations were reaching their height, the scant-leaved woods thronged with all the different varieties. Whippoorwills protested, and male thrashers and wood thrushes rivaled each other in depth of tone and in the quivering intensity of their small bodies. Down along the creek, spotted sandpipers cheeped and a few blue herons, four feet tall, with black crests hanging down over their white necks, fished the creek, hanging around for a week. They were spindle-legged and long-beaked, and roosted at night in the pines and sycamores near the delta. A few years ago Helge Lagerquist, the son of the man who owned the liquor store in Sawmill and hired by the Potawatomi Bible Clubbers to repair their cabins, came down to the beach and put a rifle ball cleanly through one of the ash-blue birds. He'd flung it over his wiry shoulder and returned to show his employers his trophy. The birdwatchers had nearly lynched him; Helge had been innocent that, using their binoculars, they'd been entering daily the exact count of the herons in their ledgers, and planned to note the day when the migrants resumed their trip, rushing along the sand to leap into the air, croaking, flapping, long beaks drawn in, legs trailing.

Mama Ardway was dying at last. She'd been moved from her cottage near Sawmill to the Lodge three weeks ago. There was no air of deep sadness in the household, for all were resigned. The mood was of acceptance that a natural thing was occurring. Dr. Bill stood at her window; he was making up his mind whether to give her a stimulant or let her alone. She'd complained of slight pain a few hours ago and now seemed to sleep. He watched a few winter-pale children run. It was Easter vacation and a few of the Chicago people who rented the same cottages year after year and felt ownership had come to do a little spring cleaning or plant something, flowers or herbs, for summer use. Any excuse would do so they could get their hands into the sandy loam. His family was up for the day, over at the Owl's Roost, doing odd jobs; they had brought a picnic for the evening. Bill would eat with the Ardways, staying close to this room.

There were three children running, two far in front of the last and smallest who cried, using up the breath she needed to reach the others, "I want to tell you something. I want to tell you *something!*" They outran her and disappeared around the bend and she slowed to a trot, squealing in a last desperation so the cry reached even the dying woman's ears, "I want to tell you something." Mama Ardway felt it was her own voice.

She lisped almost inaudibly to Dr. Bill when he turned to her, "Fooled you, eh? This time."

He smiled down at her on the white sheets in the narrow brass bed. "What's all this about, dear?"

She was like a dried-up piece of apple, shrunk small and tough. Her false teeth were in a kitchen glass on Skin's bed table. The boy had been moved in with his brothers, summoned home from Michigan State for the death Dr. Bill told Belle would occur. On the walls were the sword and gun collection, and on the floor a worn red Indian rug. The shelves Skin had set up were of his own devising, lumber planks laid across cinder block. Most of the library was second- and third-hand, spines torn, inherited; and there were new catalogs and schoolbooks.

Mama Ardway worked her mouth as if to speak and then her thoughts receded and she was closing her eyes, forgetting his presence. She wondered if she would cry because she was about to die. She felt the immense sorrow of the happenstance, and the tragedy and violence of life, the crushing and chewing of the spirit that went on, the plateaus of peace that occurred, times when one was glad to bear it. She recalled the cry of a few minutes ago, "I want to tell you something." There was no one who wanted to hear; there seldom was. Sometimes somebody listened for a little, not long. Mama Ardway resisted her drowsiness with a kind of fear. She pushed open her eyelids and wondered who the man with the cropped gray hair and stocky build, the drooped shoulders was, standing at the window, back to her. She felt he might be one of her sons, or her husband, perhaps her father. A fiery ray beamed across his pin-striped shoulder as the afternoon sun reached down around the end of the frame. The glare fell upon the brass bedstead before her eyes. She fastened herself to the hot golden color. She was a young woman again, a child, a baby; she sensed her recession into the womb, growing littler, nothing; and she died.

Dr. Bill came over slowly. He lifted her hand and let it fall. He pressed the heels of his thumbs on her tissue-paper-wrinkled eyelids; he pushed her chin up to close the slightly ajar mouth. She was like the skin of something, he thought, and took off his glasses, angry. It was the way of death; the light was on and then blinked off. But he never got used to the pain. Standing over her, his heart began to thud; he realized how he'd been cheated one more time! He left the room and went through the kitchen, telling Belle that it was over.

Belle nodded quietly. "I sure thank you for taking so much time, Dr. Bill."

"I'll drop by later, Belle, on the way back to Ideal. The family's up here for the day and they're having a picnic tonight. I'll go over. But I want to ask Monk something about the porch screens; they're rusted pretty bad. We're moving in the first week of June this year."

Belle shook her head. She worried all the time that Monk never tended to business. She knew what he'd been doing the last month instead of looking over screens on cottage porches.

He had been tearing up a spot near the tennis court that he was
going to sod for badminton. There was no earthly reason for it,
except just let some little brat mention he'd like one and Monk
broke his neck to fit it in. In place of what he'd ought to be doing.
"Well, I'll tell him," she assured Dr. Bill, "when he comes in."

"Can you take care of things, Belle? Shall I call the funeral
home?"

"No," Belle shrugged, smiling wryly. "I know what to do.
And her body's to be put out at Riverside just like she wanted.
She told me and everyone; she's been looking for this a long
time."

"I know." Dr. Bill patted her shoulder and went out. As
he got into the Volks, Herb Worth passed in a new swept-wing
sky-blue Dodge. Herb came to see Dora about every Saturday
night in Ideal; Dora wouldn't say yes or no over the years, and
Dr. Bill suspected it might upset their easy relationship if she did
either. He drew up to park beside the Dodge in the hollow by the
Owl's Roost, nodding to Herb.

The man smiled and reached back into the car, bringing out
a stuffed pheasant mounted on a pedestal. "For Gus." Herb was
coming over.

"Gus?"

"Yeah, I asked him if he wanted it. I was going to throw it
out. I guess I shot it twenty years ago and I wasn't a very good
taxidermist." Herb pointed out the twisted feet and crooked bill.
"But it's a good-size cock. Your boy thought he'd keep it here in
his room."

"Sure thing. Is this a new bus, Herb?"

"Yeah, Doctor. Some color!"

"Certainly is; the farm must be doing all right."

"I'm getting by. I trade my old car in every five years; I got
it figured. But don't you be taken in by this car's looks; it's still
just a Dodge. They make them this way to mock the fancy cars.
An auto's not just a way of getting somewheres any more; it
shows how big you are, I was telling Dora."

"What she say?"

"Says it sure puts the big shots in a spot, Doctor." Herb was
tub-chested and leather-complexioned. He'd worked hard all his
life; he felt Dora would have married him on a nickel if it weren't
for those two children; he didn't blame her not to want to put

her finger in too tight a ring. He planned to wait her out. "I saw
you've been visiting Ardway's. How's that old lady coming along?"

"Well, a matter of fact, she's gone, Herb." He stated it dryly.

"That so? Old age, wasn't it?"

"That's all."

"Dora tells me you set store by her. Now I'm sorry to hear
it." He stroked the pheasant like a live chicken, absently, forgetting, scratching it under its ears and neck.

It was April, the elm overhead not leafed fully; its unburst
branches were outlined against the sky. Two or three catbirds
meowed, alarmed by an orange-striped tomcat that padded down
the road and slunk along the foundation of the Owl's Roost and
around the corner. "You're coming to the picnic, aren't you?"
Dr. Bill asked, as they watched the animal.

"Yes, sir. Your missus invited me. Hold on while I put the
bird in a safe place for Gus." Herb leaped away and up the Owl's
Roost steps, three at a time.

Dr. Bill marveled at the farmer's command of his body. Herb
was probably a few years older than he, but seemed to get a
real whack out of life, not brooding on past present and future
like some did all the time. Dr. Bill envied Mama Ardway, who
had now settled things for herself after all. What had she whispered? "I fooled you." He wanted to knock at the door of her
grave: *"Let me in."*

Another cat, gray, prowled along, ignoring Dr. Bill, her ears
laid back twitching, her tail gliding nervously. She was hunting
and the catbirds became noisier, shouting, dipping at her, sometimes touching the flattened gray ears. She maintained her im-
passivity, hunching, sliding past Dr. Bill with no sound at all;
she disappeared along the base of the Owl's Roost, circling the
corner. A dove moaned, and a cuckoo endlessly told his one tale.
A dragonfly, the kind called the Hero, pop-eyed, its iridescent
wings spread five inches, hurled itself from a low branch over Dr.
Bill's head. Close to his face it poised, whirring a second, and
then was gone. He membered as a youngster believing that the
Heroes fed snakes who could not feed themselves. The belief
was accepted as truth among the children and passed on by them
to younger ones before they themselves reached the age of in-
credulity.

Herb jumped back down the stairs, and they started to the

beach. Then the gray cat bounded around the corner of the house, retracing her steps, scrambling up the road. In long leaps after her burst the orange tiger one, his eyes frenzied, limbs straining. The sand spattered behind them and their silent fury. By the time the two men reached the boardwalk, snarling screams sounded from the distance.

Herb grinned, "They sure have a conniption fit about it, don't they? When I was a young fellow I wished to be a cat, wild like that. But not no more. . . . This is one from the barber's this afternoon. Woman got on the South Shore bus, and it was crowded, says, will you give a poor old pregnant lady a seat? This man felt sorry for her and gave her his. How long you gone? he asks. About twenty minutes, says she, and am I wore out! Heard it?"

Dr. Bill nodded as if listening. "Never did; it's pretty good." He was thinking about the way she hadn't been able to put in her false teeth the last few days, too weak to hold them. It gave her a pinched pathetic look; she was half-embarrassed as if she knew it. The new sorrow nagged.

Herb was droning on, "Tried to get into heaven, see? And the Holy Ghost wouldn't let him, says, once you told a dirty story about me and Jesus' mother."

They were walking in the sand; it was nearly five-thirty. The family had built the fire down the beach, and Lisa and Dora were taking things from the hamper. The air was somnolent, with a hint of winter dampness yet. The lake was made of bright blue glass and it splintered when the sun rolled slowly overhead in its dome. Lisa saw them and waved; she and Clara came running, holding hands, both in Jamaicas and brilliant jersey tops. The *flicka* was sweet sixteen, and every day she came a step further from the child she had been, it seemed, for so many years. Her brown-and-gold glasses gave her a severe look, he thought, pre- ferring the old-fashioned frames they'd thrown away. During scattered moments of a day now Clara would be haughty, disdain- ful, maternal, protecting, a chameleon as it suited the chemistry of her body. She clung to Lisa too, as she'd not done since first she entered her tomboy years and declared independence. If time would only hold for a while, he reflected fervently, and the sun made a long thin shade beside each wrinkle in the worry-lines of his forehead and the smile-lines about his eyes and mouth, his cheeks and chin, if it would stop and let him enjoy this moment. He clutched it.

"She died, Lisa," he said, his arms about the two of them. "I'm sorry."

Clara hugged Daddy, snuggling into his shoulder. "You're divine."

"So are you, *Flicka.*" Lisa had slipped from Dr. Bill and walked beside. *"As the cloud is consumed and vanisheth away: so he that goeth down to the grave shall come up no more."*

"Oh, Bill!" Lisa cried. "Aren't you depressing?"

"Job. Those words couldn't be any one else's, could they? I don't remember chapter and verse."

"It's such a beautiful day," she said. "And isn't the evening going to be lovely? The sunset's going to be perfect. Think about that, Bill."

He saw her beauty sparkle, her fine hair that suddenly overcame him. He was so used to his wife, he thought; he took her for granted; that was dangerous and he vowed to remember. But instead he spoke as if needling her, "Belle said they expect Mike Paoli to come full time this next season. He's not teaching a seminar at the University."

"I know about that," Clara said. "From Al; we wrote about a hundred letters this winter. Heck."

They reached the fire and Elizabeth hadn't replied. She ran over to Dora. "Is the chicken mousse squashed?"

"Not much," Dora said, diffident. "Doctor won't even notice, time it gets to his plate. Will you look who's here!" She grinned at the farmer.

"I've got wine, Bill!" Lisa was shining. "I wanted this to be a rites of spring celebration. The ice melted but it doesn't matter." She came over to him, her slow voice appealing, "Would you uncork it? You're good at that."

He manipulated the gadget, smiled at his girl-wife, assuaged. "I'll be good, *älskling.* I'll even be entertaining. Shall I recite something? My memory's deserted me now."

"Let's make Clara. She's supposed to be the family genius."

They went over to the white-covered camp table. "A little diversion, please," Dr. Bill demanded. "Before the feast, *Flicka.*" He thought how she'd never struck attitudes easily in her boyish years, and was shy. Now sometimes he was taken aback by her flashes of female arrogance, her pleasure in herself.

Clara walked a few steps away. She held her chin like a TV dame, she thought. She'd like to be a gorgeous comedian, a real wit. Then when she started to recite, she forgot the clever patter she'd practiced in front of the mirror for the next party she might get invited to; she had to substitute something the kids at Pine Beach had been using since he beginning of time: "Ladles and Jellyspoons, I stand on this speech to make platform. The train I came on hasn't arrived yet, so I had to take a bus and walk over here. I have come before you to stand behind you. I am about to tell you something I don't know anything about."

As she paused, Gus clapped, cupping his palms to get as much volume as possible; a carrot stick hung from his mouth, and he cracked it loudly. "Do the barefoot girl with shoes on!"

"I don't remember. Oh, if I could think." She didn't want to lose her audience.

"Recite my favorite," Dr. Bill said. "For me."

"That———. I don't want to, Daddy." When she'd been seven, she'd learned the poem for his birthday, and it was the one employed frequently over the years by Daddy to show her off to guests or patients. It was as if Daddy never realized she knew at least a million others. In secret she learned the poets she wanted, Elizabeth Barrett Browning and Dorothy Parker, and modern ones like Lowell and Eberhart. She even went for that greybeard Lord Byron, her heart squeezed in a pleasant melancholy.

> *The dew of the morning*
> *Sunk chill on my brow.*
> *It felt like a warning*
> *Of what I feel now.*
> *Thy vows are all broken!*

She'd just like to recite that one, all of it, right now!

"Come on," Dr. Bill said.

She gave in, and forgot her sulkiness, feeling the admiring eyes:

> *The boy stood on the burning deck*
> *Whence all but him had fled;*

The flame that lit the battle's wreck
Shone round him over the dead!

Even Herb Worth was paying attention.

Yet beautiful and bright he stood
As born to rule the storm.
Over him fast, through sail and shroud
The wreathing fires made way.
They wrapped the ship in splendor wild
And streamed above the gallant child!

"Splendid," said Daddy.

The noblest thing that perished there
Was that young faithful heart!

"I could hear it again," cried her father.

But Mum already was handing him a plate, and Gus was going to get his. Clara watched her crowd turn away; she was a failure. She felt a lump in her throat. *Half broken-hearted, in silence and tears!* Creeps, she didn't even want to eat. She took a cigarette from the pack in her jersey pocket and lit it. She let the smoke into her mouth and out. She felt ever so much older and wiser than anyone there, than anyone anywhere. She planned a great future; either acting or writing. She wanted to deal with ideas; that was the thing; the set she went with talked about it. And she wanted to become terribly famous so her name was on people's tongues. She was going to stay up all night tonight and write poems. About yearning hearts and raining and roses and bold young men. She put the cigarette to her lips.

Dr. Bill had set his plate on the sand and was cleaning his horn-rimmed spectacles with his pocket handkerchief. His eyebrows were raised, his look quizzical. "Dulls your taste buds," he commented. "Put it out."

She kept the smoke in her fingers and walked over close to him, speaking for Daddy's ears alone. "I feel all wild today. I want to do dangerous things. If I ever do and get killed, I'd like you to remember that up to the day I died, I've been the happiest person that ever lived."

"I'll remember," he said gravely.

She dropped the cigarette with a little passionate movement and covered it with sand with her bare toes. Going over to take her plate, she tried to sway her hips the way Mum did so easily. She felt in time she'd catch on. For a dope, she was doing pretty good; she was ravenously hungry.

Later, at nearly seven, during the apricot-and-lavender sunset that absorbed lake and sky, Dora and Herb and the children set off for a hike north before they would drive home. Dr. Bill and Elizabeth had stretched themselves on the motheaten army blankets. "Should we have gone with them?" Elizabeth asked lazily.

Dr. Bill hiked himself up so he could sip at the black coffee in the paper cup anchored in sand near his elbow. It tasted bitter, lukewarm. "Not me."

"Isn't this nicer anyway?"

"I have to stop in to tell Monk about those damn screens tonight," he said, fierce. "The mosquitoes will be murder this summer."

"Won't do any good; you'll have to hire someone yourself in the end, I bet."

"Not my property. Monk will have to."

"Did you know Pine Beach is all Monk's now?"

"Wish he'd take reasonable care of it. That little Carmen Paoli's got more sense than him. All you can say for Monk is he's got a good heart; he's the most innocent full-grown man I know!"

"Innocent? Hoo!"

"In business matters; he doesn't connive. I'm aware he's not innocent in other ways. I've seen you tease him too, sidling about."

"Hoo. Will you listen?" She was good-natured.

"I wish you wouldn't do that with men. I remember you and that Bret What's-his-name at Hazel's watermelon party. It's degrading. Grow up." He spoke flatly; she didn't reply. A thrasher was up in the pines, repeating each fluid legato phrase. Dr. Bill wondered why that one species did that and no other of which he knew. Its faint voice was exquisite; where had the pattern begun, so that each piece of the song must come over again, as if proving it could be done? It almost gave one belief in a deity. *I know all the fowls of the mountain,* the mighty Lord of the Bible said.

"What is that bird?" Elizabeth asked. "What is it?"

After a while Dr. Bill said, "You heard me say Mike will be around all this summer."

"Why you keep telling me? Who cares?"

"You and he thought you were pretty clever last summer." Dr. Bill was being engulfed by a fresh wave of the agony, feeling as if *Mor* herself had just slipped away again. He couldn't endure the silence of his mind. He prodded his wife, dogged, almost unwilling, needing noise and anger. He hoped to damage himself in some irreparable way. "You ran after him," he accused. Dr. Bill didn't know why he picked Mike, except he knew Mike admired Elizabeth; he might have said as easily Monk or Fox or Philip Malraux.

"Crazy."

He had lit the fire, he thought. "Why is it women won't admit they're wrong?" He was overloud. "And want to be beaten where it doesn't show!"

"You're upset; I won't argue with you tonight. I'll talk with you any time you're not angry. I know what it is too. It's Mama Ardway's dying. Isn't it?" He wouldn't reply and lay as if listening for the bird to sing again. "You never face anything. I don't see how a man can be a sentimentalist and a physician at the same time; I can't understand it. You're just soppy. Didn't you know Mama Ardway had to die? Heavens, didn't everyone know it? Didn't you tell them to get the boys home for it? Here you've been propping her up for years, and then when what you know will happen, happens, you behave as if it's a sudden calamity." She stood up and stretched. "What a delicious evening. Why fuss?"

"I suppose you have noticed that you avoided expertly and completely the original topic: Mike." His glasses were off and everything for him was robbed of detail and clarity. The lake was an indistinct yellow haze; the outlines of Lisa's body were fuzzy, her expression vague; he couldn't tell whether she smiled or frowned. He was motionless, feeling the prickle of the wool beneath him, his body not his own. Lifting his eyes to where the apricot shading had invaded the high sky overhead, "You had an affair. And his wife worried about some girl in Chicago."

"Next he's going to say I slept with Jimmy Fox or Monk or Philip Malraux." She appealed to the air.

"Did you?"

"How can I stand here and listen? Soon he's going to ask if I want a divorce? Doesn't he usually."

"Well, do you?"

"You are impossible when you get this way. I get so furious I could scream. Haven't I been faithful to you from the time we married? You know it; next thing you'll be calling me the village bitch." Her words hovered upon the lemon-colored air, she tried to think where she'd heard or read the expression. "You'll call me that, won't you!" He wouldn't turn even to look at her righteous temper; she felt the wrench in her throat, the terrible welling tears. She sobbed and ran away on the beach toward the boardwalk. "Oh."

She couldn't very well turn to see if he were watching, could she, she thought. And she had no idea if he were following. She heard her little piteous whine, "I hate him; I hate him." Her wide-apart eyes looked down at the sand as she scuffed along, bewildered by her husband's sudden turn upon her. "Hate him, hate. Why is he the way he is?" She felt he broke her heart; hadn't he spoiled the lovely April day? Why were people black-mooded and why did they make demands? Life could be happy, she felt, weeping, if she had her way. She wanted to give pleasure! His words about Mike Paoli weren't so; they were not so. But had he said Philip Malraux in his fumbling persistence, they wouldn't be so either. Not really. She hadn't violated anything that had to do with herself and Bill; she'd been so careful at the time. And there too her happiness had turned into a bitter thing. Philip; men; she would never understand men, she knew. Always weren't they the unfathomable mystery? Dark and powerful, they thrust themselves about; they were as small children wanting mothering this minute, and great unreasonable leaders the next. Didn't she love them though! There was something so fetching about just her little Gus standing there and applauding his sister. He was still the baby, and Clara grown, though there were only two years between them. She shook her head, saying it again, nursing the tender sorrow, *"Why* is Bill that way?"

Her tears were drying and she wondered why she'd been so noisy with him. Why in the world had she got indignant and made a scene? She meant always to be calm and icy; she'd done well at first. How could she look a human being in the face again? She bit

her lip. She reached the boardwalk and decided to go on up to
the Owl's Roost and sit alone on the porch and smoke, think out
how to meet Bill and what her first words to him would be.

Eve Thwaite was approaching, slowly because Ian held her
hand, and on a long braided-leather leash she had her narrow-
nosed sedate young collie. "Mrs. Olson. Hello!" Eve waved, a red
beret perched snug on her black hair.

"Eve!" Elizabeth took in the tweed suit as she reached the
summer neighbor. Custom done, she thought, that was for sure;
three hundred dollars perhaps? "How have you been, Eve? And
hasn't your young man got big?"

"He goes to a Tom Thumb school now." The dog adored
her and waved its brush and danced up in a slow movement as if
to rest its paws on her Scotch-woven skirt. She played with its
delicate ears, pushing the head against her knee, and looked down
at Ian as she let his fat hand go.

"Bug! Bug?" the child said, as a biplane came whirring along
the shore and disappeared to the south.

The women smiled, secret, and Eve accepted one of Elizabeth's cigarettes, somewhat mashed and bent, from her shorts
pocket. "But your book comes out next week," Elizabeth cried.
"I saw the full-page ad in the *News*. I never thought I'd get to
know a real author. Please tell about it."

"Oh, the book isn't very good." Eve dismissed the subject.
"I've started another. I came down today to Pine Beach to talk
with Mr. Ardway, but I've been told his mother died and so I
won't bother him. Ian and I are taking Bobbie for a romp before we go back to Chicago."

"Are the girls here?"

"No, they're not permitted to leave Madame Moret's. We're
alone, the two of us. I came hoping Mr. Ardway will let me buy
the land Linden House is on. You see, I'd like to take it down
and build another. Or perhaps remodel, removing the upper
floor. What I have in mind is a cozy place. Have you ever seen
photographs of Hardy's cottage?"

"No. But will Monk sell?"

"Oh, it's up to him, entirely. You know, Mr. Malraux's place
borders mine and he let him buy it."

"But for a fabulous sum!"

Eve was deprecatory. "Well, there's nothing to stop me from trying, Mrs. Olson."

"Won't you call me Elizabeth? Please. Then you are coming this summer? Wonderful."

"Oh yes. I wouldn't take the girls from their friends, and I feel that Pine Beach is our other home. Of course, soon Pearl and Irene must go abroad for a year. Everyone does."

"Were you ever in Europe?"

"Once. With my husband. That was when I visited Hardy's cottage." Eve said it with a tremor, "With Boris."

"I forgot Dr. Thwaite made crusades there."

"And successful ones. Very few ministers alive have his kind of devotion to the work. Boris felt we were living in an age of moral rejuvenation, Mrs. Olson." Her eyes dropped onto the child sitting on the walkway, kicking his sandals. Eve hoped he would grow to be worthy of his father. She doubted her adequacy for the task. Sometimes forgetting, she wished for her husband's strong arm. She didn't think of Boris as Papa any more. She used his Christian name as she had not when he was living. "I'm lucky to have his little boy." She pushed out the half-smoked cigarette, kneeling, burying it. She scooped the sand with absorbed movements, playing with the child's hands.

Elizabeth watched the little widow, feeling the sting of the green-eyed one. Three merriest things under the sun, they said, a cat's kittens, a little goat's kids, a young widow. Wasn't Eve Thwaite free, though? Did she have to put up any more with strange moods and silly recriminations, and that striving for understanding that goes on in marriage, the never-ended battle. She urged, "You're going to marry again though. Sometime, Eve?"

The woman turned her face up. "What? I don't know. I haven't thought."

"You are attractive. And then think, someday you'll be all alone. Even Ian will be gone."

"Well, I know."

"It'll be lonely."

"You can be lonely in marriage, of course. My book goes into that. Two people can be at different ends of the house; the woman in the kitchen, the man in his study, and breaking their hearts. My characters are like that."

"It sounds good. I want to read it, Eve. But I think widows ought to marry. Of course only if the proper one comes along."

Eve laughed. "And how would I know that?"

"You meet a lot of men, don't you? Now that you're working and on TV and everything." Elizabeth was compounding her envy. "And autographing parties."

"Oh there aren't many of those, Mrs. Olson. I don't like gatherings. Perhaps I'm just happy now because I have my children. Though I'm almost too busy for them it seems nowadays." She sighed and unsnapped the leash of the impatient collie. "He wants to run. Now, now, Bobbie. . . . It was nice seeing you."

"Yes."

"We'll have a talk this summer perhaps." Eve picked Ian up and went down the boardwalk.

Elizabeth felt her cigarette hot on her fingers and she let it fall and lie between the boards, a blue winding stem of smoke coming from the ash. The demure figure with the baby and the huge fluffy dog was down on the sand already. Elizabeth knew what her first words to Bill would be. At least she had some news, a diversion. Wasn't Eve's outfit smart, her beret, and the suit thick and soft? Elizabeth wished it were her own. She didn't see why Bill had to be a dowdy old country GP. Didn't he have talent, looks, all the requisites for what was supposed to be one of the country's best-paid professions? She trudged up the hill.

Behind her the sky paled. Dr. Bill had fallen asleep, exhausted, lying just as he was when his wife left him. His face jerked in a little spasmodic movement now and then as his dreams bothered him, and sometimes he made a small protesting sound expelling a heavy breath. His glasses lay half-submerged in the sand by the paper cup and there would probably be a search for them when the hikers, who were now turning back, reached the picnic spot. If he had awakened now, his blind eyes would never have made out the flock of herons anyway, six or eight pair of Great Blues, far out on the glass of water. Journeying at sunrise and sunset, like shadows of mythical fowl, they raced low across the horizon. Their broad wings flapped slow, their legs dangled under the slender bodies, their long necks were crooked like umbrella handles; they made no sound.

The

SECOND SUMMER

And time has big handles on the hands,
Fields and trees a way of being themselves.
I saw battalions of the race of mankind
Standing stolid, demanding a moral answer.
I gave the moral answer and I died
And into a realm of complexity came
Where nothing is possible but necessity
And the truth wailing there like a red babe.

[13]

Out of the womb of April emerged May. The marsh marigolds threw themselves from the ground in a golden carpet that was hidden in woods. Among the lady slippers were two specimens bearing quadruple magenta-stained white blossoms but luckily no child found them. All about, from the dark caul of the past months leaped the delicate shapes of violets, white and yellow and blue ones, and wild columbine, and hepatica, whose hairy red leaves endured the winter; and triliums and Dutchman's breeches and squirrel corn and rue anemone, and now and then a pale-green hooded Jack-in-the-pulpit. The first part of the month was warm, and since the force of the migratory current of birds was closely dependent on meteorologic conditions, they were encouraged and arrived in great waves. During one week they were more abundant than at any other time of the year. In one day of field work the Potawatomi Club bird-watchers noted twelve species of waterfowl and ninety-six of land birds. Nearly all were bug-hunters, since the seed-eaters migrated earlier to clean up the last of the fall harvest; and as the flowers unrolled themselves and insects began their attack, the warblers and vireos and other diminutive species came to the blooms' defense.

May spawned June, and with seeming exhaustless vitality, the birds found nest spots, sometimes by a whim discarding half-finished ones, sometimes building on top of previous ones if a cowbird deposited an ugly immense egg among their own seed, and sometimes if robbed of their egg, maintaining stubbornly the place of their choice. One flicker, visited regularly by the gray cat, replaced her egg each day for nearly two months. Then the cat squeezed forth a litter of her own, and was adopted by Della Chapman who gave her a fruitbasket for them, and locked her in the Sand Castle's jam cellar safe from Alan's dogs, and fed her well. There was no situation, from a hole in the ground to branches in treetops, in which the birds' dwellings might not be found, formed of grasses and rootlets and twigs, from plant down, bark, leaves, lichen, clay, spider webs and horse hairs, fur and feathers, often mortared with their own saliva. Albert Paoli hung out ribbon and string and they flew off with it and used it all.

By the second week in June all the cottages had been rented and occupied and the required deposit paid—all except Paoli's, and dang it, Monk told Belle, they'd have to bring it to him; he wouldn't go after it. Angela was pregnant again. She grinned to Elizabeth, "All Mike says is 'Another year of PTA for you, little woman.' "

Mike was settled in a canvas chair fifty feet away and they held their voices down. He was writing a series of articles. "We even get paid," Angela said. "Physics is getting popular with the common classes again. Used to be they read novels all the time!"

"I'll tell Clara that," Elizabeth said. "Her appetite is totally for fiction and she thinks she's one of the elite. She doesn't know what reality is any more." They sat rocking on the tiny porch of the Eyrie. At Angela's feet, constrained by a harness tied to her chair, played the year-old baby, clad in diaper and shirt. Nearby was a tubby glass pickle-jar of brackish water containing polly-wogs which the children had got at the creek. Elizabeth said, "Isn't it too close to the last one? I don't understand you."

"I won't have to buy a stitch for it." Angela nodded and patted her stomach affectionately. "Little me. Six kids. And I even talked to your husband about doing something to hold it to five."

"Still, what are you going to do with the children? Al will be a senior next year and he'll want to go to college."

"Well, as long as Mike's teaching at the University, he can go there. And he's sure to win a scholarship. He's going out for all of them."

Carmen came dashing onto the porch, followed by Georgie, who halted at the steps. The young girl was swinging her arms, argumentative, half-gay. "Mama, he won't let me play with him and I want to!" She threw herself down by the jar and, pulling at the shining brown of her hair, stared into the clouded water where the round larvae wriggled.

Georgie's eyes flashed hate; he felt it absorb his entire husky six-year-old form. He knew that Carmen was different from other thirteens and this had been impressed upon him in the past year as he fought his way through the primary grade. But Mama wouldn't ever let him bash her as he'd like to, and he stood unable to speak, hoping to convey to Mama, by the most unpleasant expression he could contrive, the sentiment that throbbed.

"Now what?" Angela clasped her hands before the old plaid shirt of Mike's that she wore hanging out over her slacks.

"He was mean," Carmen complained. "He was mean!" She smiled over at Elizabeth, "Hi." Her dark eyes were gentle.

"Apologize, Georgie," Angela said, "And stop glaring like that."

Georgie knew, in his shame, that the mother of Clara Olson who babysat for them, was sitting there. He felt the woman put her eyes on him and wounded he shriveled and died; at the foot of the little porch steps, Georgie Paoli was dead. His evil look seeped away and he grunted blankly, "Sorry. But if she keeps breathing on the water all our pollywogs'll die. She's killing them, Mama. Everyone knows that." He looked at his brother, leashed to the chair, pounding the floor softly with a spoon. He felt a great wash of loyalty; Baby Boy wasn't queer. Love flooded him and Georgie flung himself on the porch floor on his stomach, his nose touching the baby's pudgy one.

"Come here, Carmen," Angela said. She brushed the hair back from her tall child's face. "You ought to play with your own things. Or listen to the radio."

"Okay. I'll listen to the radio. Okay!" Carmen laughed, ran swiftly into the Eyrie.

Elizabeth whispered, "I shouldn't say it, but don't you ever get afraid that you'll have another, dear?"

Angela raised her eyebrows. "Do you know what Al's Intelligence Quotient was this past winter? Over 135. He'll make a scientist, Mike says, too."

Elizabeth nodded. "Umm."

"And besides," Angela said, "Carmen's sweet. Wonder if I'm having another girl. Mike says I ought to be able to tell; female's intuition. We sure want another. Four boys is plenty."

"Still, why you want another baby at all?"

"Well, I like them." Angela laughed.

At her feet Georgie stared into his brother's pale eyes as the tiny fingers squashed his willing cheeks. "Baby Boy pooped in the lake yesterday afternoon, Mama."

"My gosh," Angela said.

Elizabeth objected, "Georgie, why do you always have to broadcast everything?"

Angela yawned. "Of course I also do it to hold onto that man of mine." She glanced out where Mike hunched over his book. "They say in love there's always one who loves more than the other. I'm so darn possessive."

"Does Mike wander?"

"A little. Sometimes. I'm sure of it." Angela shrugged. "I'd wander too, if I had time."

"Angela!"

"Umm. But being pregnant's nice in other ways; you can eat all you want and nobody minds. In fact you get urged to stuff. . . . Do you wander, Elizabeth, ever?"

"Hoo! Lucky you. Just look at me!" Elizabeth eyed her figure critically. "I wish I hated ice cream. Especially Dora's; she ruins me. By the way, Alan Malraux's going to France in August."

"He told me. Isn't he handsome, Elizabeth?"

"Clara thinks so."

"I know. She's changed abruptly from last summer. She used to tear about and yell and run and now she's all demure."

"Don't be fooled, Angela. Come see her at home."

"Wherever did Alan get his good looks? He's not a bit like his father, is he?"

"Un un."

"It must have been his mother. I wonder who she was; she's abroad somewhere. Philip was awfully taken with you. Did you know it? Have you ever thought of having an affair with anyone, Elizabeth?"

Elizabeth was looking at her hands, dreamy, her face a little indrawn, discontent. She felt the ache in her, the dissatisfactions, the wishes. She hated it when Angela talked like that. "Hum?"

"Did you ever want to hop in bed with anyone?"

Wasn't that an awful way of putting it? Elizabeth thought. She'd read yesterday of the Swiss writer, Henri Amiel, saying, *tell me what you feel when the moon's shining in your room and your lamp's dying out; and I'll tell you how old you are, and I'll know if you're happy.* Wouldn't Amiel have known for sure that she was now thirty-eight and not really at all glad? She longed to be Clara, beginning again. "I haven't thought of it." Didn't she wish that last summer with Philip were only just begun? And that they were meeting at the beach under the old green umbrella and touching hands and she feeling the hard grip of response? And all the fainting of love over again?

"He shipped out a new canoe for Alan. He spoils him so. Have you seen it? It's one of those aluminum jobs, and just ugly. That one of yours that Dr. Bill gave to Al, is much prettier, patches and all." Angela giggled, "Don't you bet Philip Malraux has a girl in the capital city of every country in the world?"

"Umm."

"Rich bachelor, not bad looking."

"As a matter of fact," Elizabeth said. "I did once."

"What?"

"This is between you and me, Angela. I don't even know if I ought to say it."

"Edit it," Angela cautioned. "I don't talk about people; you know I'm not the gossipy kind."

"Well."

"Georgie, go get some animal crackers for Baby. You can have some."

"No, Mama. I'm comfortable."

"Go on."

Georgie went, long-suffering, murmuring what the third-graders did when they jumped rope:

> *Chicago Tribune, Daily News;*
> *Did you ever see a cat in a pair of shoes?*

Angela said, "Little pitchers are clever; you'd be surprised."

"And anyway," Elizabeth said, "It's in the past."

"You had an affair with Philip Malraux."

"No. But with someone. I don't want to say the name because it's safer."

"I couldn't agree more; it protects me. But I'm sort of surprised. How long ago? Was he older, younger? Tell!"

"Oh, quite a while ago."

"Does Bill know it? Did he? How did you feel about him at the time, Elizabeth? I must say I admire you; I wish I was your kind of wife. I couldn't do it; I'm a one-man girl. It's terrible. And I'd be afraid I'd get them mixed if I started to sleep with more than one. Suppose I said the wrong name! The very first time he asked, what did you say? Did you say *yes* right off? How did you feel, Elizabeth!"

Elizabeth thought how there had been no replying of *yes* or *no*. The man had been there in his urgency and simply took her before him in a movement that could not be halted. She had completed a need, had been his answer. "Well, I only had the one affair. And it was ages and ages ago."

"But tell about it. I wouldn't repeat it," Angela vowed.

"Hoo." Elizabeth stood, laughing. "Here it is noon; I have a husband coming for lunch."

"I want to hear though. I'll see you later."

"All right." Elizabeth ran down the woods path to the Owl's Roost. She warned herself; a glass of skim milk and a piece of fruit; that was all. She'd bought a new plaid suit in Michigan City. She was considering what it was had prompted her to speak out like that. It was unwise, no question of it; Angela would tell Mike, and it would spread. Somehow she'd not been able to help it, like a small triumph. She'd felt Angela's curiosity, the friendly jealousy, Angela pregnant.

"Cripes, wish I was going for a swim like you," Gus told Elizabeth after lunch, folding three sticks of gum one after another and chewing them together.

"Well, Mr. Chapman won't be working all day long, will he?"

"I bet he will," Gus said indistinctly. "He's the whole time in a hurry, too. I liked it with Jimmy a lot better last summer. Jimmy talked to me."

"Don't call him Jimmy," Elizabeth said. "Say Mr. Fox. It's not polite."

"You have the oddest notion of what constitutes manners, Mum," Clara said. "How old-fashioned can you get? I was going to ask if I could call you Elizabeth now that I'm sixteen. Pearl's starting to call her mother Eve."

"He wants me to say Jimmy." Gus was sullen. He'd never get over to Herb Worth's orchard; he had his opinion of Daddy, he thought, for making a work-slave out of him. Skin didn't work very much, and Alan didn't work at all; he wouldn't help Ernie when he asked. Damn, damn, double-damn. This summer Gus had planned to concentrate on insects alone; he badly needed long-horned grasshoppers and true locusts, all the varieties; and he'd thought too that he'd get started on a good set of the aquatic bugs. And then there were a million beetles he didn't have. He stared at his brown thin legs thrust wearily out from the chair where he sat. He had grown almost two inches in a year; it impressed him to think of it. He chewed noisily, with passion. And then Daddy had said go to work again; every summer from now on. Work, work, work.

"I'll thank you, Clara," Elizabeth said as she busied herself putting shampoo, suntan lotion, cleansing cream, dark glasses, cigarettes in her beach bag, "not to criticize your elders. It may be a strain, but will you try? And don't try calling me Elizabeth, dear."

"I'm going to read every book of Gide's," Clara declared, sinking down on the couch, putting her feet up so her Madras skirt fell back exposing her legs; she wiggled her bare toes. "I'm reviewing books for the senior-class paper next year."

"Now, you know no one's going to read him," Elizabeth said. "Why not review something modern or a little lighter? They probably won't even print it."

"Oh yes, they will. I already thought of that. I got myself elected editor of the Ideal *Trumpet*."

"She's such a smarty," Gus said. "You don't know, Mum. She makes me sick. All the kids laugh at her. Have her way we'd have to go to school on Saturdays."

"Quit chomping your spearmint, dummox," Clara told him affably, "or I'll punch you in the gut."

"Clara," Elizabeth remonstrated.

"Why didn't you stop at one child, Mum?" Clara asked. "I'd have loved being an only child, doted over." She examined first the title page, then the colophon, then the dedication; all the pages preceding the book itself before she began. If there were a jacket she looked at everything on it first before she even lifted the cover. She wanted to devour books; she felt her conceit and how the world fell prostrate at her feet.

"I might just as well be an orphan," Gus mourned. "Having to work like I do. I can't ever do anything I want."

"Nonsense," Elizabeth said.

"I'm having a very unhappy childhood, Mum," he said.

"Run away from home," Clara suggested. "I'm doing a poem now on Gide's wife, Mum. It starts,

> *The widow clothéd all in her weed*
> *Is not so lonely as Mrs. Gide.*

Can you imagine the luck of that rhyme: Gide–weed?"

"How disgusting can she get, Mum!" Gus' voice rose in a wail.

"Bye," Elizabeth told them cheerfully as she stepped out the door. The sky was so deep a blue that it seemed nearly black. Gus' raised voice followed her.

"I hate you. You know that, Clara!"

Clara gazed at her sibling from her place of repose.

> *To love you was pleasant enough,*
> *But oh, it's delicious to hate you.*

Gus slammed the screen emphatically at her. He couldn't believe that once he'd liked his sister. She was a stuck-up big-mouth all the time. He listened to her shout after him.

"That's Shakespeare, weirdo!"

Old four-eyes Clara. He didn't dare say that in front of Daddy or Mum, but that was his private name for her when they were alone and she was like she was today. Gus whispered it, "Old goggle-eyes." He was late getting to the Sand Castle because he ran across a *Sisyphus Schoefferi*. The stout black beetle, almost an inch long, was rushing across the rising ground, struggling with a peatlike ball which he'd pressed into shape; he was employing both hind and fore legs to maneuver the object, many times his size. Hardly was it balanced at one point before it slipped from him and he lost the ground he'd gained in the past hour.

Gus thought the dung-beetles were great; he knew about the avaricious king of classic Hades, for whom the naturalist, Latreille, named them. They were the best of the *Scarabaeidae;* nothing ever got them down! Gus hoped he'd be a traveler some day. As he knelt on his bare knees and elbows beside the path, his chewing almost ceasing, he saw himself scaling mountains in faraway lands, hunting the great birdwing butterflies, or just plain getting new species of bugs not yet classified. He'd leave bloodstains from his rock-scarred hands as he toiled upward; he'd strain on the ragged stones, ever onward. His torment would never cease, he swore, until the burden he pushed toppled on his own head and he was crushed to a frightening death. He thought about the perfume of butterfly wings on one's fingers—vanilla, or lemon, or musk, or a sweetish odor hard to name at all. He fished in the back pocket of his shorts for his small killing bottle that still had a grimy label, *250 saccharin tablets.* Plucking the insect up, its six legs waving busily, seeking the burden to roll, he dropped it in. He ran all the rest of the way to the Malraux's moving dune that Ernie was halting.

Ernie's overalls and red shirt were dirty. He'd had a two-ton load of black prime soil delivered that morning in a tall moist pile at the end of the Sand Castle drive. That meant that the stuff had to be carried in buckets up the steep inland grade to the top of the dune before he could use it. He gave Gus that chore, and figured to set Alan to it if he ever managed to nail him down. Ernie used a wheelbarrow dexterously to haul the soil around. He dumped a full barrow about the root-balls of each of the spruces and dwarf hemlocks he was setting out today. He'd felt a little shaky at noon, and on Della's advice ate a palmful of salt, washing it down with lemonade. Now he felt his queasiness fading.

"Whoo-ee," he said to Gus, holding onto his sweat-wet suspender straps. "About gave you up."

"I hurried," Gus declared.

"See, the reason I'm in such a swivet, boy, is the roots is drying out. Whenever the little taproots here get that way, they're gone. And they're the ones the bush is counting on. You got to hack the dead ones all off." Ernie snipped expertly with his pruning shears, cutting all the evergreen's underground tendrils back to the quick. Spreading them out fanwise, as he held the spiny trunk erect with his other gnarled pitch-smudged hand, he dealt handfuls of the black soil about them. "Get me the hose. Step quick, boy. Got a long ways to go; we got fifty more of these nurselings. The nozzle's over there."

Gus moved, stumbling. He saw a pair of Pawpaws mounting in the air, their zebra-striped wings, pea-green and black, fluttering against the sky, high and higher, over the canyon of sand; the red and blue dots of their underwings flicked; their long swallowtails trailed. He watched while bending for the hose; they were mating, he was sure. They disappeared into the sky. He heard a crow squall and figured it would get them.

Ernie's eyes were buried in the ground. He had heard the crow too, but thought of it as a corn-thief, considering a crow-hopping excursion one morning soon, during this nesting season. If you asked Ernie, he wouldn't have known what a butterfly was, except as a bug to kill. Ernie devoted himself to war and had a bed of roses that Jack Behmelmen would have gone on the wagon for. Raising roses was hellfire nowadays; every year bred more pests, some never even heard of when he was a boy. And some coming over on ships from foreign countries. They were smarter too, hardier; they could eat DDT for breakfast, lunch, and supper and thrive on it. Ernie had a vague notion that eventually insects would gain the world. He removed the nozzle which held back the dribble of water, and pushed the wriggling hose end gently into the dirt. It would stay there, to settle the roots and overflow the dyke of sod which he'd placed around the young blue spruce. He'd water it daily until it took hold. Before he moved to follow his boy helper, he gazed at his work with the sort of engrossed look of a mother closing a nursery door.

In an hour they had set out five more of the evergreens. Della brought each a glass of grapeade made from cans of frozen liquid she bought at the grocery. "I got my suspicions of that stuff," she told the workers. "How am I going to know that's real grape in there? Couldn't those people just put in some candywater?"

"Tastes like real grape to me, Mrs. Chapman," Gus said shyly, holding his wad of gum in his palm wiped clean on a shirt sleeve. "It's good."

"Don't always be so suspicious, Della," Ernie said. "Fussing all the time, gabbing all the time," he told Gus, his mouth in a grin. "I married Della when our conversation gave out because I wanted a quiet life. And now look, ain't it?"

"Ah," Della laughed at the wiry little man, and shook her head so her gray hair flew. "Hush, you. Bring the glasses when you come in for supper if you think. I'm redding up the fruit cellar and I got to fly. You think you'd find the time to put in a few more shelves for me?"

He pounced upon it. "Yes sir! Do her this evening. You get your mind made up meanwhile to the exact what you want."

"I will." Her heavy figure plodded off; her humming audible, and then her song as she reached the Sand Castle:

> Thou great in things that make us great,
> Michigan, my Michigan!
> Our loyal voices sound thy claim,
> Upon the golden roll of Fame.
> Our loyal hands shall write the name!
> My Michigan!

Ernie saw Gus' secret gesture and proposed helpfully, "No need to go to the house. Take a leak in that pawpaw patch on your way to get the topsoil. Ain't nobody around."

Gus was embarrassed but gratified; he nodded, yet unable to participate in discussions or explanations about the part of him which he guarded jealous, from look or word. He could do no more than snicker when his contemporaries or older men sounded the subject; and when his sister demanded things of Mum outright as she did sometimes: "But how long does intercourse *last,* Mum?" Gus left the room, his ears clanging. He gazed down to the lake, hearing barking. Mum was walking past the pier posts and Chou-chou dashing up to her. Jimmy Fox had been on a walk north and stopped to talk on the way back. Gus liked Jimmy and thought how Mr. Chapman was dull as a companion. He sighed, picking up the soil-dusted pails.

Ernie glanced down at the tiny figures along the shore too. The kind of world the resorters moved in was so far removed from his that Ernie never pondered on it. He accepted it that folks differed and though he never felt a pang of true envy, now and then he spoke his instinctive disdain to Della for what he thought of as a self-indulgent and nonproductive life. He never went for a dip or washed himself in the lake. Ernie had the pride of the blue collar in his willful abstention. His mind shrank if it crept on the idea of exposing his tough ugly body to the eye of another man; and to the eye of a woman! No chance of that. Whoo-ee! When they got him ready to lay under the purple pall, someone might pull off his overalls and get a look at him, he thought, and he hoped they were quick about it. He saw the couple at the beach turn their faces in his direction; they waved. Ernie went back to work, undeterred by their frivolity.

"He didn't see us," Jimmy told Elizabeth. "How does he like working for Ernie?'"

"Did you know Gus calls you Jimmy?"

"Why not?"

"Well, aren't children getting familiar? Next he won't respect you. Why, Clara wanted to call me Elizabeth."

"It's a pretty name. She has my sympathy."

Elizabeth glanced quickly at Jimmy. She wondered if she had imagined a note of challenge. The things bruited about Jimmy Fox varied from rank homosexuality to wild bacchanalian winter parties in which he encouraged any kind of feminine wantonness. Dora had it from someone a couple of years ago that unmentionable objects were found under the hide-a-bed chair. "Hoo!" She threw a stick for Chouchou. "Go fetch it!" Her words were slow and heavy.

"The bitch hasn't the slightest idea what you want," Jimmy said. "Doesn't sit up and beg either, or shake hands, or play dead. She's uneducated for the parlor."

"I don't see why," Elizabeth objected. "Don't you think it's cute?"

"Come on walk back to Pine Beach with me," Jimmy said. "I'll tell your fortune; I read palms." His burned limbs were black-haired; it grew heavy on his chest and flat belly where the muscles were molded and taut. His brief Italian trunks housed only that part of his body at the juncture of his thighs.

Elizabeth looked sidewise at his covering, sharing the summer people's general scandalized opinion, but at the same time admiring, a little envious, his bachelor's nonchalance. "All right. I was only walking to let my hair dry. I washed it in the lake and lying on it might spoil the set." She put her little hands to the blonde waves she'd made with her fingers. "Do you think it's almost done?"

"Looks fine to me."

They began walking back. The horizon was a clear mauve band above the bright water. Far ahead where eventually one came on the soot of Michigan City and the stench of Whiting and Gary, the sky was a peach mist, partially obscuring the tier of dunes tree-green and sand-white, that disappeared south. A tern hurled itself at the water nearby and in a movement too fast to follow nipped out a silver alewife and flew up with it, in steady strokes, and away into the white flare of sun. The beach was empty; it was too early for the crowd to assemble. Elizabeth was still working on her summer tan; later when she had it to suit her, she'd lie under their umbrella. She remembered, "I forget my cream; it's in my bag; I have to get it."

"Women don't do anything I can see for the pleasure of it, Elizabeth. You do your walking to lose weight, or to dry your hair. You lie in the sun to get a tan; even reading; you do it to demonstrate your egghead qualities, which happen to be the mode these days."

"You sound like you're telling about a lot of men I know." Elizabeth mocked him.

"No; men are honest, take them as a whole. Come, let's see your palm."

His Irish face, with the heavy firm lips, was smug, she considered. "But Jimmy, you're always doing set-ups and things to keep you in shape!"

"Because I want to live to be a hundred and five. I'm fifty-four now and I intend to make it, too." His eyes ran up her, the small round toes, the thighs, her pretty face. "How old are you, Elizabeth?"

"A poodle is my favorite breed of dog." Chouchou trotted beside her.

"I know Angela's thirty-six. She told me; you're her age, aren't you?"

"Was she called Chouchou when you got her? Had that Boy Scout named her already?"

"Boy Scout? Why call Wheeler that?" Jimmy flushed, his temper touched.

"Doesn't he scoop water over his knees like a granny when he goes in?" She laughed, pleased to have turned him.

"You have a wicked tongue, Madame. Wheeler doesn't take time off to get a tan; he'd rather stay in his ancient apartment and study medieval law. He's a reader for reading's sake."

"Hoo, stop digging at women. Don't be so mad; I didn't mean it that way."

"Well you ought to see his paper, *The Pseudo-Isidorian Problem Today*."

"No thanks!"

"He wants to get over to Europe; he's applying for steward jobs to get passage; he'll never get there."

"Me either," she said. "And isn't Eve Thwaite's going to Switzerland?"

He heard the sullen note and thought how spoiled she was, and frivolous and useless. He put a hand on her soft shoulder. She had never uttered a *bon mot* or a level opinion to his knowledge. Dr. Bill was like a big worried bear on a rope, Jimmy thought. "Let's go in and swim the rest of the way."

"I'd wet my hair and I don't have my cap with me."

"Well, it's not pasted on."

"Wait till I get it."

"I'll accompany you from the sea. May I?" He plunged without waiting for her reply.

She watched his brown hard flanks submerge and waited over the seconds for him to rise. There was no ripple and she searched the surface, wetting her lips, adjusting her swim suit about her legs where it constricted. He was nowhere; she didn't like Jimmy much. When his head bobbed up though, and he waved his arm to her, she felt gay. She ran along the beach to accompany his overhand crawl.

When she'd slipped on her cap she trotted in to him, in the funny endearing way, Jimmy thought, that females run, throwing their ankles and knees, ungraceful. The Olsons' daughter Clara, did it differently; Jimmy and the other resorters had seen her sometimes, elbows close at her sides, toes straightly gripping the earth. She must have learned it at track in school, or got it watching the boys in gym. He'd rather see a woman run like her mother. Elizabeth came splashing, half-clumsy, up to him. "I

like your swim suit," he yelped after diving away from her, and
rising at the bar far away.

"You do?" she cried, and when she reached him he caught
her waist in the water a moment, perhaps accidentally.

Then she lent him her shampoo and he soaped Chouchou
thoroughly. The animal loved it, wriggling skinny-shaped under
his scrubbing fingers and later drying to a fluffed shiny black wool.
Chouchou sat on her haunches and leaned damply and heavily
against her master's shoulder while he examined Elizabeth's small
outstretched palm. He ran his index finger over the lines critically.
"Your life line is excellent, though you show parental attachment
for an undue period."

"Hoo! Didn't my father die when I was seventeen? And
Mummy never gets to visit except Christmas sometimes."

"You're religious too. Here's the money line."

"What's it say?"

"Well, it crosses the life line far down here. And that means
plenty of it, but not till very late in life. You see, you'll live to be
awfully old, Elizabeth, I'm happy to say. For a while you'll be
very ill. You'll recover and then's when you get the money." His
Irish face grinned, probing her blue-purple eyes, the quick frown.
"Really, you do have a strong hand. Tell the truth, I thought it
would be different."

"Ill? How ill?"

"A hand doesn't tell the details. But see here. Your fingers
are square; that means prudence, reasonableness—courage."

"I'm not any of those things though. I don't think so, Jimmy."

"And these two fingers here, wide apart like this, independence."

"Hoo."

"Your Mount of Venus is well developed; emotional, sensual.
Affectionate?"

"I like money," she stated, "but I hate to think of being ill.
Are you sure?"

"Get out of the habit of closing your hand, Elizabeth. You
tell the truth with your hands open."

"That's silly."

"You believe every thing I'm telling you though, don't you,
Elizabeth?"

She shrugged. "We told fortunes like this," she began to draw in the sand, "and called it *love-marry-hate-adore*. Kids don't do it any more." Getting on her knees, her hair in waves over her cheek, she printed their names with her finger, checking the letters out:

"See? You adore me. But I'm married. Poor Jimmy."

"Is that what it says?" Jimmy put his arm about the poodle. "Now if I could read Chouchou's paw. The pooch remains an enigma."

By now the beach was crowding. Monk came along. "I could rent twice as many cottages as there are, dang it." He had brought

ELIZABETH OLSON

JAMES FOX

the *Daily News* under his arm; the inside page was devoted to an article about the extent of pollution in the lake. Seven beaches in Milwaukee had been ordered closed. In Cleveland they were losing their war to keep the resorts open; and as far as Lake Erie was concerned, health officials there were flatly against any bathing at all. Buffalo had given up the lake fronting their city long ago, their present worry being the tainted taste of their drinking water. The sorriest offenders were oil and shipping interests, and of course sewage and factory waste contributed to the puzzle.

"Hell, Jimmy," Monk told them, standing like a giant against the sky above the two lying in the sun, "why, during the St. Lawrence Seaway celebration, there was eight thousand Marines and sailors stationed in naval vessels; they dumped all the shit right into the Milwaukee waters. I don't mind garbage so much."

"Ugh," Elizabeth said, "must I believe it?"

"Well, it's a fact, gal. Get your head out of the sand."

"Jimmy's been reading my hand."

"That's one path to rape," Monk leered, reaching in his trunks' pocket for his cigarettes.

"She has a very good hand too," Jimmy squinted up. "And I just discovered one more thing that fool tramp took last winter. My son's old fly rod. What'd he want with that?"

"Sell it."

"It's not worth two cents; it's twenty years old—the kid's had it since he was twelve. I sent him a card to get another if he wants to eat lake trout this summer."

"I don't like the idea at all of someone living there and nobody knowing," Elizabeth said. "What else did he take? Anything valuable?"

"I own nothing valuable, Elizabeth. I'm not much of a catch." Jimmy grinned. "Mostly he cleaned out the supplies and messed up the place. Found the key too and left the place wide open; seeing as I was his host he could have returned it to the bird box to keep out others like him!"

"Wonder why the proprietor of Pine Beach didn't find out about it. Jimmy?"

"I was tapping maples that week." Monk lit two cigarettes on his match at once, dexterous. "And repairing screens in the cottages."

"Hoo," Elizabeth laughed up at him against the blue-black sky. "Not the Owl's Roost. Bill got sore; finally hired Helge Lagerquist to fix ours."

Monk boldly handed a smoke to Elizabeth. "Then you got a good hand. I'm thinking of taking Helge on full time here. I'm about to spread out some." Monk swaggered slightly.

Jimmy raised his brows. "Elizabeth, do we smell the filthy odor of money?"

"Eve," Elizabeth replied keenly. "She wants to buy the Linden House land. Is that it?"

"Past tense," Monk said. "She bought it."

"Well, I'm not asking how much, Monk," Elizabeth said. "But I bet she's doing all right. Her book's on the best-seller list for the tenth week."

"Movies bought it, she told me," Monk said.

"*A Woman's Answer,* for God's sake," Jimmy protested. "That's all we need these days."

"Well, you're a reader, Jimmy," Monk said. "What's she answering?"

"Oh, it's wonderful," Elizabeth said. "She autographed my copy. All about the problems a young widow has adjusting."

"I can solve them in one four-letter word." Monk was crass.

"No," Elizabeth said. "The girls are all crazy about it. It's a story; she doesn't come right out with the words."

"Tell me," Monk said. "I want to hear, Mother."

"Let's see then, it's just that this widow has tensions and fears. Some man wants to marry her. She finally decides not to do it, but to go ahead with her husband's work and raise the children."

"Hell," Monk said. "And they buy that!"

The poodle bolted from Jimmy's arm. "Hey, come here."

"Well, it's a wonderful book," Elizabeth maintained, "even if I didn't make it very clear. Did you read it, Jimmy?"

"I thought it was a pack of nonsense. But it's my idea that Eve Thwaite's a lot smarter than one might suppose. She knows what she's doing." Jimmy got up, bawling, "Chouchou!"

The poodle had galloped through the creek and down to the Behmelmen beach, where Jack was coming out of the water followed by a dripping ugly yellow-white pup of a few months. "Where'd he get that, dang it," Monk said. "And what is it?"

"Don't insult me," Jimmy said. "I'm its grandfather in a way. It's Chouchou's. Jack's had it a week. Come on, I'll show you."

"I even forgot she had pups," Elizabeth said. Monk and Jimmy had her hands, helping her up, the cigarette in her lips.

"Bring your cap, Elizabeth," Jimmy said, "Don't forget." He told Monk, "She can't swim without it."

Monk said, "Everybody's getting dogs. Mrs. Thwaite had one in that old Buick she came in. One of her little gals was driving; beats me why they keep that bus now. Anyhow the little boy had been carsick and they emptied out a bathing capful. Then they let this sheepdog out and it got in a ruckus with Alan's dogs."

"It's a collie," Elizabeth said. "Bobbie. She had it way last April when she came to the beach once."

"You know she even wanted permission to remodel Linden House," Monk said. "Hell, I never got asked that before!"

As they walked down the beach Jimmy grinned, "Whatever would the Reverend have said to all these goings-on?"

"Did they bury his toupee with him?" Elizabeth asked.

"I don't know," Monk said, "but wherever he is I bet he's still in a swivet."

Jack Bchmelmen had a towel hung about his shoulders; his trunks dripped, beer-paunch protruded. He was watching Chou-chou and the pup running in crazy circles. "White Fang!" Jack sang out, ineffectual. There was a little smell of whisky on Jack. He leaned against *The Desire,* which lay with furled sail on the yellow mast.

The puppy had fur like Bosco and the same black *T* on his tail; his ears lopped in a haphazard way; White Fang was more intelligent than either his sire or dam. The three visitors joined Jack at the boat's side to observe the scurrying pair.

Jack glanced at the Glass House that sat on the dune above, naked windows glittering. "I came down early today; I'm staying here a long while. Had a row with one of Hazel's buddies." Jack rubbed his chest thoughtfully. "Say, any of you like a drink?"

"Where's it stowed?" Jimmy said.

Jack nudged the boat. "Under *The Desire.* Just a flask. Speak up if you want it. This fellow's a poet, Hazel claims. Had the gall to ask me who I was. *Me!* I punched him too."

Chouchou caught up with her puppy and they rolled over together, scrambling up and away again. "Let's go in the water," Elizabeth said.

"Hazel sure is sore," Jack said. "That fellow asked me who I was. Says, where do *you* fit in around here? Those are the words he used."

Elizabeth pulled on her cap, but the men waited, unstirring. The young dog zigzagged, wildly dashing, inviting pursuit from his mother with shining eyes and teeth, whimpering, delirious with pleasure. Chouchou followed in his footprints. The water picked up the noises, echoing. Sand flies found the people and stung their legs. Waves broke upon the wet floor. Just beyond was green-black water, far out purple-black. The sky was white at the horizon. Clouds stood so solid that their structure and dimension were felt. The sun was placed in the sky simply, like a flattened copper coin. The people stood motionless as if they had identified with the two animals and belonged to their unconfined bliss.

[14]

FOR a fortnight the weather stayed cool, almost cold. There occurred a series of summer storms, beginning with a spate that flooded the basement of the Owl's Roost. Since the floor was of dirt and the entrance from the outside stone steps, no one bothered to check the level except Gus, who claimed after checking with a contraption he'd rigged that it was over two feet. When the earth had absorbed what it could, the rest stood stagnant. At supper in the big room, Elizabeth wrinkled her nose. "Smell it, Bill?"

Dora narrowed her eyes with satisfaction as she set down the bowl of ice cream just made, "I always had a notion to scrub down that cellar some ways. Wait till that water's gone."

"I'm going up to the Lodge and complain," Bill said. "I have some rights as a tenant. He's got to bring a pump in here. Any of the others flooded?"

"We're the only place in a hollow," Gus said.

The small cellar closet had been inundated, taking with it Clara's school binder that contained a few notes saved from her special classmates as well as some of her better poems from the past years. She secretly kicked herself because she forgot to get it when the rain began. She felt a tie to them the way she used to feel for a tooth she lost when younger, collecting each for her horde, refusing to put them under her pillow as Gus did, for a quarter or a token gift. She didn't even know why she hid the binder, instead of keeping it in plain sight on her desk; there was nothing in it to conceal. "Can I go with, Daddy?" she asked. "There isn't anything to do and I'm sick and tired of books books books. Gus won't play cards or chess either."

"Because I'm busy," Gus said. He spent his time in his room, pleased that all work on the Sand Castle dune was suspended.

The next day there was a fresh burst of rain. Some of the falling drops were carried by uprushing currents into freezing altitudes where they formed balls of ice that became too heavy for the air to support and dropped with great force and speed. The children of commuting fathers dashed out to gather the hailstones, a few bigger than golf balls, and put them in the freezer to prove their assertions on the coming week end. Then, by the end of July, atmospheric pressure increased again, all the nimbus and stratus clouds were gone, and the sun rays, moteless, streamed.

Vegetation prospered from the unusual wet spell. The little pawpaw trees early in spring had opened their curious purple flowers of disagreeable odor before the leaves unfolded, drooping like giant's gloves from the small branches. Now the fruit was maturing swiftly, the four-inch oval shapes, bananalike in the way the green became spotted with brown and then turned black and soft when fully ripe. Clara brought some to her brother slumped on his bed, curly head resting against the metal bars at the head, his favorite white rat curled on the pillow. "Here." She dumped them beside him.

"Gosh, thanks." He nibbled one that he peeled back. He hated the sweetish sickening taste, but was overcome by a lonely welling of feeling for his sister. "Have a chair."

"Thanks." She pushed his tennis shoes off it onto the sandy floor, and sat, her elbows on her knees, her hands hanging listless. "Vespers in a little while." It was Sunday, almost seven. Clara thought of how she'd used to tap her foot three times, or dive under seven times; how numbers had meant special colors. She was breaking herself of the train of thought, and would deliberately mix everything up, using fours and nines, warring doggedly with her other nature. She had all sorts of new disciplines she contrived. One was to exercise, push-ups and waist-bends, till she thought she'd drop. Another was making lists of what to do for every hour of the day to improve herself. She felt she was on the verge of becoming perfect. There was only one thing that she'd have traded for being just what she was; that was to be a Catholic novice nun, who could kneel on a bare rough cold brick floor with arms spread wide all through a dark empty night and fall exhausted in a dead faint at sunrise before an enormous bloodied crucifix of some perfectly tremendous wooden god! Creeps, what she wouldn't give, she thought.

"I'm not going to go to Vespers," Gus said.

"Oh, come on."

"No."

"Come on, Gus."

"Okay."

"What you doing anyway?"

"Just lying, thinking." He put a slender finger to touch Davy's head and back by his ear.

"Why?"

They didn't talk for a while. Their life was a wheel that turned round and round over the days, and there seemed no end or beginning of it. They remained the same age forever; they were unable to conceive of themselves as adults some day. "I'll be glad when I'm grown up," said Gus, not believing it would happen, not in his presumable future. "I'll live by myself in a one-room stone house. I'll hose it down once a week. I'll do anything I please."

"Where'll you get the money?"

"I don't know, but I'll build it myself."

"What about your wife, *mon cher?*" Clara was in second-year French now.

"I'm not going to marry. If I do it'll be when I'm old; about forty."

"Forty isn't old," Clara said, thinking of Mr. Ardway.

Gus stretched out his small-boned frame and yawned. He made an ugly face pulling down the corners of his mouth with his forefingers and rolling his eyeballs up. Clara averted her eyes from the sight. Mum called from below. "Vespers? Are either of you going? Gus!"

The children sat as though the voice hadn't reached them; they didn't stir. Gus spread his arms out. "Gee you can see all Jerusalem from here." He let his arms flop. "Do you get it, Clara?"

"Here's one I learned at Uncle Jack's:

> *Dear God, you come again behind my shoulder;*
> *I had forgot. How you need me,*
> *With beating wing*
> *Rushing to see if I have called!"*

"Hand me my net," Gus said. "It's in the closet. I want to take it with. I'm immobilized. This is another sick one I got from Irene Thwaite." He lifted his arms as if they were heavy, in a cross again. "What a heck of a way to spend Easter." He yawned.

She got up and pulled aside the green denim drapes that hid the confusion within. "It's not here."

"Behind," he said.

She reached to the back wall and found it; she shook it like a spear, "Listen to me, Gus!

> *In order for You to be God,*
> *God, I am the necessity."*

"Children?" Mum gave them up and the screen slapped downstairs after her. Daddy was at the Holy Mother Hospital; he'd been called at noon.

Clara continued:

> *And by the strength of my belief*
> *In the face of mortality,*
> *I build You to a tower where*
> *I may climb in adversity!*

"Is that William Wordsworth?" Gus inquired plaintively.

"No, it isn't."

"I think I read it in my English book."

"No, you didn't. I wrote it. It's modern. You don't get ones like it in school." She began again, *"In order for you to be God, God. . . ."*

"Let's go," Gus said and got up to take Davy by his neck scruff to his cage and close the lid.

Clara shrugged and led the way. Dora had gone to the movie in Michigan City with Herb. The shell of the old house was empty except for the pair descending the creaky front stairs. They each felt a quick unnamed edge of an unknown fear; might someone be skulking behind the faded striped drapes that hung nearly to the floor beside the windows where the dusk moved? They hid their alarm, each from the other, their steps swift as they went out the door. Mum had planted a double row of garden flowers by the path. The packet of mixed seeds had come Scotch-taped to a box of breakfast cereal and she had run out and pushed them into the sand once in spring. They stood spindly, the brilliant single zinnias undersized, the three or four evening-primroses swaying, lopsided, branching over two feet like weeds, their pale yellow poppylike blooms opening at his hour with a snapping noise and an almost nervous motion. Two hawkmoths flashed down to hover above the candelabralike plants, probing with tongues longer than their bodies. One was a Sphinx, gray-mottled with a yellow-spotted body and a five-inch wing span, and the other a *catocala,* with brilliant red-and-black-banded underwings. Gus snatched the net from Clara's hand and swung it as the moths zigzagged fitfully. He missed them both and they disappeared.

"I'll wait," he said, squatting. "Did you see that *catocala cara,* that Darling Underwing? It's big and common; I really don't need it. I shouldn't have tried to catch it."

"What I can't figure is why some moths are bright-colored and yet they fly only in the night or just at dark. Why? Who can see? You think their eyes are different from ours, Gus?"

"Ye olde philosopher," Gus said. He knew the *catocalas* were rested against the trunks of trees now, their brilliance concealed by the folded gray upper wings. There were a hundred species of that genus in the country, and if it took all his life Gus intended to get one pair of each of them. He waved his sister from him, vehement, sucking at his braces, hissing. "Go on, can't you! You have to sit still, you dumb-nut."

She went into the twilight, disliking him. "Ugh."

It was lighter down at the beach, the open sky still aflame. She could hear Irene Thwaite's guitar far away, underneath the singing. Clara trudged through the sand barefoot, her hands in the pockets of her white shorts, her elbows swinging. She had decided never to cut her hair and wore it looped in a soft inverted cone that gave her height and, Clara considered, an artistic look. As she approached, she squinted in an old habit, though she could see perfectly well with the new lenses; she was deciding whom to sit by. Mum was there holding Georgie on her bare knees, and Mrs. Paoli had Chris in her arm. All the women were in Bermudas or slacks except Mrs. Thwaite, in an Italian raw silk skirt. Clara circled the people, and dropped down by Alan.

"Hi," he grinned.

Skin and his brothers were near Irene, who thumped the box of the guitar. Skin signaled his greeting to Clara by winking; she ignored him. Dick Ardway had sprouted a beard. "Why don't you grow one, *mon ami?*" she whispered to Alan. "Double dare."

"I might yet."

"Where are the dogs?"

"Jojo cut his foot and I locked Bosco with him for company. He goes in the water and gets the bandage wet."

Eve held her hand up, as the singing ceased. "Hush. Now remember, the children are going to ask questions at this time. Does anyone have one?"

Carmen's hand shot up. "I have. I *have.*"

"Well, dear?"

"Sometimes I have to get novocaine. When I'm at the dentist. I'm afraid I'll die. What about that, Mrs. Thwaite! If I get afraid I'll die."

Everyone listened, passive, tolerant, and used to standard Thwaite replies. Angela made herself be like the others, made herself not protective. Her daughter had her own way to go, she swore; but *my darling among lions!* She forced her thoughts onto Georgie and Chris beside her, half-sleeping.

Eve was saying, "That's just in your mind, Carmen. The cure is discipline. And you must pray, dear." Knowing it was silly to say it to the backward child, and yet realizing that she had a new role among the neighbors. Besides, now Eve did have a god who was palpable, close, to whom she said continual surprised thanks.

"But the dentist gives me a needle in the gum. And I'm afraid; what if I died!" Carmen tossed back her hair and her expressive mouth trembled; she put her lips together and looked down, stubborn. She had said her piece and was satisfied.

"We must drill ourselves," Eve continued, her eyes upon

Pearl, whom she never understood. Pearl was free now of the dominating influence, the tyranny of Boris, in the way the old Eve used to think that marriage would free both her daughters. Eve had looked forward to their release from their father. But the only change, as far as she could see, had been that Pearl lost the slight nervous tic of blinking her eyes. Otherwise Eve thought, it was as if the child even missed have a scapegoat for her problems. Eve sighed, frowning, "Try to think positive thoughts, Carmen. Sometimes too, just little one-sentence prayers will help— that you have decided on ahead of time." Eve's small fingers caressed the ears of the almond-eyed Collie. "Like *'Lord, I will praise Thee ever for Thou hast made me single and content!'* " Bobbie snuggled against her. "No more questions? Then we'll sing. What about 'Rock of Ages'?"

"Eve," Pearl groaned, and rolled her black eyes up at Russ Ardway.

"That's what I say," sighed Irene, strumming the strings. "Next Eve'll want 'Onward Christians.' "

"Well, I will too. How about 'Lead Kindly Light' and afterwards one of the smallest children can choose."

"Do Bill Bailey," Georgie sat up, pleading, "won't you please come home!"

Elizabeth stroked his cheek, holding him against her. "Hush. For Heaven's sake."

"Shut your big trap, Baby," Chris affectionately told his brother, Georgie, who was a year older.

Clara wasn't bothering to sing along with the group. She and Alan were behind the others and Alan had brushed her shoulder slightly. Clara waited to see whether it had been on purpose.

> *Amid the encircling gloom,*
> *Lead Thou me on.*
> *The night is dark and I am far from home!*

It was, and as he adjusted his shoulder against hers, he lightly pushed his hand along the sand too, until it came to rest against hers.

The preacher's widow wouldn't let the children choose just any song; it had to have a religious touch, she insisted. She wasn't aware that the one they picked was being rendered nightly at a candle-lit hot spot in Chicago by a black-skinned jazzman, a celebrity who had cut a disc on it which had already passed the million mark. It was "Just the Two of Us." Irene hit the box of the guitar once or twice the way the rendition on the jukebox record went.

The twilight was far gone and the parable told, when the services were over. The night was getting dark, soon would be black and the stars out. Still over the lake the bleeding hues of sunset insisted and would not be banished; the red wound remained. Fireflies were out on the dune above the people as Eve climbed the beach stairs, Bobbie dogging her heels. She wanted to see if Ian were sleeping yet, one of his father's dumbbells like a wood doll in his soft arm. She had a housekeeper that she liked, fat, homey, and unstarched. The night insects twinkled greenish about her. Some of the little boys had brought Mason jars and ran squealing to secure a supply of the soft-bodied flashing beetles. After a while the mothers led them home, some weeping in protest, others stoic and tired, willing to believe that morning should come.

There was left the scattered group of Pine Beach teen-agers and young adults. Someone spoke into the half-seen faces and limbs, "Silence reigned and they all got wet."

"Listen, everyone!" Alan almost leaped to his feet. "Silence in the court house, the monkey wants to speak. Speak, monkey, speak."

In the quiet, the German shepherds could be heard complaining in the faraway cellar, of rank desertion, "Booo-wooo-oooo!" And then an airplane droned over from Chicago, green and red lights winking. Pearl put her hand on Russ Ardway's arm. "Why not make a fire?"

"She's a monkey," Clara said to Alan with pleasure. "Pearl Thwaite's a monkey. Boy."

"Okay, Pearl, we will." Russ nudged Skin with his toe. "You heard, slave."

Skin didn't move, and Dick, edgy because he'd noticed Pearl and Russ' new interest in each other, got to his feet, rubbing his soft chin stubble, speaking unpleasantly, "Come on, Skin."

"No." Skin sat where he was, hands clasped about his brown knees, rebel.

"I'll make you," Dick warned, and the others caught the new violent undercurrent. He bent and cuffed at Skin's head lightly.

Skin scrambled to his feet with an angry grunt. "Damn your gizzard then."

"Russ," Pearl protested, "stop them."

"Come over here, Bunny." Russ pulled Pearl to her feet, whispering into her ear as he'd learned to do, worldly he felt. Russ had got a summer job in Chicago to help himself through his junior year at State; he had already lost his boyishness and developed a frown that didn't go away, not unbecoming.

"Okay." They walked to the foot of Thwaite's stairs, but Pearl heard the growling and the protests, the thuds and squeaks. She wouldn't look. "I hate it," she complained. "Murder." Her eyes were wide.

"I don't. I nearly offered to hold Skin's sweater for him. He's been Baby Brother too long."

"But how can you stand to see your own family fighting like that? They might hurt each other."

"What's being my family got to do with it? I don't feel any different about Skin than about Alan Malraux over there. Now you, Bunny," he brushed his hand along her breasts, "that's different."

She backed away, cold. "Mustn't touch." Pearl was self-assured these days; she thought she knew as much as Russ did. She didn't care for his type, anyway.

Russ put his thumbs in his belt, altering his style quickly, purposed. "Chick," he mocked, slouching, "your pardon."

"How can you stand Chicago in the summertime?" Pearl asked. "I think it's ghastly."

"There's a little item you forget, called money," he reminded her, putting a hand to tweak her nose. She slapped it away and he laughed. "And Field's is air conditioned; so's my efficiency. It's a matter of getting back and forth between two very comfortable places. See? I like it." Russ had had a few adventures; he enjoyed teasing himself with the idea of how their relation would upset this pretty little gumdrop. "I like city girls too."

"You do?"

"All a matter of taste, Chick. Some like campus girls, some country ones."

The scuffling ceased and Skin bellowed, "Russ. Russ!" at the top of his voice.

Russ instinctively ran, and Pearl with him. Skin was astraddle his brother's back, and had his arms locked behind him; Dick's face was in the sand. "I'm damned," Russ said.

"Russ, look!"

"I see, hotshot."

"Should he say uncle?"

"Let him up. No."

Skin did so, and Dick rose, spitting the sand from his mouth, wiggling a tooth gingerly with his thumb. "Anybody but you and I'd be sore. This one's loose. Ugh. Your sweater's torn, Skin."

"Oh my gosh," Skin cried, his high voice cracking, "Did I hurt you?"

"What a character," Dick said, shaking his head, his twilight-concealed face in a grin. "Sure. My feelings especially."

"Poor Dickey," Pearl's voice heavy with self-reproach. "Let me see."

"I'll make a fire for you, Pearl," Skin said grandly. "Come on, all of you. Help." He began to search for sticks, exhilarated. His upper arm was hurting, and he dabbed at his nose which bled spasmodically. His yellow hair was scrambled and he pawed it to straighten it. Skin felt it didn't even matter that sneaky Clara was making up to Alan.

Still in the sky over the lake stood the roseate stigmata that cleaved even though dark had arrived. The little fire began to crackle, and Alan handed about folded invitations he'd made.

ALAN PHILIP MALRAUX
invites you
on the 3rd day of August
at 2:30 in the afternoon
to

and inside the fold:

D R O P   D E A D !

Clara thought it was highly original, and she tried to praise him extravagantly, "I think you've got a divine first-rate mind, *mon ami.*"

Alan flushed. "You do? I think of myself as well-rounded, with the emphasis on sports. My class adviser brought it up in our last conference."

"See here," she said, "why don't you do a poem or a humor piece this summer. You'd be excellent at that. I'll see it gets printed in the *Trumpet's* alumni column. I'm senior editor next fall."

"Okay. Maybe I will."

Alan had a slight smell of vinegar about him. He'd got a severe burn a few days ago when out in the new canoe which reflected the sun; Chappy treated him nightly. He sat in front of Clara, nearer to the flame, and she studied his broad back, clad in a too-tight tan shirt which he tucked in his khaki shorts. She sighed with pleasure; a Harvard freshman and besides that, going to Paris in August. She couldn't believe she was as lucky as she was. Clara Olson had God on her side: *Dieu et mon droit!* She watched confidently, dropping her eyes as he glanced around and put a hand masterfully over hers again. All the pink left the sky.

"You know stars, Irene?" Russ questioned lazily. He'd finally capitulated, abandoning Pearl for the moment to Dick, and rested his head on Irene's lap next to the guitar. Irene was plain, Russ argued reasonably with himself, but she was an old and true friend, and it was dark. He felt very philosophical; he even read the Henry Miller books nowadays with a detached aplomb; certainly he knew all about women.

Irene said primly, "Papa used to teach us." She pointed. The sky sparkled brilliantly; the moon wouldn't come for hours. "There are the Pleiades, and they're part of the constellation Taurus the Bull."

"I don't see a bull," Russ said.

Irene ignored him. "And that's the Dog Star, Sirius."

"The Pleiades are the seven sisters." Pearl spoke from where she lay in Dick's arm.

"There's the Big Dipper," Clara said. "Going round like a wheel and always pointing to the North Star."

Alan followed her finger. "It's the Big Bear, too."

"I don't see a bear," Russ said.

"*Earth's dark forehead flings athwart the heavens, her shadow crowned with stars.*" Clara, too confused to continue, cried out, "Play something, Irene. Let's sing some more, everybody!"

Irene fingered a nickey on her cheek. She wasn't sure she liked the young man's head on her knees. "Okay. What?" She hit a chord and tapped the box.

"How about 'Last Night I Dreamed'?"

"Or 'Enchanted.' "

"Or 'I'm Happy.' "

"Did you see that falling star over there!"

"Be sure it isn't a satellite moving."

"No, it fell. Whooom!"

"Make a wish."

"What good's wishing, dumb-bunny?"

"Doesn't anyone know an *old* song?"

"We're not old *enough*, yet," Pearl said, plaintive.

"Here's one," Russ said, reckless.

> *Kiss me, she sighed,*
> *Oh no, he cried,*
> *I shouldn't even be doing this!*

Dick cut in, "Pipe down, Russ."

"Yeah. Pipe down," Skin seconded swiftly, in his newfound role. He sat apart, lonely and proud, he considered.

Irene shifted her thighs uncomfortably; her knees were going to sleep a little under the weight of Russ' head. She frowned. "Well, if you can't make up your minds, here's 'Down in the Valley.' Everyone in the wide world knows that."

> *Hear the wind blow!*
> *Hear the wind blow.*
> *Hang your head over, love!*
> *Roses of sunshine,*
> *Violets of dew*
> *Angels in heaven know I love you!*

In an hour or more the Dipper had swung its handle up in the sky, the Beta and Alpha stars yet pointing inflexible at Polaris. Russ was gaping and once Irene heard heavy breathing that could be a snore. She was conscious that Madame Moret would have a ready epithet for Russ, and adamant advice for herself. Irene felt helpless, however, to deal with the moment; she simply resigned herself to waiting. The only thing she was positive of was if Russ laid a hand on her she was going to scream.

The Olsons' whistle blew: one long blast. Dick and Pearl got up. "That for you, Clara?" Dick said.

"It's just to let me know," Clara said negligently from the dark, her hand in Alan's warm hard one.

The young people began drifting to the beach steps, the boardwalk, paths. Irene let Russ carry her guitar as he followed her up to Linden House. After a brief scuffle there, she escaped indoors, to the honey-lit room where Eve was at her desk. Irene told herself angrily, as she dashed past her mother, carrying the guitar into her room, that she'd keep her self-respect at all costs. She simply and purely could not understand the masculine mind. She was not averse to being wooed, she thought, but she didn't have to be attacked! She wept a little, and sat up in bed reading, waiting for Pearl to come home.

Alan and Clara were sitting cross-legged at the edge of the black lake which licked at the Malraux beach. Alan had an arm about her shoulder, light and awkward. When they spoke they whispered as if someone had hushed them. "I'd like to go in, I think," Clara said. "If you'll promise."

"Listen," he protested earnestly, "we'll go by the pier posts. You can't possibly miss then even when it's dark. And you stay on this side and I'll stay on the other. Swear."

"Okay, *petit chou*. Hope to die though."

He got to his feet eager. "Wet my finger, wipe it dry." He ran it across his neck where the kerchief was knotted inside his shirt collar. "Cut my throat if I tell you a lie. Do you think that's enough?"

"Umm."

At the posts, she waited until his figure and the sounds of his bare feet were both gone. Then she removed her glasses and folded her shirt about them. She felt an extraordinary comradeship toward Alan because they trusted each other. She figured that surely he would kiss her when they reached her door later. He'd know enough to walk her home to the Owl's Roost probably, although it bothered her slightly. She slipped out of her shorts and the bra she always used now. She repinned more firmly some of her long hair that had got loose. The water was silk; she could see nothing, no end of it, no sky; it was the edge of the world. And it was cold at first, warm and pleasant as soon as she slid under.

She floated on her back, her hair weighting her head as it
sponged up the water. She looked at the stars, holding her breath
high for buoyancy. There was no sound from the water beyond
the pier. It was as if one dreamed, she thought, and when she
moved her fingers and let the fluid drip, the noise came forth like
plucking piano strings. The dark, robbing one of sight, changed
the sounds of day. Then she let her feet down on the sand to find
she'd lost her direction sense; she felt panic. Where was the shore?
There was nothing anywhere but the moonless black. The fright
grasped her and she thought, what of the dead! She'd nearly forgot
the body last year at this very time by the posts. It wasn't death
itself that scared her, but the fish-nibbled swollen thing she might
run into:

> But oh, more horrible than that,
> Is the curse in a dead man's eye!

She squinted terrified in the thudding of her heart, revolving
slowly, trying frantically to pierce the obscurity. She struck her
hand on her palm; one was red. No. She hit them together again to
teach herself not to do that; and then saw the head rising. She
felt a powerful terror; it was only Alan. "You had me worried! I
thought you were a spook," she whispered.

"You did?" he hissed, pleased; his black curls hung in wet
bangs on his princely forehead. He laughed, white teeth even, and
disappeared under.

She sighed, recovering, and began to swim slow strokes, self-
enwrapped. He rose up beside her and turned his head and squirted
water in a far arc. She asked, "Want to race?"

"No, I don't feel like it."

"Nice, isn't it?"

"I thought it'd be cold."

"Me too."

He took another mouthful of water and spouted. "Can you
do that? That must have gone four feet."

"No."

His nose bumped softly against hers. "Hello. I'm Alan Malraux. What's your name?" He put his hands firm and hard on her
hips, drawing her up to stand in the water beside him. He kissed
her slowly, his lips cold and sweet. When he drew away they both
ducked under, and then swam about again, separate. Clara heard

Mum's whistle, long, repeated; she sensed the emotion contained in the tiny throbbing. "That's yours, Clara."

"Hey look! Northern lights." The sky flicked white across the lake, like lightning.

"Maybe just a storm over there."

"No. It's the *aurora borealis*." She felt she'd sounded too definite, and added conciliating, "I think."

"Let's go on shore. I've got the shivers. Where's your hand?"

"Here!"

They rushed, pushing their strong bodies, their knees, against the water that foamed. On land they ran on the beach, light-footed, pacing. "Fun," he cried.

"What if someone comes? Where's our clothes."

"Man, we'll jump in the water," he laughed. He slowed, and held her to a halt.

"What."

"Can I?" he asked, tentatively putting his hands over her little breasts, breathing fast. "I just want to know what you're like."

She submitted, like a puppy being petted. She felt nothing but light happiness that a boy liked her, a Harvard freshman-to-be, too.

"Can I feel you here? I promise." He bent.

"Okay." She felt like a goddess, admired. She had no desire at all to touch or look closely at him. She stared at the black misted water, at the stars, at the dark head that was beside her, scented yet of vinegar that lingered.

"I can hardly see you, Clara."

"It's dark." He kissed her and put his hands on her back, pulling her to him. Then she felt his abrupt shaped nudeness, and when his mouth left hers, said, "You have to take me home." She leaned away, standing from him, pulling the pins from her hair to shake it sidewise, dripping. She coiled it and wrung the water from it, flowing loudly on the caked sand.

"But I want to stay down here," he protested. "Clara."

"That was Mum's whistle. Will she ever be mad. You should see my mother. Boy." She ran her hands through her hair, happy. "You going to walk me home though, *mon ami?*"

"Sure. What you think?"

They ran back, hand in hand; he brought his clothes to hers while they dressed. He touched her breasts again, serious, slipping his hand up under her jersey, while she put on her glasses and spoke through the hair pins in her mouth, "Aren't you glad we aren't grownups, Alan!" Everything, all conquest, she felt, was ahead of them. In sensing the infinity of her existence, she forgot the one beside her; he had become all lovers, all the men who would ever enter her life.

"Wait," he was pleading. "Don't go up, Clara."

"Wonder if I love you?" she whispered. "Do I? Do you love me? What's love?"

"Let's sit down here."

"Come on, Alan."

"Wait."

It came over her that a wall stood between each person and his neighbor. Alan had his wants, she hers. He wished now to do something to her, and she was afraid. The wall reared too between her and Mum, between Mum and Daddy, between Gus and Daddy, between herself and Gus so her brother hadn't even come tonight to Vespers with her, but angrily dismissed her from him because he wanted to catch some dumb bug! She wondered how many times in a life one could break down the wall, knowing instinctively that it must happen at some point. She said, "You wouldn't want to get me in Dutch."

"You're right." He capitulated totally. "I sure wouldn't."

The oscillating auroral streamers in the north sky became tinged with green and pink. Their activity increased, the hazy colored lights flooding far up into the horizon and subsiding. The two were stumbling up the boardwalk, walking off it sometimes into the black, losing direction. "I think I'm going to get the giggles in a minute," Clara said.

A heavy-bodied owl swept above, claws drawn in, viewing them clearly with fixed yellow eyes. He shrieked, catching hold of a heavy bough. The pair hurried, wary of his intruding influence. He bayed after them in deep staccato, "Huh–huh–huh–who-o-o-o-o?"

Clara said:

When the falling stars are shooting,
And the answered owls are hooting,
And the silent leaves are still.

Alan squeezed her hand. "Say, did you write that poem?"

"No. That's old daddy Lord Byron somewhere."

"Oh." Alan kissed her at the top of the boardwalk where they parted.

She went into the Owl's Roost alone. The lights were out and she tiptoed, feeling her way up the creaky stairs. The hall switch snapped on, and Mum was at the head of the stairs in her shortie gown, whispering, "Well, young lady? Didn't I think something had happened to you? I even told Daddy you were in bed so he wouldn't worry."

"Did you blow the whistle?" Clara was surprised.

"Twice." Mum spoke *sotto voce;* her face was creamed and it shone; lipless she seemed a tiny ghost.

"We never any of us heard you. Irene had her guitar and I thought we'd never stop singing. I wish Gus had come down. It was fun."

"Will you go to bed?" Mum said severely, and she added quite irrelevantly, "Do you think I don't know that you've been using mascara since winter? I see you're starting on eyeshadow too. I wish you'd stop, and I wish you'd please not wear anything but lipstick to the beach." Mum disappeared in her room.

Clara stretched out naked on her cot. She forgot about the wall and was adoring her friend Alan. She had done her room over this summer for the first time, painting everything in it baby blue, the iron bedstead, the wood bureau, the chairs. She got some dye and tinted her bedspread and dresser scarves too. She'd stamped it all as her own! Her skin was marble cold in the dark, and her unfastened hair soaked the feathers of the pillow slowly. She dozed and slept, her body warming, her locks drying, dreams overcoming conscious thought.

[15]

ABOUT two weeks later, on a Saturday morning, a yacht appeared at dawn, like a star-struck ghost, its sails and pointed arched prow mist-enveloped. Neither Jack Behmelmen nor Clara Olson, taking early dips, noticed it. The sun was behind the dune and all the beach in a cold shadow. The rays struck only at the lake, illuminating occasional areas, the light lying like a mirror on the water for an instant before the glass broke. As the pale yellow lamp of sun lifted over the sand hills, the foam broke pinkly, and then iridescent, like a cheap jewel. The pair of swimmers emerged from the water and trotted up, not visible to anyone who might be awake on the big cruising boat. By eleven the waves were pouring their sounds rhythmically; the dog-day cicadas were calling and answering each other in lengthy urgent vibrations; the sun became brassy and hot; the yacht started to glide in, the dozen people leaning along her rails sipping Bloody Marys and watching the shore through sleepy lids.

Of course by now the Pine Beach younger members, who were digging out a four-room sand house for themselves, knew it was there and planned to swim out in the afternoon, or to get Mr. Ardway to row them in the lifeboat. They tugged at the many-colored grains with their tiny hands, a quarter the size of big Monk's.

And Monk himself, with not a shade less enthusiasm than theirs, and certainly with no more stability of intent, was shaping a house too. He had talked Helge Lagerquist into coming to work full time with him. He justified the reckless salary paid Helge to Belle by theorizing on the money that would be coming in from the new summer houses they'd construct. First he planned to do a gazebo.

"You b.s.," Belle said restrainedly because Helge was present, "what in hell is that?"

"Dang it, gal, that's a fancy name for a little place just the size for honeymooners. It'll have one room and we're building in a table and benches at the far end, and then I'll haul out that old spinning wheel and maybe Mama's little organ from the firehouse shed too. We're putting up a half-loft floor with a ladder that goes to it, and a balcony over the lake view. There'll be a box spring and mattress up there to sleep on; and we'll paint the whole thing up yellow and red and blue with black curlicues or something. I spent a lot of time thinking this one up."

"Sounds like a trailer to me. What about cooking?"

"I already ordered one of those combination stove-refrigerators. Be cute."

"*Ja,*" Helge said. "Let's go, Mister." A taciturn man of slight build with thin strong limbs and a thatch of black hair, Helge insisted on giving good value for wages received. He sensed his employer's flightiness, his gaiety; all the dark Lutheran-infested Scandinavian blood in Helge balked. "*Ja.* Let's get going."

"You know that old broken-down cabin near my boardwalk?" Monk asked him as they strode out. "Well, that's next. An authentic log cabin, hum?" Towering above his companion, he clapped his lean shoulder.

"*Ja.*" Helge clenched the shovel willingly.

They were ahead of Dr. Bill and Gus, who followed on the curving road, coming from the Sand Castle. Dr. Bill had given Alan his last shots; Alan's passport was cleared; he would go in to O'Hare Airport on Monday, and to France. He was going to stay until mid-September when matriculation was scheduled at Harvard. "Doesn't seem very keen on the trip, does he?" Dr. Bill said to his son. "I thought he'd be wild."

Gus scuffed his tennis shoes in the dust. He was grateful that he'd been rescued from the work with Mr. Chapman. They were going to pick up lunch and head for a swim. "I'll carry your bag," Gus offered, extending a topsoil-smirched hand.

Dr. Bill handed it over. He spotted the men ahead with their shovels, climbing the bare dune bordering the Wigwam. "Let's take a look, Gus."

"Yeah."

Dr. Bill stepped briskly. He'd wakened Lisa for the first time in weeks last night when he'd come into the bedroom, and the tenderness he felt for her still lay in him. They dug their toes in the slippery grains, aiming for the spots where the spiked beach grass grew sturdy. The great mound was smoothly rounded, a few trees and shrubs held firm on its pockets. On the surface were fixed imprints of wind-waves; the tracks of the men before them looked like hooves of mammoths. "*God dag,* Helge!" Dr. Bill hailed. "What's it going to be this time, Monk?"

"A gazebo. Know what that is?"

"*God afton,* Doctor, Sonny." Helge was somber, viewing the problem.

"Good idea. Fine view."

"See, I wanted something different, dang it." Monk plunged his spade to the hilt beside him.

Gus stood, breathing hard from the climb, behind his father. "There's a ship." He pointed to the motionless yacht in the blue beyond the people-flecked sand. While the men talked Gus gazed at it; tired, he sank upon the sand to wait, the satchel between his insteps. Beside him was a spindly butternut and Gus' eyes came to center slowly upon an enormous caterpillar, a Hickory Horn-devil, making a straight and ponderous way up the trunk. Gus decided to get it before it got very much higher; it might not shake down. It was a beaut, over a third of a foot long, greenish brown, with three pairs of horns, more than an inch each, red and tipped with black. Its front legs and head, which were rearing and waving about as if to determine direction, were reddish too, and its squat prolegs yellow-and-black striped. It seemed in haste, ready to spin. He looked about for a branch on which to coax it, to get it home and into his cage. As he bent over, he heard Helge yelp in his high-pitched foreign tongue.

"Vad är detta? Son of a bitch!" And Helge's shovel was slamming against the butternut.

"Wait," Gus screamed, "it's a larva!" as the insect dropped, curled into a ball. He dived into the hot sand beside it.

Helge shoved him from the way with a stringy hand. "It's a poison worm, Sonny! *Gå er väg!"* And he struck the Horn-devil so the fluid oozed from it and the red protuberances crumpled like bent flower stems.

Gus got up from his position of indignity. No use talking, he felt. Daddy was already shrugging to let him know that the man just didn't understand, and Mr. Ardway was thinking it was funny. They were starting down the sand slope past the bushes to the road, half-sliding. Helge was turning the caterpillar over with his tool to get a good look before he covered with sand what he'd destroyed. Without plan or judgment Gus ran at him. "Double-double-double-damn bastard!" Gus' short-cut blond hair was damp; he was half a head taller than the wiry Swede, a third his age. Gus hurled himself at the dark bent face and, before the startled man could duck, had bruised his cheek; clumsily they grappled; Helge, angered at the unreasonable act, but deferent because this was the son of the doctor, hit with but a part of his strength.

Dr. Bill, after his first reaction, which was to move to rescue his heedless son, stopped scrambling back up the duneside in his sand-lumpy shoes, and put his hand on Monk's shoulder behind him. "What the devil?" he asked.

"Beats me. He collects them things though, doesn't he?"

Dr. Bill blinked in the noon haze, heaving because of his wade through the sand and his need for decision. Was that his *pojke* flailing like a little windmill, half-pinned by Monk's sweating black-haired helper? He saw the boy's face in a set frown which didn't alter when Helge's slaps on the shoulder and side felled him, sprawling at the edge of the dune. "I'll kick you down there, Sonny, lessen you stop now. You crazy in the head?" Helge appealed to Monk. "Time we get started to work, *ja?"*

"You're right," Monk boomed, passing Dr. Bill. He dragged Gus to his feet.

"Your hands off me," Gus grumbled. "Damn. Double." He stood surly, his mouth swelling where the braces had cut.

"Well, act your ago, boy. Huh, Doc?"

Dr. Bill grinned, "He is." He gazed around. "Christamighty, I forgot my kit. Where is it, *Pojke?*"

Gus shuffled, his hurt mouth pouted, his thin shoulders self-conscious. He brushed down at the sand with his fingers in an aimless dipping movement as he searched. "There it is." He ran for it, his limbs ungainly from a charley horse in his thigh which had twisted as he fell. Gus' throat was swelling so he feared mightily that he'd cry.

"How you doing?" Monk asked Helge.

The man was rubbing his dark-stained cheek, grinning, shouldering his tool. He touched his hand saluting the doctor half-way up the slope. "Quiet banty kicks the hardest. *Ja,* Sonny?" Helge wrinkled his face, anxious.

Gus wouldn't look at him, and slid after Dr. Bill, who waved, *"God dag!"*

As they gained the road, Dr. Bill spoke, bashful before his son. "I never thought I'd be praising you of all people for spirit, Gus. Always trying to understand you." He looked over at the grubby lip-swelled lanky one. "Don't know whether you're aware of it," he offered conversationally, "but I was reading that the old-fashioned country doctors were the original naturalists. You ever think of that?"

"Well, I don't care," Gus cried. "You know what that was? The larva of the Royal Walnut moth. That's what. They're plenty hard to find; that's the first one I've seen this year." He stamped his feet walking. "That darn boob."

"I was certainly impressed that you'd tackle a man. Where'd you learn such language?"

"I bet it was going up to spin a pupa. That's the way they do. It looked fully mature. I just bet."

"I only got a glimpse, but it was a fantastic-looking thing; you'll have to admit Helge picked one that did look poisonous, now. Are you sure it couldn't sting?"

"Daddy," Gus groaned. "They're as harmless as an angle-worm; looks don't ever mean anything." And his father's hand laid affectionately on his shoulder was nothing at all at this hour to Gus. What was done, he knew, was done. As he grinned painfully, the despair trembled within him again; he could still see it crawling, the suction pads of the prolegs gripping the butternut bark. It had raised up and fanned the air with the red front legs that later became the six of the insect that hatched. Its brilliant horns had fluttered, the wee head peered blindly up where the green protection grew. That Horn-devil was fully five inches.

"Ever tell you they used to call me the Black Swede?"

"Umm."

"That was in med school. I was a wild kid lots of ways."

"Oh."

"I don't see how you got mad enough to tackle that Scandehoovian there." The man was ebullient, swinging his bag, "Over a worm."

They went up on the Owl's Roost porch. Dora was in the kitchen. "Everybody's down at the beach," she declared. "You hear about the rich man's boat down there, Gus? Oho!" She sobered, "What's the matter? He been in an accident?"

Dr. Bill winked at the maid. "On purpose. Been in a fight. Let him alone, Dora."

They watched the boy turn, half hiding a limp, heard him running up the stairs, shouting, "Be down in a sec to go swimming, Daddy. I'm not hungry, Dora."

"All right, child." She looked at the doctor. "I'll fix him sandwiches. He never knows is he hungry or not."

"Well, I do. And I am. I'll be changed in a minute. I want to make a few notes first." He took his bag over to the settee and Dora followed, chattering, clearing away the lemonade glasses Clara and the missus had left.

"That young one's an eater from eatersville when nobody's around." Dora said.

He looked up at her. "Haven't changed your mind, Dora? About Herb?"

"No. I said I would and I will."

"I keep getting my hopes up that you'll back down." Dr. Bill grinned at her.

"I don't know what got into me. I'm packed and ready." She was going to hitch up to Herb the next evening, Sunday, at the Ideal rectory. Dora brushed back her wispy hair.

"The thing I don't get is why after keeping him standing on one leg for more than seven years, Dora, you have to get it over so fast."

"That's the way I'm constituted. I made up my mind. My grandmother used to say, you can take all day to boil an egg, but still you've only boiled an egg. Eh?"

"I can tell you right now, Dora, we'll never get on with your cousin Mable."

"You'll like Mable once you get used to her ways. She's what I call a quiet type. Not like me. I'll get your sandwiches for you." She rattled the glasses and hurried away.

Dr. Bill pulled off his horn-rims and laid them aside. He leaned forward, face in his palms. Slowly he rubbed his forehead with his fingertips, to ease the tiredness. He felt the thrill in him still; this was an entirely new piece of Gus he'd glimpsed. He'd thought all along his progeny was a real namby-pamby; he'd been disabused beautifully.

When they were down at the beach, Gus thought Daddy would never leave him alone. All kinds of people were out for the weekend and he had to tell everybody, "My boy got into a scrap with Helge Lagerquist. Surprised me! Listen to this." Daddy, who was always so quiet.

When Gus started into the water, Mum called to stop him, "Has it been an hour since you had that sandwich? You'll get cramps!"

The pain in Gus' thigh was intense now, and his lips ached on the thick-puffed inside where they were cut. Miserable, he knew he'd not do any of the things he wished: weep and lay his head on Mum's soft tan knees; ask Daddy to stop the pain; walk out into the cool lake. He slapped at the stinging flat speckled beach fly and sat alone on the sand at the shore edge, as if he were watching the moored yacht. The insect flew up in quick erratic circles, heading over to the chattering group behind Gus who were being photographed.

Belle Ardway was insisting, "Now I want to shoot a pyramid next. Now I mean it!" She had a pictorial history of her three boys—beginning with Russ, chubby, bald, toothless, out of focus, on his stomach upon grass in front of a plot of iris plants.

"*Cheese,* everybody," Mike Paoli called.

Smiling mothers knelt in front, holding the children before them; in back the older ones and the fathers, sheepish, jocular. Two of Jimmy Fox's offspring were in the photograph just taken, the older a balding thirtyish broker and the other a spinsterish woman clinging to her pair of children, a husband somewhere about. Clara Olson was babysitting for Angela, who was at the doctor's, and she held the yearling boy in his hand-me-down outfit tenderly, casually.

"Dickle-dickle, *petit chou!* Let me have a copy of that one, Belle, will you?" Clara asked.

"Bill," Elizabeth objected. "Will you tell Clara to stop calling everyone by their first name?"

"Flicka," Dr. Bill said.

"Okay. But be sure and let me have it for Angela, Mrs. Ardway?" Clara smiled deceitful.

"Jimmy," Someone called, "can't someone stand on your shoulders? Skin, will you? And put one of those Fox grandchildren on top of Skin. Let's cram the film with everybody!"

Clara went into the Paoli umbrella's shade, holding the baby against her woolish bright-blue suit. When she sat down and propped back on an elbow, she snuggled him against her. Secretly she let the baby's mouth lie close to her breast the way she'd used to do, experimenting, with her dolls. The head was so enormous; she wondered how it ever got out. Every time she thought of birthing she refused it. She knew the facts, but they had nothing to do with herself. As long as it was someone else, Angela for instance, she found it easy to understand. Boy, she didn't see how she ever could; she hated things to hurt her. The curtain drew across, dark and complete. She put her mind on his exquisite nose and the self-enraptured way the diminutive hands clutched each other.

"I have a brilliant idea," said Jimmy. "All of you lie flat. Mrs. Ardway, you set the camera on the sand here. Put Chouchou in the center. Now make a low shot of us all with tongues out, panting like dogs. Get it?"

"Down, everyone," Monk shouted, hiking up his Tussah silk trunks.

"Down, Chouchou. Here!" Jimmy laid his hand on Elizabeth's soft neck, threatening, "Down, now."

Elizabeth giggled, shrugging, "Don't, crazy."

Skin glanced at them. He wondered if Clara's mother ever kissed with Jimmy Fox. Ever since he'd seen her do it with Mr.

Malraux last year he'd been watching her. He hunted for Clara and saw her close by under the red-and-blue-striped umbrella with the Paoli baby. Skin had been talking with her just before Mom began this drippy picture-taking; for once Alan hadn't been hanging around. Last night Clara had let Skin kiss her down by the creek for a minute. He'd been surprised; she went off and on like a light; now friendly, then hostile. He'd been accusing her of hedonism before she'd told him to do it. "All you have in mind," he'd accused, "is the seeking of pleasure." This afternoon he felt he hadn't made his point at all. He sprinted over to her, as the adults began drifting out to the water. His father was hauling out the leaky lifeboat to give the smaller kids a treat; they were hollering dutifully in squeaky voices after him, having abandoned their sand castle. *"Hoh, hoh, hoh!"*

"Hi, Skin," Clara said. "I saw you standing on Jimmy's shoulders. And that kid on top of you. You looked like Mr. America. You've got good muscles, you know."

"Let's talk." He knelt, giving the baby a knobby forefinger to clutch and study.

"Oh you. Talk talk. Next it'll be moral relativism." She mocked him, lazy.

"Well, what's wrong?" he inquired. "I took that dumb ethics course too." He knelt on both knees over the girl and child, and felt the barrier; he struck it wantonly aside with his sword, "You're beautiful. But you know it, don't you!"

Her warm brown eyes were caught in his brittle blue ones and for the moment she was in love with Skin Ardway. It might not last, she told herself, but for right now, wasn't he cool? The noise seemed distant, of the people in the water, of Monk's roar as he overtook the swimming Jimmy Fox, of Pearl Thwaite's minute transistor radio tinkling within its leather case, as she went by with her new *amour*, Russ. Clara waited until Skin at last looked away from her, down at Angela's baby. The calescent sun flamed outside; the sand was ablaze. "Creeps, *mon ami,*" she whispered softly.

And suddenly the umbrella jolted, and there stood Alan, rude. He stopped so suddenly that sand sprayed up before him on the two inside and the baby. The two dogs followed pell-mell, and recognizing Clara rushed to greet her, long red tongues hanging.

The baby began to wail in a long-drawn culminating way. "Oh jeeps." Alan pulled the shepherds back by their studded harnesses.

"If you don't mind; this is private property." Clara slipped the baby about on her knee and jounced him so he lulled into a singing whine. She turned her dark frown on Alan, who'd plopped down on the sand, the dogs behind him. "This doesn't happen to be your umbrella, Alan Malraux."

"I'm sorry," Alan said hastily. "Man, Clara!"

She stared away and then looked to Skin; she patted the back of the hiccoughing baby. "Sure is plenty stuffy in here, Skin."

"Clara. I've got something for you!" Alan pounded his fist on the sand. "I left it with Dora. I've just been at the Owl's Roost. It's a present. I won't tell what it is but it's something you said you wanted bad."

"There's nothing I want. Except to be deprived of present certain company. Ugh."

Georgie Paoli came up behind Skin and put his little hands on Skin's shoulders. "My sister ate her lunch in a wet suit. I think she'll get sick and die, Clara."

Clara patted the sand. "Sit here, Georgie. No she won't."

The child relaxed with a sigh, leaning against her; he jigged his baby brother with an elbow. "One two three alari."

"It's because I'm going away, Clara." Alan put his hand out to the girl's leg and circled her ankle with his fingers. "And I'll miss the tennis court dance!" He hadn't been swimming and his hair was dry and stood up rumpled; the scent of sweat was yet on him.

She felt an anger within her, born of a small guilt because she'd loved Alan best only last week. It was a careless temper, and she dallied with Alan because he was nothing at all to her at the moment. She looked at Skin, cruel, "How will we ever endure life at Pine Beach without Alan?" She moved her foot to free it.

Skin warned Alan, grinning, "Clara's mean when she wants to be. Look out."

Alan clung to Clara's ankle. "I don't even like to go away. Man!" He hurled everything he was at her feet, feeling how precious she was, how well-made, how unattainable.

"Why go then?"

"Father says. But you ought to see what I got you." He tempted her. "It's what you want! Guess, Clara."

"Why don't you go swimming?" She wrinkled her face a little, and wriggled her foot loose. "Phew."

"I just will." He was scrambling up and going, offended, from their sight. His dogs slunk behind.

Five minutes later he had started throwing a baseball with the full-bearded Dick. The solid small globe whacked into the boys' cupped hands. Alan yelled, "Harder! Man," his voice pitched on a higher key than usual. The dogs barked faintly, racing after sandpipers with White Fang and Chouchou clear down to Behmelmens' beach and then up to the other end where the old pier stood.

"He's got a thing on me right now," Clara complained to Skin.

"How do you feel about him? I know you had a crush last year."

"I don't know. I sure don't." She hugged the baby and impulsively kissed the soft folds of his neck where the tuft of hair was downy. "Look how he is here, Skin."

"Ten alari, postman!" Georgie said, making a silly face up at Clara so she would nuzzle him too.

Within the umbrella all was still, and the four children scarcely heeded the noises outside. After a while Elizabeth came to look after Angela's baby, so Clara and Skin could dash into the water. Alan and Dick still doggedly tried their strength out, like brown giants, seeking somehow to wear down a part of the powerful river of energy that came in them in an unbid way, owning their bodies.

Elizabeth was half asleep, the baby in her arm crook, the little boy's head by hers. Pretty soon Angela was walking down the shore to join her. Angela smoothed back her short dripping locks. She was distended and made herself comfortable with a beach pillow on the huge white chenille towel decorated with a design of black footprints.

"Go and play, Georgie," Angela said, "so we can talk."

"When should I come back, Mama?"

"In an hour or so."

"What time will it be?"

"It's about four now, isn't it, Elizabeth? Come on back about five; then we'll go up."

"I don't know what five is, Mama," Georgie sighed, "so I better stay."

"Why don't you just keep within earshot," Elizabeth asked, "and we'll holler for you?"

"That'll be okay." Georgie strolled into the world.

"Who's is the yacht?" Angela asked.

"Someone from Chicago."

"Everybody's been going out there. Jimmy insisted I swim to it with him, Angela."

"He's got a thing on for you, Elizabeth, hasn't he?" Angela stirred. "I'll be glad when I can breathe normally again."

"Hoo. Jimmy's insane. And would I do it? No." Elizabeth laughed, and wondered why, even if there were no pressure, she just went ahead lying. She looked at the fist she'd made with her small hand, and remembered what Jimmy Fox had said about that. Even if it were something she didn't care a fig about, she always slightly extended the truth. Sometimes in her favor, sometimes not, just so the story were more colored than the reality, and her life seeming more exciting, herself as well. She would hear herself doing it and not be able to stop. They weren't ever black lies, never to Bill, or before that to her father, never anything largely mean but petty ones that didn't matter. She thought how she was small-natured, wondered at the paucity of what she gave to anyone. Bill had waked her last night, but there'd been no sense of prologue or even participation. Hadn't it been a dull event, bounded by habit even in the way she repeated the words of surfeit, pleasure? "I'm coming," she said, perfidious, for she wasn't and cared less. "Hoo, Angela, Jimmy hates to be told no." She almost asked it, bored with herself. She lit a cigarette, surprised to see her hand trembling so that the cardboard match broke. What was she upset about? she wondered.

Angela leaned over to take a cigarette. "I forget what it is to have men look at me. I feel about as exciting as a cocoon and just as maneuverable."

"Hoo." Elizabeth's wide eyes were hurt, unpurposed.

"I stopped by the Owl's Roost coming down," Angela said. And Dora had a big stuffed white lamb in the kitchen. She says someone just brought it over for Clara. It's all floppy and its eyes are closed, had a blue ribbon and bow!"

"And I just got her to pack her last doll away last fall," Elizabeth said. "Now the new parade starts."

"Do you remember!"

"Do I? What wouldn't I give to be Clara and sixteen? I can remember the first toy a boy gave me."

"Me too, a brown panda."

"Mine was a rag doll. I can even see its red-checked dress. The apron was tied on; it wasn't sewed to her." Elizabeth looked into her palm that had such a long life line, and an illness besides. "What I'd give."

"Not me." Angela patted herself. "No thanks. I like the real thing. Babies, Elizabeth."

They could hear the thudding of Alan and Dick's baseball. The hot sand stung the bare feet of the two young men. They had cigarettes clenched between their white teeth, and they half-laughed as they breathed in the smoke and hurled the missile.

[16]

On SUNDAY night, seven-thirty, Dora did take the muscle-chested, lean-faced Herb Worth to husband. Half-way through the words she thought, oho, she ought to walk out right now. All she was doing was trading one job for the next. She was getting twenty-seven dollars and board and time off when she pleased; she was a fool. She'd kept her maidenhead successfully through thirty-nine and a half years, and while the black-garbed chubby man recited, for better or worse till death do thee, she just realized that she'd made this decision largely as a matter of pride, wanting the title *mistress,* Mrs., before her name. She felt she'd pay for it, her mind uneasy on the night ahead. Her eyes touched over Herb's children standing behind the rector, a little lost-looking. Their grandmother had been unable to leave her bed at the farmhouse. Dora looked down at the heavy gold circle which fit loosely behind the large knuckle as Herb pushed it past with some difficulty.

"I do," he said loud, victorious.

"All right," she told the preacher, "I will too then."

They whirled toward the farm then in the sky-blue long Dodge, the boy and girl in the back seat, Herb driving a little too fast. For the first time in the couple's acquaintance, both were speechless, indrawn. The children hummed and softly chanted to themselves in unison, "Stagger Lee," as near as they could recall the jukebox version. Dora made herself quit thinking about whether Cousin Mable would get along with the boy Gus. If you didn't know people real good, it was easy to fancy they were something they weren't, Dora considered. Gus might seem babyish to some. She knew things like the missus Olson was unhappy and she'd stepped out on the doctor last summer; and was thinking of stepping out again with almost anyone who came along. And the doctor loved his children and there wasn't a time he didn't say the wrong thing to the boy, so they never got on; the girl child was just being kissed for the first time and was all in a pother, up and down, like a heifer. Cousin Mable would have to pick it all up slowly.

"Hot," Herb said. "Rain tomorrow. What you think?"

"Due for a true storm. It's the second week of August now."

"One's making up somewheres." He hammered the accelerator a little nervously and they spun the curve in a cloud of dust.

And the man was right. The heated westerly wind blew gently at seventeen miles an hour over the lake, which was now scarcely making whitecaps. This was the first wind, the later, made of heavier cooler air, would carry in it a yellowish dust from the stretches of South Dakota and Nebraska where the present high was. But it wouldn't reach Chicago until ten in the morning. The Weather Bureau put out warnings of course, during the night, regarding the front coming, and mentioned the seiche-breeding aspect which might develop after the storm. In Minnesota at nine-thirty in the morning, temperatures plunged and the Rochester streets were flooded; in Frankfort, Indiana, a lightning bolt caused a ten-room farmhouse to go up in flames, the housewife telling reporters later that she and the four children watched the bolt tear apart the breakfront in the dining room where they sat, before scrambling out through a whirl of dust and smoke. Down in Florida in the rain-swollen Hillsborough River area, a fourteen-year-old girl was swept to her death and a hundred families fled their homes, with a damage estimated near three million to the two local counties.

Alan Malraux had slouched down to the lake after a late breakfast, wearing his light black jacket and swim trunks. The wind was increasing a little, the water ruffling, as he dragged the seventy-six-pound metal canoe down for the season's last time. He was taking the 3:02 South Shore in the afternoon, and at O'Hare International Airport, had been booked on a jet Constellation. When he reached home in September, Chappy would have him packed and he'd go at once to Cambridge. Ernie'd have stored the metal canoe with his old orange cedar one in the garage by then, up on the rafters. Alan yawned as he directed the dogs to jump in the craft before he pushed free of the sand. He'd been up late in the night, wanting to finish the humor piece for the *Trumpet's* alumni column. Clara would probably think it was pretty crumby; which it was, he thought. It was supposed to be a radio dialogue, where you switched stations:

ANNOUNCER: This is the Kentucky Derby and it's a great day in Louisville. They're off and the horses now are—
LADY: Scrambled well. Add a dash of salt and a very tiny pinch of *fines herbes* and one—
SINGER: Bride, tall, fat and wide! Here comes the groom who's as thin as a—
COMEDIAN: President in the White House, having tea with the ladies, while the V.P.'s in the basement, washing nigger ba—

And so on. Alan had got hysterical composing it at midnight, but he knew even then that by the true light of dawn it would be flat as a flapjack. He really didn't care, because he was slightly sore at Clara anyway for her unaccountable snootiness under the umbrella yesterday.

He hopped in and paddled down the shore, past the Pine Beach raft, which was bobbing and smacking heavily in the young waves. Jojo barked when a flock of gulls swirled overhead with voices like lost children, but obedient lay down at the boy's word. Alan hadn't really cared to go see Father, but now that the time was upon him, he felt a shivering of excitement. He had no idea what he might experience. His mind hung back on Clara's body again, which she'd let him touch that night, thank gosh. He felt entirely friendly toward her even in rebuff, a feeling related to that part of him which had begun to assume such high import.

Ernie, a few years before, had explained a procedure he called jacking off, which was supposed, Ernie claimed, to keep your mind clean. Alan felt now that his life was moving swiftly forward and Ernie's rustic rules were left far behind.

He moved the boat down the shore a long way, forgetting time. He was close to Michigan City. The lake bottom began to take on the aspect of bedrock rather than sand. The water was roughing heavily as he made a rudder of the oar and wheeled for the return. The dogs stirred uneasily on the metal floor, crouched as commanded, but on bent haunches, eyes on his face, braced as the canoe bumped on landing after each wave. Alan loved this sort of sea! If there was one thing Alan considered dreary, it was constant calm. He knelt against the thwart and thought how he preferred the cedar canoe though. Father said no, because he thought Alan careless and this one was unsinkable. But it didn't handle as well for it was too heavy; and he didn't like the welded bottom where rivets cut his bare knees.

His jacket was open at his bare silky-skinned chest, the brown hair soft yet, lengthening. Jojo's growl rumbled as they dipped into a wave and the spray scattered over him. Alan laughed at the animal, "Easy, fellow." He was scornful of summer people who wanted the lake to be their private indoor swim-pool, he thought, warmed to the right degree! When lightning would lick down, they ran frightened of electricity. He didn't. He sneaked away and swam in storms, loving the quick-moving drama, the hot rain spattering, and the dark mutter of thunder.

The sun was a lightbulb overhead where the soaked rugs of clouds bagged low, lifting and falling again as the warm and cool air, the light and heavy, fought, mingled, whirled, seeking stability. Storm warnings were up, of course, in Benton Harbor, Michigan City, circling the Great Lake, three hundred and seven miles around. The signal was a white pennant above a square red flag with black center; it indicated a front of marked violence approaching, the winds birthed in the northwest. At the Potawatomi Bible Club beach, the guard on duty at ten-thirty hoisted their yellow flag. He chased a few resentful teen-age boys off the beach when they insisted on leaping into the breakers. Alan meanwhile, down the shoreline, decided to ride his canoe in and beach it at a deserted spot while the flurry passed through. He stripped his jacket off inside out, onto the sand, and the German shepherds lay on it while he took a short swim. They refused to accompany him.

There was no rain in the Pine Beach area, although Milwaukee was doused by three inches, including one downpouring of half an inch in seven minutes. The temperature, between ten and ten-thirty, dropped in Chicago from ninety-three to sixty-eight. At O'Hare Airport the gale was measured at seventy-five miles per hour. All airlines canceled their flights until further notice. Trees in the city suburbs were toppled and branches torn; wires tangled and power connections became disrupted. The Ideal Telephone Company ceased service to Pine Beach, Sawmill, Ideal; the operator went home for the day. Bell Company had difficulties too, restoring service to their customers by late in the afternoon.

Angela Paoli set about mopping the kitchen floor while Albert limped through the rushing air to tell Dr. Bill. Angela was in no hurry, having been through it five times. She planned to give the baby a bath and put the cabin in shape to while away the time. The phone was dead and she was unable to call Mike long distance in Chicago, or her doctor in Michigan City. Mike had been gazing out of his high-floor classroom at the time, at the sudden-darkened streets, rain-lashed, pierced by auto headbeams. Thunder pounded and lightning cracked about the *most glorious view in Chicago,* the Observation Deck of the Prudential Building. Water hammered at the city's mountains of windows. Then, as suddenly as it had pounced upon Chicago, the storm fled east-southeast. The sun unveiled its face and people everywhere came into doorways to stare at the quick stillness.

A seiche-spawning condition was being confirmed by the Weather Bureau, which issued continual fresh warnings that violent swells were expected to commence near one in the afternoon. The barometer dived nineteen inches. The northwest gale, which had been piling the lake water at the opposite side, abruptly died. At the same time a new slow wind, a seventeen-miler, arrived from the east. As the released uninhibited water dashed back, across the one-hundred-eighteen-mile expanse, the young wind aggravated its fury. The swell went plunging sixty yards as far as the sidewalk at the North Avenue beach in Chicago. Then the wall like a tidal wave returned to the other shore, causing the lake level at a

Michigan City pier to drop over nine feet in three minutes. A series of swings was setting in. A seiche. That first wave had trapped fifty-three fishermen out on a breakwater at Benton Harbor; six lost their lives, hanging to the rope. An account appeared in the *Trib* the next day, describing the event and mentioning things they dug out of their morgue of files, one being that scientists reported Lake Michigan having dropped three hundred and fifty feet below the present level six thousand years ago during one remarkably extended seiche, so that Indian shore dwellers had difficulty keeping abreast of the receding levels.

After Alan's dip in the sea, he'd gone to slip on his jacket and lie on the sand to take a short snooze and wait out the squall. He had been weary from the late hours the night before, and from the violent morning exertions. He had slept deeply. His watch read near one o'clock when he awakened, hungry. Racing down to the angry sea, damp trunks scratchy, sand in his teeth and ingrained in his heavy hair. Shoving the canoe out, the dogs scrambling in between the thwarts. The water line had noticeably withdrawn and the edge, formerly lake bottom, was soft and gravelly. But he paid no heed; the sign meant nothing to him. He paddled far out on the choppy waves, seeking to avoid the short surf, unthoughtful of danger. He bent the craft northward toward home. Ernie would be put out at his tardiness.

It was 1:16 when the tall vicious returning roller approached slowly. Alan saw its strength like Armageddon. "Man," he spoke into the terror, never having seen one like it except in a dream. He dug his paddle to wheel and attempt riding the huge thing in; he saw that was his only chance. His canoe responded, and halfway in its turn, the whirling foam came spilling and spinning. Boy and dogs were sucked into its motion. Alan met the enemy bold and stubborn. He fought it even as he was dragged down to the sandy stirred-up bottom. The tremendous undertow held him there until it filled his struggling lungs.

Jojo and Bosco, guided by instinct, half-drowned, strong-muscled through their master's training, pawed their way to shore. They were two hours reaching it, for the swell charged at them and then past them in its strong backwash. They landed unnoticed just below the Potawatomi area where the Clubbers were assembling to deplore the carnage. It was as if some beast of legend had visited from the ocean; boats were mauled, the life-guard stand tilted foolishly, one sailboat was dragged off, and small craft gnawed and disgorged high on the bank.

The dogs whined on finding each other, and then went trotting back and forth, their harnesses heavy upon them, slick-skinned like wet rats, along the water edge, not certain of what they sought. They dodged, growling when a last comber plunged and gushed at them. As it receded they stood in the half-cool, noses lowered, sniffing, nudging each other's shoulders, forepaws motionless in the water. At length they shook themselves, spattering, fluffing their fur, and began to lope toward the Sand Castle. They passed the scattered people of the Potawatomi Bible Club, and Behmelmens' property, where *The Desire* had been whirled about and driftwood was caught in sand washed in the boat. They padded through the shallow creek that had fanned in backwash, and along the unmarked sand of Pine Beach, at length scratching tiredly in the grooves they'd dug since puppyhood in the side entry door.

When Della Chapman saw them there, her singing ceased, her heart quailed, and she felt she was done. She let them in, to plop exhausted on the linoleum, ribs standing out where the wet hair clung, harnesses appearing too large. Chappy had many times feared for her charge, and as many times seen him return, boshing her for her silliness, indignant slightly at her attempt to unman him. She screamed smally, and then ran up the stairs. Ernie was out on the roof where the crows-nest perched, restoring a broken lightning rod. "Alan," she said. "The dogs are back; just the dogs."

"Whoo-eee." Ernie paled and his hammer slipped and slid from him, knocking all the way until it softly gained the ground below. "You sure?"

Trembling, the over-mid-aged pair stumbled down into the house. Ernie tried the phone to be certain it was dead, and then trotted down the steps to the drive. He got into the Chrysler and drove over to Sawmill, trying to locate the sheriff who, they said, was away at another drowning. Della, her gray hair fluttering about her round screwed-up face, hustled down the beach stairs. She kept pausing at each landing and shading her eyes, squinting at the shore and the white-freckled gray expanse. What was she doing, fussing about, coming down here? Perfectly foolish, she thought, and came to a halt at the dune's foot. Were Alan alive, or were his body somewhere on land, wouldn't Jojo and Bosco have stayed by it? If there were any hope even, wouldn't the two of them be here at the shore? She could hear the boy asking the questions. "Chappy, how loony can you get!" She began to cry openly and went one foot at a time back the long steep way. She couldn't go into the house though, where the bedraggled dogs would thump their tails on the floor, affectionate, hopeful of food. She wandered over to Thwaites' next door where the new Linden House was nearly completed. The pretentious top storey had been removed and the ground floor redesigned to resemble an old-fashioned English cottage.

She could hear the widow's typewriter as she stood on the stone slabs. When it paused she went up and pulled the little string, making the bell tinkle inside. Mrs. Thwaite, pencil in hand, wearing gray Bermudas and a frilly blouse, welcomed her absently. The collie rose from the rug to greet Della, who pushed it away with a rough hand. "Go on!"

"Behave, Bobbie," Eve said; the dog paid her no heed, shoving its smooth head against Della's fingers.

"Alan," the housekeeper began in a plaintive whine. The lower part of her face crumpled and her lips folded in.

The door dashed open, and Irene and Dick strolled in. "Hi, Eve," Irene said. "Hullo, Chappy. Back in a sec with my racket, Dick." Irene ran into the other room.

Eve nodded to Dick, their eyes meeting, the woman's cool and retired, the bearded young man's a little afraid. "Sorry to bust in on you like that."

"It's Alan Malraux; he's missing, I believe."

"Does my dad know!"

"Mrs. Chapman? Does he?" Eve patted the shoulder of the woman who sat with hands crossed in her lap, gazing down, whimpering. "I guess not, Dick."

"I'll go get him." He was gone, light-footed on tennis shoes.

Dick had a time hunting down his father. He bellowed for him from the top of the high dune where the gazebo was being completed; neither Helge nor his dad was there and it smelled of fresh paint. He yelled into his home at the front-porch door,

"Dad! Where you!" Belle came out peeved from the bedroom where she'd been trying to catch a nap. Dick left his mother open-mouthed and ran down the hollow to the Owl's Roost.

There he learned from Mrs. Olson that Dr. Bill had asked Monk to go in to Ideal and find a phone that was working, to let Mrs. Paoli's doctor in Michigan City know that she'd had her child at home, and that he might come to call at his leisure; meantime Dr. Bill was going to pick up Murdock, who'd move into the Paoli's cabin for a few days. Monk was also to send a wire to the father at the University, advising that all was very well and that Angela had already given the baby its name: Billy. Monk wouldn't be back until at least four o'clock, Elizabeth informed Dick as they talked out on the porch.

"Isn't that a nice little beard." She reached a gentle hand to feel it. "Think I ought to let Gus grow one some day? He's not old enough yet, is he?"

"Alan!" Dick stuttered at last, protesting her casual gesture, clutching to him his moment of glory. "They think he's drowned, Mrs. Olson!"

"Where's Gus?" Elizabeth said immediately. "Mable." She ran to the kitchen. "Where are the children!"

"Here, Mum," Clara called from the couch in the front room. "Hey, why?"

Mable was leaning at the counter with a pink mug of coffee, leafing through a cookbook. "The boy's upstairs in his room, missus. He wouldn't even help me close them windows, when the wind came up. Said he was busy." Mable was aggrieved, thinking Cousin Dora sure had spoiled the kids in this house.

Elizabeth was putting her hand to her forehead. "Why did I do that? Poor Philip." She was smitten with her reaction, aghast that she'd thought first of her own. She hurried back and put her fingers on Dick's arm, urgent. "Stay a moment and tell me."

"I have to go. I better find Jimmy Fox. I hope he's not gone somewhere too. We got to get the lifeboat out. We got to do something!" He wheeled and his footfalls scudded down the stairs.

Clara came in the doorway, in faded shorts and an old shirt of Daddy's, pencil in hand. "What's wrong?"

Elizabeth looked over, uncertain. "I don't know exactly. Something may have happened to Alan Malraux."

"Like what."

"Could he really have drowned?"

"I don't believe it, Mum."

"Well that's what Dick said. But he exaggerates."

"I don't believe it a minute. Ugh." Clara flushed. "He's flying today. France. Remember?"

"Don't you think the flight was canceled? I've been so excited about Angela's time coming I forgot he was going today." Elizabeth had given Alan a message for Philip. *Tell him we're fine here, but we wish he'd come back. Everyone in Pine Beach misses him.* She had wanted her former lover to know she hoped him happy.

"Besides," Clara declared flatly, "he wouldn't take the canoe out in this weather; Alan's no dope. He's probably gone for a beach hike. Heck." She walked into the house. "I might go down and see what's going on, though." She dropped her pencil suddenly and went.

Elizabeth didn't hear; her hands were at her cheeks. "This was what you always were afraid of, Philip. Poor Philip."

Then she heard the new sound and so did Gus upstairs and Mable in the kitchen; the siren scream flowing from the Studebaker in which the sheriff and three of his uniformed men traveled. And so did Clara, running to the beach. When she reached it Ernie and Jimmy Fox and Dick were with the officers in a group on the sunlit glaring flooded sand. She caught up with them and trailed after as they walked north and almost an hour later south. They decided there was no point in taking any boat out, since the storm had churned up the cold deep water, and the body would surely remain on the bottom a while.

Weather had a lot to do with it, the rumple-shirted sheriff affirmed; a hot day sometimes brought them bouncing right up. A couple of metal oil drums had been washed ashore and two of the troopers were rolling them down the wet beach, walking on the sides, fooling around like noisy kids, their boss thought.

"Want to give it a try?" one of them called to Clara, friendly.

She shook her head, frowning, and smiled slightly, "Guess not."

When the Potawatomi Clubbers were questioned, some of them had noticed the dogs running down the beach, but thought nothing of it. The sheriff went on his way then, advising Ernie that they'd send a man over to do some searching every day or two. Clara watched all of them go up; it was six-thirty, and Mable would be peeved because she'd missed supper. She gazed at the long gray stretching water, under which Alan's body rolled. She had no notion, she thought, why she'd been so mean to him the day before yesterday under the umbrella; she couldn't fathom it. She shoved her bare feet into the cold grains, feeling chilly as she mounted the boardwalk.

She dreamed that night of protecting things from enemies, human or fire or vague beasts. There were great blazes and yelling and she dashed about fighting and saving something. She awoke in a small hour, hearing herself speak, and turned over impatient at her uncontrol. She began to think about Alan, listening to the fog horns in one of the harbors down the thick-misted lake, blahing raucous all the dark long. She thought about that humor piece he'd forgot to write for the school paper; she considered how he'd have been over the ocean by now, droning to Paris. In the pocket of her arm was the woolly drowsing lamb. She cried herself to sleep.

When she awoke at five, she sprang from the bed vigorous, determined. She knew she'd find it, getting into her suit. The lucent moon over the black sand in the insecure light was split in half, mounted very high. She felt the chill scene as she struck southward. Daylight overcame the orb's brilliance; by six it faded into the sky. She met Ernie Chapman returning from the north, Jojo on his heels, Bosco ranging up by the beach grass. The dogs reared up on Clara's blue soft-fabric suit and licked her face, claws digging in her flesh; she patted them. Their coats were drenched, and Bosco's leatherish pads left on her shoulder strap a smudge of tarry stuff that came from oil barrels tossed by the furious surf. A little later Jojo threw up a dead sea thing he'd eaten. His cheeks puffed and he erupted it casually, his tail to the humans. He sighed and trotted away, sneezing and wrinkling his lips. Clara rumpled his fur, "What'samatter, huh?"

Ernie was shrunken-faced, his beard cropping out, uneven. "Mr. Malraux'll be here on the 10:20."

"You think he might be alive some place?"

"The wire came through at three a.m. this morning."

"Maybe he swam in somewhere, Mr. Chapman, that we don't know about. Creeps."

"*I don't know.* Whoo-ee, though."

"Your dune looks good up there." Clara waved generously at the slope where Ernie and Gus had been busy dealing with the movement of sand grains and wind.

"None of that son-a-bitching kudzu choking out the evergreens like that damn bastard from Chicago, Mr. Jim Fox, plants, either," Ernie said viciously, wondering at his anger.

"Yeah," Clara agreed, her throat constricted suddenly, liking his vehemence. She repeated the swear-words to herself. *Roll on, thou deep and dark blue son-a-bitching bastard damn Lake Michigan, roll. Ten thousand fleets sweep over thee in vain. For a moment like a drop of rain man sinks into thy depths with bubbling groan, unknelled, uncoffined, and unknown! Without a grave even.* Or something like that. Bastard damn anyway.

There were all sorts of debris on the mirror-shining shore. The dogs found a small battered sturgeon and growling with each other tugged at it, one pulling the suckerlike mouth, the other the bony tail. Ernie cast one more glance at the horizon and walked up to the Sand Castle steps, not speaking again to the girl. She watched him go and sat down on a piece of dampish driftwood and threw sticks for the German shepherds to retrieve with eagerness, instantly obedient, their brute eyes slavishly fastened to her moving arm. When it got near breakfast time she had trouble with them sneaking after to follow her, and she had to yell at them before they'd stay at their own beach, tails wagging, heads low, fawning.

Later, Ernie was somehow again enraged as he sat on the nicked bench in the South Shore station in Michigan City, reading the headline: SON OF FAMED NEWSMAN DROWNED. Neither he nor his wife had spoken to one of the biggety britches who came around last night asking questions. That brown-nose sheriff, Ernie thought, sucked right up to them and told them what they wanted to hear. His employer was due on the next coach from Chicago, and Ernie had come in the Chrysler so they could beat the bus to Pokagon. He squirmed, miserable, on the seat. The line was always late, ten minutes past due now. He'd abandoned the comfort of his used overalls for a town pair of brown pants and a starched shirt, the collar of which irritated his leathery neck. He got up and circled the almost-empty room; he purchased a bar of Ex-lax from the cashier and chewed two squares of the chocolate while he stood at the glass door. All his joints ached; he decided he was getting the all-overs and it was a sign it was about time for Ernie Chapman to stretch out on the little slab in the undertaker's parlor. The far whistle hooted.

He handed Mr. Malraux the Michigan City News while they drove homeward on Highway 12. "We ain't neither of us spoke to them reporters either," he said.

The man just stared at the page after looking it over. Ernie somehow had expected him to rip it or something. But he only ran his long fingers through the bushed red hair. "And how's our Chappy making out, Ernie?"

"Della's all right. What else, ain't it?"

"It was unsinkable," Malraux stated it firmly, folding the newspaper compactly.

He repeated the words in the afternoon when he stood on the smooth-brick terrace with a pair of troopers the sheriff sent over. They came with the news that the aluminum canoe had been towed in by an early-rising fisherman. The three walked down and halted on the hummock above the gray-headed pier posts. Fully clothed, even to footwear, the men appeared strange in contrast to the sunning resorters down the sand in scant suits dyed in primary colors.

"That don't matter, sir," the deputy answered him, "see there's all kinds of things. He could of been hit by the boat and knocked out. More likely the canoe got thrown one way and him the other. We figure the kid thought the squall past and then's when he made a mistake. See, the seiche don't work like a regular storm. It's the sudden swells are dangerous. He must of went straight into one. The Bureau'd warned all small boats off the harbors and all swimmers off beaches. Clear up the Great Lakes. Lots of folks drowned though. All here and there. They always do; they don't pay attention."

"He's right," the younger one said, "there was six drowned at the Benton Harbor breakwater. A pier full of fishermen had allowed the storm was done when the wind quit blowing and the rain went around. They was out there with casting poles."

"A baby tornado banged through Kalamazoo. Know that?"
They dwelt on the performance, hashing it about.

"This has been what I call a year. Set a record. Man!"

Philip glanced at the young man; he had black wavy hair
and Philip thought he talked the way Alan did, challenging, abandoned.

"I understand your son was about to take a trip. It's a
shame, sir."

"There's nothing for me to do then?"

"You just wait."

"In other words, the body might never turn up."

"That's right, sir. Sometimes they don't."

"Ridiculous! What about sounding over the water. Aren't
there new methods for this sort of thing?"

"No sir. Get some real hot weather, once in a while it helps.
But you can't tell. See, it's fifty-fifty, sir."

Philip felt the thing like a rat in his belly that turned and
twisted, dissatisfied. He fought it. He'd seen death of every kind
and told himself, this was a clean way for anyone to go. The
boy had had no unhappiness; he'd had his freedom; his death was
quick. Philip had seen men who'd taken a week at dying, tor-
tured, broken-toothed, swollen-fingered, cast into a yellow dust of
a road in a loin rag as a pregnant lesson to others. He'd seen men
bent and broken; a man was a man, Philip considered, and his son
no better than they. Alan hadn't had time to make a hero.

Philip battled the rat down. He walked with the men as far
as the first landing and while they went on their way, he rested at
the log bench. My Lord, he thought, will I ever bear it. He was
amazed at his hurt and how it enfeebled him.

The lake was a bright blue jewel and the sand sculptured in
swirled lines where the combers had rolled up for the first time in
years. Philip hoped the body was never found. Let it stay in its
wet grave. How could you stuff Alan into the ground! If the
sheriff's men did find the corpse, he'd have it cremated and the
ashes thrown back in. He would not look at it. The boy always
had gone to the lake like it were his mother, riding the old cedar
boat that he loved on its breast. The slow way of inland waters
was fetching, never conveying the brutality of brine-tasting oceans

where tides ran and depths were unmeasurable. The lake was a small woman, slow-spoken.

There'd been a woman Philip had had who didn't care enough for him, of leisurely foolish words, with a little body and rather small longish breasts and a habit of making questions where there were none. In the lands he'd gone to, in noisy squalid places flanked by stone splendors, and in cold quiet worried countries, he couldn't rid himself of her somehow. She had remained with him. He'd awake and fold and refold in his mind a night, and what she'd done and he, and recall the soft near-drawl, "Hoo!" Until he was angry after a while at himself. How foolish she was, her lips light and her laugh deliberate always and pleased. She stirred him no more. He'd noted her down the beach in a plaid suit, half an hour ago, tanned face within the yellow frame of hair turned toward where he was with the troopers. He'd felt only tiredness, bent from any emotion.

He was a little frightened of the rat that was awake. He crooked his head onto his hands, sitting quietly. A few indigo buntings, the males colored and the females like drab sparrows, came into the pine boughs in the tops of the tall narrow trunks shooting into the sky above the stair landing. There was no eye to appreciate the effect of their colors playing against the prickly green needles and the polished piece of lapis lazuli that was set beyond.

[17]

A COUPLE of days went by and late in the afternoon of the second Dr. Bill came down to join his wife and daughter for a dip before supper. He had brought along a bar of soap and Clara watched him standing in the shallow water up to his knees, rubbing the white lather under his arms and over the hairs of his torso and on his broad shoulders. It came upon her with abruptness that Daddy was getting older each day and there would be the time she would look for him and he would be gone. The wave of love for him that came rode in upon the current of despair, because wasn't she older too? He laved the water on himself in a slow happy movement that told her of his comfort. He turned and grinned, "Catch, *Flicka!*" tossing the soap to her.

She laughed back, eager. "Dopey!"

"Bill," Elizabeth got up and ran down to the edge of the lake. "There's Philip walking. Come on, let's go talk to him. Shall we?"

"Fine. One minute." He plunged under and the soap foam dissolved in his wake. Then he walked out, pushing his legs slowly. "I'm beat." He put an arm about Clara's shoulder.

She hugged his bareness; her bright suit became her dark

hair and eyes, she knew. "Divine, divine man. Oh, Mum, how did you ever catch Bill Olson," she giggled.

"Flattery will get you nowhere."

Elizabeth walked a little ahead of them, stepping quickly. She waved, "Philip! Oh?"

"He sees us," Dr. Bill said. "He's not going to run away, Lisa."

"Do you think they'll *ever* find him?" she whispered back, demanding.

"Who can tell, Lisa."

"Don't talk about it, will you, Bill?" She frowned.

Clara set her mouth and scuffed the sand as she walked, clinging to Daddy's waist. She looked to Mr. Malraux through her lowered lashes, eyes nearsighted, unable to glean if he were unchanged. She didn't like him. She had no doubt she was the one who'd find Alan. No point talking about it, but she would. The new sensation like a blade sliced in her, and she set mind upon closing the wound, leaning her hair upon the close shoulder, bumping it.

Philip had walked north for half an hour, and since he'd forgotten his sunshade, his freckles stood out large in his long pale face, a little sweated. He wore a shabby green pair of swim trunks, a size too small, that he'd found in a drawer in the guest room. His dark glasses hid his eyes, and he seemed somewhat frail to Elizabeth. The sun near the people was standing on a fan of white rays that the Pine Beach children said meant the water was being sucked into the sky. "Hello, Bill. Elizabeth."

"Well." Dr. Bill took his hand, warm.

"Hello?" Elizabeth said.

"Dammit to hell, Bill," Philip essayed a chuckle, folding his arms, clasping his ribs. "Shows there's no sense trying to thwart fate. Very thing I was most afraid of, so I got him one that was self-righting, flat-bottomed. Ernie says he didn't even like it and was always after him for the cedar one. Try and make up a philosophy out of that."

"Lordamighty, it's no time for philosophy, Philip. I lost someone this last spring. You sort of wade your way through." Dr. Bill gestured to the acting sun. "Sometimes that sort of thing helps. Beauty. And then again it makes it harder."

"Maybe I'm bothered because he's not been found," Philip said. "Think he'll float up? You ought to know. Doesn't he have to rise to the surface?"

Dr. Bill held Clara tightly. *"Lord, how long shall I cry and Thou will not hear; even cry out unto thee of violence and Thou will not save."*

Elizabeth was impatient, slapping her small round hip where the suit was smooth-fit. "He asked you a question!"

"Alan gave me a lamb, a big white one," Clara said. "It was expensive and I love it, Mr. Malraux. It's beautiful, with a ribbon. Alan and me had a good time on the beach the day before. I'm glad I was nice to him. Belle took photographs of everybody!" She ended helplessly, and looked down at her legs. She leaned on Daddy; a liar, and bird-witted besides, she thought.

"Philip, what are you going to do now?" Elizabeth asked. "Are you going to stay the summer? What about the Chapmans?"

"I had no relationship at all with that kid." Philip looked at Bill. "Dammit to hell. My son. I thought bringing him to Paris would be good. We'd kind of be on my ground and it'd perk him up, so we'd find each other maybe. I don't know why I didn't do it earlier in the summer."

"He worshiped you," Elizabeth said.

"If the body's close in where it's shallow," Dr. Bill shrugged, "it'll come up quickly, but if it's drifted far out, and so on, it could just never be found. It doesn't really matter to you, does it?"

"What was that from the Bible, Bill? *Even cry out unto Thee of violence and Thou will not save.*" Philip pulled off his tinted glasses and blinked his gray eyes.

"This spring Monk Ardway's mother died." Dr. Bill almost shook his fist. "Funny thing, too, she died of old age, nothing more. But it was as if she were torn away, ripped from my hand. I can't explain it. The thing I'm saying is, don't let the fact of his youth increase the grief. Death's always terrible."

"Bill," Elizabeth whispered. "You're hurting him. Will you not talk like that?"

"One has to talk, *älskling.*"

"You always say that; do I believe it?"

Philip looked at Elizabeth dully. "Still ever asking questions, isn't she?"

"What do you mean?" Elizabeth sounded hurt.

Philip spoke to her, "When you heard my son was lost did you think of me or your own?"

"Didn't I think what anyone would?" she cried. "Of the father of the child?" She turned to Bill. "Didn't you?"

"I thought about Mama Ardway," Dr. Bill said. "And how I'd like just a visit with her."

"You *must* have thought of your own son," Phillip said nearly desperately to Elizabeth.

"No. You think I should have, Philip?"

"Everyone turns to his own," Philip said. "I'd have thought of Alan. I always did when I saw hurt children. I wanted him safe and normal."

"Alan was an unusual kid," Dr. Bill told him. "He came hunting with Gus and me last winter. A blizzard had started and the ducks were bedded past the ice. Alan shot the only greenback we got. My boy can't fire a shotgun and hit a barn door."

"Let's see, Gus wants to be a scientist?" Philip asked.

"An entomologist," Clara stated, "of the first rank. Ugh."

"But I was amazed at Alan's skill," Dr. Bill said. "He told me Ernie Chapman trained him. Brought it down with a single shot and reloaded in the same movement. And the dog was trained to retrieve too."

"Never cared for hunting," Philip said. "One time I blew apart a turtle with someone's gun just for fun, and it almost destroyed me that I was responsible. Of course, I've seen a lot of man-killing too."

"Well, your boy was a true Viking that day, I thought. We got along fine. I was wishing he were Gus even."

"You were?" Philip was pleased.

"Look there," Clara told them.

The spikes of rays on which the sun was pierced had become a mixture of purple, rose, pink, violet, and the wool clouds behind were colored too, and in back of them streaks of azure shone through.

"I don't know your boy at all," Philip said.

"You two would get along good," Elizabeth cried. "Wouldn't they, Clara? Gus and him?"

"Yeah."

"I'm Swedish," Dr. Bill said. "My mother was a down-to-earth Lutheran. She drilled the Word into me until I thought I hated it. King James. Children don't get that nowadays. Ever read the Bible, Philip?"

"I'd like to."

"Revelation. You don't have to believe to like the words: *and God shall wipe away all tears from their eyes; and there shall be no more death, neither sorrow, nor crying, neither shall there be any more pain: for the former things are passed away.*"

"I'll hunt down my Bible; there's one in the library here." Philip's mouth smiled.

"We hope we'll see you some more, Philip?" Elizabeth said.

"I don't know." He stumbled on the shelf of sand that the eating waves made as he turned from them up toward the Sand Castle.

The Olsons walked back down to the Pine Beach shore; Elizabeth was furious. "Why did you have to keep talking about death? *Why?* Didn't I tell you!"

"He wanted me to, *älskling*. He needs it said."

Clara was running ahead in one of her spurts of energy, unable to endure standing still and walking slowly for so long. Their eyes trailed her, absorbed. Elizabeth accused her husband of more. "And you were disloyal to Gus, too. You said you wished he were Alan!"

"Well, I did wish it that day, if it makes you any happier to know it." He set his mouth, wretched.

Elizabeth swung her hands, and lifted one and glanced into the palm; she wondered if ever they forecast rightly. She'd give anything to have looked into young Alan's life lines. Didn't she bet they hadn't predicted a thing!

At the supper table, Dr. Bill looked at Gus, remorseful that he'd made comparisons. It was the old point that always fit, he thought, equality where some are more equal than others. Alan could shoot, and Gus could net bugs. The boy was picking at the meat balls and whispering with Mum. "Secrets?" Dr. Bill said. "Speak up, now."

Elizabeth murmured, "We were just saying we miss Dora. Mable has a heavy hand with pepper and she never met a mild herb."

"Can't you instruct her, Lisa?"

"She isn't a bit nice. How can she be Dora's relative? And she spends just hours at that counter drinking coffee and looking at cookbooks."

"I think it's pretty good," Clara said. "Make out that you're in Mexico, *petit chou*," she advised her brother.

"Okay." He gulped a mouthful and spilled the red sauce on his shirt.

Dr. Bill thought the kerchief knotted at Gus' neck must have been there at least a week. "How's the collecting coming this summer, *Pojke?*"

Gus glanced up as if caught. "Okay." He took his glass of milk and drained the full contents, remembering as he set it back that he'd just broken the law; one sipped milk, he'd been told since first he learned the meaning of the instruction; it had to do with digestion. He sighed and sucked silently at his braces.

Dr. Bill thought, adoring the boy, this was his dearly beloved. *As the cloud is consumed and vanisheth away.* He remembered Philip's eyes in the rainbowed sunset. He felt a deep need to do something for Gus. "Have you everything you need? Is your cyanide fresh? It wears out, you know. And the stuff has a tendency to deliquesce, melt down. Had any trouble?"

"The poison jar is fine," Gus said with hasty finality.

Dr. Bill recognized the curtains; he wondered why he was never able to lift them; they were simply there between the two of them. "Will you let me know if you need anything I can get for you?"

"I don't care for any, Mable, thanks," Gus was saying.

"You ought to eat, your age," Mable said to him. "Want some, Missus?" She offered the dish of red sweet gelatin in which solidified canned fruit shivered.

"Sorry. I'm not eating desserts," Elizabeth felt she sounded positively groveling.

"Me neither," Clara said. "I'm getting a tummy."

"I thought you always had one," Gus told her.

"Shut up. Shut your mouth, dodo, and you'll catch no flies."

"I'll make the vote unanimous," Dr. Bill smiled at Mable. "I'm just not hungry."

The maid returned to the kitchen defeated and the family

rose, drifting their ways. Clara slipped out the door and down to the beach. She walked in the uneven low terrain of the dune hillocks instead of by the lake while it was yet light, to avoid meeting Jack Behmelmen taking his dip or any of the various beach strollers. When dusk fell she would go down to the water. There was no sign of anything ever, though. The first two evenings she'd been sure she would come on it, wincing at each driftwood piece ahead. By tonight she felt only the desire of the hunter, and she believed fear was not in her longer. She'd stopped swimming out to the raft in the afternoons, and refused to go in the lifeboat even with Skin. She paddled about within the first bar or sunned or sat reading under the umbrella. She had a continual sense of prelude.

Dark was gathering. She could see the distant Uncle Jack followed by White Fang, for whom he threw countless sticks to be chewed and not retrieved. And Russ Ardway, who was rushing Pearl Thwaite this summer, was following her, carrying her transistor radio, four cans of beer, and a candle wrapped in a blanket. Pearl tossed her hair and led. "Beatniks," Clara whispered, half-envious.

She followed the shore for a mile, almost reaching the spot where Alan had slept on Monday afternoon while the storm spent itself. She turned back and by the time she reached the creek it was pitch-dark. Over the horizon Chicago was a faint mirage and the Wrigley Building lights winked and the Lindbergh beacon flashed. She went up on the sand and to the end board of the walkway. A few youngsters had a small blazing fire down the way and were singing:

> *There was an old woman*
> *Who had a pig;*
> *He wasn't very little*
> *And he wasn't very big.*

Feeling the lump mount in her throat in back of her tongue, she proceeded toward the Owl's Roost where there would be a large lighted room and one would sit among people and listen to the buzzing insects that thrashed against screens out beyond where fear was. She hurried. The children were sweet-voiced:

The little old woman
Fed him on clover;
And when he died
He died all over!

The party was breaking up and someone squealed as they doused the flames with sand; the voices faded.

She was going by the cabin that Monk was planning to rebuild. Dr. Bill called out to her, and she saw his flashlight beam. *"Flicka?"*

"God afton, Daddy!" She ran directly to him.

He sat on the splintery bench inside the low-ceilinged, sand-dusted hovel; the light made odd shadows on his grin. "Where you been?"

"Oh, walking." She was sitting beside him. "What are you doing?"

"Good question." He had quarreled again with Lisa on returning from a call and finding that Clara was out and nobody knew where. "You're an unnatural mother," he'd berated his wife, knowing as the words came that he was wrong. Lisa had run weeping up the stair, flinging herself. "Oh. One of these days!" Dr. Bill knew from previous lessons that it was well to give her temper time to wear itself, and then he would apologize. He'd swear whatever was needed. As he went from house to house, from patient to patient, Dr. Bill saw every kind of relationship between husband and wife. Why was it that as long as another outside his own needed aid or advice, he was able to give it in measure? But with his own, he seemed unavailing, small of spirit. He felt his puzzle, tired. Then Clara's step came on the walk. He flashed the light, calling. "I wish you wouldn't go out on the beach alone, Clara."

"All right. I promise." The words slipped readily out. "There's a mirage tonight."

"Is there?" He cut off his light, and they sat in the blackness; the dark was warm and the walls and ceiling of the falling house protected them from the dangerous stars and anything nescient of night or life or death. Somewhere near Pokagon, the Pere Marquette locomotive squalled, and the howls of the two German shepherds responded, lamenting.

"No one's ever going to find him." Clara stated it.

"What's the difference? Look at the matter, *Flicka*. You don't believe it's important what happens to the body, do you? If you know the spirit's gone."

"But it's spooky somehow. You ought to know where things are."

He smoothed her hair. "My tidy child."

She threw herself on him all at once, dismantled by his touch of affection. Sobbing, "I can't bear it. I was mean to him on Saturday, before."

"Oh, *Flicka*."

Her voice keened uncaring, "I told him the umbrella was private property. I told him Skin and me wouldn't miss him at all!"

There was nothing for him to do, he felt, holding her to him, but pat her shoulders. That was all the sustenance a father could be. He was nothing ever availing to the three he loved. He stroked her hair upward into the way she wore it now like a young woman. He felt how tiny her breasts were against him, shaped like Lisa's, but young and firm. She was all confused; there'd been too many sudden deaths in these last two summers.

He totted them up: one two three four—the Bible Club girl, Preacher Thwaite, Mama Ardway, young Alan. All tipped from warm beds into the cool graves. He felt how Clara knew more of dying than he at her age. Until the war came he had known no death, was unprepared for even his parents' going. Nothing had harmed him at Clara's tender age. She had lost a young companion now, and he had no way of knowing how she had thought of Alan; he'd never find it out, not through her, he thought, bitter.

Clara leaned back on his arm, subsiding. "What would I do without you, Daddy? You're the only person I can just say anything I want to."

He grasped it. "Do you feel that!"

"Yes, don't you know it? The only one."

"I know how worried you are right now."

They sat quietly; she slapped a mosquito; far away a plane whirred like a beetle. The kudzu vines planted by Monk, on Jimmy Fox's advice, grew in the sand mounded outside the cabin. The subtle odor of artificial candy came from the flowers deprived by the dark of their purple color and concealed by the gigantic leaves and by the night over the leaves. Clara breathed in the scent and recalled the day by the bridge at the Wigwam. She'd been picking sandburs from Chouchou's leg ruffs when Bosco had dashed up; as the preacher fell she smelled the same odor and ran at once to tell Alan.

"I don't like Mr. Malraux." She spoke her problem to the blackness, feeling Daddy another part of herself.

"Philip's a good man. He writes well and works hard. It's not his fault he's had to leave Alan alone so much. Try to understand, Clara. He felt that a permanent home for his son here was better than trotting him all about the world."

"What about Alan's mother?"

"They divorced years ago."

"Why didn't he marry someone else then? Did you know he liked Mum?"

"What you mean, Clara? They never got along. Mum always teased Philip Malraux, and I never liked the way he treated her."

"How?"

"Impolitely, as if what she had to say was too trivial for his attention."

"Well, all I know is I saw them together at the Sand Castle. In the library. And he'd got Mum's shirt unbuttoned." She continued headlong; the words had been restrained a long time. "And Skin saw them kissing together once, too."

The dark fell down upon them and they breathed into its thickness. "Of course I don't believe it."

"Well, I don't know," she said weakly. "I don't know." She began to cry again softly, pushing her face into his shoulder, seeking a place to go to escape everything, to be let alone. "I don't know anything, Daddy. What do I know?"

He held her closely. It was the kind of thing there was no point exploring. If they did at the Sand Castle or if they didn't, and if Skin saw them or not, why should he care? It was very possible, he told himself, aching a little as the stab receded. He was no chivalrous fool, and cuckoldry was as old as man; it predated suburbia, Victorianism, and the ancient Chinese. And he wasn't going to go into his bruised pride yet. He sighed. "I suppose you and your brother talk about these things all the time."

"Boy no, Daddy. Gus is funny. He never even asks questions about stuff. And if I ask Mum any little thing in front of him, does he get mad."

"I see."

"He's dopey. And he thinks I'm terrible."

"I see."

"And I never said it to anybody about Mum. Not even to Skin that time. Promise." It was true.

"I see. Well, I think we ought to get to bed. Let's go see if there's some store-bought ice cream in the freezer. I wish we had a new batch of Dora's homemade."

"Me too. I'm not hungry, though."

"I'm not either. Come on." He held the flashlight, leading the way, the yellow light at his heels. He probed himself for indignance. Ought he not to be outraged? He assured himself he should, but sensed only weariness and if anything rewarded that he'd discovered his daughter had a use for him of sorts. "You won't go out early to the lake tomorrow, Clara? Give me your word. It's not good for you. Let the police do their proper work. Let things go their way."

"All right." Her voice was small; she was blaming herself; was she a goon, though! Why did she tell! She was a real dumb bunny from the word go. Clara heaped the coals.

When they entered the Owl's Roost, Elizabeth was on the couch in Clara's favorite position, reading, sandaled feet propped up, a half-empty dish of ice cream on the floor by her. "Hi, you two."

"Hi, Mum."

"*Älskling.* I'm sorry I was cranky earlier. Clara's not going out before breakfast tomorrow. She's given her word on it."

"Hoo. I'm glad to hear it. Can I get you a bowl, Bill? It's called lemon-marbled butter pecan."

"All right. But only a little."

She got up and ran into the kitchen, calling, "Like a dash of chocolate sauce?"

"Well." He felt anything Lisa wanted to do for him he'd accept. He thought of all her services, the breakfast trays, the midnight meals, the clean sheets, the ways of marriage, since the months ago when Philip Malraux undid her and felt his wife's breasts; he went no further than that. "Go on to bed, Clara." He kissed her cheek. *"God natt."*

She flicked her hand tiredly, her shirt hanging out of her shorts, mounting the stairs. "I'll sleep like a log, Daddy!"

He spooned the ice cream to his mouth, smiling, the gorge up in him. "Thanks, Lisa."

Elizabeth slipped onto the couch again and picked up the book she'd spread flat on its face. "Is there any use in counting calories in ice cream? Isn't it phenomenal!" She opened the volume, settling herself. "I'm glad you and she had a talk. You were right. I should have watched out for Clara."

[18]

IN THE morning Clara over-
slept. It was nearly seven by the hands of the Donald Duck clock
when the loon screamed. The girl stirred, dreaming she'd found
what she sought. The call rose again, lifting and dying. She
opened her eyes and exhaled heavily, thinking it was afternoon
and she'd dozed; she struggled to locate herself in time and place.
The room was cool; her scant nightclothes were sweat-damp. She
sensed that everything happening had happened before sometime.
She hunted for the dream which had disappeared. She sprawled
drowsing until the shriek throbbed again outside the window. Immediately she kicked away the sheet and light quilt, knocking
the toy lamb from the bed.

"Creeps, it's a loon."

She groped for her glasses and swim suit. She was running
over the sandy hallway and down the stairs, hearing Mable banging about in the kitchen. The screen whacked as she hurried into
the foggy daylight.

Over the water it was cool and misting heavily. The shore
breeze had begun to stir. The big goose-shaped bird was plain to
see, off the delta of the creek, its handsome checkered body, its

black head and collar. She was rewarded, "Finally!" It dived and
appeared again, and made its way into the fog, voice trembling.
"Whoooo-oooo-looooo!"

Her hair was coming down, the pins slipping from it. Clara
pulled the remaining few out and kept them in her hand, going
north, shaking her head so her locks fell free. She knew a spurt of
almost giddy happiness as she walked steadily on her usual errand.
She hiked nearly an hour up the lake until at last she halted. For
a while she stood kicking in the gravelly water at the edge. The
mist had lifted. There was nothing at all. She felt suddenly how
there was nothing to be found at all. Pine Beach was a pinpoint
down the shore, alien to her. She was conceding that it was over
and Alan was nothing now.

As she neared the home beach, a few of the children were
coming down over the dune in a trickle; they stopped at its foot.
One, Carmen Paoli, separated and went to play solitary at the
water where the pebbles would be colored. Carmen came in
Clara's direction and then was running.

"Clara!" It was not until she nearly reached her that Clara
saw the wildness in her manner and that she was weeping, face
contorted. She flung herself on Clara. "Was I scared."

"Well, come on!" Clara said and ran with Carmen's hand
in hers.

Alan was half in the water, almost hid, shoved by the wavelets that had brought the body against the sandbank of the edge.
"Now stop crying, Carmen. It can't hurt us."

"I was scared," the girl said. "Clara."

"You stay here."

"Boy, was I though!"

"Wait."

Clara went to it and hesitant, laid back the bruised arm to
see the face in the wetness. He wasn't really ugly, or very changed,
only worn somewhat by the billows' treatment. She knew him;
eyes closed and sunken, sopping sand-grained hair in curls, his
flesh colorless, a little puffy. His black trunks were torn, clinging;
he wore no jacket; his shoulder blades protruded thinly.

"*Petit chou,*" she sighed.

Cautious, as if he might fall apart, she dragged him from the
shallow sea onto the bank. She didn't want to leave and stood by

the shell a moment. Carmen was sniffling, and Clara felt her obligation to the living.

"Come with me, now."

"I was scared. And I want my mother."

"I'll take you to your mother."

They trudged up the dune toward the Malraux stairs, hand in hand. When they were in shouting distance, Clara faced the other small children. The group was busy at shaping a cave of pine boughs and sticks.

Clara yelled, "That's Alan's body! Don't dare anyone go down there. Anyone does and I'll get you after. See!"

They all stood looking over at her and she felt her authority and hoped she could keep from crying. She repeated hoarsely, "See?"

They made no reply, but ceased their play and came to stand in a silent row where they could view the far-off lump. Some of them sat down to wait among the Marram-grass clumps.

The two went up the steps, waiting on the middle landing to get their second wind. At the brick terrace Clara banged the gargoyle knocker from Boulogne. Jojo and Bosco snuffled at the bottom crack, recognizing them.

The door opened and Alan's father was there in a short silk Korean robe he was tying about him. His light eyes wavered from hers. "You found him."

Clara pushed at her glasses, ducking her head as if frightened. Carmen was clutching her hand tighter. The dogs jumped up to lick them. "Don't. Hey!"

"I'll think what to do." He looked down at Clara and let his useless hands fall at his sides.

"Go call the sheriff."

"Yes. How is it done, child? Will you help me? These country phones. Do I crank it before I lift the receiver down?"

"Here." She said, "You wait, Carmen." And went past him into the side entry, the shepherds following, toes clicking on the wood, noses at her heels. She turned the handle and the bell pealed. She told the operator and then went to the kitchen to latch the dogs in. She returned to the man still standing in the hall.

Carmen was going to cry. "I want my mother."

Clara looked up at Philip and felt how she hated the man

because of Mum. She wondered why she'd spilled the beans last night to Daddy, and it made her hate increase. The dogs began to yammer in the kitchen, running back and forth, knowing their abandonment. "Don't let them out. I have to go down and stay with the body till they come. You tell Mrs. Chapman to take Carmen home."

"Yes." Philip didn't try to stop her, but just watched all the things she did and the assured and steady way with which her young body flowed, and how she was fearless, her long dark hair about her brown shoulders and the blue bathing suit. Her brows frowned angrily and she walked away. He stayed in the open door, the child sobbing beside him, looking at the empty sky where the early rays were coming to lick at the great pale water below.

[19]

AND then three days passed and the sun shot up and stood winding its horn upon the final day of August. The summer people would be gone after the Labor Day weekend; many of them were busy already, rolling up rugs and packing trunks and hunting about their homes for keys to doors so they could turn them over to Monk Ardway. The final event of the season, the tennis court dance, was to be held that evening rain or shine, Monk announced to everyone; come hell or high water, dang it.

Philip Malraux had refused to see any of his neighbors since the discovery of the body. He spent his daylight hours in the Sand Castle library, hearing the dogs padding outside the door, or Chappy and Ernie moving in whispers on the stairs and in the kitchen. Philip consumed a good deal of alcohol while he was completing the business of decisions; where the body was to be cremated, which agency should handle the sale of the Sand Castle, what to do with Alan's German shepherds, and when to tell the Chapmans to go away. At length there seemed to be nothing more undone; no tie existed longer to hold him to any place in the world, Philip thought.

The previous afternoon Chappy had carried him a tray of food and urged him to go to the coming festivities. He was prepared to do what she or anyone asked. He sat dry-faced, unable to eat. She brought him ice then and water, and a new bottle of bourbon and left him. He spent a lot of time gazing through the large windows overlooking the lake. Up ahead the shore bent like the bay at Napoli. Neither the beauty of it nor the soft cooling breeze touched him. He watched a group of Pine Beach men walking along the shoreway. One of them wore white duck sailor trousers and a blue-striped shirt; Jimmy Fox.

"Omnibus hominibus moriendum est," Jimmy was saying.

"That from your pig-Latin friend Wheeler?" Monk queried, hostile.

"Sure. All men must die. The poor kid."

"Yeah," Mike agreed. "But how about my Carmen finding it like that?"

"Wheeler's going to Europe," Jimmy said. "Not as a steward on any ship either. He's been awarded a fellowship." He folded his arms; his flared trousers were tight about the loins and emphasized his small hips.

Jack Behmelmen kicked at the sand, his florid face wrinkled like an old piece of fruit. "Does it worry the little girl, Mike?"

"Not that I can tell. How do you know? She's just as noisy as ever. I agree with everything she says to keep the peace." Mike sighed, permissive. "It's Al we're concerned about. Angela had to put him to bed last year when that girl was washed up on the beach. He had nightmares for a long time. And the minister's death bothered him too."

"That day was crazy. Remember that storm?" Jack said. "And all the time the gulls kept tearing out over the lake into it. Wonder why they do that."

"And Angela says Al's having bad dreams again," Mike said. "Talks in his sleep."

"Well, Carmen had guts," Monk said, "anyway."

"She's a good girl," Mike said. "And the only one I'm going to get, looks like. I got five sons!"

"That's just the way the gulls acted forty years ago," Jack said. "When my little kid drowned."

"Take it easy," Jimmy told him. "We know."

Dick spoke up from the rear. "Sure glad they found Alan at last!"

"It's over now," Russ said smoothly.

"All but the shouting." Dick blinked at the tears that continued to gush whenever he thought he was in full control. "Let's dive in, Russ!"

"Watch it, boys." Monk's eyes like a lover's went on them, safe for the time. They disappeared in the white-ruffled water.

The group listened while a crow hawked somewhere off above the shifting sand and the weather-shaped pines. The sight of the dead buffeted form of Alan being taken up the sandy path by the ambulance men lingered in the brain of each. Each felt his luck. As he did every time death touched him, and as he would continue to do while his good fortune held.

The two boys leaped from the water. Chouchou and White Fang bounded and sprang at them. Dick and Russ thumped the animals, affectionate, enthusiastic. They almost strutted, as if defying the thing which had passed them by and claimed their untried friend. They came after the older men.

At the Sand Castle, Philip, in his window saw the group disappear from sight. He became conscious of Jojo and Bosco scratching at the library door. He let them in, and heads drooping they slipped by to go to the old chest. They reared up, staring in the glass, tails wagging, heads cocked. "Why do you do that?" Philip sounded annoyed and he wondered at himself. "Go away." They left their game, dropping down and coming to shove their noses at his freckled hand. He saw how he had not the energy even to move his fingers to stroke their heads.

When Chappy came to the door to call the dogs to their meal, he said, "Dammit to hell, tomorrow I must step down to the beach and say good-bye to everyone. But Chappy, I'm not going to any dance. What you think? Tell me what to do."

"I reckon you're right," she sighed. "Do I know?"

Right after breakfast in the morning, the young people appeared to prepare the court for the fun. They came bearing brooms and crêpe paper. Dick swung a length of wire to connect his record player. He dropped his armful and waltzed onto the court with the broom in his embrace, inquiring of it, "And how do you feel about appearance and reality, Mademoiselle?"

He squealed for the broom in falsetto reply, "But if the reality is not what appears, have we any means of knowing if there's any reality at all!"

"He's simply insane, Snooky," Pearl said to Russ.

"Give him a few years, Cookie," Russ told her through his cigarette. "He'll wear down."

"To think. Last year it was Papa. And we didn't have the dance at all." But Russ had already turned away and Pearl remembered that everyone wanted to talk and hear of themselves, that no one really shared anything. "Snooky, you've got the most super tan," she murmured and Russ came directly again to her side.

"And you," he said, "are fascinating." He crumbled his cigarette with his fingers. "You write me from Switzerland."

She nodded. "And we'll be back in spring. Eve says we're coming here every summer. My mother always has everything planned these days."

"And you know what, Bunny?" Russ viewed her coolly. "You're just like her; you're a planner too."

"No." She was veiling her eyes, kneeling to lift the red crêpe ribbon. "Nail this end up to the catalpa trunk there, will you?"

"Yeah." He gazed at her pretty shape and struck another cigarette, leashing himself with learned patience.

By noon they were finished and everyone met down at the beach. The raft had drifted down the lake shore during the night, and all the group trudged south in the dampish cool wind to retrieve it. Clara wore over her swim suit a heavy gray cotton jacket with a parka hood. She had Georgie Paoli by one hand and Skin had the other. They tramped along, digging their toes into the many-colored fine grains that appeared yellow-white. "I never got to go after the raft before," Georgie said. "Nobody ever let me come. This is keen."

"Don't say keen," Clara chided.

"Okay." The child was placid.

"Why not?" Skin asked.

"It's bad language, *mon cher,*" Clara told Skin. She spoke to

Georgie, "Two words you use all the time you have to promise not to say any more. One's *keen* and one's *stinky.*"

"Okay," Georgie said. "What are they?"

"I give up," Clara said. "One thing, I'll never be a school-teacher, Skin."

They swung the little boy between them, lifting his feet off the ground; he squealed with pleasure. The current had been rough and the raft was shoving its nose like an ancient undecided sea beast against the bank. It was guided back, through resistant churning waves, to Pine Beach; the smaller children and Clara and Irene rode on it, while the others stayed in the water or ran on land. Pearl, feeling her near separation from Russ, was beside him, her small sturdy hands up on the rough creosoted wood. Her summer steady was so gay, Pearl knew it meant nothing to him that she and her beauty would be gone for many months. It went through her mind that he enjoyed himself too much. She made an effort to seem to equal his nonchalance, crying against the breakers, "We ought to sing a round."

"Okay. Which one?"

"Down at the station?"

"Not that grandaddy."

But they were already chanting, taking different parts, mixing it up.

> *Down at the station*
> *Early in the morning,*
> *See the little pug-a-bellies all in a row.*

From the shore of the main beach the grownups were watching the raft approach. Most of them had sweaters or jackets over their suits.

"Why, here comes Philip," Hazel exclaimed, and everyone turned.

He wore a plaid mackinaw over his thin shoulders, the buttons undone, exposing his freckled red-haired chest. "Hazel."

She noticed he was a little high. "We're so happy you came down."

"Hello all," he said.

After the chorus of greeting there was a lull, awkward, and Hazel, settling down on a log, spoke into it, "Elizabeth, what do you hear from Dora, darling? How does she like being Mrs. Herb Worth?"

"I don't know," Elizabeth said, "but Gus is desolate. Mable gets into his room. The other day I found him crying."

"I didn't hear about that," Dr. Bill said.

"Yes, you did. I told you the whole thing at breakfast. First time Gus let me comfort him for years."

"She break something?" Belle asked.

"No, she made order in his things. Gus was going to leave home, Belle."

"Lisa," Dr. Bill objected. "You're exaggerating."

"Wonder how Herb is for a husband?" Hazel said.

"Women's minds run on one track," Jimmy said.

"You noticed that too," Mike Paoli laughed.

"I think it's just that women speak their thoughts out while men hide them, darling," Hazel said. "What you think, Philip?"

"I agree," Philip told her, "to whatever you just said."

"I bet Herb's a bull in bed." Monk spoke coarsely. "He's built up that wad for a dozen years while Dora kept him waiting."

"You b.s.," Belle nudged him, "now watch your language in front of Mr. Malraux."

"Don't mind me, Mrs. Ardway," Philip said, swaying slightly. He felt his grief made him naked before the group, none of whom he knew very well. He wished he'd not felt compelled to come.

"You see the article in the paper, Mr. Malraux?" Belle queried. "And there was a notice in *Time*, too."

Philip had read it that morning when Ernie brought the mail:

Died. Alan Philip Malraux, 17, son of newswriter Philip Malraux; by drowning during the recent seiche, off the shore of Pokagon, Michigan. The body has not been recovered.

Suddenly feeling his isolation, his exposure, and without will to start or halt them, the tears began to run down Philip's face.

The group stunned, watched. He didn't resist; his mouth bent down and his eyes closed. Elizabeth felt how he was defenseless. She saw that she was always cruel and empty-headed; her mind opened up like a light upon her own being. Was she of any good at all, she thought, fluttering about for what gratified her, grasping upon the past, avoiding the future? She felt how the hurt person there needed solace. Someone ought to give him back himself. There was no need for him to battle alone, feeling them all strangers circled about, all the world. Bill was watching nearby, and the eyes of her neighbors were gathered. Elizabeth felt how her husband would never forgive her if she went over and took a strange suffering man's head in her soft hands, if she whispered while listening ears grasped, "Dear? Is there anything to do but cry. Don't mind."

She was reaching up to stroke the funny harsh red hair which felt familiar, remembering. "Is it poor Philip then?" Surrounding him who needed her, touching him with tender arms. Feeling her husband's self-esteem shattering, as he turned embarrassed, toward the scornful grin of Jimmy Fox and then the incredulous gasp of Hazel.

"But darling," Hazel protested, "What's wrong with him?"

Elizabeth felt the way she had toward Gus last week when Mable got the labels and beetles all mixed up that Gus had arranged on his table, dumping them into the drawer. "Why not just let him alone a minute?" she asked Hazel.

Restless, the men shifted on their feet. Monk reached down for a skipping stone and walked toward the water. Jimmy drifted after him. "What you make of that?"

"Hell." Monk skimmed the stone on top of the little billows that rose and fell. "Didn't you know he had that little gal made last season?" Monk wondered at his own wrath, his words that fell as if he were jealous. "Why Jimmy, he even wanted her to divorce the doctor and marry him. I heard them quarrel on it."

"I'll believe all but that last," Jimmy said.

Jack stood behind them, unhappy. "She's a real fine wife, Elizabeth Olson. I respect her."

"Don't get your dander up," Jimmy said. "Everyone's edgy here."

"That was a fine fellow, that young Alan." Jack's eyes were reddening. "Look, I lost a little boy. Robin. Directly after the war. There were the three of us."

Jimmy put a muscular hand on Jack's shoulder. "Don't get started on that, will you? Take it easy. I'm getting pretty jumpy."

"Yeah," Jack consented. "Okay. Anyone think to bring a flask down?"

"Monk?" Jimmy said. "I know he's got one stowed in that natty new jacket."

"Matter of fact," Monk pulled it out. "There's a built-in pocket for the very purpose."

As they returned, Philip was scrubbing his fingers in his hair. "Really, I have to go."

"Philip?" Elizabeth looked at him, barefaced, so Dr. Bill watching knew these two had been one.

"Have some brandy, Malraux?" Jack offered him Monk's flask.

Philip spoke tiredly, shaking his head. "Thanks. I've overstayed. And I have some things I must do. I only came to say good-bye." He put out his hand to Hazel.

"What about the little dance tonight, darling?" she worried. "It would be good for you."

"No." Philip turned to Dr. Bill. "I appreciate what you said the other day. I got into the Bible too. You remember? Revelation, you said. *No more death, neither sorrow.*"

"You staying on long here?" Dr. Bill spoke without warmth, crisp. "Got plans?"

"I don't know, Bill. My Lord." Philip knit his forehead and looked around. "Good-bye, everyone." He reached over and caught Elizabeth's fingers with his. "You too, dear one." And he was plodding away.

Dr. Bill asked, "Is that your perfume, Lisa! You always put on too much."

"It's me, darling," Hazel informed him. "*Les Fleurs du Mal.* Doesn't it incite you even a little bit?"

"Who knows a good joke?" Jimmy said.

"Only ones I can think of are decent," Monk told him.

"Have some brandy, Dr. Bill," Jack said generously.

"Is there any?" Monk asked. "You leave any?"

As the group separated, Hazel whispered to Elizabeth, "What were you trying to do? What *was* that?"

"Do I care?" Elizabeth defied her friend, refusing to speak of it.

"Better watch out, darling. You'll lose your nice Dr. Bill. There aren't very many steady husbands like him."

"Do I!" Elizabeth thought she was still sounding like a child.

Gulls were calling like humans, darting in a sweeping arc upon the watery world. Far out it was brown-green as if angry and some of the waves were long, building themselves. The air was so clear that the whitecaps near the horizon appeared as distinct to the eye as those churning upon the close sandbar. The noise of breaking for the big ones was a long crescendo of break, roar, pause, and *sssssssh*. All the while under lay the hiss of the foam. "Bump, splash, fissssshunk! Fishshshshhh." Some of the gulls remained riding on the lake, mistaken for whitecaps. Others were returning; scavenger birds, their eyes swept the surface for anything dead to scoop, or dying. Their whiteness glinted.

Dr. Bill in the upstairs of the Owl's Roost could hear their childlike voices. It was late afternoon and he walked down the hallway to his room and flung open the door so it slammed upon the back wall. He hadn't noticed Elizabeth there, napping on the bed in her underthings. She came awake, sitting up, her hands going promptly to her hair and the waves in it. Pale-lipped, she glanced at him, bridling, "Do you have to bash the house down?"

"Mable's packing. You can drive her down to the bus."

"All right. What she do?"

"Christamighty, I'm not going into it."

She was still sleepy and fumbled her way to the dresser, to lipstick, almost without knowing what she did. "What time?"

"Five." He laughed. "*Älskling*, if a bomb were dropped to end the world, all the women would still run to their mirrors."

She stepped back to the bed and snuggled down into the pillow that was washed in the sunlight. "I hate to wake up suddenly. Gives me a headache." She closed her eyes.

He didn't reply, sitting in the stiff cane-bottom summer chair. That Mable. Goddam everything. He put his elbows on his knees, hating even the yellow haze of light that lay about him and over his unclothed wife and her soft hair. He understood Lisa and her gesture toward Philip, but out of pride he would not accept it. It made no matter that Malraux was in grief; nothing mattered except that Lisa, flagrant, had stripped Dr. Bill before their neighbors. He would never forgive her, he knew. The Grey Swede, he thought, grim. He'd not spoken of it and never would, he vowed. And she would not dare bring it up. It would hang heavily between them forever, made of hate. Her breathing arose and fell, perfectly even, unconscious. He could never rest like that, composed easily; how he resented her!

"Everyone but me knew about last summer." He spoke loud and sudden, darkly.

Her eyes came open, purple-blue in the sun. "What you mean!"

"About your big affair."

"Did Clara tell you something?"

"Yes she did."

"Do you want to divorce me?"

"Don't be melodramatic."

"I'm not; do you?"

"I don't know."

"Because else won't you have to forgive me? Hoo!" She laughed, winning, somewhat tense, her head remaining on the sunny down. "We're so silly, Bill. It's like a movie, isn't it? Only really we're us and it doesn't matter. Don't let's fight. I can't bear it."

"I wish you'd grow up."

"Don't you see? That's the thing, I *am* grown. Did I really hurt us? And would I go away and marry anyone who asked me? Philip did."

"No."

"I don't care if you believe or not. Do I care?" She turned her face to look at the ceiling. "Oh."

"Some day you'll leave me, Lisa."

"No." She declared it and got up and went to him. She sat on his knee, inundated with all kinds of old known love. Her bare arms folded about his angry familiar form, and she felt him sigh. He made such a thing of nothing always, didn't he? she thought.

"Some day you'll leave. You'll be carried away by these ridiculous infantile emotions of yours." He spoke fiercely, so tears almost sprang, but yet held her on his knees, grasping her rounded barely clothed limbs.

"What if I do?"

"How can you say that!"

"Oh." She pushed her face into the back of his neck, trying to cheer him, to make him play and forget this indistinct woe. "You know what, Bill? We aren't going to have a maid any more."

"How's that?"

"What did Mable do wrong, though."

"Nothing at all. Damned woman sitting there drinking her coffee and sand in the vegetables. I said pack and get out of here!" He shrugged. "I lost my temper."

"You funny man!"

"Take her down to the bus, Lisa."

"Okay."

"And you can't do her work. You can't even iron properly."

"Yes, I can."

"Maybe Dora would come back part time."

"No. Won't you see? I can do it."

He said nothing for a moment. "I'll buy you that Porsche, älskling." They stayed silent, and Dr. Bill thought he said that as if she were Clara and it were a bribe, not as if his wife had any mind at all of her own.

She was pleased and giggled, on his knee. "A white one?"

"Umm."

"Oh, didn't I forget to tell you! Monk came after those lanterns again. Did you notice them gone downstairs? I tried to tell him no, but next thing I was saying he could have them and you wouldn't care."

"Lisa." He felt it rile him. He knew that somehow his wife had twisted the talk so that he was now upon the defensive. "I don't mind if you did."

"Come lie down a while." She persuaded him, and drew him to their bed. She lay waiting in his bended arm until his breathing turned to sleep. She crept quietly away and slipped into shorts and a pullover, going to take Mable to the bus.

In the little Volks neither spoke, until Mable finally said flatly, "I washed the sand off of that spinach, Missus." She made a dusting movement at her print frock.

"Don't I know you did, Mable?" Lisa sensed her subservience and the incongruity of her soft sweater and bare tan legs against the woman's conservative attire. She was eager to unload the unwanted one at the highway.

"I expect you'll be trying to get Cousin Dora to come back. She sure did spoil the boy and the girl bad." Mable got out lugubrious, slightly venemous, swinging her large bulging bag. "Thanks for the check, Missus."

Elizabeth had overpaid her; she smiled good-bye and drove away, crossing the four cement lanes to get the mail at the Pokagon post office. The American flag on its pole snapped occasionally in the September breeze. The hinged wood flaps that covered the windowed front of the square building at night were raised and hooked to the wide eaves, making shade. Inside, Elizabeth worked the dial; besides a paper, she took out a handful of advertisements: medical bargains and offers of free samples for Dr. Olson, end-of-summer clothing and shoe sales for her. While she leafed through them, the husband of the postmistress edged around the bank of mailboxes and sniffed.

"Day, Mrs. Olson. There's no first class there."

"I see."

He frowned, "Mable leaving?"

She nodded, without looking up. "We like her very much, though."

"Why she going?"

"Do I know? We just let her go. We go back to Ideal tomorrow."

He digested the information and offered in fair return, "Watched your VIP neighbor clear out not ten minutes ago. Ernie was driving and the bags piled in back."

"Umm."

"Ernie's starting him a nursery other side of Benton Harbor too. Says Mr. Malraux is staking him. And he gave Alan's pair of dogs away too, to the Ardways."

"I know. They're Skin's."

"Oh?" He said, and sniffed in his habit; he gazed down at her white wool-covered breasts.

She went out of the building, arms full of the mail which she dumped on the seat. She went speeding past the tennis court where Belle, solitary, was laying a cloth on the table Monk had set up. Colored paper ribbon was strewn and the Japanese paper globes hung. Elizabeth didn't notice the Volks tires cartwheeling the dust so it drifted over the festive scene and on Belle who raised her head sharply.

Now that it was final, she sighed at the sharpness of the pain

of Philip's departure; she felt a need to be with Bill. She ran up
the porch steps and up the inner stairs to wake him.

"You have to help me finish the packing since we haven't a
maid, Bill! School starts already on Wednesday." She was breathless, throwing herself on the bed beside him.

He sat up and swung his legs around, rubbing his eyes, feeling for his glasses. "Hellamighty. And I'll wager Mable hasn't
done a thing."

"She did a little."

"What?"

"Well, she folded the sisal rugs. And I asked her to roll them
instead."

"Let's go do it over again, Lisa."

"Want a beer?"

"Umm."

"We don't want to go to the tennis court till late, do we?
Monk's sure to have the small-children things first. It wouldn't
be any fun till dark anyway. Don't you agree? I can't wait to see
your lanterns lit up, Bill. Can you?" She followed him down into
the cellar, talking all the while, in questions.

[20]

AND Monk did do the little-children things first. He dusted the cobwebs from the ancient red fire-wagon and gave them all a ride about Pine Beach, screaming as they circled the Owl's Roost, where Elizabeth came out to wave. Chris Paoli pulled the rope, so the bell went "Pling! Plinnggg!" Then Monk unloaded them by the tennis court and parked. He took cigarettes out of Carmen's ears and found a penny in Ian Thwaite's curls. He had balloons and a Go-Fish bowl of wrapped gifts, too. "Dang it," he complained to Mike in the early autumn-like dark that dropped with suddenness, "try and buy a nickel toy nowadays."

"You're talking to one who knows." Mike chewed his cigar and glanced over to his new son in a French tote-basket by the bench.

Angela was explaining to Belle. "Billy's fine there. I always pick the noisiest spot to put my children when they're that age. They don't sleep well where it's quiet; noise must mean home, don't you think?"

"It's unnatural, though, not to fuss with babies," Belle

[300]

said. She blew fastidiously at the dust to remove it from the paper cups. "My, at the dirt here; Monk ought to of sprinkled that road like I said. Or got the boys to. Those four big *I*'s; they're too busy to do anything for anybody." Belle complained, enjoying herself, presiding over the soft drinks, the salted chips, the pretzels.

There was a dogfight just at dark. Eve's collie had rushed in with head and dazzling white ruff lowered to attack Bosco's front legs. White Fang had watched the scuffle from the sidelines, obedient to Jack's order, on his haunches; his two ears loped unevenly as he held them alert. Jack had strolled over to see the festivities. Jimmy said, "First time you ever appeared at one of these functions. What is it?"

"I suppose it's the pup. He wants to see the world," Jack said. "He looks to me for guidance." White Fang wore a wide red bow on his collar; it hung frayed below his neck, giving him a clownish look. "Hazel put it there," Jack said. "It's his birthday. He has one every month; this is the ninth."

"Ought to hang a whisky barrel on him," Jimmy said. "He's big enough." The crossbred was half again as large as Chouchou.

"Yeah." Jack and his dog ambled away.

In the confusion of the fight only Skin had got nipped. He wore a few purple-red bruises on his arm. Eve leashed the restive Bobbie and there was no more trouble. Alan's pair followed Skin, and when he leaned against the backdrop arguing with Gus Olson, they crouched slavish by his new-pressed slacks. Monk went about lighting the candles in Dr. Bill's Kawasaki lanterns. The flames burned straight, pointed, almost unflickering. Monk put his hand to the pocket of his swaggy sportscoat to check that his plastic nip flask was there. Chris Paoli carried the matches for him, and let Monk have a look at the gap in his mouth where a tooth had stood a day or two ago. Chris carried a purse mirror of Angela's in the pocket of his shorts; he took it out now and then, to screw his face about and examine the loss with emotion. He murmured to himself:

> *Spanish dancer, take a glass of wine,*
> *Close your eyes and count to nine!*

Dick was adjusting the record player, which had developed a bug; weird thumps and squeaks came over the loudspeaker as he endeavored to pinpoint the problem. He tested a record and the music shrieked:

> *Teen angel, can you hear me cry?*
> *Have you gone to that place in the sky?*
> *Am I yet your own true love?*
> *Teen angel!*

Pearl came over to where he was tinkering; her eyes wavered over Dick's cat pants, green-yellow shirt, beard. He was dressing beat this summer, while Russ looked, she thought, more like a well-heeled stockbroker. "Hi." She rubbed a tiny bump on her temple. "What's this, Dick?"

He laughed at her. "It's just a little nickey; it isn't anything." He stood by her beautiful upturned face.

"Do you want me to write you from Switzerland?"

"You want to dance, Pearl? I'll change this record to a smooth one I got if you do."

"Okay."

The new minor chords beat out slowly, the nasal jazz voice:

> *Um daddy cool,*
> *Um daddy cool,*
> *Daddy cool daddy cool!*

"That's a pretty sweater, Pearl."

"But do you want me to write?"

"Did you ever see the new cottage my Dad built. It's called a gazebo."

"A what?"

They were on the court, their feet grating on the cement. The drums backed up the bass:

> *Um body,*
> *Um body um body!*

"I'll show you after a while, Pearl. And write me a long letter about whatever you're doing, will you?"

Others were out on the shadowy area. Mike Paoli, cigar discarded, was holding Elizabeth Olson, in a pale orange dress, tightly to his black turtle-neck sweater, face impassive, loins tight to hers, silent. His son, Albert, wan, almost handsome, was managing well despite his shortened limb, with Clara.

"You taking Trig or Physics this year?" Al inquired.

"Both; and there's only one other girl in my Trig class. I'm in Physics honors section too," she boasted, "but I'm not very good. Boy, have I been loafing. And I've got German too. Ugh, *mein Herr*. You Chicago kids getting the Sequential Tests?"

Al shrugged. "Probably. We get everything there is."

"Do you have SCATS, school-and-college-ability-tests? We get measured for everything, *mon ami,* even how good we listen."

"Stop talking about school, Clara."

"Yeah."

"See, when I get interested in what you're saying, I do something wrong. I miscounted there and stepped on your foot." Albert felt his chivalry.

"I didn't notice. I hope Dick doesn't put on his favorite record about that drag-strip driver who wrecks his heap and then has to sing to the girl of sweet sixteen while he burns. Heck, if he does, you want to sit it out and hold our ears?"

"I sure agree."

And the balladeer brayed of adolescent perpetual love, of high school wedding rings, of the faithful and permanent quality of death. Albert and Clara went over to the table where Belle was and got Cokes. The wind stirred; the candle points fluttered a little and stood still. Clara wore a short white silk gown, gathered over her small bosom. She'd dressed her dark hair low in a French knot and felt her sophistication. She had on mascara, eyebrow pencil, eyeshadow, to the limit of what Mum would tolerate; Mum had held firm on the pancake makeup, tossing it in the garbage can, claiming that Clara would get acne. She crossed her legs sitting with Albert on the bench; thinking that right now Alan would have been in Paris with his father, maybe going out to a night club or somewhere. She allowed the familiar feeling to engulf her, pushing it back only when the hard lump came in her throat and the water to her eyes. "Are you fond of sociology, Al?" she cried thickly.

"It's all right."

"I like it very much." She spoke unhappily, hearing his German shepherds, now someone else's, Skin Ardway's, playing behind them in the grass, snarling softly, nuzzling their noses in each other's fur.

She could see her mother and Mr. Paoli dancing, and Gus went by with plain old Irene Thwaite, and Pearl cheek-to-cheek with Dick again; and Georgie, six and a half, with his mother. Daddy was talking with Belle Ardway and was holding the namesake infant he'd taken from the Paoli basket. Eve was with them, Ian at her side. Ian pulled loose and flung himself on the collie. "Puththycat! Puththycat."

Eve's protest came, "Why does he say that, Dr. Bill; he understands perfectly well that it's a dog!" And her father laughed.

Clara turned back to Albert, mourning, "And I like English and Government. I only really have trouble with math."

"Write if you want any special point explained. I'll answer by return mail. Yours till the board walks and the kitchen sinks!"

Clara held her soft drink in a studied exquisite way. When Skin dashed up and cried uncourtly, "Come on, Clara! Dance," she turned from him unspeaking and shook her head.

Skin walked off, grim.

Clara Olson, Ideal, Mich,
Stuck her head in a pickle dish!

He shuffled over to his mother and squired Belle out onto the dimmed area, putting his angular young hand, marked by the collie's teeth, about her thick waist. He vowed silently to dance only with Mom tonight. Over and over; nobody else. He decided not to ask Clara to go to any of the senior hops with him. He also would refuse to answer to his nickname any more; he'd go by his given name, Sinclair.

"Pay attention, Skin," Belle said, patient, when her corn was bumped.

"Say Sinclair, Mom. From now on."

"I figured you'd be telling me that soon."

Skin thought how he'd go to the Downtown Drug Store across the tracks next chance he had in Ideal, and buy a full gross of prophylactic rubbers. He knew what his brother Russ and Pearl Thwaite had done this summer. He felt the snake within his chest, the venom, the just-realized eternal perfidy of the female.

Belle sighed, "Sinclair!"

"My gosh, I'm sorry, Mom."

Then the music ended and there was a sprinkle of applause while the record was being changed. "Dick, please," Georgie Paoli called hoarsely, earnest, "do Bill Bailey won't you please come home! Pearl, you make him."

"Be still," Angela ordered. "I'll be glad when it's next year and you get a new favorite." A Tokyo swing band took over. "Here we go. The next one's with Chris. And then I hope to stop and visit Billy!" Angela could see Carmen arguing with Gus Olson; her hair was like a silver stream, her olive skin heightened the brightness of her eyes. With resolve, Angela put her mind on the child she was dancing with and away from the other. She felt a wave of premonition which she recognized as false, that something horrible, devastating, would occur to Carmen one day which would destroy all of them.

Gus felt Carmen was being difficult and ovcrloud. But he was used to her and she always roused his protective feelings, much the same as did Davy, his beloved white rat. "Concentrate, will you? On the music."

"Okay. Okay." Carmen smiled, distracted. "Did you know I was the one found Alan?"

"I know; doesn't everyone? Now guess this one, Carmen. Two legs sat upon three legs with one leg in his lap." His voice slid treble and bass. "In comes four legs and runs away with one leg. Up jumps two legs, catches up three legs, throws it after four legs and makes him drop one leg! It isn't hard."

"I don't know but what's the difference between a sewing machine and a kiss?"

"I forget," Gus lied. "Pay attention to the rhythm, though."

"I am. I *am.*" Her confident laugh rang like a bell and they stepped on each other's feet. "And boy, was I ever scared, Gus."

Dr. Bill passed them, hurrying over to Elizabeth. "Remember, Lisa, I'll be home late."

"Umm." She stood in the shadow while the music was being changed.

"Have a good time now, *älskling.* Summer's over."

"I know." She kissed his cheek.

He was going up the road, blending to the dark. Monk approached in the flickering light. "What?"

"Oh, he's just got calls to make."

Monk slid his arm about her. "Hi, little gal."

"You're such a good dancer. Hoo! Where'd you ever learn."

Monk smelled her fine blonde hair and thought how it was scented like lake water after the long season. He felt a thing charge through him that was like nostalgia; he'd always wanted a piece of this small warm gal. Her bright frock was slippery under his sun-darkened strong hand. "Bill won't be back till early in the morning, *hausfrau.*"

"Hoo."

"Want a smoke?" He fingered for his pack in the bright sports coat.

"No." She was shaking her head, desiring nothing of Monk but his long-lived praise, his approbation.

In the night, on the court where the white lines that delineated boundaries for the game, were indistinct, they moved, slow, to the tempo, the haze from Monk's cigarette over them. "What you thinking?" Monk urged.

She didn't hear. "What's that song?"

He sighed, sensing her slip away. "I don't ever hear the words. It's sure to be about love though, dang it."

Love, she thought, and dusk, and miss, and baby mine, and birds sing. Out of dark crushing centuries, Sappho saying, *the beings that I've toiled to please they've wounded me the most; the moon sets, the Pleiades are gone; it's midnight; the time goes by and I sleep alone.* Elizabeth turned to Monk, laughing, so he felt again that the doctor's wife was the prettiest gayest thing there.

The music was whining so loudly that Dr. Bill, striding through the woods, could hear:

> *Hey nonny nonny;*
> *In the moon's blue light!*

He fumbled down the path lit only by the dim stars. He went into the great shell of the Owl's Roost, where the quiet was a resting animal. Going up the stairs to change he heard a whispering in Gus' room. He looked in, snapping on the wall switch. The twenty-five-watt bulb in the ceiling glowed over the table where beside the stuffed pheasant was an insect mounting rack. In it one of the three stretched Fritillaries had come alive, its wings struggling and body writhing, arched with effort. Dr. Bill bent over to free the cardboard strips that held the brown speckled-and-silvered wings. He checked to see that the other two insects were quite dead. The butterfly flapped blindly about; he persuaded it onto his fingers and unlatched the screen to loose it into the dark. Its tiny tarsus claws were hooked upon his skin, but at length it dropped fumbling below. He turned off the light and left the room.

A few minutes later the Volks was scampering through the hollow and past the sandy road that led to the Malraux place, the headbeams illuminating the *For Sale* placard nailed to the splintery Ideal Line telephone post. Dr. Bill felt fine. Whether his wife stayed or went home faithful, whether she loved by his rules or hers, whether some day even she left him, seemed unimportant. In the morning it might again become essential. And then he might feel deeply too about understanding his two children as he felt he should. But now he was complete within himself; there was a triumphant wave that went through his body down to his fingers. He had no need for philosophy or companions; his only mild hunger was to insure the health of his latest namesake, William Paoli.

The noises from the tennis court swam out, the blare of a syncopated beat and a shout as one of the bright huge lanterns ignited. Dr. Bill hadn't seen.

It had caught because of a low-burning candle and Dick Ardway stamped it out, bellowing, "Where's Dad!"

Clara, on the grass near the side of the woods, watched the blackened paper frizzle and waft downward. She was looking away toward the dark road where the fire engine loomed hulking and stilled. She listened to the music chatter:

> *In the moon's blue light;*
> *Hey nonny, hey.*

Her back was to the court and her eyes into the blackness. "Hey, Clara!" someone called. But she lingered; she didn't know for sure about anything any more. Not even how she felt about death. One time, not long past, she'd been immortal, secure. The lump was in her throat; she felt the wound of her loss, the sharp endurance of her loyalty. She would never stop grieving after him.

She put her hand into the tiny bag Mum had given her once and took the lipstick and fixed herself. She understood her dark beauty in the pale thin dress, and the way it tucked low at her breasts. In the woods not an owl was hooting or insect trilling. She knew how prey was being seized in there by quick-darting night birds or by the clever weasels and foxes. She almost caught the cry as a mole or shrew or baby mouse was snatched and borne off in the teeth or talons.

Clara wanted to say what she was thinking to Al, to Skin, someone. Russ Ardway came sauntering up, a dark red sweater over his trim white shirt and tie. He dragged on a cigarette while he grinned at Clara, and reached for her hand. "May I, Bunny?" He dropped the butt and put it out with his shoe in a practiced lazy way.

She responded almost without thought, quickly going to the boy who was over twenty and had been unattainable before. She was sensible of the homage done her. Smelling the tobacco on his breath and the slight taint of whisky. Russ danced with a languid air and only when they were at the edge of the court did his arm tighten about her. Almost casually his fingers came to touch her, pinching her nipple softly the way his father had done at Uncle Jack's party. Was that last winter, she thought, or years ago?

She was rather patronizing, "Be good, *petit chou.*"

Russ was pleased, "The chick has grown into a cool cookie."

Clara felt as if the present were a thousand years ago and she a piece of the pattern. As if it had happened time and time over, to one and another. The soft happy noises were about them, the tinkle, *"Hey nonny nonny!"* As if some other girl had moved as she, wet-eyed, in a young man's arms. In the night, dancers shuffling nearby, having had a young companion washed away in the tide of the sea.

She sighed, "Maybe. But anyhow, watch yourself." Thinking how she was content, complete, how everything was beginning.